THE KING'S QUEEN

Gate of Myth and Power Book 3

K. M. SHEA

For my Champions. I'm well aware that this series has a really weird premise. Thank you so much for trusting me and giving it a try. You all really know how to Win Friends and Influence People!

THE KING'S QUEEN

Cover Art by Trif Book Design
Edited by Deborah Grace White

ISBN: 978-1-950635-22-1

www.kmshea.com

CHAPTER ONE

Chloe

Thunder rolled in the distance. It hadn't started raining yet, but when I cracked open the front door of Book Nookery—the twenty-four-hour bookstore that I worked at—and stuck my nose out into the inky night, I could smell that it was coming.

"A dark and stormy night, that's two to put down for my *moody atmosphere bingo card*." I closed the door, then shuffled back to my desk.

I grabbed my new favorite hot beverage, a steamer of hot milk with amaretto flavoring, and took a swig. It was so hot I nearly burned my tongue, and it wasn't exactly comforting since it was so hot outside we had to run the air conditioner, but that was September for you.

Even if the hot and sticky summer was clinging to Magiford, I was determined to welcome fall and slam the door on what had been a chaotic and heart twisting summer.

The front door opened, making the bell connected to the door jingle.

I carefully set my steamer down—Mr. Gleevers had brought it in for me, so if I spilled it I couldn't get a replacement until my shift ended at five in the morning, and it was barely midnight—then slapped on my employee smile.

"Welcome to Book Nookery!" I chirped.

I only saw ebony darkness through the door, before an unassuming man slipped inside the bookstore.

He was average height, and while he had a sort of liquid grace to him, his shoulders were hunched slightly in a way that I recognized came with spending too many hours sitting at a desk. His hair was black and his skin was pale, but it was the red eyes that marked this unlikely guy as a vampire.

My smile turned sincere. "Josh." I waved as he stepped deeper into the store. "I saw two of the books you ordered came in—is that what you're here for?"

Josh was a semi-regular, and perhaps the oddest vampire I'd ever met. He almost looked nerdy—like he'd be more at home in an office than in a vampire den. But his crisp, black and white suit was the calling card of the *deadliest* vampire Family in the Midwest, the Drakes, and he'd paraded a museum's worth of weapons through Book Nookery over the years he'd visited.

"Greetings, Chloe Anderson." Josh slightly bowed his head. He set a hand on the pommel of his sword so it didn't bob when he moved. "Yes, I am here for my books."

"Great, let me just get them..." I trailed off when the bell rang, and two more vampires skulked into Book Nookery.

One was a beautiful woman with blond hair, a perfectly tailored suit, and a smile that flashed her pronounced vampire fang teeth. The other was a red-haired guy, who was also a vampire based on his red eyes. He, though, was scowling, and looked like he lived life with a perpetually sour expression.

Both vampires—each well over six feet—fell in line behind Josh, watching him with the attention of underlings.

I paused in the middle of pulling the first of Josh's books from the drawer in the desk where we stored reserved materials.

Wait...is Josh a higher rank than them?

Josh was so competent in the way he carried himself that it wouldn't surprise me too much. But it was a funny juxtaposition: the shorter, nerdy guy with a thing for books and weapons, would be a higher rank than the model-tall vampires behind him?

"Here's the special edition volume of Edgar Allan Poe poetry." I set the book—a leather cover embossed with gold lettering—on the desk. "Do you want to look it over to make sure you still want it?"

"A sagacious suggestion," Josh said. "But I already know I want it. Edgar Allan Poe was truly capable of capturing the darkness that so often envelops this delicate world of ours and steeps into the hearts of the living." He sighed deeply. "It is forever my sorrow that I was not in America when he was alive."

Behind him, the gorgeous blond vampire had a benevolent smile on. The sour red-haired vampire mashed his lips together and shook his head.

"He can't really be that good," the red-haired vampire said. "France had so many better poets and thinkers. The United States is dreadfully *young*."

Josh peered back at the taller vampire. "The age of a civilization is not indicative of the size of its talent pool. But, to your point, I must admit there is very little that can beat a Gregorian Monk Chant. When we get back to Drake Hall, I will play some for you. Perhaps it will help you explore new depths to your soul."

The red-haired vampire opened his mouth, but the blond violently elbowed his side.

"How very educational!" she said in a sing-song voice.

Oh, yeah. They're definitely his underlings. But exactly how high is he in the Drake hierarchy?

I retrieved the second book—a much smaller nonfiction book about Japanese katanas—and set it on my desk. It was heavy—the paper was thicker to better render the glossy photographs that filled the book. "And here's the book on katanas."

"How perfect." Josh inspected the nonfiction book, then nodded his satisfaction. "What do I owe you for them?"

"Let me ring you up, and we'll find out." I scanned the books in and processed Josh's credit card payment before wrapping both books in tissue paper—Ms. Booker encouraged me to go the extra mile for our regular customers—and packing them in a brown paper bag that had a book design printed over it.

I passed the bag over to Josh. "I hope you enjoy the books. Can I help you with anything else?"

"I don't suppose you happen to stock hymnals of Gregorian Monk Chants?" Josh asked.

"Um, no." I blinked. "I could see if there are any books we could order for you, though?"

Josh checked his watch and shook his head. "No, I'm afraid we are due at House Medeis in a few minutes. It is nearly time for a surprise night training session with Hazel, and I have so been looking forward to it. She makes amusing noises when properly surprised, and that makes His Eminence laugh."

I struggled to make my laugh even a little realistic and not robotic with fear. "His Eminence" could only refer to the leader of the Drake Family and the vampires of the Midwest, Killian Drake. The "Hazel" Josh referred to had to be Hazel Medeis, the protégé of the top wizard in the Midwest.

The exact kind of people I've been avoiding since I told the Curia Cloisters what I was.

After my adopted siblings—Pat and Joy—had been kidnapped by the now ex-Unseelie Queen and ex-Seelie King—I had told the Curia Cloisters that I'd recently discovered I was a shadow.

Initially, I'd faced a lot of doubt—shadows had been considered extinct for centuries since the elves had killed them long before the elven war that had taken out the elves.

The Curia Cloisters dragged their feet all summer in researching it, but in mid-August they'd finally concluded that I was what Noctus said I was.

What I hadn't expected was their sudden renewed interest in me. When I'd been an outcast/freak of nature, the Curia Cloisters had been very little help. Now I was constantly getting invitations to meetings as they were desperate to find out how my parents had survived—as if I knew; they'd dropped me off at a hospital when I was a baby, and a human family had adopted me!

I hadn't agreed to any meetings for several reasons. First off, I was a little bitter that the Cloisters was magically interested in me now that I was a shadow when I'd spent my entire life desperately trying to get help from them before discovering what I was.

Secondly, the invitations I kept getting were from supernaturals with high standing in the Cloisters. I preferred a trouble free, quiet life and wanted to avoid political ploys at all costs. Meeting with highflyers would not help me succeed at that goal.

And finally, when I'd left Noctus, the King of the Mors elves who was hiding his existence from supernatural society, I had promised him I wouldn't let anyone find out about him, or the city of elves that lived in his proverbial shadow.

I was going to keep that promise, no matter the sacrifice.

But I need to focus on work, now, not Noctus, I reminded myself.

I pushed my shoulders back and refocused on Josh the unlikely vampire. "Do you train Hazel often?"

Josh tilted his head as he thought. "Frequently enough, I suppose, as I am her firearm instructor. Celestina trains with her more, but that is understandable given that she is the First Knight of the Drake Family, and I am only the Second Knight."

"*Second Knight?*" I repeated, my eyes bulging so much I was going to need eyedrops to hydrate them after Josh left.

The First Knight and Second Knight were terms used to refer

to the vampire family's first and second strongest members after the Family Elder.

Which means Josh is the third strongest vampire in the Drake Family?!

I stared at the even-tempered vampire, who smiled at me, looking very benign even though he had to be deadly beyond my reckoning to have that kind of rank.

Josh checked his watch. "Regardless, we had best leave—being late is a stain I do not wish to add to my soul. Good evening, Chloe Anderson. May the light of life puncture the darkness of this bleak existence for you."

A wave, and he was gone, his two underlings trotting along behind him—though they shoved each other when they tried to get through the door at the same time.

"Huh." I dubiously glanced at the accounting software that was open on my work computer's screen. "I guess that will teach me for judging a book by its cover."

I finished processing the last few purchase orders for the day, before exiting out of the software.

Since I finished that, I'd better check and see if there are any customers who need to be informed that their orders are in.

Usually, the task was left to the day shift, unless a supernatural indicated they preferred to be notified during the night hours.

I fished around in the drawer and grabbed the printed-out list, frowning when I saw it was just one specific customer: Mr. Ferryman.

I'd been trying to contact this particular customer all summer long for the many books he'd ordered—and purchased over the phone with a credit card—but had failed to come in and pick up.

The stack was growing big enough to be a tripping hazard, which I didn't mind so much, except it made me exceedingly nervous to be holding on to books that technically already belonged to the customer. (It just wasn't a good business practice.)

But no matter how many times I tried calling this mysterious patron, they didn't come in. The only identifier they left with the order was "Mr. Ferryman," and the phone number. Even the internet wasn't a help with so little information to go on.

I checked the spot under the desk where we were storing the mystery customer's order. He'd purchased books on short swords, modern fashion, daggers, and a donut cookbook that I had peeked at with jealousy when it had first come in.

It looks like he bought a book about housecats this time. He's certainly interested in a wide variety of topics.

Still, it upset me that we were failing to give this customer their order and kept taking their money. Besides, Ms. Booker—the owner of Book Nookery—did not abide with disorder, and while this wasn't causing disorder in the store per se, it caused disorder in the accounting books!

"I left a note for the day shift that they shouldn't take any more orders for Mr. Ferryman until they come in and get their books, didn't they see it?" I grumbled.

I fortified myself with a swig of the deliciousness that was my amaretto steamer—which was even tastier now that it didn't scald my mouth—when the doorbell jingled again.

Struggling to swallow, I glanced at the new customer, and almost spat out my drink.

Shiloh, a pretty blond whom I knew had a thing for lawn care, entered Book Nookery, a smile blooming on her face when she saw me.

"Chloe! Hello!"

I attempted to force my customer service smile, but my nerves were so rattled I'm pretty sure my expression was closer to a twisted grimace. "Shiloh! Hello!"

Shiloh happened to be the neighbor of Noctus—whom I was maybe still pining over even though we'd been forced to face the reality that our priorities in life meant we couldn't be together. I'd met her while staying at his home, and she'd pushed me to date

Noctus, who *told* her we were as a cover story to explain my constant presence.

I knew that was going to bite me in the butt someday...

"What brings you to Book Nookery?" I set my hands on the desk to stabilize myself. "Or, as I should say, can I help you with anything?"

"I do need a book, but I'm really here to see you," Shiloh said. "It took me a while to figure out that you work the night shift, or I would have been here sooner. And when I *did* realize it, I had really bad luck and visited twice when you happened to have off." She made a face that still managed to look cute with her button-like features.

"Well, here I am," I lamely said. I started to pick up my steamer, then realized my hand was shaking so badly I was going to slosh the drink, so I set it back down.

"Yes!" Shiloh turned in a circle, peering through the doors and hallways that split off from the main entrance where the desk and I were stationed. "I can see why you'd like working here! I mean, a bookstore would be a fun place to work no matter what, but magic feels extra potent here."

I blinked in surprise.

Shiloh was human, and humans were typically ignorant to the presence of magic. Magic could be tricky even for supernaturals to process. Vampires couldn't sense it at all, and while magic caused sensations in me—fae magic tickled my elbow, whereas the presence of werewolves was more of a furry feeling—I couldn't do more than sense its presence.

Shiloh did pick me out as a supernatural the minute I met her as a human, though. She even figured out Noctus is a supernatural—though with his looks I guess it would be weirder if he wasn't. Some humans are extra perceptive. Shiloh must be one of those.

"The Book Nookery is a very rewarding and fun place to work," I slowly said. "I'm very lucky to be able to embrace the supernatural as part of my job, since Book Nookery does specialize in books on the magical, in addition to offering popular fiction and nonfiction."

"Got any books about cheese?" Shiloh asked with a teasing smile.

I laughed—I'd become acquainted with Shiloh's love of cheese while living at Calor Villa. "Actually, we do. Though they're recipe books. Is that what you're looking for, or were you thinking of something more informational?"

"While I'd love to say I'd take a recipe book, I have no idea when I'd find the time to make any cheese," Shiloh sighed.

"Busy as usual, are you?" I asked.

"Yeah." Shiloh rubbed her eyes, and for a moment I saw beyond her sunny disposition to the tiredness she hid with her bright smiles. "Things will slow down now that I won't have to mow and weed, but I need to get sidewalk salt and see if the snowblower needs a tune up."

Both of Shiloh's parents had died, leaving her a very young homeowner while she attended the local community college.

The sheer hours she spent maintaining her house had me grateful I just rented a studio apartment.

"Actually, instead of a cheese book, I don't suppose you have a copy of *How to Win Friends and Influence People*?" Shiloh asked.

I froze.

"Oh? Did you hear about Dale Carnegie from someone?" I tried to keep my voice casual, but it cracked in the middle of my question.

Ker—a werewolf friend of Noctus's who had been around longer than America was a country—*loved* that book, and its author, Dale Carnegie.

Even thinking about her made a lump form in my throat. I'd vastly underestimated how much I'd miss her, Aristide, and Charon when I left Calor Villa.

"Yeah, one of my professors recommended it," Shiloh said. "Do you have it in stock?"

"We do." I stepped out from behind my desk. "It's over here."

"Wow, you don't even have to check the computer? You're a book magician," Shiloh joked as she followed me into the "drawing room," which contained all of Book Nookery's biographies, self-help books, books on languages, and any nonfiction books about supernaturals.

"I'm not that good." I ducked under a hanging glass lantern that glowed a forest green color and hung from a hook fashioned in a vine shape. "I just know where it is because I recommended to Ms. Booker—the owner—that we stock it."

And I had been inspired by thoughts of Ker, but Shiloh doesn't need to know that.

"Thanks—talk about convenient." Shiloh almost rammed into me when I stopped at the long row that marked all our self-help bookshelves.

"Is this your last semester at community college?" I scanned the shelves as I looked for the right book. "Last time I saw you, you said you were almost done with all the classes you could take."

"Yeah," Shiloh sighed. "I'm still trying to figure out what to do next."

"Don't rush it," I advised. "It's a big decision. And here we go." I plucked the thin volume from the shelf and held it out to Shiloh.

Shiloh took it, then danced nervously from foot to foot. "Hey, um. I might be overstepping my boundaries, so you don't have to answer, but...are you okay?"

Ahh, yes. May the butt biting commence.

I made myself blink, as if I was confused. "Yes?"

"I mean...Noctus told me you two broke up," Shiloh said.

Good. He invented that stupid cover story, I'm glad he at least broke the news of our fake break up to her.

"We did," I confirmed. "In early summer."

"I know, but—are you really okay with that? You seemed great together."

"Great? You never even saw us together when we were... dating," I said.

"Yeah, okay, but Noctus seemed so...happy," Shiloh said. "And you're an amazing person, so I can't fathom what happened. You two just seemed to have such a magical connection. Noctus is a great guy—I know he'd treat you like a queen."

I felt all the blood drain from my face at her casual choice of words.

She has no idea how close she is with that statement.

Noctus was a king, after all. If he ever had a romantic dalliance, she'd be his queen.

But even at my most delusional, I had never pondered that. Noctus and I hadn't even been a *thing*. I'd been caught up in the feeling of belonging and—even more dangerous—the warm feelings the magic bond between us inspired, but before we even got to the point of becoming...anything, I'd been forced to realize that the things we both held most precious—him with his kingdom and me with my human family—were opposing forces. It would never work—as I swiftly learned when Pat and Joy were kidnapped and Noctus couldn't risk moving to help and possibly reveal his people in the process.

And while I loved my family, being human meant they were inherently delicate—and easily manipulated with magic. All it would take was a fae spell or some vampire pheromones, and they'd spill every detail they knew about Noctus if they were asked—even if they didn't want to.

Since neither Noctus nor I could budge on what was most important to us, we didn't work—or rather, we *couldn't* work.

"It wasn't a bad break up," I said, truthfully. "It was just that we realized we want different things, and those wants weren't going to mesh."

"And you couldn't compromise?" Shiloh asked.

I smiled sadly. "Romantic love is important, Shiloh, but there's so much in my life that is equally as important, like family. I wouldn't compromise in loving someone—whether it's my boyfriend or my brother and sister."

Shiloh frowned at a shelf of self-help books that were about organizing and decluttering. "That makes sense. I figured it had to be something adult-ish and unfortunate. Noctus wasn't angry about your breakup, he just seemed..." She sighed. "Regretful."

"I was sad about it—I still am if I'm being honest," I admitted. There was something about Shiloh's warm eyes that made me open up, or maybe it was that she *knew* Noctus, when I hadn't even told Pat or Joy about him. "But there wasn't any other way. Sometimes, life just says 'no,'" I said.

Shiloh pressed her lips together, making her cheeks pucker a little. "It still seems silly when he's clearly pining for you, and you obviously miss him. But, yeah. Sometimes life likes to take a swing at you, and other times it jumps you from behind, grabs you in a choke hold, and then slams you into the ground."

Don't ask—don't open the door. Don't do it!

"How is he doing?" I asked.

Why did I ask?!

"Did you miss the part where I said he's pining for you?" Shiloh asked. "But, he's okay, I think. Back to his usual stoic, blank faced self. Though—no offense, I know you were his girlfriend and all, but I think something's wrong with Ama and that's why he's detached again."

"Ama?" I repeated, blinking in surprise.

"Yeah. I haven't seen her in months, and she used to pop out at least once a week. I asked him how she was, though, and he said she was fine. But he comes outside a lot less now than he did in the spring."

Well...she said he's fine. And she's right, "detached" is kind of his modus operandi. He'll recover, if he hasn't already.

Shiloh drummed her fingers on her book. "But, hey, you should come visit the neighborhood sometime."

I immediately shook my head. "I really shouldn't go back to your neighborhood."

Her frown was back. "Why not?"

Shoot—I can't exactly tell her that Noctus and I are pretending we don't know each other...what do I say?

My shoulders hunched as my finely tuned survival instincts pitter pattered toward anxiety. "It wouldn't be emotionally healthy," I said. "I'm working on moving on. Seeing him would... make things worse."

I was going to leave it at that, but Shiloh looked so crestfallen.

"But I'd love to meet for lunch sometime—or breakfast," I offered before I realized what I was saying. "Since I have night shifts I'm available in early mornings if you don't have class."

She knows Noctus, this could be a potential information breach... except, would it really be? If we stay friends, it's not like we'll be frequently talking about Noctus.

Shiloh clutched her Dale Carnegie book to her chest and beamed. "That would be great! I mostly have night classes this semester. It's why I could drop by tonight after I did my grocery shopping. I could do some mornings—here's my number."

I pulled my phone out of my pocket, still mentally arguing the risks as we exchanged numbers.

There can't be any harm in staying in touch with her...I just can't let my siblings meet her, and if we stay away from the Curia Cloisters and her cul-de-sac, there shouldn't be any risk for Noctus.

Shiloh left a few minutes later, leaving me to finish my now lukewarm steamer—which was still delicious—before once again turning my attention to calling the mystery customer.

I only got their robotic voicemail—as I always did—so I was left feeling dissatisfied after I stored their books again.

Pondering what to do next, I saw the few newspapers Ms.

Booker kept for customers to peruse were messed up, so I stopped to reorganize them.

On the front page of the Magiford local newspaper was a giant article. "*Ten Injured in Magical Artifact Explosion*," the headline shouted in bold font.

My forehead wrinkled with worry as I skimmed the article—Pat had told me about the incident; he'd initially been concerned it was from the tracker.

A magical artifact went off, releasing a shadow monster that injured ten people—one of whom was hospitalized, although is expected to make a full recovery...Curia Cloisters investigating, artifact appears to use fae magic...following leads with no formal announcement to make at this time, except to promise that the perpetrator will be caught...

"Yeah, that's not the tracker. I was at home that day, and he only comes out to play when he knows I'm around." I refolded the newspaper and straightened the stack.

In fact, it seems more likely to be connected to the illegal artifact ring Noctus, Charon, Ker, and Aristide busted.

There wasn't anything that jumped out at me to make me suspect the issues had a common mastermind. It was just that the organizers of the illegal artifact manufacturers hadn't ever been caught, and they'd purposely rigged their artifacts to fail after a few months or weeks and either burn or explode—on a tiny scale.

It seemed weird that there would be *two* groups of crazies who were using exploding spells for nefarious reasons, especially when—as a whole—supernaturals were pretty good at pulling together to pretend we were all civil and harmless to keep the humans from getting spooked.

Pat's going to be on this case—they'll use him to represent human interests.

Pat had joined the Curia Cloisters task force department, to help them learn how to handle humans and to act as a go-between for the city and the Curia Cloisters.

I turned my gaze on to the rack of magazines we sold, when my text ringtone chimed.

I opened my messages—if it was anyone besides my family I'd ignore it, but it was Pat.

Eurydice

AT THE SIGHT of the code word, anxiety—followed by a surge of adrenaline—spiked through my body. I speed dialed my brother while sprinting through the house, sliding into the kitchen.

I grabbed my short sword, daggers, and leather harness—given the tracker's continued presence in Magiford, Ms. Booker let me bring my weapons to work with me—and tossed my ringing phone on the table while I started to strap my gear into place.

Pat picked up the phone, and I frantically tapped the speakerphone button. "What happened? Did he try for Joy again?" I pinched my finger in one of my harness's buckles and barely noticed the pain.

"*Orpheus*!" Pat shouted through the phone. "*Orpheus, Chloe.*"

I sagged, and all the fear in my body dissipated when I recognized the second code word. "Orpheus—this was just a drill? Joy's fine? You're fine?"

"*Yes. I just wanted to test your response time while you're on the clock.*"

I would have dropped the dagger I was holding, except it was elven made, and even though my relief was making me lightheaded, there was no way I was going to just *drop* something so precious.

Especially since Charon and Noctus gave it to me—

"I hope I reacted fast enough?" I asked.

"Yeah—you were very satisfactory. Last week I tested Joy, and she took five minutes to respond, which is terrible. I gave her an improvement plan sheet, and she drove over to my apartment, used her spare key to get inside, and put bird feed on my patio. It's still *overrun by pigeons!"*

I laughed. "Yeah, she told me about that—I'm just glad she is still so fiery!"

At the end of July, the tracker attacked Joy outside her new workplace in Magiford City Hall.

A visiting werewolf Pack heard Joy screaming and intervened, but the incident had left my siblings and me shaken.

Maybe I should stop avoiding the Curia Cloisters. If the tracker hurts Pat or Joy, I don't know if I could forgive myself.

Since August, it seemed like the tracker had changed tactics. Now he was laying traps around Magiford for me instead of any kind of direct confrontation.

It was maddening—that he was so consumed with getting me that he would observe and change tactics, that he even *cared* so much! I mean, I never did anything to him! Why was he obsessed with getting me?

Noctus and the others said he was a half elf; does he hate me just because shadows are the elves' natural enemies? But we weren't even involved in the elven war—everyone thought we were dead!

"*Just stay alert,*" Pat told me, snapping my attention back to him. "*Things have been a bit tense in Magiford, and it's only ramping up.*"

"Okay," I slowly said, trying to sense if there were any undertones to his warning. "I saw an article about the artifact incident downtown...has something new happened at the Cloisters that you can't tell me about?"

"*Nah,*" Pat said. "*Unless you count the new big threat the Cloisters is experiencing: a gopher infestation.*"

I relaxed, some of my tension leaving me. "A gopher infestation?"

"*Yep. Or maybe moles or groundhogs—I haven't seen the little buggers.*

Whatever they are, they keep digging holes in the lawn and flower beds. It's driving the groundskeeper crazy."

"That's oddly wholesome," I said. "But since this was just a drill, I should get back to work. Ms. Booker has been very understanding, but I don't want to waste time I should be spending stocking shelves."

"*Right, right. Just be safe, baby sis.*"

"You too, Pat."

He hung up without acknowledging my request—typical older brother.

I sighed as I put my weapons back, my nerves still twitchy.

I need to take care of the tracker. One way or another.

CHAPTER TWO

Noctus

I walked around the freshly scrubbed pavement that marked the spot where the rigged spell—attached to a jewel brooch that acted as a low-level artifact—had gone off. When the brooch released the shadow monster, it had also liberally dosed a five-foot area around it in blood, *human* blood.

The area had been meticulously cleaned—to prevent the blood from causing any unpleasantries with vampires, who weren't always the best at controlling themselves when surrounded by so much of their sustenance.

Rumor had it the Curia Cloisters suspected the bloodbath was done to cause chaos and make the situation seem even worse than appeared to spread panic, but it seemed like an odd way to establish intimidation when—without the blood spell—the artifact probably could have unleashed another shadow monster.

It was possible it was an attack aimed specifically at vampires, except vampires weren't the type to mingle with humans, and it had gone off during the day, so only two vampires were in the area at the time. Thankfully, one of them was a Drake vampire, who restrained the younger, more easily influenced second vampire until backup from the Cloisters arrived.

I finished my inspection of the sidewalk, then turned on my cellphone flashlight.

The sky was a swirl of dark clouds, blocking out the midnight moon and stars, and only one lamp had survived the monster's rampage, so the street was dimly lit.

But I had good enough night vision, and night was the safest time to investigate. During the daylight hours we'd be noticed.

Besides, night is when it's worse.

I shut the thought down and forced myself to stare at the evidence before me—or what little was left.

The claw marks left in the sidewalk from the shadow monster hadn't yet been repaired, so I was able to study the jagged lines carefully.

The brooch had been hidden under a bench positioned at a bus stop, with a giant sign that contained the bus schedule next to it.

The monster had only injured six of the victims—the remaining four had been hurt in the ensuing stampede.

I raised my gaze, looking across the street where a new apartment building—one that had been touted in the supernatural community as a safe haven for the likes of lone wolves, unclaimed vampires, and Court-less fae—had been due to open in mere weeks.

Luckily, a Court-less fae and a lone wolf had been about to tour the building when the monster was released, and they'd been the ones to kill the monster before it truly started to rampage.

"A bus stop, huh," Aristide said, his voice invading my careful focus. "I guess these creeps are declaring the humans as their targets for this round."

The vampire gazed unseeingly down the street, tilting his head as he listened to the sounds of our surroundings.

"That is what the Curia Cloisters seem to think, according to their published information—although they might be holding some back for the sake of the ongoing investigation," Charon said.

"Mmhmm. What do you think, Noctus?" Aristide asked.

"I am not convinced." I felt a few raindrops on my skin and glanced up at the gloomy sky that would likely loosen a downpour on us any moment. "Its location near the apartment building is too close to be ignored, and including the blood seems an oddly *specific* choice for intimidation when a second creature would have caused even more panic."

"Then do you think they were aiming for the outcasts of supernatural society?" Aristide staggered a little when Ker—in her wolf form—started walking, leading him forward. "That would be a pretty big veer from their campaign with their illegal artifact ring we cracked earlier—if it's the same guys, that is."

Aristide followed Ker as she led him up a little closer to me, so intent on smelling she almost scraped her nose on the sidewalk.

"It is," I said, certainty weighing down my voice.

Charon glanced at his tiny notebook. "The manufacturers that we caught are still in Ghast Prison."

"Yes, but they weren't the ringleaders. We have the video footage of the fae—who we believe set the illegal ring up—that put him on this street. There's a good chance he planted the brooch." I paused, then continued. "It's most likely he works for the group the Paragon warned us of."

"The one that backed a wizard coup, and attempted to take out the fae empress back when she had just been made Queen of the Night Court?" Charon asked.

"Yes. The poorly manufactured artifacts fit their style," I said. "Though I don't fully understand why they're attempting a similar scheme a second time."

"They're not selling them, just planting them," Aristide pointed out, turning to speak in my general direction when Ker led him past me. "Maybe the first ring was a practice run that they learned on."

"Possibly," I said. "They're certainly scaling up. We can be certain the monster released was a shadow creature, forged by elf magic."

I knew the type well. I'd forbidden my people from using it.

Early in the summer two idiot juvenile elves had made several of the monsters, but I'd found them shortly after the attempt.

"Shadow magic isn't something that can be hidden," Charon said. "Whoever made it can't be from Calor Villa—they'd never be able to disguise it. So there must be elves working for the organization the Paragon is chasing, if not leading it."

"Yes." Aristide adjusted his hold on Ker's guide dog harness. "So isn't it a good thing the Curia Cloisters have been investing in greater magic-power, and the Midwest Regional Committee of Magic is the strongest in North America, if not the Northern Hemisphere? They should be able to deal with this shady group."

"Yes," I agreed.

"So *why*," Aristide drawled, "are we out here, about to get rained on, for a situation that doesn't even involve your people?!"

Thunder growled in the distance, underlining the vampire's irritation.

"An elf from Calor Villa witnessed the event," Charon said.

"*Witnessed*—she wasn't even on the block." Aristide turned in a circle as Ker guided him back toward Charon and me. "We could easily let this pass by. So. What are we doing out here?"

Raindrops started to spatter my jacket as I rubbed at the shackle on my wrist—it would be helpful to try to sense the magic in the area, but I was doing my best to block out all magic. I'd had to, ever since Chloe left.

"We're here because I'm bored," I announced.

"Bored?" Aristide squawked. "*Bored?* That's your reasoning?

Forget investing your time in meaningful projects, let's just sit out here in the rain in the middle of the night like a bunch of creeps."

"The night is your natural time of comfort," I said. "I'm being thoughtful."

"No—no, don't try that one on me! If you were being thoughtful, you'd take a vacation," Aristide said. "Like normal people do when they don't have work looming over them. Maybe go to Hawaii, or Australia. It's spring for them right now, isn't it? We could go hug koalas or something instead of pretending to be a crime solving ragtag group of supernaturals."

Charon narrowed his eyes. "His Majesty is *not* ragtag."

I rubbed my ears, only half listening. As if it had sensed my attitude toward it, the wild magic in the area was starting to stir.

"Whatever, we could have still taken a vacation instead of... whatever this is." Aristide yanked up the hood of his rain jacket. "But if you insist on adding more make-work projects to your already towering and unhealthy number of responsibilities, might I suggest a pet—we at least have positive proof they have an impact on you."

I eyed my longtime friend. *Is he attempting to ascertain if I'm wounded by Chloe's exit? Surely he can't think I'm that delicate—it's been months.*

Ker whined and bounced next to Aristide.

Aristide's nose twitched—likely with the scent of wet wolf as the light rain started to sink through Ker's coat. "Yes, I know, a cat or dog wouldn't work because of you. I was going to suggest he start with something easy—maybe a pet fish."

"No pets," I said.

"Not even a rabbit? How about a ferret?" Aristide asked.

I swung back to Charon. "Let's stop by the clocktower before we head home."

Charon glanced from me to the apartment building across the street. "Do you think it could be a potential target if these villains aren't caught?"

I looked back at the apartment building and frowned. "No. You and Aristide successfully convinced the city that the clock-tower investor is human, and the elves running businesses out of it do not publicize that they are supernaturals."

My people generally pretended to be humans, unless cornered by another supernatural and asked why they had a glamour, then they would confess to being fae. It was a ruse we had practiced for centuries.

"Okay, fine," Aristide said. "I didn't want to suggest this, but how about a bird?"

Ker made a questioning noise.

"They sing all the time and sound generally happy, so yes, birds are *not* my aesthetic, but I'm getting desperate," Aristide said.

"Aristide, I'm not getting a pet," I said. "Go back to the car, we're leaving soon."

Aristide scratched Ker's neck for her. "Sorry, did I hit a sore spot?"

I rolled my eyes. Even though the vampire wouldn't be able to see it, he knew me well enough to guess my reaction.

"And now you have nothing to say except to—I imagine—roll your eyes like some kind of impatient prepubescent human being. Charming." Aristide turned on his heels so he pointed in the direction of the SUV Charon had parked on the street. "Just tell me this, Noctus. Are you *really* so desperate to forget about Chloe that you intend to muck around in things that don't involve us, and work yourself into a dangerous level of fatigue?"

I opened my mouth to respond, but at that moment the wild magic in the area managed to crack through the wall of control I'd mentally erected to hold it back.

It *wailed*, filling my senses with a ringing sound that vibrated my bones.

Aristide jostled Ker's guide dog harness. "Nothing to say, hmm? What do you think, Charon?"

Charon shut his notebook and tucked it away into the cloak-like shirt he always wore. "I wouldn't presume to ponder what His Majesty is thinking."

"You're just as much fun as ever, Charon. Good talk," Aristide said. "Fine—you win, Noctus. I won't push any more. Tonight. Let's get out of this rain and check out the clocktower."

As Aristide walked off, Charon bowed to me. "Is everything alright, Your Majesty?"

"Yes," I said through gritted teeth as I tried not to visibly react to the soul-crushing weeping of wild magic. "Start the car."

"Very well." Charon stepped into the street and jogged off, passing Aristide and Ker.

I shut my eyes as I tried to shut out the melodramatics of wild magic once again.

After all these months, it still mourns Chloe.

Which was idiotic. She was still alive. Magic had just decided it wanted us bound together—a trick I had stupidly fallen for when I believed Chloe was a mere cat. But I'd successfully freed her—thwarting magic in the process.

Enough! I internally snarled as I slammed down on my magic once more, cutting off the quivering choir of wild magic mid note.

I exhaled; my skull once again silent.

I could admit that I missed Chloe, but regardless of any feelings of affection, it didn't change that she'd left. That she *had* to leave. Our lives were never going to comfortably fit together. I knew that and understood it.

If only wild magic realized it as well.

I took a step toward the now running car, and the skies opened. Rain poured down, filling the air with the acidic scent of rain on pavement.

It will come to accept it. I ignored the rain as I headed toward the car. *It won't have a choice, because nothing is going to change.*

"Oh great," Aristide yowled farther down the street. "And now it's raining. *Fantastic*! I hate this city!"

CHAPTER THREE

Chloe

A gust of wind blew down the street, yanking at my light jacket.

Septembers were warm in Magiford, but I was stuck wearing a jacket that was a size too big for me so it would cover up my sword harness and give me enough stretch to grab my sword from the scabbard on my back if I needed to.

Just another reason why I need to take care of the tracker, I grimly thought as I automatically ducked French Fry when he attempted to land on my shoulder and instead almost smacked into my head. *It's bad enough that I'm hot right now, but when the weather changes, I'll freeze to death in this jacket.*

Wet grit scraped the sidewalk under my shoes—sensible boots with reinforced toes and heels for extra kicking power—and I wrestled my jacket back into place.

I'll have to straighten my clothes when I get to the Curia Cloisters. If I ask for help while looking like an untidy rat, they'll say no—shadow or not.

It was my day off, and I was heading to the Curia Cloisters with the vague hope of making arrangements for all the meetings I'd been studiously avoiding, and planned to surprise Pat with lunch after I finished.

I was nervous—my stomach was already flopping around in my gut, and I was just walking. I needed to make sure I didn't say anything to give away Noctus's presence, but I couldn't wait any longer. The tracker needed to be taken care of, for the sake of my siblings.

Maybe this will go better than I'm thinking. They've been requesting meetings, but they haven't really been pressuring me. The Cloisters know where I live and work, and while I am a shadow, I won't really be useful for supernatural society at large as a solo shadow.

I adjusted the way my jacket fell on my shoulders—it was starting to slide to one side—and glanced to the south.

The clocktower rose above all the other shorter downtown buildings.

I was passing closer to it than I technically needed to since the Curia Cloisters were on the northwest side of Magiford, but... there was something reassuring about the clocktower.

Not a word. I vowed. *Not a single word about him. They never really asked how I figured out I was a shadow. If this meeting goes the way I want it to, whoever the Curia assigns to speak to me will do all the talking, so they'll never think to ask me.*

A thumping noise that sounded suspiciously like a trash griffin getting into trouble yanked my attention to the sidewalk in front of me.

About half a block up, French Fry was shoving his pigeon feet between the gaps of a wooden garbage can. He must have spied a piece of trash or fast food that had missed the garbage bag and fallen between the wooden frame and the bag.

"French Fry," I called. "Stop it."

The greedy little thing refused to let go, so I sighed and jogged to catch up to him. I knelt down and tried to pick him up, but I couldn't stand since he still refused to let go of the scrap of food—a French fry, of course.

I poked my fingers through the gap in the garbage can and had to rip the French fry from his grasping bird feet. He tried to shove his head through the gap, but his aim was off, so instead he smacked his head on the wooden siding.

He made a short, staccato grumbling noise as I tipped him onto his back and whisked him away from the can.

"Don't be piggy." I grabbed the coveted French fry and stood up, cradling him like a baby.

French Fry grumbled some more and flicked himself in the face with his raccoon tail. He immediately switched to happy, cooing noises, however, when I offered him the flattened and probably week-old fry.

He grabbed it with one of his pigeon feet, then fell out of my arms, splatting on the cement where he stuffed the fry in his orange beak and promptly choked.

I wiped my hands off on my jacket and stepped around him. "It's amazing your species has continued surviving all these years."

I shoved my hands into my pockets as I started walking again, marching through the heart of downtown Magiford.

I smiled to the rare person who met my gaze, and paid close attention to my senses as I shouldered my way through crowded sidewalks.

I didn't feel any supernaturals in the area, which was expected. Supernaturals didn't exactly hang out downtown—it was why I had staked out the territory for myself.

Well, the Seelie and Unseelie Courts used to have occasional turf wars downtown, but that had stopped since I'd overthrown the monarchs of both Courts.

It still feels crazy to think that I stopped them. I was stiff with anxiety the whole time. But, then again, they shouldn't have messed with my siblings.

I turned north, following one of the two lakes that sprawled across Magiford. Another few blocks, and the downtown area thinned out to parks and businesses with bigger lots like auto body shops, a gas station, and a car wash, before turning residential.

The Curia Cloisters were still far away, but I walked everywhere in this city, so the distance didn't bother me.

French Fry flapped along with me, but after we'd gone a block he abruptly banked and crash landed.

He probably saw something edible.

"French Fry," I started. "You are going to get hurt if you keep —" I snapped my jaw shut so hard my teeth clicked.

Fear. An oppressive fear that rode all my instincts so hard I froze, a tangle of desperation that made me want to run and terror so tangible I couldn't move.

I instantly recognized the sensation: it was the tracker.

Experience let me override my waffling instincts. I turned around, already reaching for the hilt of my short sword that barely poked up out of my floppy jacket.

The tracker—elf-tall and lanky—was a block behind me, boldly standing in the middle of the sidewalk. He wasn't even bothering to use his usual weird, shadowy magic to cover himself, so I could see the black swirls of his neck tattoo, and his box-dyed hair color of the month: acid green.

He most likely wasn't using the shadows because he didn't need the advantage they gave him. He had an even bigger one, today: he was holding a young woman and had a knife at her throat.

"Don't move, shadow," he called, ignoring the young woman who squirmed in his grasp. "And let go of that sword I know you're drawing—or she'll pay for it." The tracker flicked his eyes to the panicked woman.

No, no, no, no.

I was a scaredy-cat all the way to my bones, but I'd never forgive myself if he hurt her because I fled.

I must face him. But how?

I could hear my heartbeat in my eardrums as I tried to think.

The young woman—she had to be human as I couldn't feel any magic coming from her—had eyes wide with panic, but as soon as the tracker pulled the knife from her throat, she tried smashing the back of her head into his face.

He dodged her head, but he staggered a step, and growled under his breath.

Good, she's fighting. That means if I get her free, she'll make a run for it.

"Shadow, I am not *patient*," the tracker warned.

I let go of my sword's hilt and held my hands out in front of me.

The tracker changed his grip on the young woman so he held her by the neck, and kept his knife pointed at me. He shoved her ahead of him, using her like a shield as they approached me.

It's okay, it's okay. I tried to calm my rapidly rising hysteria. *I'm trained for close combat—my fast shifting from cat to human makes it better for me. I will do this. I must do this. I can't leave her.*

"Of all of the shadows I've hunted, you have been the most problematic," the tracker drawled as he stalked closer, dragging the young woman with him. "You don't act anything like you should. Which is no excuse for why it took me so long to figure out how to get you. But, in my defense, any other shadow would have turned tail, caring only for themselves."

He hunts shadows? Why? We've been gone so long, and Noctus said this guy is half elf at best.

I gulped and tried to remember which pocket I'd stuffed my cellphone in.

The tracker and his hostage staggered close enough that I could see the whites of the young woman's eyes.

"But once you're gone, I can track down the humans who adopted you," he sneered. "A bit of pain, and I'm *sure* they'll suddenly remember more about the circumstances of your adoption."

My parents, he's talking about my parents.

Anxiety still flooded my body, making me knock-kneed, and I started breathing faster.

He's going to torture my parents for information.

The tracker's smile was cruel.

No. The word rippled through my entire body. *Never. He's never going to touch them.*

I glanced at his hostage. She met my gaze and nodded imperceptibly.

"Don't move an inch, shadow," the tracker warned me.

He wrapped his hand around the woman's neck and held her away from me, then lunged forward, his knife aimed at my heart.

I shifted into my cat form, so he staggered and almost fell over.

The young woman kicked him in the shins and dug her manicured, acrylic nails into the tendons of his hands.

I turned back into a human and smashed into him, grabbing his hand with the knife and thrusting it behind his back.

"Run!" I shouted to the young woman.

Freed, she ran, her purse slung over her arm and smacking her on the side as she sprinted down the sidewalk.

The tracker roared and yanked his arm out of my grasp.

I turned into a cat and darted between his feet. Once behind him, I shifted back into a human and kicked at his lower back.

The tracker staggered from the pain, and I used the moment to unsheathe my short sword.

The tracker—hearing the sound—darted forward, getting out of range, then peered back at me. "What, aren't you going to flee with her?" The tracker tossed his head in the direction the young woman had run.

"No," I said. "Because I'm going to stop you. *Now.*"

Confusion flickered across his face.

I lunged forward, stabbing my sword at him in one of the patterns Charon had meticulously drilled into my muscle memory.

He lunged to the side, avoiding the elven blade.

I shifted to my cat body, snuck underneath him, then turned back into my human form while underneath him, slamming into him with the force of my body-swapping magic behind me.

He fell, knocked straight off his feet, and a flicker of fear skittered across his face.

I swapped my grip on my sword, narrowing in on the tracker as I looked for any weaknesses I could take advantage of.

Ear. Max shock factor.

I stepped into his space before he could stand, and slashed my sword along the side of his head.

He thrashed, so my blade only sliced through the top fold of his ear. He yelped in pain and tried to scramble backwards.

Disarm him.

With his hands on the ground, it was easy to step on the knife and pin it to the asphalt, then stab my sword down at his hand.

The tracker let go of the knife and rolled away. He lurched to his feet while I kicked his knife under a bush—I certainly wasn't picking it up, he'd probably poisoned it or something.

The tracker tried to adopt a fighting stance, but he was so angry he couldn't settle. "Why don't you fight like a shadow?" he shouted. "You're more like—"

An elf, right? It made sense, given who'd taught me.

But I couldn't give him a chance to end the sentence. He was a half elf. If he realized who Noctus was, it would be a disaster.

Ridden by desperation, I leaped across the gap he'd put between us.

The tracker raised his arm, blocking my sword strike with a leather arm bracer.

Unfortunately for him, elven forged blades were ridiculously sharp, so the edge of my sword cut through the armor piece.

His eyes widened, and his body shook, leaving him wide open.

"Leave my parents alone," I hissed. I shifted my center of balance, leaning back so I could kick him in the groin.

The tracker groaned and fell to his knees.

I raised my voice to a growl. "Leave my *siblings* alone!"

I moved to knee him in the chin. He tried to raise his arm—the one with the now ruined arm bracer—but I had too much momentum, and he was too weak from pain, so my kick just made him punch himself in the throat.

He toppled backwards.

"Leave the *humans* alone!" I shouted as I kicked the side of his head.

He's effectively brained. I just need to get him bleeding to keep him weak, and then I can call Pat and the Curia Cloisters.

Normally the thought would have made me queasy. I was all for self-defense and justice, but stabbing a guy was not my usual speed.

He threatened my parents and hurt Pat and Joy.

I rotated my wrist, adjusting the blade of my elven sword, then stabbed it straight through his boot—and foot.

He didn't have reinforced boots—a major miscalculation. Or maybe not, I only stabbed him in the foot because there are a lot of major arteries in the leg, and I didn't want to risk nicking any of them. (This information was brought to you by Charon, who had instructed me *to* cut up an enemy's leg for that very reason. But I wanted the Curia Cloisters to question him. I didn't want him to bleed out before they arrived.)

The tracker yelled—his voice raw from pain—and rolled on the ground.

I retreated a few feet and swapped my sword for a dagger. Since I needed to use my phone, a one-handed dagger was a better choice instead of a sword that could potentially be swiped.

I fumbled to pull my phone from my left pocket, then swiped my cellphone screen open when the tracker yelled. "*Your parents—the shadows—used you as a decoy!*"

I paused, then suspiciously raised my dagger to a defensive position, but the tracker was still on the ground. "What?"

"Your real parents—the shadows." The tracker groaned, a vein popping in his neck. "They dumped you with humans to cover their tracks. I was able to follow them all the way to the human city where they dropped you."

Oohh I get it, he's trying to play a mental game. I warily navigated through my phone's screens, pulling up Pat's number.

I had thought a lot about my parents as a kid—why would they have given me up, did they know what I was, did they not want me? But in the end I'd grown up in a loving family, and I was thankful that my birth parents—whatever the circumstances—had loved me enough to see that I was safe.

"Hiding with a newborn would have been more difficult." The tracker whimpered as he tried to stand, but his stabbed foot wasn't cooperating. "So they abandoned you—in a public way so your presence was recorded with humans while their trail disappeared. They sacrificed you, used you as a decoy, so they could stay hidden."

I paused, my thumb hovering over the dial button.

Used me as a decoy? No. If they wanted to make my existence public they would have dumped me among supernaturals, not humans. Right?

Except...if their trail disappeared after they left me...

My gut instinct roared to life. Without thinking I jumped backwards, barely avoiding the dagger the tracker threw at me.

I snapped back to attention, thrusting my dagger out so I caught the tracker—who'd used my moment of uncertainty to get to his feet—in the shoulder.

He roared in pain, and I sensed more than I saw a change in his neck tattoo. Black, shadowy magic wrapped around his fist, which he swung at me, catching me on my left temple.

I felt the magic scrape my skin, trying to dig its claws into me, but my natural magic defenses ripped it apart so it couldn't affect me. But the magic must have somehow boosted the tracker's natural strength, because it felt like I'd gotten kicked in the head by a horse.

I was flung backwards, pain crackling through my skull.

I heard the tracker shout—his voice twisted with anguish, and I didn't think it was just because of his new shoulder wound.

Get safe, I must get safe.

Still blind from the pain, I turned into a cat and dragged myself across the sidewalk.

I think I managed to get half under one of the shrubs lining the sidewalk, because I felt branches pull at my fur.

The tracker alternated cursing and groaning. I heard something dragging on the sidewalk—his injured foot, I think—as his voice grew distant.

"I need backup—help!" the tracker spat.

Is he on the phone?

I tried to clear my eyes, but a new wave of pain made my stomach swirl, and I settled for digging my claws into the turf.

"I *know* I wasn't assigned to go after her, but shadows are a liability even if our leaders refuse to realize it! She jumped me, and now I don't know where she ran off! Send someone—with potions!"

His voice grew quieter and quieter as he fled, until I couldn't hear his voice at all.

I stayed under the shrub, squinting as I could finally start to see again. I moved an inch, and pain jolted through my body, knocking me flat again.

This is bad. I have to change. I have to call Pat, or Joy. Someone!

I tried to reach for my magic to change, not caring that I was going to pop into my human form while sprawled on the ground, half under a bush. But the pain was so bad it made spots dance in my eyes, and it felt like the world tilted around me. My body tingled unpleasantly, and I fought to stay conscious.

No, no!

Minutes passed, and I panted—so sick and hurt I couldn't tell directions anymore.

"Oh, my. Is that a cat?" The voice was fuzzy and distorted thanks to the ringing in my ears.

"I think it's injured—its eyes aren't focusing."

Something brushed at my neck.

No, no. I weakly meowed, trying to protest, but even that tiny movement made my stomach flop unpleasantly in my gut.

"No collar...do you think it's a stray?"

"Must be. Here—run back to the car. I have a sweater in the back seat. Grab it, we can wrap it up and take it to a rescue."

Call...Pat...Joy...

It was getting harder and harder to remain conscious. I needed to stay awake and change back—no one knew I was out. Pat and Joy wouldn't realize I was missing for hours.

Help, I thought, feeling tiny and helpless as the world turned black again. *Noctus, help*.

THE NEXT TIME I woke up, I was in a metal cage, sitting on a cat bed covered by a piece of red flannel decorated with yellow birds.

What...?

I had just enough time to pick my head off the flannel before the waves of pain and nausea hit me.

Ugh, just how badly did the tracker hit me? I must have a concussion...

My thoughts felt thick and slow. It was a struggle to think, and when I moved the smallest bit—even just to flex my paws—it made pain swim through my body.

Where am I? What time is it? Did the tracker come back and find me?

I heard a door open. "We're thrilled you chose us. At Paw-Pals

Rescue, we love matching up furry friends with their forever homes, and I can tell you'll be a wonderful family," a woman said.

A rescue? That's right—someone found me under the bush. They must have brought me in. It was too hard to keep my head up, so I rested my chin on my bed again.

A woman wearing blue jeans and a fleece pullover walked past my cage. "This way to the cat room. We've picked out a few potential friends for you. You can interact with them in here."

She said this place is called Paw-Pals Rescue...that means it's not the humane society. It's probably going to take Pat and Joy longer to find me.

My stomach lurched, and I closed my eyes, trying to block out my vision in the vain hope it would stop my stomach from rolling.

Two sets of footsteps passed my cage. Or one set passed my cage. The other stopped in front of it.

I cracked an eye open to find a little girl crouched in front of me. She was maybe five or six and looked vaguely familiar with her tawny colored hair. Her eyebrows knitted together as she studied me.

"Mom, doesn't this cat look like Ama?"

"She does." A woman knelt next to the little girl. She squinted at me, her forehead bunching in what appeared to be confusion.

As I looked at her my magic—still working despite my rattled skull—peeled away at the glamour the mother and daughter were wearing, showing their pointed ears and the black spirals that cut through their eyes.

Oh. They're elves. How about that? Statistically that's, wait, she called me Ama.

"Do you think it *is* Ama?" the little girl whispered.

"No, my love," her mother said, her voice even quieter. "That's impossible?" She sounded unsure—my magic at work, most likely.

I can't let an elf adopt me—that would bring me back into Calor Villa. Noctus would be furious. Gotta hide.

I struggled, trying to stand in hopes that I could crawl toward the back of my metal crate, but the pain in my skull made me collapse. I couldn't give up—I couldn't fail Noctus like this. So I hissed instead, then growled deep in my throat.

"I'm sorry—I know you mentioned you were particularly interested in a black cat, but that one isn't available yet." The woman in the blue fleece joined them outside my cage. "She was brought in this afternoon—injured. We're waiting for a vet to take a look at her, but she won't be ready for a new home until we get her healed up." She worriedly glanced at my puffed-up fur. "Although we'll also have to see how good she is with people, kids in particular. We do have two well socialized black kittens available, though. They're waiting for us in the cat room."

"I hope she gets better fast." The elf girl blinked at me a few times, then slowly trudged toward the door—though she stopped to look back at me. "...I *think* she looks like Ama?"

"Ama?" The woman in the blue fleece smiled kindly as she bustled across the room. "Is that a cat you know?"

"Yes! She's the best cat ever." The little girl traipsed after her.

The elf mother, however, stayed in front of my cage. Her expression warred between concern and confusion, especially when the cat in the cage above me stuck its paw out of the grate of its gate and patted my door, meowing.

Of course, my magic is calling to them. Sorry, cats.

My head ached, and I gave a very un-cat-like sigh as I tried to brace myself against the swirling sensation my head was producing.

"You're not Ama," the elf mother said, her voice certain. "But...just in case." She fumbled with her coat pockets and pulled out a cellphone.

My eyes fluttered shut.

A commemorative photo? Great. It's too bad I can't ask for help, but you don't know Pat or Joy, and I'm strictly no-contact with your king...

I heard the click of a camera shutter, and the quiet taps as the elf hurried after her daughter and the woman from the rescue.

I cracked an eye open—this time a cat in the cage next to mine meowed.

I just have to wait it out. Pat and Joy will find me.

My stomach soured, the blackness that had been invading the edges of my vision swallowed everything up, and I drifted off into the comfort of unconsciousness.

CHAPTER FOUR

Noctus

Wild magic was wailing again.

This time it had opted for annoyance instead of a theatrical performance, and was vibrating at a high pitched, keening noise.

Ignore it. If I let it know I'm irritated, it will only act out worse.

I kept my expression neutral as I poured my magic into the portal, cementing it to the ground, and making certain it was properly connected to the other gates in the clocktower.

I was only passable at portal magic, unlike a number of my subjects. Charon in particular was brilliant at it. But since the Paragon was sniffing around Magiford, and since Auron had sent a few unwanted messengers, I'd decided that my magic should be used to power the portals, in the hopes that anyone capable of sensing elven magic behind the screens of fae spells we'd set up would only detect my presence.

Thankfully, my vast magic could brute force make up for my

lack of skill when it came to gates. They just had to work; they didn't have to be beautiful. But my poor abilities meant I had to drop by every so often to top the gates off.

That task only took a few moments, and it gave me a chance to inspect the building while Ker dragged Aristide off to see her flower shop.

As if summoned by my thoughts, I heard the click of Ker's nails on the smooth floor, and the tap of Aristide's shoes followed by the noisy gurgle his straws made whenever he finished draining a blood pack.

"Back so soon?" I cocked my head, studying the gate, then pushed a little more magic into it.

"Indeed," Aristide said. "We went to check out the flower shop, and three customers immediately left, their hearts pounding as if they were going to explode. Can't understand why for the life of me."

"It's definitely not the blood pack you're sipping on, or the werewolf of Hades that serves as your guide dog." I glanced back at my friends.

I'd always liked Ker's werewolf form. With her brown-black undercoat and red overcoat, she looked like a mixture of coal and fire. But, matched with her werewolf physique—which was especially impressive as she was larger than most modern American werewolves—she looked fierce even if she wagged her tail.

"Humans." Aristide sniffed. "Always afraid of the wrong things. Ker, I need to throw this in the bins."

"Trash cans," I called to him as I added one last swirl of magic to the gate, then stepped back. "We're in America, at the moment."

"Oh, don't I *know it*?" Aristide grouched as Ker led him to a trashcan pushed against the wall. We were in the basement, so the floor was relatively empty, having been built solely for my people to use the gate—the biggest of all the ones in the building.

"Charon?" I called. "I'm nearly done. What—"

Wild magic's keening rose to what could only be described as the high-pitched scream of a red-faced toddler.

I frowned as the magic in the gate sloshed, destabilized.

"*Enough*," I hissed at wild magic. "Why can't you just go back to *silence*? You were perfectly content with that for centuries."

Wild magic, miraculously, cut itself off. For the first time possibly ever, it listened to my request.

Why does this not feel like victory? Suspicious, I studied the gate again.

It had stabilized, and its power would hold out until my next inspection.

"Is everything well, Your Majesty?" Charon asked, stepping out of the shadows with his customary tiny notebook in hand.

"It's fine," I said. "I've finished with the gates. Did you check the security footage for any visuals on the fae?"

Charon bowed, making his hood drape deeper over his head. "I have. He passed the clocktower the morning of the artifact accident."

"You think he's doing this solo?" Aristide asked. "We haven't caught anyone accompanying him."

Ker violently sneezed in her disagreement.

"We might not recognize his partners even if we caught them on our security footage," Charon said. "Given that—as organized as he appears to be—it seems unlikely he'd bandy about with his cohorts and openly consort with them."

I strolled away from the gate, heading for the staircase that led out of the basement and into an employees only section of the clocktower. "If he's attached to the organization the Paragon spoke of like we've theorized, it's probable that he's working with others."

Ker guided Aristide along, her ears swiveling as she listened to us.

I started to climb the stairs, but waited until Aristide was at the base to call back to him. "Stair, Aristide."

"Thanks." Aristide used his foot to find the first step, then gripped Ker's harness with one hand and the stair banister with the other.

Ker waited until we reached the top of the staircase before she prodded Aristide in the hip as Charon climbed the last stair behind them.

Prompted, Aristide asked, "Yes, we've theorized about it, but do we have any proof he's connected with them?"

"Solid proof? No. But there is logic to the theory. Why else would he return to Magiford—a city in which he's already been foiled, that only grows more and more dangerous for criminals as the Regional Committee of Magic continues to unify—if it's not for some larger purpose?" I approached the private elevator—it wasn't open to the public as it stopped at the various floors the gates were on, and could also go up to the walkway outside the clock faces, as Chloe and I had once done.

"But maybe you're overestimating the fae's intelligence," Aristide said. "Supernaturals do stupid things all the time—good and bad."

"True," I said. "Which is why more surveillance is necessary."

Charon's phone beeped, announcing an incoming message.

I ignored the sound and pressed the call button for the elevator.

"Another cat picture, Charon?" Aristide asked.

"What?" I turned back to my friends, my eyebrows furrowing.

Charon gave Aristide a rare side eye—something I witnessed possibly once a decade. "Your Majesty," he said. "It's..." He trailed off, and I could see he was mentally warring with himself by the way he imperceptibly flattened his lips.

"Your people keep sending him pictures of black cats," Aristide said. "As in: *every* black cat they see in Magiford, wondering if it's Chloe."

"I see," I said.

"They're very enthusiastic." Charon paused, and his lips flattened so much it was almost noticeable.

"Is something wrong?" I asked.

Charon recovered enough to bow to me. "No, Your Majesty. It's merely Galla—Prydwen's wife—and their daughter. They went to some animal rescue and found an injured black cat. Of course, it's not Chloe—"

I held out my hand before realizing what I was doing.

This is stupid. She's gone. We can't have anything to do with each other, and she's not so poorly trained that she'd get herself hurt unless the tracker—

I glanced at the picture—a snapshot of a cat with luxurious black fur lying on a lumpy cat bed, her eyes closed in obvious pain.

Chloe.

I knew it with every beat of my heart—I knew it better than I knew my own magic. That sick, injured cat was Chloe.

"Where is this?" I asked.

"I don't know," Charon said.

"Find out," I said. "We're going there. *Now*."

"What is it?" Aristide asked. "It's not really her, is it?"

"It is," I grimly said. "She's injured."

Charon, his thumbs raised over the screen of his cellphone, glanced at me. "I requested the location, shall I fetch the car?"

"Yes."

Charon bowed, then sprinted off, going so fast the employees only door groaned when he slammed into it.

Aristide's forehead wrinkled with worry. "Did she look bad?"

"Yes," I admitted, the word tasting like blood.

"How do you know it's her?" Aristide asked. "Her magic should make her hard to recognize."

"I just know," I impatiently said, my voice almost a snap.

I thought he'd push me, but Aristide nodded and adjusted his hold on the harness. "Ker," he said. "After Charon—shortest path possible. Noctus, be a pal and warn me if I'm about to walk off a step, would you?"

I relaxed. "Of course. I'll get the door."

THE FRONT DOOR OF "PAW-PALS RESCUE" groaned when I yanked it open.

Control, I reminded myself. *This is already a huge risk. I need to reduce any variable that could make it worse. That means I can't flash my magic around, either.*

Charon held the door open for Aristide and Ker, slipping in after them.

A human poked her head into the reception room, blinking in confusion when she saw me, then my friends.

"Hello, welcome to Paw-Pals Rescue. I'd love to help you, Mr..." She trailed off and smiled brightly.

I held out Charon's cellphone, with Chloe's picture pulled up. "I'd like to see this cat."

The woman took the phone, her lips forming an 'o'. "I'm sorry, but this cat is injured—she isn't available for adoption just yet. We have a vet coming to see her shortly. Once he gives a diagnosis and health plan, I'd be happy to call you if you'd like to leave your information—"

"She's my cat," I interrupted, trying to mentally throw the woman off balance. "Her name is Ama. I've been looking for her."

"Oh." The woman blinked. "I guess I could bring her out to see if she recognizes you, but she's quite upset. She's been growling and hissing at potential adopters whenever she wakes up." She glanced worriedly at Ker.

"The dog is well socialized with cats." I burned with the desire to flash my powers at this woman and dazzle her, just so I could get back to Chloe faster, but I couldn't give in to the juvenile thought.

"The dog's name is *Spot*," Aristide announced with a haughtiness typically reserved for royalty. "And she will be perfectly behaved." He nudged Ker, who brought him a few steps closer to the woman until he stood directly in front of her. "As for Ama, I'm sure she must be terrified and is deeply missing her...owner. My friend has been working himself to death with missing her since they have a bond beyond regular pethood. Could you please find it in your heart to take us back to her?"

Aristide's not-so-subtle attempts to needle me were washed out by the vampire pheromones he was positively oozing as he smiled in the woman's direction, magnifying his vampiric powers.

Charon, myself, and even Ker looked up at Aristide in surprise. He rarely used his vampire pheromones—a sort of vampiric version of my own dazzle powers that essentially let him twitterpate his way into manipulating humans. That he was using them now...

The woman's jaw slackened. "Sure," she said, sounding dazed. "This way."

My shoulders relaxed as the woman shuffled off to a door. I glanced at Aristide, who was shivering in revulsion. "Thank you."

Aristide reached out, and I shifted so he could put his hand on my shoulder. "We've got you, Noctus," he said in a quiet, serious voice. "Let's go get Chloe."

We followed the woman into a back room, where there was a wall lined with metal cages, each occupied by a feline.

I scanned the wall, searching for Chloe. Initially, a couple of the cats pressed their faces against their cage doors in curiosity, until they sensed Ker and immediately backed into a corner.

Only one cage was still, and it was occupied by a black lump.

Chloe.

I had to clench my hands in impatience as the human unlocked the cage door, revealing Chloe, limply splayed across a bed.

"Here she is. Is she really your Ama?"

Chloe raised her head—her eyes weren't focusing correctly, and if I had to guess, she wasn't standing because she *couldn't*—and hissed.

The human raised an eyebrow at me, but I ignored her and reached into the cage.

Chloe growled, her fur puffing up, and plastered her black ears against her skull.

I ignored the warning and picked her up, cradling her against my chest.

"Wait," the woman said. "That's not safe..."

She trailed off when Chloe's growls quieted.

Her ears relaxed, and she stretched her paws up to me as she started purring. I maneuvered Chloe so she could hook the claws of one paw into my shirt, and I could hold her stable with her head snuggled into my neck.

"Oh. I guess she is yours after all," the woman said, surprised.

I automatically reached for the magic that once bound us together, before remembering she wasn't wearing the collar.

That means I can't heal her. Do we have any healing potions in the car?

I turned on my heel, and although I wanted to storm out, Chloe had mentioned previously how bouncy it was being held, so I walked as smoothly as possible back to the reception room.

"Wait," the woman called, hurrying after me. "Where are you going?"

"Thank you for what I'm sure must be a touching reunion," Aristide said. "We'll take it from here."

"Indeed," Charon echoed, skirting a desk positioned in the center of the reception room.

"But she still needs to see a vet," the woman protested. "And she didn't have a collar on her. Is she even fixed—"

"She gets the finest medical attention, I assure you," Aristide said, his voice edged with a hint of desperation as Ker deftly led him around a cat tower. "We will see to her injuries immediately."

He trotted out the pheromones—I could feel them in the air like a thick, warm blanket.

The woman must have been a genuine animal lover, because even with all of Aristide's pheromones aimed at her, she anxiously wrung her hands as she peered from me down to Chloe.

I flicked my sunglasses down and tapped my own magic. "She will be fine. Thank you for caring for her. My assistant will give you a generous donation in appreciation."

The woman stared blankly at me as my magic took root.

I nodded to Charon, then shoved the door open, stepping into the warm September sunlight.

Chloe hadn't stopped purring, and when the outside air hit her, she pushed her head against my neck, trying to get as close as possible.

I'll have to let her go after we get her healed, I reminded myself. *It's risky to save her like this. I* must *let her go—for her sake and the sake of my people.*

But as I cradled her, making my way to the SUV, I finally realized that the wild magic floating in the air had stopped moaning. In fact—in a sound barely above a whisper—it was singing.

CHAPTER FIVE

Chloe

I was in a car. I recognized the hum of the engine and the earthy smell of leather upholstery. That was all I knew for certain.

I *thought* Noctus was holding me, but there was a good chance that was a fever dream. Noctus would never risk getting involved with me—not when any outside person interacting with him was a threat to his hidden kingdom.

But the familiar warmth wrapped around me, and the way my back was being supported? Only Noctus was that thoughtful.

My mind must be overlaying his presence as a comfort. Am I in worse shape than I thought? Maybe I should go to the doctor after I finally get free.

I kept my eyes shut—the world swirled uncontrollably whenever I had them open.

"*—safe to feed her a healing potion in this form?*"

"Her form isn't a problem. Her ability or willingness to drink is. Unless, Charon, you happen to carry syringes in the car?"

"No, but I shall endeavor to do so in the future."

"Maybe we can get her to change into her human form?"

The voices were so muffled, I couldn't tell who was talking, except for Noctus—if it really was Noctus. I felt his voice in my bones as his chest vibrated when he spoke.

"Chloe? Can you hear me? It's safe to change into your human form," Noctus said.

I mashed my head into his jaw.

I just want to sleep.

"—need to get her back to her apartment."

"Can't you heal her?"

"There's no bond without the collar."

"Her sister lives in the same building. We should be able to alert her."

"Try dribbling some potion on her head. Her skin might absorb it and at least kickstart healing whatever's got her ill."

Something wet wiped my back.

"I'd advise against licking her, Ker. We don't know what happened to her."

Nothing happened. I messed up and let myself get distracted. If Charon ever found out about it, he'd make me climb stairs for an entire week of practice.

I was starting to think it really was Noctus holding me, and it was Aristide and Charon I could hear. But the hours of my unattended head injury had only made the nausea worse, and the aching pain in my head had sharpened to a knife-like sensation.

I needed a fae potion. I wanted Pat and Joy. Or my mom and dad.

What about Noctus?

The dangerous thought rang through my aching head, and a pained breath of air wheezed out of me.

"Chloe?"

I was pulled back from my warm nook.

Half dreading what I would see, I cracked an eye open.

Noctus, impeccably dressed in a tailor-made suit with his artfully styled golden hair and perfect face that was marred by a tiny line between his eyebrows—one that I knew meant he was worried—studied me.

He's here. He's really here. I'm safe. Noctus is here.

With that reassurance, the tension that had been keeping me awake evaporated, and I sagged in Noctus's arms, falling asleep.

When I woke up, I was sitting on my own bed, wrapped in blankets.

"Come on, Chloe. Drink." Noctus was crouched next to my bed, holding a saucer that had a pink colored liquid poured into it.

He bumped the saucer against my mouth, getting my nose wet.

I licked my nose off and recognized the fizzy drink as one of the three fae potions from the shoebox I'd hidden in my closet. I'd purchased a lower grade fae potion; it tasted like cream soda and fizzed on my tongue.

He brought me home? He brought me home, and he dug out a fae potion from my closet—this is the best possible outcome I could have ever hoped for. But...how did we get in the building?

My thoughts were slow—clearer, but cumbersome.

How did he even find out I was in trouble? Did those elves tell him?

It seemed probable, but it didn't explain what he was doing here.

This was Noctus, he'd never do anything to risk exposing his people. Busting me, a shadow with a brother who worked for the Curia Cloisters, out of an animal shelter was the *definition* of risk.

"Chloe," Noctus said, naturally drawing my attention. He

caressed my cheek, and the line between his eyebrows was still there. "You *need* to get more potion in you. Drink."

Sorry, you're right.

It took a lot of focus, but I managed to drink the potion. A couple times I dunked my nose too far in, but Noctus moved the saucer so I didn't face plant.

I didn't lick the saucer clean, but I drank most of it.

Since it was a lower grade potion it would take a while to heal my head injury, but my stomach was already starting to feel better. That went a long way in helping, even if the light in my studio apartment stung my eyes, and things still seemed to be moving while I was lying down.

Charon appeared at the foot of my bed. "I have alerted her sister, as you instructed. I believe she'll be here shortly."

"Then let's head out," Noctus said. "The SUV needs to be gone before she or the brother get here."

Charon bowed to Noctus, then disappeared around the partition I used to screen my bed off from the rest of my apartment.

Noctus set the nearly empty saucer down next to me, then stood up.

I peered up at him, my head lolling.

I have to thank him. Can I change back?

I reached for my human form, but the pain in my head was so overwhelming I had to shut my eyes again.

"Be more careful in the future, Amalourne," Noctus said, his voice deep and rolling.

I peeled my eyes open just in time to see him start to walk away.

Wait, thank you! Thank you for the rescue, for coming for me. I never thought I'd see you again, and I know this was dangerous. Thank you.

I meowed.

It was such a stupid thing, but I didn't know what else to do.

Noctus froze, his back facing me. I could see his shoulders tense the longer he stood there.

Shoot, you don't get it. I'm saying thank you—it's okay!

I tried to struggle out of the blanket burrito he'd wrapped me in, but I was too weak. So I settled for purring.

Noctus continued to stand with his back to me for several long moments. Eventually, he placed a hand on the wall. I saw the tendons in his hand flex as he clenched it.

It's okay, Noctus. I know you have to go.

I didn't have the collar anymore, but hopefully Noctus knew my purrs well enough to realize what I was trying to say.

Noctus pushed off the wall and disappeared around the partition. A moment later my apartment door shut.

I closed my eyes—the sour feeling in my stomach was entirely gone and had been replaced by a bubbly sensation.

I'm home. I'm safe. I just have to rest until the potion kicks in. I survived...because of Noctus.

"Here, drink this one, too." Pat shook a bottled fae potion in my face. This one was green, and I was pretty sure Pat had swiped it from his work at the Curia Cloisters.

"No thanks," I said. "I've already drunk three. Any more and my bladder is going to explode."

"Should have thought of that before you let yourself get decked in the head," Pat said with zero sympathy. "Drink it."

I took the olive green drink and uncorked it. "My concussion is gone, guys. I'm fine. It wasn't even that bad." I took a slug of the drink, which had a strong, minty flavor.

"Not that *bad*?" Joy flung down the latest copy of the Curia Cloisters' newsletter that she'd been perusing. "You were stuck in your cat form when I got here! You couldn't even sit up straight!"

I was starting to sweat, so I peeled off one of the many blankets tucked around me—my siblings still hadn't let me get off my bed, which made for a comfortable but hot nest. "I meant it wasn't life threatening."

Pat grimly shook his head. "That's not right, Chloe, and you know it. The only reason you're okay is because a Book Nookery customer somehow recognized you. That shouldn't even be possible with your magic. You had to have been at death's doorstep for that to happen."

No, I just have a soul deep connection with an elf king I haven't told you about.

The thought made me squirm, but I wasn't going to budge on telling my siblings about Noctus.

"How do you know a customer recognized me?" I asked, trying to figure out what kind of cover story my ex-friends had weaved for my rescue.

"He buzzed my apartment," Joy said. "Said you'd managed to turn human long enough to unlock your door. You can't even remember that much?"

"Everything is really fuzzy," I truthfully said. "I mostly remember coming in and out of it at the rescue."

"And yet you don't get why we're upset that you're treating this so casually?" Pat groaned as he sat on the foot of my bed, his knees touching the partition that screened my bed off from the rest of my studio apartment.

"I'm sorry," I said. "I shouldn't have let the tracker distract me. I almost had him." I balled my hand into a fist and had to bite back the desire to scream.

He was down! If I'd stayed focused, he'd be in the Curia Cloisters' custody! Now who knows what he'll try next, and my siblings are in more danger than ever!

Joy picked up the newsletter again—I think it was just to keep her hands busy, so she didn't strangle me like she wanted to. "You said he distracted you, then decked you in the head. What did he say?"

I hesitated.

After I'd recovered enough that I could see straight, I'd told them the bare points about the fight so Pat could phone the incident in. But I hadn't said anything about my birth family, and I wasn't sure how they'd react.

"He said...that my parents used me as a decoy. They dropped me at the hospital in a way that would get attention from humans but not supernaturals, then disappeared. There was a public record of my existence, but not theirs, so I'd be easy to find, and their trail ended with me." The explanation tasted sour, maybe even truthful.

Pat, unable to sit still, jiggled his foot. "That means someone is still hunting your family, too. Nobody knew shadows had managed to survive—much less what they are—and yet someone is still hunting them. Why bear a grudge that long?"

"And *who* could bear a grudge that long?" Joy asked. "You said elves were the ones who hunted shadows to extinction, but they're gone. Who else would hate shadows enough to carry on the elves' goal?"

I rubbed my head as I tried to remember the muddled moments after failing to grab the tracker. "It might just be the tracker. He called someone after I stabbed him."

Joy rolled the Curia Cloisters' newsletter up and tapped it on her knee. "It is a little odd he didn't just finish you off right then and there."

"Not really," I said. "He was in even worse condition than I was. He was going to pass out and probably die from blood loss if he didn't get help fast enough, and I managed to scramble under a bush without him seeing."

A smile twitched across Pat's face, wiping away the worry that crinkled around the corners of his eyes. "That's our Chloe," he said. "You got him good!"

"Not good enough to actually catch him." I glanced at the window—the only one in my apartment—and stared at the makeshift nest built out of ripped strips of paper take-out bags and twigs. It was French Fry's occasional home that he roosted in maybe once a week.

It was empty at the moment, but he must have dropped by relatively recently, because there was a saltwater taffy wrapper in it that hadn't been there when I'd woken up this morning.

Pat pulled me into a hug. "You survived. That's what we care most about."

I relaxed as he patted my back. "Thanks, Pat."

He awkwardly cleared his throat, let me go, then ruffled my hair. "You're okay, kid. And don't overthink what he said. He's a psycho. There's no way he'd tell the truth."

"Yeah," Joy agreed. "Besides, if you were a 'decoy' like he said, it wouldn't have taken him your entire life to realize you existed."

"True," Pat said. "We didn't even know you were a supernatural until you were a toddler, and working at the Curia Cloisters has only furthered my belief that supernaturals are snobby and self-absorbed. Your birth parents probably dropped you at the human hospital because they thought you'd be safer. Plus..." He hesitated and awkwardly scratched the back of his head.

"What?" I asked.

"Well...your birth parents' trail might have ended with you... because they *died*," Pat said.

"Pat," Joy hissed.

"She has a right to know," Pat said. "It's a possibility."

"It's fine, Joy," I said. "I already knew it was a possibility, even before I knew I was a shadow."

I couldn't stand their looks of sadness and pity, so I finished off the potion Pat had given me and set the empty bottle on my nightstand. "There, happy?"

"Not until that crazy killer is off the streets," Joy darkly muttered.

"Speaking of him..." Pat unearthed his cellphone and opened an app. "I need to ask you a few more questions for the report. You said he had a hostage, right?" Pat asked. "That's a new tactic."

"He's done that before," Joy said. "Like when he manipulated the Seelie and Unseelie fae into kidnapping you and me."

"Yeah," Pat agreed. "Except this is possibly worse. It's not that shocking that Chloe would care about us. But if he's realized she cares enough about humans that using one as a hostage will make her comply with whatever he wants...he's really hunting you, Chloe. In the truest sense of the word."

"I know." I rubbed my forehead and kicked the last of my blankets off. "But what more can we do? He's careful with his approach. The only way we could possibly ensure our safety is if I quit my job and Joy and I moved into the Curia Cloisters, and that's not happening."

Joy hit her knee harder and harder with the rolled-up newsletter. "I know you didn't want to do this...but maybe you should go ahead and meet with the higher-ups from the Cloisters. Playing politics can be dangerous, but hopefully this is temporary. If you can get some leverage, they might help more. Don't you think so, Pat?"

Pat frowned. "It's hard to say. They might just want to use her, to learn more about shadows. However..." He rocked to his feet, shuffling out of the way so I could scoot past the partition and step into the other half of my apartment. "I will say the attitude of the Regional Committee of Magic has changed over the past couple years to have a more favorable outlook of wizards, magic humans, and humans in general. Talking to them is likely the best shot we have at getting actual help."

"I came to the same conclusion." I padded toward my kitchen, the tiled flooring cold on my feet. "I was on my way to make arrangements at the Curia Cloisters to talk more about being a shadow when the tracker got me."

"It's just as well, then. We'll need the extra help." Pat rested his hand on the top of my partition. "Because while you might have almost had him, you did effectively confirm his guess that humans matter to you. Whatever he does in the future, he knows, now, that the easiest way to stop you is to get someone innocent involved."

I sighed and leaned against my fridge. "Yeah, he's escalating. I'll call the Curia Cloisters—after I use the bathroom."

Pat made a face. "Thanks for the announcement."

"Pat and I will figure out what to eat—I'm assuming you're hungry?"

"I probably will be once my stomach empties from all the potions," I said.

"Good." Pat grinned, and some of the tightness that had been in his face since he'd arrived at the apartment disappeared. "While we eat, I'll tell you what new antics the Curia Cloisters' groundkeeper tried in his war on the gophers, or whatever it is that keeps tearing the place up. Hint, the story involves an ultrasonic spike, and some really unhappy werewolves."

I laughed as I stepped into my tiny bathroom, flicked on the lights, and closed the door in his face.

I did a quick study of my face via the mirror. Surprisingly I wasn't bruised, but it looked like I'd been dragged around a gravel parking lot by a werewolf. My brown hair was less wavy and frizzier and wilder than usual, I was ghostly pale, and my brown eyes were bloodshot.

The makeup I'd used on the beauty mark beneath my left eye was gone—it wasn't that I disliked the mark, it just added a bit of sophistication to my otherwise blandly cute/girl-next-door appearance. I'd started covering it up as a defense mechanism when I moved to Magiford to make myself even harder to recognize.

Woah. No wonder Pat kept shoving potions at me. I look rough.

I tied my hair back and splashed water in my face.

After wiping the water away with a soft towel—it had a black cat embroidered on it. My mom made it for me with her embroidery machine as a Christmas gift two years ago—I rested my hands on the edge of the sink.

Noctus came for me.

The thought had been roosting on the far edge of my mind while I'd been occupied with everything Joy and Pat had to say. Alone, I couldn't avoid it any longer.

When I left, he said we'd have to be strangers. I knew we'd never see each other again, because we wanted opposite things. And yet, he still came for me.

I stared into the mirror.

I hadn't changed much since my stay at Calor Villa. Oh sure, I was stronger now, and I could use a sword and could be a threat in combat if the battle wasn't too uneven. But I was still the same anxious, overly cautious person.

Except...in one very dangerous way.

Life in Calor Villa had taught me to hope. Between Noctus letting me off after discovering I'd been posing as his cat, learning that my powers were more useful than I'd ever thought, and making my first supernatural friends besides Ms. Booker and French Fry, my pessimism had softened just enough to let me hope for big things—things normally beyond me—without the instinct to crush it.

And now, as I stood in my bathroom—having survived the tracker and the aftermath with my siblings—a very dangerous hope started to take up residence in my chest.

I left Calor Villa because my need to protect my family and Noctus's need to protect his people aren't things that can cohabitate. But...Noctus still came for me. What does that mean?

CHAPTER SIX

Chloe

Two days passed, during which my dangerous new hope frolicked in my brain while I made arrangements for my first official meeting at the Curia Cloisters.

I was a strange jumble of emotions by the time I arrived for the scheduled meeting, but I was determined to tuck everything away, as this meeting had the potential to be very, very dangerous.

Pausing outside the meeting room I'd been directed to for the occasion, I took a deep breath and forced my shoulders up.

I was mentally preparing for battle, because in some twisted, screwy chance of luck, the official I was meeting with to discuss shadows, was *the Paragon.*

I wasn't entirely sure why the Curia Cloisters had decided he was the person I needed to see. I was a human, not a fae. Frankly, I'd assumed the Cloisters would unearth a vampire who remembered shadows to talk to me, but no. It was the Paragon, *who I had met as Ama*.

Be polite and chill, I coached myself. *But not too chill, because he's the Paragon. But I can't let him realize I'm* pretending *to be chill and that I'm really scared stiff trying to make sure I don't mess up and say something I—as Chloe, having never met him—shouldn't know.*

My head was spinning with how weird and complex my life had become as I gloomily opened the door.

Inside, sitting at a table and taking selfies with his cellphone, was the Paragon, making the universal peace sign as he beamed at his phone.

I was struck dumb for a moment so I just stared, until my ever-so-helpful powers kicked in and tried to peel back the layers of the extremely intricate and powerful glamour the Paragon wore.

Hold it! Stop—no! This isn't what I want!

I mentally clamped down on my magic as the sheer strength of the Paragon's glamour made my eyes water. I sneezed three times in quick succession, and for a moment I didn't see the Paragon's white hair, but rather—*no! Put the glamour back! I'm already keeping too many secrets. I will not pick up anymore!*

I squeezed my eyes shut until I was certain my magic had sulkily given up.

Cautiously, I cracked one eye open, and was relieved to see that the Paragon—with his white hair and long, waterfall-like mustache—was in his old man guise.

He was wearing blue robes that had dove gray flowers and vines stitched on them, and eyeglasses that I was positive he didn't need.

I heard the click of a camera, and the Paragon stopped posing and tapped away on his phone. "Hey, bestie," he muttered to his phone as he typed, seemingly unaware of my presence—an example of my magic being useful. "Bought a new robe. Feeling cute. Might drop by later." Only after he sent his message did he look up and notice me.

"Aha! You must be Chloe Anderson!" He stood up, pushing his chair back. "Lovely to meet you!"

"Hello, Paragon," I said. "It's an honor. Thank you for being willing to speak with me."

"Yes, of course," the Paragon said. "We must all help where we can. But let's get out of here, shall we?" He adjusted his spectacles as he approached me, and I realized he was taller than I thought he was when I'd been Ama.

"Get out of here?" I echoed. "What do you mean?"

"This place is so dingy and boring. Plus, there's no drinks!" He peered around the room with a scowl, then turned back to me and smiled brightly. "I thought we could go to my pocket realm!"

"Um." I wanted to refuse, but how could I politely go about telling the *Paragon*—the most powerful fae in the USA—that I was rejecting his personal invitation?

"Just a moment and we'll be right there—try to stay standing." The Paragon winked at me as he pulled a pink coin purse covered with white unicorns out of one of his voluminous sleeves and snapped it open.

It must have somehow contained a gate, because I felt the tingly sensation of portal magic before wind blasted me in the face and I automatically shut my eyes. The ground morphed under my feet, changing from the standard tile the Curia Cloisters used throughout its buildings, to what felt like a wooden floor.

The temperature warmed, and the fragrant scent of lavender filled the air. I opened my eyes, surprised to find myself in a pleasantly dim room.

At the far side of the room I spied what I think was meant to be a desk, except it appeared to be made out of living tree trunks. One of the branches that made up the desk leg grew a few leaves while I was watching, and then gave them a tinge of red so they matched the fall colors I'd started seeing on some of the trees around Magiford.

A model of a phoenix was set precariously on top of a giant, golden statue of a dragon head. Next to it was some sort of kitchen area, with a closed cupboard and racks of glittering fae potions arranged on top of a counter space.

A ping-pong table was covered with what appeared to be drying herbs and a half-finished Lego set of what I was fairly certain was a castle.

But what I really loved about the room was that it was basically wall to wall bookshelves. Some were filled with modern things—one, planted by his living desk, had a tv and what appeared to be video games and DVDs—while others were stuffed with books. Some of the tomes were covered in brightly woven cloth while others were made of such faded and worn leather they must have been centuries old.

"*Mmert?*"

Oh no. I forgot about the cat!

I watched with bugging eyes as a pink skinned, hairless cat poked her head over the top of the Paragon's desk. "*Mmert*!" The cat repeated her purring, chirp-like noise and hopped on the desk. Consumed by my inner panic, I noticed with only a vague recognition that the sweet sphinx cat was wearing a blue baby onesie. It had cute little cartoon wolves on it and said "Will Howl For Food," which seemed kind of odd for a fae pet to have, but then again the Paragon was mostly odd.

I'd met the Paragon's cat before, as Ama, when the Paragon had toted her over to Noctus's Cape Cod home. The problem I'd learned, was cats were the sole creature that could recognize me no matter my shape, and were naturally drawn to me as a result.

She's going to know who I am!

I was mostly sure the Paragon's cat was normal. At least, I was certain she couldn't talk to him. No, the real danger was whether the Paragon would notice if Aphrodite's demeanor was different with me.

"Aphrodite!" the Paragon boomed. "Thank you for greeting me—what's this?"

Aphrodite trotted past the Paragon, coming to a stop at my feet. She didn't pause to sniff me or show any sign of hesitation that any cat would show a stranger—no matter how magical.

Instead, she immediately began to rub her head into my legs, purring intently.

The Paragon frowned, watching us.

I laughed nervously as I crouched down and petted Aphrodite's head, then patted her onesie-clad back. "Sorry. Cats just like me. I guess it's part of the magic that comes with being a shadow."

It's true, and a reasonable explanation. Maybe he'll buy it.

The Paragon's forehead puckered into deep furrows. "Oh, yes, that makes sense. It is merely that, that is the kind of greeting she reserves for friends."

Nope, of course he would notice the difference in his cat's behavior. He's the only cat dad on the entire planet that's even more intense than Noctus.

I forced a smile—because otherwise my expression was going to freeze in place. "Oh really?" I asked.

Aphrodite, meanwhile, placed a paw on my knee and stretched up, attempting to tap my chin with her other paw so I'd start petting her again.

"But," he continued, his expression turning stormy, "what I cannot fathom is..." The Paragon's long mustache somehow drooped, and his spectacles slid down his nose. "Aphrodite, no matter what kind of magic she has, how could you just ignore me like that?!" he complained.

I relaxed—the danger was over. Almost lightheaded with relief, I petted Aphrodite, who purred deeply as she ignored her overly doting owner. She boosted herself up just enough to touch her nose to mine, "*Mmert*"-ed to me, then ambled back to her owner, who was holding a hand over his heart.

"No," he declared. "It's too late to console me. You walked

right past me and—youch!" He yelped when Aphrodite stretched a paw up over her head, pressed it into his robes so it sat on his inner thigh, then hooked her claws through the material, presumably into his leg.

When she let him go, the Paragon stooped over and scooped her up like a large baby, going so far as to adjust her onesie for her. "You are a mercurial feline, but you deserve all my love and adoration."

"Wow, wow, wow," someone said behind us. "That was a sight I never thought I'd see."

I whipped around, my jaw dropping.

Leaning against one of the many bookshelves—this one was covered by globes with land formations that looked nothing like earth—was a beautiful woman with silky black hair and the most gorgeous purple-blue eyes I'd ever seen. Gifted with fae grace, but lacking their too-perfect beauty with her smile that had too much sass and warmth in it, I knew on sight who this woman was. Her picture had been plastered all over Magiford for the past two years.

This was Queen Leila—fae ruler of the Night Court, who was slowly rallying the fae Courts in the USA and becoming the first fae emperor in years.

...and the fae empress was wearing jeans, farm boots, and a blue flannel shirt, and had dark bags under her eyes. She clutched two large Karuba coffees that I was pretty sure she must have bought at a Kwik Trip gas station—one in each hand.

"Hey!" Queen Leila smiled at me before taking a slurp from her coffees—or lattes? I couldn't tell which. "You must be Chloe Anderson. I'm Leila, Queen of the Night Court."

"Queen Leila, it's an honor to meet you." I bowed to the fae queen, who stopped guzzling her drink long enough to shake her head.

"Oh, formalities aren't necessary. Believe me, it's fine." Leila gestured at me with one of her coffees. "We're just so excited to talk with you—Paragon, if you take even a *step* toward your tea cabinet I will smack you with so much paperwork you'll have to get an office at the Cloisters."

The Paragon had been scooting toward the kitchen space, but he guiltily twirled around at Leila's growl. "Whatever do you mean, Queen Leila?" He cuddled Aphrodite against his chest, and the bald cat purred.

"I mean I'm not letting you drug your guest."

The Paragon huffed. "We've been over this. My teas are not *drugged*, they are sprinkled with a variety of charms that seek to help and aid a person!"

"Yeah, but that person isn't necessarily the poor soul who *drinks* the tea." Leila glared at the Paragon over the top of one of her drinks before taking a slug of it.

The Paragon sniffed. "You've been touchy ever since you came back from your most recent excursion to the other fae Courts in America. Was it because the golden eagle of the Mountain West Summer Court bestowed a fae kiss upon you after eating carrion?"

"I'm not touchy, I'm tired," Leila said. "All the fae word-smithing and politics is enough to drive a person insane. But!" The pretty queen straightened up and smiled at me. "This is an important meeting, not just because you're a shadow, Chloe, but because I owe you my personal thanks for taking care of the Seelie and Unseelie Courts this summer. I didn't know how much chaos they were causing, or I would have come back." The slant of her smile shifted, tinging it with regret. "Thank you for taking care of Harel and Darina. I'm so sorry for what they did to you and your siblings."

"Um," I said, wilting slightly under the intensity of Leila's purple-y eyes. "You're welcome?"

The Paragon must have sensed my discomfort. He propped Aphrodite against his side—she was a hefty cat, so his arms were probably starting to get tired—and made a noise in the back of his throat. "I see how it is," he said. "I do so much for fae kind, and I don't even get a thank you!"

Leila rolled her eyes. "That's because you're a fae, not a human, and I know Chloe won't use my words against me. Now let's get this chat started. I have a meeting with some of my fae lords in an hour to squelch a Court uprising against me."

I widened my eyes at the statement, until Leila tapped one of her Karuba cups. "They're trying to bring back the dratted Court ski trip—over my dead body. That trip is ridiculously expensive. The Court budget says: never!"

The Paragon nodded. "I see. In that case, let me just brew a pot of tea, and—"

"*What*," Leila barked, "did I say about the tea?"

"You're being rude and answering for my guest," the Paragon said. "Chloe, don't you want tea, personally selected by Aphrodite and brewed by...a machine I own?" The Paragon pointed at a glass teapot that sat on a special base and seemed to have a brewing basket—the tea version of a coffee maker.

"It's charmed," Leila warned me. "It'll make you talk, or maybe make you goofy for an hour. I wouldn't recommend it."

I awkwardly shifted where I stood. "Actually, charms don't work on me."

Both the Paragon and the fae empress stared at me.

"Really?" the Paragon asked. "All charms?"

I nodded. "Healing magic is pretty much the only magic that affects me."

Leila whistled. "Wow. Now that's a neat trick."

"Oh." The Paragon drooped. I guess he really had wanted to charm me.

That's not too surprising, based on what I saw of him at Noctus's place.

The older fae abruptly straightened. "Well, it matters not. You are still a guest. Tea?"

I briefly rubbed my eyes—they were watering again from the

strength of his glamour. "Yes, please. Thank you, Aphrodite, for picking out a tea."

Aphrodite extended her two front paws at me, reaching for me.

The Paragon squawked and marched over to the cabinet by the kitchen area, muttering under his breath. "You capricious creature! How dare you be so willing to abandon me? Now, choose the proper tea for your new friend—and perhaps a cup for myself."

"*Mmert!*"

When the Paragon opened the cabinet, the bald cat climbed into the wooden structure, nosing through the shelves and shelves that were lined with little metal canisters covered in gauzy blue fabric.

"You're braver than I am," Leila told me before she took a sip from one of her cups, then a swig from the second. "My general rule is to never consume anything the Paragon gives me."

I shrugged. "The last three years have stress-tested my immunity to magic," I said. "I've had just about every fae magic in existence thrown at me. The tracker that harmed my family has had his fair share of throwing weird magic at me, too."

"Ahh, yes. Him." The Paragon—in a move that looked far too young for his elderly appearance—folded his arms across his chest. He glanced at Leila, who had paused with one of her Karuba cups raised halfway to her lips. "I'm afraid I have some... shocking news regarding him."

I tensed up. *Did they find him? Is he registered with the Cloisters somehow? What has both of them acting like this?*

The Paragon moved a tin of tea that Aphrodite almost knocked over as she climbed onto the next shelf. "I don't quite know how to tell you this, but I suspect that your tracker...is an elf."

I paused for a moment at the non-revelation. *And...? I've*

known this all summer—OH. I'm not supposed to know elves are still alive!

"It must be a shock," Leila said.

"Yes," I slowly said. It was easy enough to act like the Paragon's words gave me anxiety—I mean, nearly everything gave me anxiety. In fact, I was anxious about having to act anxious now that I thought of it. "I mean...based on what little information I've been able to find, elves wiped the shadows out."

"They did," the Paragon grimly said.

"*Mmert*," Aphrodite pawed at a tin.

"This one is for our guest?" he asked.

Aphrodite purred, then jumped down to a lower level of the cabinet as the Paragon scooped the dried, loose leaf tea leaves into a metal basket in his glass teapot.

"It would be easy to assume he is stalking you solely to continue the hunt his forefathers began," the Paragon continued. "Based on the tattoos around his neck, his elf ancestry is from the Auron family—the royals of that family specialized in summoning, as did the elves who chose to settle in their lands." He plugged the base in and pressed a few buttons, causing the tea maker to beep, then stepped back.

I bit the inside of my cheek. I remembered Noctus and the others had said as much when I'd first described the tracker to them. "The Auron family survived, then?"

"No. The Auron lands were wiped out," the Paragon said. "It's possible one or two survived, but for the most part, the elves really are gone. I saw a photo of your tracker from a security camera taken during your recent tussle with him, and I suspect he's only half elf—there are a few specific features elves have that he lacks, unless he's covering it up with a glamour, which is unlikely given the presence of his tattoos. But, half elf or otherwise, he is still dangerous." The Paragon retreated to the cabinet, where Aphrodite was digging around.

I carefully replayed the Paragon's words in my mind, trying to pick apart what he was dancing around without giving away that I already knew all of this. "Earlier you said it would be easy to assume he's coming after me just because I'm a shadow...does that mean you think there's another reason he might be chasing me?"

"Sort of." Leila pressed her lips together. "It's possible he is a part of an organization the Paragon has identified. Although the organization seems to exist at a national level in the USA, it's been particularly active in Magiford. Members of the organization have manipulated fae and wizard politics, and are behind the largest incidents that have rocked our city."

Ahhh yes, the Paragon briefly mentioned this the last time I saw him, when he introduced me to Aphrodite. Though he said specifically they've tried killing Queen Leila. But! I'm not supposed to know any of this.

I didn't even have to act anxious, my heartbeat jumped from the stress of the situation, and I hunched my shoulders. "Why would they want to mess with fae and wizards?"

"We don't know," the Paragon grimly said. "I haven't been able to find a pattern to their behavior or discern any kind of motive. It seems they particularly enjoy chaos and destruction, but I'm of a mind to suspect they seem mostly intent on tearing our society apart."

"Do you think they're all elves?" I asked. "And they want to get back at supernaturals? Is that why you believe the tracker might be working with them?"

"No, as the Paragon said earlier, the war did wipe out the elves, with a few exceptions," Leila said.

There are way more exceptions than you think.

"The organization has members of supernatural races—werewolves, fae, vampires—though it seems like they target the outsiders, who either don't want to join Packs, Families, or Courts, or who cannot," Leila explained. "Last summer, an illegal artifact manufacturing ring was discovered. One of the fae who belonged to it, I had personally banned from joining any Courts as they had made an attempt on the life of Consort Flora of the

Summer Court. I'd hoped that would bring about reformation, but apparently it only drove them off the deep end."

"You won't change them all." The Paragon selected an elegant, clay cup glazed a dark blue and painted with pink Sakura flowers for me. "Some fae—as it is with all supernaturals—will not choose the better path. Their choice is not your responsibility." The tea maker beeped, and the Paragon poured the tea into the mug, then rinsed his machine.

"I know," Leila said. "But it's still disappointing." She stared at her coffee cups for a moment, her posture sagging. When she straightened up, I briefly spotted a necklace—a tiny white feather secured into a gold base and hanging from a delicate gold chain—peeking through the collar of her flannel shirt.

"Returning to the organization, they seem to have access to elven magic, but it would only take the existence of one half elf or two to be able to cast spells for them," Leila continued. "And that is why we suspect your tracker might be attached to the group."

"That, and the conversation you reported hearing as he fled, before you passed out." The Paragon, holding the stem-less clay cup—carefully approached me. "Here, your tea."

"Thank you." I carefully took the warm cup, inhaling the puffs of steam that wafted from the tea. I wasn't a big tea drinker—especially since I'd discovered the wonders of milk steamers—but the slightly bitter scent and olive hue of the tea made me suspect this was a green tea.

"Normally I don't tell a person what Aphrodite picks out for them—the discovery is half of the fun—but I suppose I can bend this rule for a fellow cat-hearted person," the Paragon said. "It's '*Lament-Be-Gone*,' a green tea with an earthy flavor and a touch of nuttiness, warmed by an under-note of ginger."

I cautiously sipped the tea. It had the somewhat grassy taste a good green tea had, that, with the zing of ginger the Paragon had pointed out, was somehow soothing. The familiar, ticklish silk sensation on my elbow let me know the tea was indeed laced with magic, but the sensation washed over me, unable to stick thanks to my immunity to magic. "Thank you. It's delicious," I said.

"I call it Lament-Be-Gone because it warms one from the inside out and raises one's spirits." The Paragon trundled over to the cabinet, where Aphrodite was pawing at a particular canister of tea leaves. "But I've been thinking I should be calling it 'Lost Lover,' since Aphrodite seems to particularly offer it to those nursing a broken heart. I don't suppose you went through a sad breakup recently?"

CHAPTER SEVEN

Chloe

I'd been in the middle of taking another sip, and the Paragon's question caught me so off guard I inhaled some of the hot tea, burning my lungs and making me break out in a wet cough.

The Paragon had his head stuck inside the tea cabinet, so he didn't notice, and Leila was thankfully chugging one of her lattes at the moment.

"Nope." I wiped tea off my nose. "No heartbreak here," I squeaked.

"Really? Because—I beg your pardon! Aphrodite, what is the meaning of this?" The Paragon shook the tea canister that Aphrodite had selected for him. "You can't really think *I* need this?"

Aphrodite purred and hopped out of the cabinet.

"You get back here and choose a different tea. Aphrodite!" the Paragon called.

Aphrodite ignored him and toddled over to me, leaning

against my legs and purring. I crouched down—careful to hold my cup out of her reach—and scratched under her chin, trying to convey my thanks.

Noctus and I weren't...we weren't even a thing. Or maybe we weren't a thing by human standards, but the bond we had from the collar was pretty intense, and leaving him was a deep loss. But the last thing I need is the Paragon picking up on my emotions and snooping when he's already craftier than I like dealing with.

Leila tapped her fingers on her cups. "What did Aphrodite choose for you?"

"*Calm the Heck Down*," the Paragon read off the container.

"Isn't that the tea you lace with some kind of sleeping spell?"

"It's for relaxation purposes!" the Paragon insisted. "But Aphrodite, you have deeply wounded me! I have no need to *chill*! I am already so chill!" The Paragon tossed the tea tin inside his cabinet and shut it with a huff.

"Are you going to grab a coffee or something?" Leila asked. "Because the clock is ticking."

"No," the Paragon sourly said. "I shall simply have to survive without a beverage. What about you? I thought you usually chose to patronize the Queen's Court Café." The Paragon eyed her Karuba drinks. "It *is* your namesake."

Leila toasted him with one of her cups. "I got a coupon for a free drink from Kwik Trip. There's no way I'm going to pass up that kind of deal."

"And you have two, because?" the Paragon asked.

Leila smiled affectionately at her drinks. "Rigel also got a free drink coupon. He got it and gave it to me," she said, casually naming her husband, the King of the Night Court. "Now, to the garden?"

"To the garden," the Paragon grudgingly said.

He trudged over to a bookcase, browsing through the titles. "Fairy Tales, Chronicles of Narnia—ah-hah! Recipe books!" The Paragon pulled on a book, then stepped back.

Nothing happened.

The Paragon frowned, then tugged on the book again. "I adjusted it some time ago so it wouldn't be so *violent*. Since then it's just been persnickety." He grumbled as he yanked hard on the recipe book—a Better Homes and Gardens recipe book. He pulled twice more before something clicked in the wall, and the bookshelf was slowly pulled up, disappearing into the ceiling.

"Wow." I clutched my mug of tea as I watched—not a single book on the shelf was disturbed. "That's some fancy magic."

"'Tis only a trifle—nothing complex." The Paragon waved a hand at me, but I could tell by the extra bounce to his step that he was pleased.

Leila marched past the Paragon, leading me into the garden. We passed under a dozen wooden arches that were covered in vine-y plants and dotted with tiny, paisley-colored flowers.

The arches opened into the aforementioned garden—a swathe of brilliant green hemmed in by an orange and red brick wall with a glass ceiling that was hazy with frost.

I was fascinated to find that the garden wasn't grassy, but instead was covered with moss. A little waterfall burst out of the brick wall, falling into a pond, and I was pretty sure I saw a few koi fish in the depths of the water.

Rose bushes with flowers that were unbelievably bright shades of red, pink, and dusty orange were beautifully arranged in front of a wall of ivy—just staring at the flowers tickled my elbow with the sensation of fae magic.

But I particularly loved the ferns and the moss-covered rock formation tucked away from flowers.

The garden was a little chaotic—as if it couldn't decide if it was an English tea garden or a Japanese moss garden—but that suited the Paragon's style.

The Paragon led the way to a black bistro set of outdoor furniture. I sat down on a chair with a back design of roses, while Leila plunked her drinks down on the table—which also had a rose motif—and sat on a chair decorated with irises.

"Okay, let's get serious about our discussion," Leila said.

So all of this was considered small talk? I'm not sure if that's a good thing or a bad thing.

"Very well." The Paragon took the last seat—this one had a thistle design—then folded his hands and eyed me over the rims of his glasses. "Naturally, I wish to help you discover more about your powers, Chloe, but I want to give you a proper warning first."

Aphrodite jumped onto the Paragon's lap, and he adjusted his sitting position so he could pet her.

"The organization Queen Leila and I have mentioned is top secret. Very few know of its existence, because we are still trying to sort out their mission as well as their identity. We didn't believe elves were involved in the organization until I saw your statement regarding the attack on you. You said the tracker made a call."

"If you don't mind me quoting you, I have the statement you gave to the Curia Cloisters on my cellphone." Leila dug her phone out of a pocket on her blue jeans. "Here we go, you said '*I can't recall exactly what he said due to my head injury, but I know he requested backup, and mentioned that he hadn't been assigned to me, but thought shadows were dangerous even if leadership didn't acknowledge it.*'"

"It's the reference to leadership that makes us think he is likely part of this organization," the Paragon said. "After a joint session with those who are in the know here in Magiford, it was voted that you should be brought into the fold in the hope that we might capture this tracker of yours, given that his obsession with hunting you brings him into the public. He's an easier target —a welcome change given that we haven't been able to uncover any new Magiford operatives."

"You think they were behind the exploding artifact from downtown," I guessed.

Leila raised an eyebrow. "How'd you guess?"

Because I was with the guys who flushed out the donut shop manufacturers, and this is a build up from that.

I couldn't say that, obviously. Thank goodness I had an explanation prepared!

"My brother works for the Curia Cloisters task force." I stared into my cup of tea.

Leila's expression cleared. "That's right. I'd forgotten about that. But you are correct. I have two of my best people investigating the issue."

"The Drake vampires and a few Medeis wizards are working the case, too," the Paragon added. "I believe the Pre-Dominant is going to lend out a few wolves for the investigation, too, isn't she?"

"It's actually the Pre-Dominant's protégé," Leila corrected. "But, yes, he is."

"And you think the guy after me is part of the organization you've uncovered—just because of my statement?" I asked.

"Well, that, and the fact that he's probably an elf—or at least an elf descendant." Leila set her phone down, then took a final swig of one of her coffees, tipping it all the way back to get every last drop. "It's a safe bet he hates all supernaturals, not just shadows."

I frowned. "Just because he's an elf doesn't necessarily mean he's evil."

Both the Paragon and Queen Leila stared at me. "Yes, it does," Queen Leila flatly said. "He's an elf. We fought a war against them to keep supernaturals *alive*."

"They did attempt to completely wipe your people out," the Paragon added.

I awakened to my mistake as more wrinkles spread across the Paragon's forehead.

Oh no. I showed my hand. That was a mistake. Reverse!

"Of course!" I croaked, my voice gurgling in my fear. "I don't know much of anything about elves besides what we learn about regarding the war. I thought maybe some were nicer—statistically speaking, there would have to be at least a few kind ones. Right?" I forced myself to take a sip of my now lukewarm tea and tried to look casual by slouching in my seat.

The Paragon leaned over Aphrodite, stretching his fingers out so he could pat my arm. "You are too kind," he said. "And so naïve. But I'm glad—there is hope for supernaturals if you can be this kind after everything you've gone through."

Leila thoughtfully pressed her lips together. "I don't know. She's right that there would be a rare elf who was decent—we know that for ourselves. But, as a race?" She shivered. "Let's just say I'm glad they're gone so we don't have to think about it."

I laughed nervously to fill the silence. *I don't understand how my ancestors were so famous for this subterfuge stuff. It is so much easier to just pretend to be a cat.*

"Regardless, there is no need to get philosophical," the Paragon said. "All of this is to say, we'd like to work with you on capturing this tracker of yours. Obviously because he's a danger to your life, and you are possibly the last shadow alive, but also because even though it's only a small chance, if we *can* capture him, and he is a part of the organization, it will give us an edge and perhaps let us discover what their true motive is."

I carefully sifted through the offer, thinking it over.

There's no reason to refuse. The tracker needs to be taken out fast since he keeps on escalating, and I don't want anyone put in danger. It's maybe a little disappointing that they're mostly interested in me because of him, but I guess it's not that surprising. I might be a shadow, but I'm still just me.

"You said you'd like to work together...what did you have in mind?" I asked.

"I'd say we fae could give you all the spells you want, but I suppose they won't work for you, will they?" Queen Leila asked.

"Anything that's an 'effects' spell won't work," I said. "But I'd appreciate fae potions."

"I can make potions myself," the queen said. "But they're

pretty weak. I'll see if I can get any of my people to brew some up, they'll be stronger, then."

"Thank you," I said.

"Are there any other spells you can use?" the Paragon asked.

"I guess any spell that is contained and activates once released I could technically use, but I'm not at all familiar with handling magic," I said. "I wouldn't know how to use it." I took another sip of my tea—even though it was lukewarm, the drink was a consolation to my frazzled nerves.

The bigger problem is Charon didn't train me to use magic spells, so adapting them into my sword and dagger fighting style without his help would be impossible. I can't be fumbling with potion bottles when the tracker is threatening humans, I have to rely on reacting fast.

"With your permission, we'll speak to your brother," Queen Leila said. "Or, really, the Paragon will speak to him. I must leave for another trip in a week or two."

"Yes, yes," the Paragon said. "We're aware Pat is most concerned with the safety of you and your sister. I'll inquire with him to see what resources he'd like access to."

"Maybe a tracking spell," Queen Leila said.

My fingers instinctively tightened, pressing my teacup into my palm, and I couldn't even say for certain why.

A tracking spell would be helpful. Then I wouldn't have to mess around with trying to call someone while running. And it wasn't like Noctus's tracking spell brought up bad memories. Yes, I'd lost a good amount of hair in my fright whenever Noctus found me in Magiford as a cat before I realized he *was* tracking me, but it wasn't a traumatic experience.

Maybe it's just that it reminds me of Noctus.

Oof, I had it bad. At least I'd be motivated when I got a chance to try planning some more.

"I'll ask," the Paragon said. "Since he's a human, he might appreciate a primer in available magics—though I suppose he's been experiencing that firsthand with his workplace being what it is."

"Yes," I absently agreed, then slightly shook my head and made myself refocus. "But did you only want to talk to me about the tracker? I thought this was also supposed to be a conversation about shadows, so I could learn more about them."

"Well, *I'm* here for the tracker conversation, but you're right. The Paragon wanted to talk to you about your existence." Queen Leila looked from me to the Paragon and waved a hand at him.

"What is that supposed to mean?" the Paragon asked.

"You know, you were going to tell her about the thing," Queen Leila said.

"No, I don't know. I don't speak whatever *this* is." The Paragon grandiosely waved his hand.

Leila sighed. "*Him*. I thought you were going to tell her about *him*! Unless you changed your mind?"

"Oh! Him!" The Paragon abruptly straightened up, sliding Aphrodite across his lap. The cat was remarkably calm and merely yawned despite the manhandling. "Yes, I suppose I should. Chloe."

"Yes?" I took a final sip from my cold—and now empty—cup of tea.

"There's someone I know that I'd like to introduce you to, who might have a better idea about what you're capable of than any book or dusty old windbag of a vampire might be able to say. But, I should warn you, he's an elf."

I'd thankfully swallowed my sip of tea, but at the Paragon's words, all the air in my body left in a wheeze.

No, no, no, no. He only knows one elf—well, technically, two—but I don't want to see either of them!

Yes, I was finally letting myself hope that maybe, his saving me was a sign that someday things would work out.

However!

I didn't want to pop around—mere *days* after he'd already

saved my sorry carcass—when I still didn't have any plans to put into play, risking blowing our covers and doing the very thing I promised I wouldn't!

Hope is a distant thing. This is too much!

Queen Leila must have interpreted my gurgles of shock as fear, because she set a hand on my arm. "You might feel weird about meeting an elf since you've got one chasing you, and elves are responsible for the extinction of shadows, but he's safe. He's not the *nice* elf you mentioned you were hoping for earlier, but he is an outlier in that he's decent and trustworthy enough that we know he won't harm you. He's helped the Paragon before in identifying elf magic."

Yep. Yep, it's definitely Noctus they're talking about.

My fingers shook a little, but I determinedly tightened my grip on my mug—I had to be with it so I could steer the Paragon away from this insane idea.

"I can't imagine how big of a deal this is...but, I'm sorry, I don't think I'd feel comfortable meeting an elf," I said.

Especially not that *one!*

"I can understand, but, I'm afraid, Chloe, he is the greatest source of information available to us when it comes to shadows," the Paragon said. "He might even have some materials from when shadows used to be more numerous."

"Couldn't you just ask him if there's a book?" I asked.

"Yes, but I'll have to introduce you. I can't just tell him, 'I have a shadow, please give me some priceless resources that aren't supposed to exist anymore, thanks!'" The Paragon punctuated his sentence with a big, cheesy wink.

Nope, I'm not giving up. I am not going to be so bad at my personal vows that I'm now just going to show up on Noctus's doorstep!

"I just found out I'm a shadow," I said. "And that elves are still alive. This is a lot to take in." I pushed my clay cup across the bistro table then folded my hands on my lap.

"I suppose it would be overwhelming," the Paragon said. "But allow me to assure you that he is the best possible source for information, and I don't take telling you what he is lightly."

Queen Leila tilted her head. "What is it about the situation that makes you uneasy, Chloe? A few minutes ago you were hoping elves weren't evil."

"Aha! Yes! He might surprise you! In a way he can fulfill that hope of yours. He isn't evil—though he certainly isn't kind." The Paragon frowned. "Except to his cat. Oh—but you can *turn into* a cat! Maybe he'll actually like you!"

My hands spontaneously twitched, and I was pretty sure I'd just sweated through my shirt.

I hope I wore enough deodorant, because this is getting ugly.

"Can't I hope for peace between us, and still be reluctant to meet an elf?" I asked. "I was just brained by one a few days ago. Plus, who's to say this contact of yours wants to meet a *shadow*?"

The Paragon scratched his ear.

Queen Leila stared at him.

"I mean, she's not wrong," he said.

Queen Leila rolled her eyes. "If you're that set against meeting the Paragon's contact, our opportunities for knowledge about shadows shrink drastically. I can have the fae check our libraries, but I'm not very hopeful. Fae kept elven relics—money, artifacts, weapons and the like—more than books." She drummed her fingers on the table. "Maybe we can rib Killian Drake into finding the oldest vampire in the Midwest and waking them up to see if they remember anything about shadows?"

"I'd rather face the elf," the Paragon said. "Old, crusty vampires are so disagreeable."

"I would really appreciate it if you reached out to the vampires," I said. "Thank you."

Queen Leila set her empty cups on the table. "It's no trouble. Thank you for cooperating with us about this tracker."

"Of course," I said. "He's hurt my family. I want him caught more than anything."

A funny, slanted smile skipped across Leila's lips. "You're an interesting one."

"What do you mean?"

She shook her head. "It's fine. Paragon, are you satisfied that she can't be spelled or charmed?"

"Yes." The Paragon sighed. "Though the side effects of Lament-Be-Gone aren't that obvious."

"What kind of charm is in it?" I asked as I hid my legs and hands under the table so any unexpected reactions to the revelation wouldn't be visible.

"It's a memory charm," the Paragon said.

A memory charm...I get it. There was a small, ridiculous part of me that was disappointed the charm hadn't worked on me. Life would be so much easier if I could just forcibly disconnect from my memories of Noctus, Charon, Ker, and Aristide. But they meant too much to me.

"A *memory* charm? Is that even legal?" Queen Leila growled.

"It's temporary," the Paragon insisted. "And quite mild—it's meant to help you forget your troubles. I assume your memory is fine as ever?"

I made myself smile. "Yep. It's just fine."

"You are unbelievable." Queen Leila scowled at the Paragon. "And your drugged teas must be against some kind of law. Do the Dominant, the Ancient, and the Magister know you have them?" she asked, referring to the top werewolf, vampire, and wizard officials in the USA.

"Of course," the Paragon chortled. "Why do you think I developed the teas in the first place? And they are perfectly legal, I'll have you know. I don't force anyone to drink them—it's a *gift*. Anyone who doesn't think twice about a fae gift deserves what they get!" His laughter shook Aphrodite, who leaped off his lap with an agility that surprised me considering her rotund shape.

"I can't argue with that." Queen Leila leaned back in her chair and grinned at me. "But you don't have to worry about us, Chloe. Your powers will keep the Paragon honest!"

"I am honest," the Paragon complained. "I'm a fae! Fae can't lie, and Aphrodite, are you truly abandoning me?"

The pink skinned cat ignored her owner and instead hooked her claws into my jeans and purred.

I smiled—a real one, not a forced one or the kind I used for customers at the Book Nookery—and picked Aphrodite up, setting her in my lap where she purred so hard I could feel it in my legs. "Thank you." I fiddled with Aphrodite's onesie, straightening it on her. "For everything. I don't want to make a big deal out of this—I just want to live a quiet life and keep my family safe. But I really appreciate the help."

"Of course," Queen Leila said. "You've been alone for so long. It's high time supernaturals help you."

"Yes," the Paragon said. "Also, Aphrodite likes you, so I am honor bound to help you regardless!" There was a gleam in his eyes that had my gut instinct hissing. "And help you *I shall*. Let me make some inquiries, and let's set up another meeting to discuss my findings."

Queen Leila didn't seem to notice, but the vow would have had me puffed up if I was in my cat form.

I hope I don't regret this meeting. But they're offering to help catch the tracker, and Pat and Joy's safety is the most important thing to me.

I TRIED NOT to salivate and hyperventilate at the same time as one of the most amazing scents in the world tickled my nose while I passed a customer a paper bag that contained their book purchase and a Book Nookery business card. "Thanks for your business, come see our store," I managed to say.

The customer waved as they walked away.

Ms. Booker delicately adjusted her glasses as she peered up at me. "You're smelling the apple cider donuts again, aren't you?"

I owlishly blinked in the afternoon sunlight and self-consciously checked to make sure the bun I'd pulled my hair back into was still neat. "They made a fresh batch."

"I would guess that you have werewolf blood in your family tree if your ability to smell things didn't seem limited to fresh bakery items," Ms. Booker dryly said. "Go take your break. See the market—and bring me back a tea from the bakery stall the brownies are running."

"Yes, Ms. Booker. Thank you!"

I grabbed my backpack—I could no longer carry just a purse since I had too much to carry, including my weapons, my weapon harness, and two spare fae potions—then slipped out of Book Nookery's stall, joining the crowd that strolled around the closed off main street.

Today was the fall supernatural market—it was always held in mid-September, and it had crept up on me this year between the drama with the tracker and my meeting with the Paragon and Queen Leila.

The supernatural market was held once per season, and was supposed to be the magical version of a local farmer's market. Realistically, it was a marketing campaign that let supernaturals promote our good side to humans.

It bought a lot of goodwill as it was one of the only ways for humans to purchase supernatural goods, and it was a great opportunity for the handful of supernatural businesses that had human clientele—like Book Nookery.

Ms. Booker had a stall at every supernatural market—it was a great way to drum up new patrons—and we staff members rotated through helping her.

I followed the scent of apple cider donuts as it led me past a fae selling skincare and hair potions, a pumpkin-smashing game run by a troll who helped his customers swing a massive hammer at the ill-fated squashes, and a wizard who was using her fire magic to roast ears of sweet corn before dipping them in a vat of melted butter.

I slowed down, however, when I passed by a stand of handmade leather goods.

Wallets stamped with werewolf designs, journals with unicorns and dragons embossed on the covers, knife sheaths, and belts that were studded with different metals for ornamentation were carefully arranged on a table or hung from a wire rack on the side.

What I noticed was what could only be described as a necklace.

It was thin—maybe about as wide as my thumbnail—and was dyed black. It was inconspicuous, and had a magnetic buckle as a fastener.

There was something about the sleek, minimalistic design that reminded me of the collar-necklace Noctus had put on me, even though the two looked nothing alike.

My collar—a lacy thing with three pomegranate red gems on it—had cemented a bond between us—one Noctus had taken off me before I left Calor Villa.

He'd slipped the collar in my backpack before I left, and I had unknowingly taken it with me.

It was currently stuffed in a pocket of the backpack I was carrying. I didn't have the heart to put it on—it wouldn't reconnect even if I did, so it would only remind me of what I'd left—but I also was too stubborn to just leave it in my apartment.

"Do you want to see it?"

I jumped where I stood, surprised by the comment—people usually didn't notice me—then guiltily swiveled to face the seller. He was a werewolf—very evident by his wide shoulders and the arm muscles that stood out under his t-shirt, along with his amber colored eyes that screamed "predator." But despite his slightly grizzled hair and beard, there was a genuineness to his eyes that let me relax.

"No, but thank you." I tried to smile. "Your work is very beautiful."

"Thank you." The werewolf tilted his head, and I could tell he was trying to scent me out by the way his nostrils flared. "But are you sure you don't want me to get the necklace off the rack for you? You seemed drawn to it. It might be a bit big for you, though."

"Oh, I wasn't thinking of it for myself. He has a much bigger neck, though, so I think it would fit him okay," I confessed before I realized what I was saying and clammed up.

Woah, what am *I thinking? I might have hope that maybe somehow things will work out, but hoping and buying Noctus a necklace are two totally different things.*

The werewolf seller rested his hands on his table and opened his mouth to respond to my spontaneous confession.

Unwilling to embarrass myself anymore, I hurriedly blurted out, "Thanks again, but no thanks, enjoy the market," and lunged at the next stall.

It wasn't until I was two stands down that my heartbeat started to return to normal and I could breathe again. Relieved, I peered at the new stall I stood in front of.

It had a small, innocuous sign that was printed on copier paper and laminated. "Life Advice?" I read, slightly confused.

A woman sat behind the stall, seated on a folding chair and a thick cushion. She was reading a paperback copy of Pride and Prejudice and had a bookmark pinched between her fingers.

She was beautiful with delicate facial features and silky black hair that was pulled back in a clip, and she was wearing a blue and white kimono that had a sea motif with bright red flowers to contrast.

She must be a vampire, I thought as I studied her clothes.

Given vampires' near immortality, they didn't usually follow modern fashion and wore whatever they felt comfortable in—usually something historical. Aristide and the Drake Family were the only vampires I knew of who followed modern convention when it came to clothes.

My guess was proved correct when the woman removed her reading glasses and glanced up at me, revealing dark red eyes.

"Yep, life advice," she confirmed.

I slightly bowed my head—this vampire was out in the middle of the day, a time vampires usually avoided as daylight made them ill, which meant she was probably very powerful. "You must be very wise," I said.

"Not really." The vampire tapped her fingers on her book's cover. "But history—and general behaviors—are cyclical. They repeat. You live as long as I have, and you see repeat after repeat, and all the reboots you never wanted but got anyway. We're still making the same mistakes everyone was making hundreds of years ago."

Thinking of all that I'd encountered over the spring and summer, I grimaced. "I can see how that would be true."

She arched both her eyebrows at me. "In that case, it's you who are the wise one." She narrowed her eyes. "You're the clerk that was working the Book Nookery stand, aren't you?"

"Yes."

"Ah, that explains it. Book people are always clever. I'll tell you what, just for that, I'll give you a piece of advice for free."

"Okay," I slowly said—I wasn't used to being treated this nicely by supernaturals. "Thank you very much."

"I give all kinds of advice—fashion advice, financial advice, decorating advice, but in this case, I'll give you romantic advice."

I sucked my neck into my shoulders. "I'm sorry?"

"Get the necklace," the vampire said.

I gulped. "W-what?"

The vampire leaned over the tabletop of her stall so she could point down the row. "Get the necklace you were eyeing up—for the man you were thinking of."

"But, but," I tried to jumpstart my thoughts, but I couldn't seem to form sentences.

"Yes," the vampire said. "I know. You're scared. Relationships are scary things—you're putting yourself in a position to be hurt." She narrowed her eyes, then added, "Again."

My eyes bulged as I gaped at her. *Woah, she's good.*

"But then again, you're always scared, aren't you?" she asked.

"Yes," I replied quickly and honestly.

"Good girl. At least you're aware of it." She nodded at me, her smile tinted with a hint of pride—as if she knew me, or at least recognized my struggles.

"And that's the first step to getting over all my fears?" I guessed.

"No." The vampire sighed, and the casualness left her voice for something that sounded sympathetic. "No, I'm sorry to say that your fears will try to rule you for the rest of your life." She glanced at me again, her red eyes holding me in place. "It will be your lifelong battle to act despite all those fears. But just because you are afraid, doesn't mean you won't be victorious. Slay your inner dragons; get the necklace."

With that, she picked up her book, put her glasses back on, and immersed herself in the world of Jane Austen, seemingly finished with me.

She's right. I'm always going to be afraid—my shadow instincts will always have me two moments away from puffing up and running.

I stared at her "Life Advice" sign for several long moments, then looked down the row at the leatherworker's stall.

But what if I didn't just hope and wonder. What if...I tried to think of a way Noctus and I could be together?

I took one step, then another toward the werewolf's stand.

This is insane. I'm insane! But...what if she's right? What if I give up on Noctus, when there really is a way I can be with him—and Aristide, Ker, and Charon—and I didn't even take the time to consider it?

I squared my shoulders as I reached the werewolf's stall, the smell of leather filling my nose. "Excuse me, could I take a look at that necklace after all?"

I WAS WAITING in the park where the Paragon had said to meet him, when an SUV with tinted windows pulled up to the curb, practically screaming "suspicious!"

I stiffened, until the front passenger window rolled down, and the Paragon popped his head out of the car.

"Greetings, Chloe Anderson! I procured us a ride—hop in!"

The invitation went against everything parents teach their kids about stranger danger, so I slowly approached the vehicle, reluctantly opening the back door, to reveal a leather interior bench seat, the Paragon sitting in the front passenger seat, and a big, hulking guy in a tailor-fitted suit and sunglasses driving the car.

I still wasn't going to get in, until I saw the golden dragon insignia emblazoned on the SUV's dashboard.

The dragon—that's the emblem of Killian Drake, the vampire Eminence of the Midwest.

I sneezed twice—compliments of the Paragon's overpowering glamour—then looked to the suited man driving—he had to be a vampire.

I cautiously pushed my magic down, used to the process I needed to follow to keep from accidentally peeking under the Paragon's glamour. "Does this car belong to the Drake family?" I asked.

"Yes!" The Paragon twisted around in his seat to smile at me. "Killian is my bestie—this is one of the many perks of being his only friend!"

I cautiously climbed into the car, closing the door behind me, and jumping when the car's doors automatically locked after the driver shifted gears.

"Does Killian Drake *know* you're using the car...and his driver?" My seatbelt clicked into place as I settled into my seat, and the car rolled away from the park.

The Paragon made a noise in the back of his throat. "He's got loads of cars and drivers. He won't notice."

In other words, Killian Drake doesn't know the Paragon uses his cars as a taxi service. But I'm surprised his vampires are willing to play along with it.

I studied the vampire driver through the rearview mirror. He took off his sunglasses—revealing his bright red eyes—and glanced back at me. "His Eminence prefers the Paragon to be *occupied* instead of freely wandering around Drake Hall," he said, correctly interpreting my expression.

"I see." I dropped my gaze to my hands, and tried to find a way to settle them in my lap that didn't feel awkward. "Paragon? When you texted me our meeting place, you said you found a new source of information. Who is it?"

"Ahh, yes! I'm pleased to say the vampires have pulled through." The Paragon wobbled in his chair as the SUV turned a corner, leaving the downtown area and heading into the more human, residential parts of town. "There is a vampire who lives in Magiford who pre-dates shadows!"

Surprised, I braced myself on the door. "Really? Is he awake?"

"Oh yes, he's awake and functioning," the Paragon assured me. "He's connected to Killian Drake, actually, and he's quite knowledgeable. Wouldn't you agree, Gavino?" he asked the driver.

"He's terrifying," was Gavino's reply.

"Hush—you'll scare her," the Paragon scolded him.

"Are we going to meet him?" I asked.

"Yes," the Paragon said.

I nodded and glanced out the window, frowning when I realized I recognized the neighborhood.

We're getting close to Noctus's cul-de-sac. Another turn, and we'll be on the street his neighborhood connects to.

The car slowed, and the driver turned the car.

...the Paragon is a fae and can't lie, but he can use loopholes with his words.

"....Paragon," I said, my voice calm even though I was starting to hear a ringing in my ears. "Are we going to meet that vampire *right now?*"

"Well...He is rather busy at the moment. In fact, he's not actually in Magiford—he was called away with his partner for a family emergency."

The car turned into Noctus's cul-de-sac.

He's taking me to Noctus!

CHAPTER EIGHT

Chloe

Despite impulsively buying the leather necklace at the fall market, I had exactly zero steps in my plan to reunite with Noctus, but I knew one thing: this was not the way to do it.

All the acting and lying that would have to go into this—the chance of a trip up was too great, and the *Paragon* would be the one to witness any mix ups.

Not to mention I had promised I wouldn't come back!

I can't do this. This is the worst-case scenario!

Panic flooded my system. My heartbeat must have tripled, because the vampire driver turned to look back at me. "Are you alright, miss?" he asked.

I'm not going to be able to hide my reactions, I must do something!

So I did what I always do whenever I was terrified, I turned into a cat.

"Chloe?" The Paragon turned around in his chair. "Look, you

don't have to be scared. Yes, we're going to meet..." he paused as he glanced at the vampire driver. "Er, my contact that I mentioned to you in the meeting with Leila that you indicated you did not want to meet, but he's not going to hurt you. His powers are contained—he even agreed to speak directly with you!"

No, no, no, no!

As a cat I struggled out of my seatbelt and jumped to the floor of the car as it rolled to a stop.

"Chloe—you'll be fine. I vow it!" the Paragon said.

I ignored him as I tried to crawl under his seat.

"Chloe!" The Paragon unclipped his seatbelt and got out of the car. He opened my door and stood in front of it. "I know you're afraid, but it's going to be fine."

The car was too well made, so I could only wedge half of my body under the seat. When the Paragon reached for me I hissed and batted at him with a paw—though I made sure I didn't use my claws.

"Are you making a human do something they don't wish to do?" The vampire driver's voice was smooth and terrifying.

The Paragon groaned. "She doesn't wish to, but she *needs* to. Chloe—woah!"

I slipped past the Paragon, springing out of the car. Every hair on my body was puffed up, and I skittered around the Paragon, dodging his arms.

"Chloe, wait a moment!" the Paragon called after me.

I was disoriented as I sprinted down the sidewalk, but my cat agility kept me balanced as I glanced back, making sure I was far ahead of the sneaky fae.

The Paragon's expression shifted from concern to surprise.

Uh-oh, that can't be good.

As soon as the thought illuminated my brain, I felt hands around my shoulders, and I was lifted off my paws.

No, please, no. If there is any justice in this world...no!

Slowly, with dread weighing down every ounce of my small body, I looked up at who'd caught me.

Staring down at me, with his dark, golden hair fanning across his forehead, his perfect, sculpted features, and his hazel eyes that were shot through with the familiar elven spiral...was Noctus.

He was wearing a suit—black with a black undershirt and the top two buttons undone—and there was almost a cruel edge to his smile. "Greetings, *shadow*," he said.

Oh, he's not happy I'm here.

I was so defeated and so upset; all I could do was limply hang from his grasp.

"Noctus!" the Paragon shouted as he hustled up to us, hitching his robes high to reveal his skinny legs and knobby knees. "Good show—and excellent catch! Though I must warn you, the cat you are holding is, in fact, the shadow I called you about. Here."

The Paragon slipped his hands under my armpits.

He tried to tug me from Noctus's grasp. Noctus continued to hold me snug against him, his expression flat.

"Hm?" The Paragon peered up at him.

Something flickered across Noctus's face and he slowly released me, letting the Paragon hold me up by my armpits.

The Paragon gave him a curious glance, then turned his focus onto me, rotating me so I faced him. "You see, Chloe, you have nothing to fear. Noctus is very cat hearted, I assure you. He has a cat of his own, a black one, just like you." He tilted his head and peered at me over his glasses. "In fact, now that I'm seeing you like this...you do look similar to Noctus's Ama."

I stiffened in the Paragon's hands. *Oooh, this is why I knew this was a terrible idea! This is turning into the worst day of my life. Work, magic, work!*

The Paragon stared at me for three full seconds, then twirled in a circle, still holding me. "Ama, however, is better looking—sorry, but her coat is glossier and fuller. Noctus's doing, you know.

He's a terrific pet parent—if not a tad overbearing," he stage whispered to me.

"*I beg your pardon?*" Noctus growled.

"What, what? Did you say something, Noctus?" The Paragon beamed at the elf king.

I hung from the Paragon's hands, my heart recovering. *I'm so glad the Paragon has the attention span of a goldfish.* With my heart beginning to slow to something near a normal rate, I waited until the Paragon wilted under Noctus's glare before I expertly wriggled out of his hands.

I landed paws first on the sidewalk, then took off, sprinting toward the cul-de-sac entrance.

Noctus—with his expert cat wrangling skills—stepped into my way so I smashed into his legs and picked me up before I could recover. "Why does the shadow keep attempting to run away?"

"Funny thing, I neglected to tell her we were coming to see you today. Haha, oops!" The Paragon sheepishly scratched the back of his head.

Noctus cradled me like he used to when I was Ama. I stiffly let him roll me onto my back, my paws pointed up to the air.

I don't know what to do. I didn't want to come here like this, and now it's going to be even more complicated. How do I even act? I'm going to have to overthink every action and word I say to make sure I don't give anything away. I was such an idiot for trusting the Paragon!

"There's a difference between not expecting to meet someone, and being terrified," Noctus said.

"Mmm." The Paragon held his hands out to take me. "She might have said, previously, she didn't want to meet you. She's just a tad scared of you—don't take it personally, she did just find out elves exist, and one is actively trying to kill her."

"So you've said." Noctus turned away from the Paragon, blocking his sight of me. "Why, then, would you bring her here when you *knew* she didn't want to?"

"Because she's a shadow." The fun and jokes left the Paragon's voice. He sighed as he fell in line with Noctus, glancing at me. "It was underhanded to bring her—and I apologize for it, Chloe. But if your tracker is involved with the organization, and even seems to be knowledgeable of the leadership within it, you're the best lead we have."

So it's all about the organization. Not me.

He'd been obvious about it during the meeting with Queen Leila, but I'd thought the Cloisters would still attempt to help me in some way that didn't directly benefit their ongoing search. Silly me.

"We cannot afford any mistakes," the Paragon continued. "You need every possible advantage you can get in this situation, which includes consorting with elves." He held his hand out, palm up.

Thankfully I hadn't pretended to be Ama in months, or I would have automatically tapped my paw to his palm in a high five. But, when the Paragon glanced from me to Noctus, I realized I probably appeared to be a little too relaxed in the arms of someone I'd been desperate not to meet.

Right, I need to focus. I must get through this meeting with a convincing enough act that the Paragon doesn't get suspicious. Here I go!

I squirmed in Noctus's arms, wriggling fiercely enough that I should have been able to slip out of a less experienced grasp.

Noctus, however, was well versed with my typical antics. He ignored me and shifted me to one arm so he could open the front door.

He stepped through the gate built behind the front door of his Cape Cod home, and for a moment the dizzying swirl of portal magic made my stomach flop.

Noctus emerged in his villa, gliding past the gold gate with its ornamental flourishes that he pushed back into place once the Paragon popped out of the portal.

"This way, Paragon." Noctus continued to ignore my struggles as I tried to wriggle out of his grasp, leading the Paragon to the drawing room he was usually received in—I think it was an effort to limit the view of the villa.

This particular drawing room was opulent, but not to the point of being gaudy.

Cathedral ceilings, decorated with golden fleurs-de-lis, were lit up by four extravagant chandeliers that sent tiny rainbows cascading through the room.

"Now, then. Noctus, please allow me to introduce you to Chloe Anderson, who was recently revealed to be a shadow. Chloe, this is Noctus, the elf contact I spoke of," the Paragon gestured from me to Noctus—who was still holding me.

So he's not planning on telling me Noctus is a Mors elf. Interesting.

I paddled my paws in the air, signaling my desire to be put down.

Noctus set me on a settee, his hand familiarly grazing under my chin in a gesture the Paragon didn't see—he was scowling so deeply his fluffy white eyebrows were squatting low over his eyes.

"I already told Noctus all about the tracker and how he's threatened your family..." The Paragon trailed off. "Er...Chloe, if you would return to your human shape, I imagine it would make this conversation easier."

It will make it harder, actually, to keep you fooled since I'm not convinced I can keep all my expressions in, but I should try to get this over with as quickly as possible.

I hopped off the settee and trotted over to the enormous windows on the far side of the room, taking shelter in the comfort of the gold curtains before I reluctantly swapped to my human form.

I set my hand on the mantel of a marble fireplace—one of three in the room—and stepped around the gold drapes.

These windows must be spelled, I realized as I glanced outside, where part of the elven city built into Calor sprawled. *I mean, they obviously are. This view of the mountain and the elven city shouldn't be possible in this room. But they must also have some kind of screening glamour on them. The Paragon's been in here every time he's visited, and he hasn't noticed the view.*

I felt the prickle of elf magic in my ribs, but I wasn't sure if it was the windows, or just being back in Calor.

Noctus and the Paragon sat down, Noctus selecting the gold settee covered in tasseled pillows that I'd abandoned, while the Paragon plopped down in an armchair.

When he saw I was back in my human shape, the Paragon waved to me. "Excellent. Say hello, Chloe."

I turned on my heel and pointed myself in Noctus's direction, but I stared at his neck instead of risking looking into his eyes. "Hel-lo." I didn't have to feign awkwardness as I shifted my weight from one foot to the other. "Th-thank you for agreeing to this meeting."

Noctus leaned back in the settee, resting his arms across the top of it. "Despite your reluctance to meet me?"

"Noctus, don't tease the girl. She's already scared out of her mind," the Paragon lectured him.

Noctus shrugged. "You don't have room to criticize given you were the one who dragged her here unwillingly."

"You are in a *mood*, aren't you?" the Paragon tisked. "And what's up with your clothes? Usually, whenever I see you you're dressed up like a hitman looking to break someone's teeth."

"Wearing black, moveable clothing is hardly the mark of a hitman." Noctus shrugged, the movement emphasized by his black suitcoat.

He was dressed, I recognized, for going out into Magiford, most likely. He was more comfortable in his training clothes—the outfit the Paragon had mentioned. He dressed like this when he needed to impress, without using his magic.

"Whatever," the Paragon said. "Can we get started?"

"Fine. But you've already told me everything about her, don't waste my time repeating it. Why are you here today?" Noctus asked.

Slowly, I edged over so I was standing next to the Paragon's chair, across from Noctus. I couldn't tell his expression—I was keeping my eyes on his neck.

"To ask for your help—or rather, your resources," the Paragon said. "Chloe is the first known shadow in centuries, and she's adopted by humans. No one has taught her about shadow abilities or magic. Supernatural society as a whole doesn't know much about her, though we are exploring fae libraries and there is a vampire contact, though he's not available at the moment."

"Not the dragon shifters?" Noctus asked.

The Paragon shrugged. "None are in Magiford at the moment. I've notified the Dominant, the Magister, and the Ancient. They'll be asking their acquaintances, so I imagine it will reach the dragon shifters eventually, but Chloe doesn't have time to spare. She needs to know how to defend herself now."

"I see," Noctus said. "Is that your request, shadow?"

I shut my eyes. *He's angry. Yes, he came to save me, but this is way worse than breaking me out of an animal shelter. I messed up.*

When I opened my eyes, I kept my gaze on the top, open button of his black dress shirt. "I would appreciate any resources you could share. I work for a bookstore; if there is a book title you know that could help, the owner and I might be able to track it down."

My clothes felt scratchy and uncomfortable, even though I was wearing my favorite long sleeved blouse. "I'm sorry to intrude on you like this. I'm sorry, I..." I trailed off as a chalky taste filled my mouth, and I didn't know what to say that wouldn't make the Paragon suspicious but would still tell Noctus just how bad I felt about this.

Here I was, thinking I'm smart enough that I could lay out a plan that would make this possible and safe, and days later I let him down. Him, and Charon, Aristide, Ker, and everyone in Calor—

"Chloe," Noctus said, his voice warm and familiar. He said my name like a caress, just as he had the night on the clocktower when we nearly kissed.

Surprised, I let myself look up into his face.

The spirals in his eyes were swirling. Not with anger, but something painfully close to affection. The set of his lips had softened, and he tilted his head in what I recognized as a playful gesture, holding my gaze.

I couldn't look away from him. It was *Noctus*, and I'd been missing him fiercely even though it had been months.

Ohhh I shouldn't have looked. I should not have looked. Big mistake. Big one. Stop looking!

Noctus's barely-there smile grew a little, but his eyes changed—from warmth to regret. He—

The Paragon stuck his head up in between us. "Hello?" he said. "Is this what is called, according to those chick flicks the Drake vampires use for punishments, 'love-at-first-sight'?"

That broke me out of it like a bucket of ice-cold water.

I sucked in a deep breath. "*What?*"

"A supernatural long thought extinct, a handsome elf," the Paragon ticked off on his fingers. "Seems like the start of a good meet-cute. Except you should know, he's crusty and boring beyond all belief. The best part of his personality is that he's a pet owner."

"You're always so charming whenever you're asking for something, Paragon," Noctus said.

The Paragon sat back down and folded his arms across his chest with a grunt. "I was nice to you at first. But it's been *years*, and you're still a tight-fisted, frosty wall. Now. What was that?" He waggled his fingers at Noctus and me.

"Um," I said.

It would have been convenient to blame Noctus's elf magic, except I was a *shadow*, and magic didn't work on me!

I wanted to look at Noctus to nonverbally ask for help, but that was only going to make this so much worse.

THINK! What would distract the Paragon?

"Sorry, it just occurred to me, he's very different from the tracker, who you think is also an elf," I squeaked.

"Oh?" The Paragon perked up.

"Yes. The tracker is more agile and graceful than a human but..." I dared to glance at Noctus, but this time I smartly looked *over* his head. "Nothing like Noctus. Noctus is much more..." I waved frantically.

"Yes, he is quite impressive." The Paragon tapped his fingers on his chin, frowning when his pointer finger got tangled in his mustache's long hairs. "So you're saying Noctus has a more intense feeling of elfness?"

"Yes," I said. "*Much* more intense."

"Well I suppose, he is Noctus," the Paragon mused, which was probably more him thinking of Noctus's kingship and bloodlines than any personal thoughts about the royal elf.

"He's likely from a different family," Noctus said, deigning to help me. "Or—more likely—he's only part elf."

"Perhaps," the Paragon said. "Could a part elf still use full elven magic?"

Noctus shrugged—I think, I still wasn't risking looking at him straight on. "It's possible, particularly if he was a half-blood."

I relaxed—we'd safely moved on. This was good.

"That sounds possible." The Paragon narrowed his eyes as he studied Noctus. "But while that explains why Chloe was staring at you, it doesn't explain why she so fully captured *your* attention."

It was a good thing the Paragon was only a fae, because my heart thumped in my chest with so much force that it physically hurt.

Why does the Paragon have to be so persistent? Why, why, why?

Noctus slowly blinked in the unhurried fashion of a large cat. "I beg your pardon?"

"You were staring at her," the Paragon said. "And the way you said her name. It was..."

A thud that came from the hallway outside the room made us all look over at the door.

It swung open, and Charon—wearing his customary cloak-like shirt and hood—slipped in, carrying a tea tray balanced on one hand while he tried to wrestle the door shut with the other.

I heard what sounded like a dog's nails on the smooth flooring—Ker, probably—and some scathing whispers.

"Let me in, you expressionless twerp—"

Charon backed into the door, slamming it shut before Aristide could hiss any more insults at him.

The door rattled behind him, and there was a muffled wolf's "*Awoo*—" which abruptly cut off.

Charon corrected his hold of the tea tray, but otherwise was unbothered by the scuffle. "Refreshments," he announced tonelessly.

"Thank you, Charon," Noctus said.

Charon bowed and approached the coffee table, setting the tray on it.

"The reason why I was interested in Chloe Anderson," Noctus began, taking control of the conversation before the Paragon could, "is the reason why I even allowed you to come today."

"Oh?" The Paragon leaned back in his chair, the rims of his eyeglasses gleaming.

"I once considered a shadow in my acquaintance as a companion," Noctus said. "Moreover, it has always been my sorrow that the elves wiped out such a talented group of supernaturals. I am glad there is at least one survivor."

I was fairly certain he was talking about me, but I wasn't as skilled at hiding my expressions—or recovering—as Noctus was, so I opted to watch Charon, instead.

"You can be sentimental," the Paragon said. "Interesting—I didn't know you had it in you."

Charon took the opportunity to pour Noctus a cup of tea,

serving him first, then poured one for the Paragon and set it in front of him.

The whole time he never glanced at me, or gave any indication he was aware of my presence.

Of course, he wouldn't. I left. It's not that he hates me, I'm simply not part of the group anymore.

My hope—and decision to make a plan—rattled around in my heart.

I missed Noctus fiercely, but it was more than him that made me dream of Calor Villa.

Charon poured tea in the last remaining teacup. "Sugar or cream, miss?" he asked, his voice lacking inflection—at least I could be comforted by knowing that was usually how he talked.

"Cream, please. Thank you." I awkwardly cleared my throat and tried to smile at him, hoping he could read the apology in my eyes.

Charon's expression was bland as ever as he poured some cream into my cup of tea.

Drooping, I took the cup from him when he offered it, holding it as I gawkily stood by the Paragon's chair, still feeling too awkward to sit. I sipped at my tea, even though it wasn't really my thing.

It was then that Charon uncovered the silver platter of treats he'd brought, revealing a crystal plate filled with neatly arranged donuts.

There were cake donuts flecked with blue-ish purple bits that smelled like sugar coated blueberries, round chocolate donut holes that were covered with a glazed frosting that had *just* set with a slight crust to it, a cake donut that was a dark green that I was willing to bet was green tea flavored, and three intricately arranged cinnamon twists.

Donuts. He brought donuts, my favorite food.

"Donuts? What prompted this sudden bout of VIP treatment? Normally you won't offer me any kind of food!" The

Paragon eagerly grabbed the green tea donut and two of the chocolate donut holes.

"We don't typically offer you food because I don't wish for you to stay longer than needed," Noctus said. "In this case, it hardly seems like it will be necessary to starve you out."

I barely heard him—I was busy trying to fight back the unexpected tears that stung my eyes. I hurriedly took another sip of my tea to buy me time to fix my expression before picking a blueberry cake donut.

This is torture. Because they're so understanding. But I suppose they've been doing this for centuries. They've experienced this before.

The thought made my heart hurt worse—not for me, but for them.

Noctus, Charon, Ker, and Aristide made so many sacrifices because Noctus was the last elven king.

But he was a good king precisely because he was willing to make those sacrifices, and he didn't force them on anyone—as I knew firsthand.

I must find a way to make us work. I must.

"So." The Paragon popped a chocolate donut hole, then slurped his tea. "Since you're pleased that there's a shadow left, are you willing to help?"

"Certainly," Noctus said.

The Paragon jolted in his seat as he seemed to simultaneously inhale and choke on his tea. He coughed so hard he had to cling to the arms of his chair so he didn't throw himself out of his seat. I set my tea and donut down and patted his back.

I stopped, immediately, as my fingers could feel toned muscle under his robes that my eyes couldn't *see*, and the itchy, sneeze-inducing feeling of his glamour smacked me, so I had to back off to get my magic to leave the glamour be rather than peel it back like it wanted to.

The Paragon recovered without my help, though he nearly

emptied his teacup in the process. "What did you say?" he asked, his voice rough from all the coughing.

Noctus studied his teacup with a relaxedness he typically reserved for baiting Aristide with jokes about nostalgia vampires. "I said certainly."

"You mean you'll actually help?" the Paragon asked.

"Why wouldn't I?"

"Because when *I* ask you for help, you say no!"

"The shadow was a very dear companion. And I have helped you—I have identified elven magic for you before. Just because I refuse to answer the question of your obsession hardly makes me unwilling to help," Noctus said.

The Paragon made a snuffling noise and stuffed a donut in his mouth—probably to keep from blurting out something offensive.

Noctus's shoulders moved in a barely noticeable shrug before he turned his gaze on me. "I'm afraid there isn't a book that would be of help to you, Chloe Anderson, given the shadows' extinction predates the invention of the printing press. There are, however, elven records. Charon will have to translate them for you as they'll be in elvish."

I really wish he'd stop saying my name. He sounds so...familiar.

"Thank you," I said to the space above his head. "That would be very helpful, and much appreciated." I mechanically turned on my heels so I was pointed at Charon—who had positioned himself by the door. "Thank you in advance for your translation work." I didn't let myself look at Charon's face, either. I fixated on his left shoulder.

"Of course." Charon started to bow. "As—"

The door popped open. It would have smashed Charon flat, except he caught it with his hand and braced himself for the impact.

Aristide, tapping his white cane on the ground, entered the drawing room and kicked the door shut behind him so quickly that I barely had time to register the blur of black and red fur before the door closed on Ker, locking her out.

"What's that, we have visitors?" Aristide declared, looking in the Paragon's and my general direction—most likely tracking our heartbeats. "How stupendous. I *love* visitors." He threw his arms wide with the declaration, whacking Charon in the shins with his cane—revenge, I was betting, for shutting the door on him when Charon arrived with the tea and donuts.

"Aristide," Noctus acknowledged. "You've met the Paragon before. He brought the newly discovered shadow over."

"Yes, you mentioned that. How wonderful to meet you, shadow," Aristide said. "Are you healthy? Your heartbeat is going so fast I'm concerned for you."

Charon stepped in front of Aristide. "If you'll excuse us, we'll be going. Aristide can help me find the scrolls and sources that mention shadows in the library."

"And how," Aristide began, "am I going to do that when I can't *see* anything in the scrolls?"

"Perhaps you can track them by scent," Noctus said. "You do have an affinity for old things, after all. I imagine they remind you of yourself."

"Ha-ha-ho!" Aristide belly laughed. "Aren't you crabby—maybe I should call for Ama?"

"Oh, yes!" The Paragon wriggled in his chair. "I haven't seen Ama for months. I do so miss her—you'll love her, Chloe. She is absolutely charming, nothing like her owner!"

Noctus, proving he was a thousand times better at this subterfuge stuff than me, yawned as he reclined on the settee. "I believe I told you Ama would not be present for your demands because you stress her out."

"I would never!" the Paragon declared.

Safely positioned just behind the Paragon, I absently shook my head. *Mm, no, Noctus is right. You are more stressful than my clock-tower training sessions.*

"If you leave an address with Charon at which you can be reached, he will deliver the materials to you when he is finished with the translation," Noctus abruptly said, his voice the tiniest bit flat.

The room felt a degree cooler—the change so slight it was barely noticeable. But the Paragon must have picked up on it, too, because he stood up. "Understood. Thank you, Noctus, for the use of your resources. Chloe appreciates it, as do I."

"Yes, thank you so much." I bowed my head to avoid looking at Noctus, then started marching toward the door, sensing now was the time to leave.

Charon opened the door for me and stepped into the hallway first, but Aristide remained in the drawing room, his head cocked as he listened.

Ker wasn't in the hallway, but I did feel the furry sensation of werewolf magic, so she was probably changing in a nearby room.

I have to get out of here, I don't think I can face her. She's too kind.

Charon waited until the Paragon passed through—the fae paused in the doorframe to wave at Noctus before he charged after me—then closed the door.

"Where can you be reached?" Charon asked as he led the way back to the gold gate.

"I have an apartment, so you'd have to drop the translations off at the main office. Otherwise, I work at the Book Nookery book store, so it might be easiest to drop everything off there," I said, knowing Charon knew exactly where I lived and worked. "My boss knows what I am, and that I'm working with the Curia Cloisters to find out more about my heritage. The material would be safer there, too."

"Book Nookery," Charon repeated. "Very well. It will be sent there. Good day to you, Paragon, Miss Chloe."

Charon opened the golden gate, and practically shooed the Paragon and me through the portal so we stepped out onto the cement front porch of the Cape Cod.

"Well, that went marvelously!" the Paragon declared as he scuttled down the sidewalk.

"Marvelous?" I repeated, incredulous.

"Oh yes," the Paragon said. "I was fully prepared to beg and cry and have to come back at least twice more before he shared any resources with you. He's an elf, but he's as stubborn as a goat." He glanced back at the Cape Cod, then led the way to the Drake SUV that was parked on the street. "It's astounding, really, that he was so affable today. Something good must have happened to him. Unless maybe he really does like shadows?"

"Is that possible?" I asked. "He's an elf."

The Paragon squinted in the afternoon sun. "Maybe, but he's unusual—he's got a conscience, and the legacy to prove it."

I blinked in surprise. *What, exactly, is that supposed to mean?*

"Come along, then. We'll drop you off at home. And congratulations on your good luck," the Paragon added. "Those translations will be your best resource—the elves were *obsessed* with shadows. If anyone remembers them, it would be the elves."

I opened the back door of the SUV as I planned how to drive a very necessary point home. "Yes, except they're all gone."

"Yes," the Paragon sighed. "They are."

Reluctantly, I glanced back at the home I'd vowed to avoid. I thought I saw something move in the window that was connected to Noctus's office, but I couldn't be sure.

I miss having a place among supernaturals—a place with them. But how could I make it happen? Should I become a vampire blood donor and hope that the vampire would be willing to lengthen my life, and then when my family gets old I disappear myself? But that'll be decades...

"Chloe?"

"Yes, sorry." I hopped in the car, closing the door behind me, and focused on the Paragon, forcibly dragging my mind from thoughts of Noctus, and his friends.

CHAPTER NINE

Noctus

The day Chloe and the Paragon visited, I knew Aristide was going to be intolerable and Charon would barely be any better. So, as soon as they left, I arranged to do a barrier patrol and eliminate a few monsters that had attempted to intrude on Calor's boundaries to take myself out of the house.

I stayed out until the late evening, and then loitered in the shadows of the town—hiding, because if my people knew I was present they'd stiffen up, bow at me, and generally be afraid.

It wasn't until after midnight—when I knew Aristide would be busy with his podcasts and Charon would have stopped working—that I wandered up to the highest level of the town.

I sat on a stone bench near one of the back door entrances to my villa, to all appearances watching the way the starlight struck the waters of the gurgling phoenix fountain that my bench was planted in front of.

In reality, I was enjoying the silence—since seeing Chloe, wild magic had, mercifully, shut up. Though I was betting the effect was temporary since already I heard the occasional chirp and note.

It's probably realizing that yes, she came here, but she's left again and isn't coming back.

I'd been resting my hand on the pommel of the sword I'd taken with me, but at the thought, I reflexively tightened my grip.

Footsteps echoed across the courtyard. "Noctus?"

"Hello, Kerberos," I said without looking at my longtime friend.

She stopped next to me and rested a warm hand on my shoulder. "Are you okay?"

"Just fine," I wryly said, shifting to make room on the bench so she could join me.

Ker sat down, leaning forward so she rested her elbows on her knees. She stayed silent, though she glanced at me, a sad smile flitting across her lips. "You don't have to pretend, you know. We know what Chloe meant to you. No one will criticize you."

"For inviting my heartache back into my own house?" I asked.

Ker shrugged. "It was a chance to see her—something we didn't think we'd get."

"You don't think I was insane for letting the Paragon bring her? It had the potential for disaster."

"Nah," Ker said. "Charon's been dying to find a way to help her despite the separation. And what better way to do it than right under the Paragon's nose? It was safer than you might think. Chloe is good enough at acting that we knew she'd be able to roll with it. Though I don't think she appreciated the Paragon dragging her here without telling her."

"Yes," I agreed. "She seemed...upset."

Ker snorted. "She would have gotten away if you hadn't been there with your expert Ama-catching skills."

"Experience," I said. *And maybe a bit of desperation.*

I'd thought I was processing Chloe's absence just fine. It had been hard after she left, but I'd dealt with loss in my life before—it was a constant companion in long lived supernaturals like myself. But after rescuing her from Paw-Pals, even though it was just her cat form, her absence haunted me.

It took everything I had to leave her in her apartment and go. I'd told myself it was because she was injured, and I'd hoped that maybe, if I saw her safe and whole, I could let her go.

But no. Now, I wanted her more than ever, to the point where I knew I wouldn't be able to handle any good-natured ribbing from my friends.

"Noctus." Ker paused as she stretched her long legs out in front of her. "Isn't there any way it could work?"

I listened to the gurgle of the fountain as I tried to recall what we'd been talking about. "Make what work?"

"Chloe, and you," Ker said. "Since the Paragon officially introduced her to us, don't we now have a reason to reach out to her? I don't think the Paragon will be overly suspicious. He'd report it back to the Regional Committee of Magic, but none of them seem interested in you if they think the Paragon has control over you."

"It's a wonderful dream," I said. "But it's a temporary solution. I believe we'll soon be leaving Magiford, and while the Paragon might follow us due to his bulldog attitude toward his pointless quest, we *cannot* let the Regional Committee of Magic or any supernaturals note our move with interest—something they definitely would do if the last shadow was connected to me."

"Noctus, you're an elf," Ker said. "Chloe wouldn't *have* to move with us—you could use gates to port yourself to her. You'd need to keep portals to Magiford active for a while, anyway, or all the Calor elves quitting their jobs within the same month would possibly raise some suspicions."

"Not necessarily," I said. "Humans and supernaturals don't talk. My people all work for humans—it's unlikely supernatural society would even notice their absence. But I see what you mean.

It's still..." I stopped talking—I missed Chloe so badly, I didn't even want to voice just how impossible our situation was.

"You don't have to be so perfect a king that you become unfeeling, Noctus," Ker said. "It's okay to take some risks for Chloe. She means a lot to you, and it's important to embrace whatever love you can find in life, or you'll lose yourself. You won't be a king, you'll just be a husk."

"That's an alluring thought, Ker, but it's more than just myself that I'm risking. It's even more than Calor." I shut my eyes, contemplating just how I could make her understand.

The largest of my duties was that of a king. It was a ball and chain, one destined to drag me under and eventually drown me.

But it was more than that. I'd changed the course of supernatural society when I'd killed my family, and I intended to see through the consequences of those actions, no matter how widespread they were.

Perhaps I should tell her. I'll have to explain to Aristide and Charon eventually if we do move.

I opened my eyes and glared down at the shackles on my wrists. "I know where the elf princess that the Paragon seeks is."

Ker straightened up. "You what?"

"She's a Vitas princess—a member of the displaced branch," I said. "And if the Paragon or any other supernatural finds her, they will destroy her. She'll be a sacrifice in the name of slowing the death of magic. If found, her suffering is inevitable; the Paragon is about as good a fae as can be found, and he's so bent on the idea of using her, he refuses to investigate any alternatives."

"Are there alternatives?" Ker asked.

I tilted my head, listening to magic. It hadn't started screaming yet—it was still too pleased with Chloe's dwindling presence. "Maybe. Though I couldn't give any certain theories."

Ker nodded her head. "And Chloe's presence as the last shadow could be a threat to the princess because she would draw more attention to you than just the Paragon."

"Precisely," I said.

"If the elves of Calor Villa went public, it'd be extremely easy to hide the princess," Ker said.

"Perhaps, but that's not going to happen. The only way I can see it working is if Chloe were to abandon her family and her life—as you have. But she's already indicated she's unwilling to do that. And I can't blame her for that. She *should* treasure her family. What she has with them is indeed special."

"Maybe," Ker agreed. "But I can't help but think that what you have with her is also special."

I shrugged. "Perhaps it is for me—I've lived longer and am all too aware of what I lack. But Chloe isn't the same. She'll have more opportunities."

Ker stared at me, her gaze relentlessly sympathetic.

"And I care for her enough to know that those other opportunities will be more beneficial for her," I belatedly added.

Ker shook her head and sat up straight. "I don't know how you can take all of this loss and not go crazy."

"I'm hardly alone in this," I said. "I could argue you have lost more than me—you actually *loved* your Pack. No matter how one were to construe the definition of love, there is no way one could say I shared any kind of similar bond with my family."

"Yeah, except I get to spend my days with my new Pack, living off your wealth, generally having fun," Ker said. "I'm not being forced to give up the love of my life."

I rolled my eyes. "Now you're being dramatic."

"You'd argue that Chloe, whom you *still* call Amalourne—and don't deny it because as much as I pretended not to hear you calling her that, we both know I could hear you when we thought she was a cat—is not the love of your life?"

I was silent—more out of self-preservation than anything else.

Because, yes. I would say Chloe wasn't the love of my life... because that was too tame and shallow a description.

Yes, she was my Amalourne, but she was more than that. In

the future, no matter what she did or whom she ended up with, she would unknowingly carry a piece of me with her. Even though our bond was dormant, she'd still have me.

Kerberos, most likely sensing my inner struggle, patted my back.

A wry grin twitched across my lips—she was treating me like an upset pup—but my humor disappeared when I felt a bone deep groan.

For a moment, I assumed it was magic—restarting its tired chorus. It was only when I looked at the sky that I realized wild magic was still quiet, and it was the sorrow in my own soul I was hearing.

CHAPTER TEN

Chloe

Three nights later, when Joy dropped me off at the Book Nookery for my night shift, she followed me inside.

"Good evening, Chloe, Joy." Ms. Booker, wearing a belted, fitted dress designed with geometric patterns and a navy-blue woolen overcoat, rested her hands on the store's front desk as I hung up my jacket and stowed my purse. "How goes the new security measures?"

"Good evening, Ms. Booker. It's going just fine." Joy smiled at my employer. "Knowing she's made it safely to the Book Nookery takes quite the cognitive load off my mind—and Pat's."

Although I preferred to walk to work—and I was perfectly capable of driving—after the previous incident with the tracker, Pat and Joy had decided I now required an escort to and from Book Nookery.

I was willing to do it for their sake—the tracker did have a history of attacking when I was on foot and alone.

Besides, I had my own security measures I made sure of, that they didn't know about. I had an emergency bag in which I kept a stash of their dirty clothes, just in case I needed to ask a werewolf to smell them out, but my siblings didn't have to know about that.

"I understand," Ms. Booker said. "Although, please allow me to assure you that once she is inside Book Nookery, she's perfectly safe."

"I'm sure she is," Joy said. "It's why we're thrilled she's working here." Her phone beeped. Joy glanced down at it and tsked. "I need to run. Be safe, Chloe."

"I will be." I joined Ms. Booker behind the large desk and tucked my water bottle away. "Have a great night, see you in the morning?"

"Yep. I'm on pickup. See you then!" Joy waved, then hurried out the store's front door, the bell jingling with her exit.

I picked up the clipboard that held the list of books that needed restocking. "How was the afternoon shift?"

"Quite fine." Ms. Booker adjusted her ever-present string of pearls. "It was busy, until a touch after six. A wolf Pack came through, that was most interesting indeed." She glanced at me. "Any news from the Curia Cloisters?"

I shook my head. "There's a vampire in Magiford who is more than old enough to remember shadows, but apparently he's still out of the area due to an emergency. I'm not sure they will arrange for a meeting anyway. In the latest message I received from the Curia Cloisters, he said he never interacted much with shadows. I doubt he can tell me anything more than I already know from my time with Noctus," I said.

Ms. Booker knew about my time with Noctus, and had been surprisingly fine with keeping Noctus's existence a secret from my siblings. It was a relief to be able to tell her—I couldn't even tell Pat or Joy about my latest visit to Noctus's place since the Paragon had been clear only he knew Noctus's location, and only those on the Regional Committee of Magic were aware there was an elf in the city.

"That's a disappointment," Ms. Booker said. "I thought the Curia Cloisters were making an effort to help you—finally."

I shook my head. "I think they're more desperate to find whoever is responsible for the shadow monster and blood spell that were set off by that artifact earlier this month."

Which is probably that shadowy organization the Paragon told me about, which would make them even more *desperate to uncover them and end this.*

"I'm just one shadow," I said. "I can't help them with everything that's going on. Magiford is only just recovering from all the wizard House drama they've been talking about in the Curia Cloisters' newsletter," I said.

Ms. Booker slightly pursed her lips as she studied me. "You are, perhaps, too understanding."

I laughed. "No, I'm just thankful they're letting Pat use Cloisters resources to look for the tracker."

I trailed off when I heard the unmistakable sound of a loud engine idle outside.

"Do you hear that?" I asked. "It sounds like a bus."

The front door flew open, and a handsome man—fae, going by his appearance and the slight tapering of his ears—stepped inside.

His long black hair was pulled back in a ponytail, and he had blue-ish-purple eyes that were so striking they reminded me of Queen Leila's. His white smile was turned dazzling by the warm tone of his olive skin, and with his black trousers, pinstriped vest, and a black bowtie, he looked fashionable, but from a different time.

"Night Court," he declared in a loud voice that had a sort of raw charisma to it. "This is Book Nookery, the bookstore and workplace of Chloe Anderson, the last known living shadow!" He pointed to me with a wooden stick that had a purple pennant flag attached to it, and was topped with a plastic crescent moon.

I leaned to the side so I could peer out the open door into the inky night. Shapes of other people were clustered out on the front porch, and a large bus was parked in front of the store. "What?" I said.

People began to pour into the store, dressed in what I vaguely recognized as 1920s fashion. The women wore black, purple, or dark blue beaded evening dresses with hemlines that went just past their knees, matched with plain pumps, pearl necklaces, and silk wraps. The men wore tweed or pinstripe, sheep's wool suits with matching fedoras or flat caps.

It took me a moment to place the new flood of customers with otherworldly beauty, oddly colored eyes and hair that ranged from platinum blond to streaked pink, and olive skin as fae nobles from the Night Court.

"Oh my," Ms. Booker said at my side as the front room was rapidly filled with fae—all of them wielding cellphones. "You said you were curious, Lord Linus. You didn't say you intended to turn my place of business into a zoo."

"Ahh yes, perhaps I should have warned you." The handsome fae with the wooden stick and purple flag forged his way through the crowd. "But, then again, the demand for a meet and greet greatly outweighed my expectations." He flashed a smile at me and rested his forearms on my desk. "Chloe Anderson, it is lovely to finally make your acquaintance."

I looked from the charismatic fae to the rest of the fae nobles who were gawking at me. I could hear the click of their phones' camera apps. "I'm sorry, what's going on?"

"Chloe, this is Lord Linus—the father of the highly esteemed Queen Leila," Ms. Booker said. "He's become something of a regular at Book Nookery these days. I realized during his last visit it was because he was keen on seeing *you*, and informed him of your night shifts."

Lord Linus—who looked barely older than his daughter, but that was fae aging for you—grinned at me, oozing charm. "Officially I am here to send my greetings on behalf of my daughter. She instructed me to introduce myself, as I am the unfortunate soul left in charge of the Night Court when my dear daughter and her deadly husband leave to visit other Courts."

"I'm Chloe Anderson," I said. "You have a lovely daughter. The fae are lucky to have her."

As much as my parents would have chided me for not thanking the fae lord, thank yous and fae were tricky. Fae were master wordsmiths who could contrive favors from words.

Queen Leila wasn't like that, so I doubted her father would be, but it was better to be safe than sorry.

"Leila is quite amazing isn't she?" Lord Linus pulled his cellphone out of a pocket in his trousers and swiped it open, proudly showing his display screen—a photograph of Leila eating a pretzel the size of her head. "I took this yesterday—she's too cute. She has my boldness, you know, but that kindness in her is all her mother. And her step-father—he's probably why she turned out not at all like a proper fae and more of a decent human being."

I set my hands on the desk, unsure of how I was supposed to respond to that kind of judgment on his own people. "Okay?"

"At any rate." Lord Linus put his phone away. "If you run into trouble while my darling daughter is away, I'm your contact for the Night Court. Naturally, we should exchange phone numbers."

My shadow instincts prickled in my gut, so I was already suspiciously eyeing Lord Linus when Ms. Booker politely interjected.

"Excuse me but, Chloe, you should be aware that in exchanging contact methods with Lord Linus, that will be considered an open invitation for him to contact you whenever *he* wishes. A dangerous thing considering this." Ms. Booker gracefully gestured to the packed foyer.

"Ah," I said, thankful again for my innate suspicion. "And who, might I ask, are they?" I blinked when one of the fae nobles used their flash, blasting me in the face with light.

Lord Linus turned around. "Ahhh, yes. They are my unofficial reason for being here. In addition to aiding my daughter with the Night Court, I also run the Night Court Tour Bus. We mostly visit Timber Ridge in northern Wisconsin, but I've been attempting to expand our offerings. We're experimenting with a tour that focuses on places of interest within Magiford." Lord Linus flashed me a charming smile that was extra enticing given it had more warmth and laughter than any fae usually displayed in a lifetime. "You, I believe, will make that list."

"Even though I'm a person, not a place?" I asked.

"Yes." Lord Linus tapped his fingers on the desk. "The only known shadow is simply too good a marketing line to miss out on. Isn't that so, Night Court?" he asked his Court.

They responded with murmurs and more pictures.

"—would be an excellent addition to the photobook I'm making. I can put her picture next to the one I took with the werewolf in Timber Ridge!"

"—must share this with my cousin in Europe. She will be positively green with envy."

"So!" Lord Linus turned back to me, his cellphone in his hands once again. "Might you share your phone number?"

Not so easily swindled, I straightened my shoulders. "I'm afraid I must defer to my employer on whether your tour bus can stop here. The bus itself might be considered a nuisance on the street." I glanced at Ms. Booker, but she merely raised a penciled-in eyebrow at me.

I shifted my weight back and forth on my flats, surprised she hadn't chimed in with me. "Wouldn't this be disruptive to our regular customers?" I asked her in a lowered voice.

"It's your shift," Ms. Booker said. "And your reputation."

Ah. She's leaving this up to me since the Night Court is already friendly with me. I might be able to turn them into an outright ally. Lord Linus is the better target to focus on than Queen Leila since she's busy as the fae empress.

My stomach churned. I didn't think the Night Court was dangerous—tricky, yes, self-serving, yes, but they wouldn't hurt me with Leila as their ruler. But these were issues I never thought I'd deal with—this was a league on par with Noctus's.

But. At least that means I've seen this before.

I made my shoulders square. "How often do you hold these tours?" I asked.

Lord Linus's eyes gleamed. "Oh, only occasionally."

"Once per month?"

"Hmm," Lord Linus shrugged.

"Once per week?" I guessed.

"Bravo," Lord Linus said. "No wonder you were able to take down Darina and Harel—I hope you tore Harel's ruddy cape. It was so *gaudy*. Yes, once per week." He settled into place, apparently done testing me. "I'd want to know your schedule so we can drop by when you are here."

"And?"

"And, pictures are required," Lord Linus said. "Leila has gotten everyone into social media. They'll want to take pictures of you."

I narrowed my eyes. "I need to be able to complete my work."

Lord Linus glanced back at his fellow fae, who had progressed to taking pictures of Book Nookery's decorations. "Surprisingly, they *can* be patient if it means getting what they want. But you'll have to decide if you want to charge anything. The Northern Lakes Pack charge a mint for wolf photos."

I pressed my lips together as I thought. "The Northern Lakes Pack is famous for owning multiple businesses and a Pack LLC. They have a way to collect the funds and report it for taxes. I don't. However..." I glanced at Ms. Booker, who was the picture of elegance as she adjusted her coat. "I'll only take pictures with paying customers," I decided. "As long as they buy something—anything—from Book Nookery, they can get a free picture."

"In the form—cat or human—that she chooses," Ms. Booker added, closing the verbal loophole I hadn't considered.

"Deal," Lord Linus said. "Now, for phone numbers..."

We exchanged numbers—it felt more than a little surreal as I entered the fae lord's contact information into my contacts list—and then the fae lord turned to address the nobles.

"You heard the bargain," he said. "Fetch something to purchase if you want a picture with her."

The fae scattered, drifting off into the other rooms.

I watched Lord Linus with fascination. Fae were charming, but Lord Linus was charismatic to an extreme.

It's too bad Ker can't meet him. She'd turn him into a case study.

A few fae still milled around the foyer, perusing the rack of book related stickers, keychains, magnets, and pins with more interest than I would have imagined a fae noble would have for common merchandise.

Lord Linus pushed off the desk. "I'll go help the night mares move the bus away from the street—wouldn't want to upset your neighbors if it really is a nuisance," he said.

"Night mares? The Night Court's selected animal?" I asked, picturing the silvery and black unicorns that had become famous. "The ones that can create portals?"

"Yes," Lord Linus said. "Two of them travel with the bus to transport us from location to location."

"So you don't even drive around in the bus?" I asked, confused.

"Goodness, no," Lord Linus said. "Why waste hours of life when the night mares will make a portal in exchange for an apple or carrot? Besides, I'd never be willing to spend so many hours in an enclosed space with other nobles." He winked, then strolled away, slipping through the door with a jingle of the bell.

Ms. Booker waited until the general volume of the Book Nookery lowered to a quiet murmur before speaking. "You handled that well."

"Thank you," I said. "But...you knew?"

"About the tours? No," Ms. Booker said. "But I knew Lord

Linus wanted to meet you. You are wondering why I didn't warn you?"

I debated pretending otherwise, but I had a good relationship with my boss, and she'd been helpful to me in far more dangerous situations. "Yes."

"As a shadow, you're going to find you command more respect and interest than you've previously encountered," Ms. Booker said. "You need to learn how to navigate it. Lord Linus and the Night Court are relatively innocuous. If you bungled your meeting with them, at worst you'd be fielding fae popping up and bothering you across Magiford until you struck a new bargain with them."

I pressed on my clipboard's silver clip, opening and closing it. "I get it."

Ms. Booker brushed at a nonexistent crease in her dress. "However?"

I glanced out at the gorgeous, well dressed fae who still populated the foyer. "I just want to protect my family. I didn't really want...this."

"Life rarely gives us what we want," Ms. Booker said. "Which is why it is important to learn and shift with what you are dealt. Otherwise you will forever be unhappy, or missing the greatest opportunity of your life because you are certain you could not handle it."

Her warning seemed particularly heavy for the moment, so I glanced at her in surprise.

Unfortunately, at that moment a fae lord perusing the keychains cleared his throat and doffed his flat cap at my employer.

"I beg your pardon, do you have any cat and book related merchandise?" he asked.

Ms. Booker stepped out from behind the desk and approached the fae lord. "There is a sticker of a black cat on a stack of books—rather fitting as Chloe's feline form is a black cat." She minced over to him, turning the rack to point out the sticker as fae nobles crowded around her.

I fiddled with my clipboard as I watched.

There was something familiar about the fae lord who had made the request. Like I'd seen him before...

Wait. I recognize him! He was the fae lord who tried to lure me into his house when he thought I was a stray cat!

I'd attempted staking out several areas as safe zones in Magiford before settling for downtown. One of the areas had been the Night Court Territory—which I'd been forced to abandon after several of the nobles developed a weird obsession with obtaining a pet.

My instincts screamed at me to duck down behind the desk, but I settled for clutching the clipboard to my chest like it was a shield.

Thank goodness Ms. Booker specified that I get to choose the shape I take the picture in. Magic or not, there's no way I'm using my cat shape with these guys. It's not worth the risk!

The bell attached to the door jingled, and I shiftily pointed myself toward it, expecting Lord Linus's return.

Instead, to my surprise, Charon stepped through the door, then paused to hold it open for Aristide and Ker—in her guise of guide-werewolf and wearing her special harness that Aristide held on to.

CHAPTER ELEVEN

Chloe

I dropped my clipboard on the desk with a clatter as emotion clogged my throat, just at the sight of my friends. "H-hello. Welcome to Book Nookery." I glanced nervously at all the fae, but none of them seemed to take notice of the trio.

Charon approached the desk, carrying a thick, three-ring binder. "Miss Chloe," he greeted me.

The tingle of elf magic that prickled at my ribs said Charon was thankfully wearing a glamour of some sort—probably one that altered his eyes and ears, but I couldn't see it.

Aristide tilted his head as he listened to the sounds of the bookstore, but Ker started wagging her tail faster and faster.

They stopped when they reached the desk. Ker set her front paws on the edge and stretched up so she could look at me over the desk.

"*Ker*," Aristide hissed. "Stop it! Guide dogs aren't supposed to be friendly while working."

Ker ignored him, and her tail wagged even harder as she gave me her best "I'm-just-a-fluffy-dog-don't-you-want-to-pet-me?" look. It was surprising considering how massive she was—but that was a werewolf for you. Stretched up like this, she was taller than I was.

I smiled at her—she was the only one I hadn't seen when the Paragon busted into Noctus's place. Impulsively, I leaned across the desk to quickly scratch her neck before I picked up my clipboard and tried to gather my sense of professionalism. "How can I help you?"

Charon placed the hefty binder on the desk. It was so heavy it rattled my plastic cup of pens and pencils. "I have brought the translated information."

"Already?" I reached for the binder then hesitated, glancing around the bookstore.

Despite their interest in taking a picture with me, at the moment the fae seemed more interested in perusing Book Nookery's wares.

That's good. If they don't pay attention, we can play this off. Come on, magic. Kick it up.

Praying my magic that made me hard to notice would kick in, I smiled at Charon. "Thank you. I didn't think it would be possible to get translations done this quickly."

Charon shrugged—a movement so small and imperceptible the only reason I didn't miss it was because I was used to the closed mouthed elf's lack of reaction.

"Because of Noctus's...hmm...*loyalty* to the shadow that was once his companion, he'd recently charged Charon with pulling all information on shadows from the library," Aristide tattled.

Wow, they must have started on this when the Paragon started asking Noctus about meeting me.

"Still, thank you for so quickly getting the information to me." I smiled.

Charon completely ignored me and flipped the binder cover

open. "Everything has been organized, color coded, and tabulated."

I leaned over my desk so I could peer at the printed-out sheets—which also contained scanned images from the scrolls and whatever other reference material had been used.

Ah, now I know *Charon was the one who did all of this. Noctus's desk is a mess, there's no way he'd be this organized.*

"Don't be fooled by stone face here. We *do* hope you find it useful." Aristide smiled sunnily at me.

I glanced at Charon and couldn't help but smile again. "I'm sure I will," I said. "This was very kind of you. I hope this wasn't too much of a bother. Really, truly, thank you." I tried to infuse my thanks with as much sincerity as possible, hoping to get through to Charon, Aristide, and Ker.

I knew Charon wasn't angry with me—I remembered the donuts—but I hadn't had a chance to thank the trio for everything they'd done before I left Calor Villa. I'd been so worried about my siblings at the time that I could barely think straight.

Charon didn't react, he just turned another page in the binder. Ker set her muzzle on the desk and peered up at me, her tail thumping on the wooden flooring, while Aristide traced the edge of the desk with his fingers.

"It was never a bother," Aristide said. He smiled in my direction, but there was something unusually *gentle* about his voice—like me, he wasn't referring to the binder. "In fact, it was quite interesting. And it gave our venerated leader something to distract him—a fact I now mourn since he seems intent on turning us into a crime solving gang despite the fact that one with a dog already exists in human pop culture." Aristide reached out and set his hand on Ker's head, who made a happy snuffling noise. "I've told him we'd need to rebrand, but he just won't listen."

"Crime solving?" My instincts turned on edge, but I kept my body language casual—or as casual as I could make it. "Are you looking into current events?" I glanced at the local newspaper—

which had a bold headline about the ongoing investigation in the broken artifact situation.

Aristide was incapable of seeing the gesture; Charon did, though. He glanced at the newspaper as well, which was probably the biggest confirmation I could ever hope to get from him.

"What Noctus needs is a new hobby. Or another pet," Aristide groused.

Ker snorted, which I suspected was her way of agreeing.

"We've delivered the binder," Charon said, his tone dry and emotionless. "It's time we leave."

"I suppose," said Aristide. "Come on, Spot."

"Wait," I said as they started to turn away. "I just want you to know...I didn't mean...I'm going to keep my word," I said.

I'm not going to reveal anything about Noctus or Calor Villa. I'm sorry, I didn't mean to show up and cause trouble.

The words burned at my lips, but I couldn't say them—not publicly.

Charon slightly bowed his head. "We know."

The trio turned away from me. Aristide and Charon headed for the door with Ker following faithfully at Aristide's side, though she looked back to gaze at me with her sad, wolfish eyes.

"Then you should also know," I blurted out, "that I'm not giving up."

There, that's about as close as I can come to saying that I'm trying to get back to them, somehow.

They peered back at me—expressions showing varying levels of shock and confusion.

The corners of Charon's lips twisted. "Very good, Miss Chloe," he said, before leading Aristide and Ker out.

"Did you just smile?" Aristide asked as they made their way through the foyer.

"Nonsense," Charon said.

"No, I'm pretty sure you just smiled."

"You couldn't possibly know if I did or not."

"Of course I can!"

"You're blind."

"*Obviously*. But you can hear a person smile with their voice, you know, even if they have the personality of a toad."

"Watch the door."

The twisting pain in my heart lessened as I watched the three disappear through the door, then glanced down at the binder.

I wasn't sure if it was the lingering effects of Charon's glamour, but I could feel the sharp needling of elf magic as I paged through the binder.

"Chloe, dear, I'm retiring for the evening." Ms. Booker's heels clicked as she glided past the desk, pausing when she saw the binder. "I take it this is the information you were waiting for?"

"Yes," I confirmed. "I'll have to let the Paragon know I got it."

Ms. Booker eyed the binder. "It's a shame he didn't collect much, but I suppose he must have worked quickly considering that it hasn't been long since your visit."

Didn't collect much?

I furrowed my eyebrows as I stared at the fat three-ring binder that weighed enough to rattle the contents of the desk.

What is she talking about? This is a lot!

"Though I suppose it's also possible he didn't share everything he had with you," Ms. Booker continued. "Considering your...*interesting* history together. At the very least it is a start. If they included references I might be able to help you track down additional materials."

I stared at the painted picture copied from the scroll that took up most of the page, and included an elvish title in the bottom corner.

She can't see everything, I realized. *It must be spelled.*

"I think they did include some titles," I said. "But whatever sources they used were in elvish, so I can't be certain. I'll look through it and copy out anything useful."

"See that you do." Ms. Booker turned on her heel and started up the stairs.

"Ms. Booker?" I called after her, retreating to the far end of the desk and half stepping out of it. "Thank you—for your help."

"Of course, dear," Ms. Booker said. "Just make certain you don't let anyone pressure you." She glanced meaningfully at the fae still cluttering up the foyer.

"I won't. Goodnight."

I waited until she disappeared up the stairs before I returned to the binder, flipping through it with even more eagerness than before.

Charon had used page dividers and tabs to mark out the different sections. One was entirely about history—mostly about the enmity between shadows and elves, and information on how the shadows were hunted down. The next section was a basic rundown of abilities—something I was already relatively schooled on, though I grinned when I saw Charon had underlined and bolded my ability to fall from heights, something I had unwillingly practiced with Noctus.

I flipped to the last section—which oddly wasn't labeled—and was surprised to find this section included information on fighting. Not as a shadow, but an elf.

There were clearly labeled and organized exercises—for swords and daggers—with perfect illustrations and handwritten notes in the margins that suggested moments for swapping my shape.

He's continuing my training. This is a training guide—or the closest thing Charon could make.

Charon had been teaching me how to fight—it was why the tracker found my techniques so upsetting.

I had stalled in my sword and dagger training ever since I'd left...but this would help me learn additional tactics and techniques.

No wonder he spelled it. Elves never willingly gave up information about their own race. I can't believe he even made this for me.

I laughed when I flipped a page and saw that someone had drawn a round cat into the exercises, showing how I could exploit my agility in fighting.

I assumed it was Charon, until I saw the handwriting in the margins and recognized it as Noctus's penmanship.

I flipped through another page, and another, then five, then ten.

Page after page had Noctus's careful handwriting—and crudely drawn cats that were so horrible they were cute—decorating the page.

I bit my tongue to keep from sighing—or feeling, I wasn't sure which.

Could this...if he's willing to do this for me, doesn't that mean he also hasn't really given up? Does he also wonder if our story could end differently?

My motivation burning bright in my gut, I pulled out my cellphone and opened the notes app—where I'd started recording every idea, no matter how stupid, that I thought of that could possibly bring Noctus and me back together.

A lot of them I didn't like, for example, the idea I had to ask my family to go into hiding with me and we all lived in Calor Villa. (That would be grossly unfair to my siblings, and was definitely one of the more selfish ideas I had.)

Even more of my plots were improbable, like the one I was hesitating to type out.

I said every idea. I need everything I can come up with.

I shook my head and typed into the app: **Noctus and his people go public?**

I followed the note with three laughing emojis to note it was *not* going to happen, then recorded another idea: **Get job w/Paragon so I have excuse to interact w/Noctus?**

That's an idea that has potential, but a lot of danger. Either way, I'm not to the point where I'm evaluating ideas yet, just brainstorming.

"Excuse me, but I am ready to make a purchase." A beautiful fae woman set a recipe book on coffee drinks and beverages on the desk, as well as a book about gardening, then immediately pulled out her phone. "Since I am buying two books, could I take two pictures?"

I hastily stored my binder on a shelf of my desk. "Sure," I said. "But could I ring you up first?"

"I'M STUFFED." Pat rubbed his belly as he tottered down the sidewalk, weaving his way toward his parked car. "I overate for sure."

"The food was amazing as usual," I agreed, thinking of the donut breakfast sandwich I'd had.

Pat groaned and held his stomach. "I've put on at least ten pounds since I moved to Magiford."

Joy noisily sucked on the straw of her iced latte that was mostly ice by this point. "The food in Magiford is ridiculously good. I'd blame it on the supernaturals, but all the places we've been to on our food tour are human owned and run."

Since Joy had moved to Magiford, we tried to have a sibling outing at least once per week where we met and went out for either breakfast or dinner. Today we'd opted for breakfast—it was easy for me since we went out after my shift, and Pat and Joy were already up since they were determined we travel in packs these days.

I ruffled my light jacket—as we crept toward October, the weather was starting to get a little too cold for me to handle with such a lightweight coat. "My working theory is the restaurants have to be good—fae are naturally pretty choosy, and while werewolves need to eat a lot because of their metabolisms, they also have heightened senses," I said.

"What about vampires?" Joy asked.

I veered around a fire hydrant as we continued our stroll down main street. "Most vampires don't eat human cuisine—it comes down to personal taste for them—but yeah, those who do are even pickier than fae."

"Either way, if we're settling here long term, I'm going to have to work out more." Pat dug his car keys out of his jacket pocket. "If I get too out of shape I won't be able to even pretend to keep up with all my supernatural coworkers. Okay, Chloe. I'll take you home. Joy, where's your car?" Pat peered up and down the street.

"I'm in public parking over by City Hall—I have a meeting there, so no need to worry about escorting me." Joy stepped to the far side of the sidewalk, making way for a few pedestrians going the opposite direction. The orange light of the weak morning sun made Joy's blond hair glow, and her bright smile had the human pedestrians automatically returning it.

Traffic—both foot traffic and street traffic—was starting to pick up as people were beginning to head into work.

"You'll call when you get there?" Pat asked.

Joy frowned. "It's less than three blocks away."

"We can't be too cautious," Pat said.

"Yes, we can," I mutinously muttered as I hiked my backpack farther up my shoulders while being thoroughly ignored.

"Fine." Joy swung her purse with a sigh. "I'll call. Sleep well, Chloe. Have a good day at work, Pat. See you tonight, little sis!" Joy waved as she hurried ahead of us to a crosswalk—even Joy wouldn't jaywalk in front of Pat—and crossed the road.

I checked my phone as Pat held his hands up, shielding his eyes so he could see through the growing sunlight and watch our sister. "Hey, Pat, do we have enough time to head to the Curia Cloisters and back to my apartment before you work today? I want to buy a few potions."

Pat spun around to face me so quickly he almost knocked into me. "You're out of potions? Why? Did you get hurt somehow and didn't tell us?"

"I'm not out," I assured him. "It's just that today's the day my favorite potion vender is selling this month, so I thought I could stock up on a few extra."

Pat folded his arms across his chest. "Your favorite potion vender, or the *cheapest* potion vender?"

"His potions are very affordable," I acknowledged.

Pat's scowl grew. "You can't fool me anymore—I have contacts now. Cheap potions mean they don't work as well!"

It was a lot easier to do supernatural stuff before they learned so much. Then again, he's not wrong.

"It could be worse," I said. "I could try ordering them online."

"No!" Pat chopped his hand down. "That stuff isn't regulated by the FDA, you have no idea what actually goes into those potions you find on the internet. They could be some weirdo human who is posing as a wizard and is running a scam!"

"Wizards can't make potions," I said. "Only fae can."

And elves...

"Whatever, the point is, it's way more dangerous," Pat declared.

"So then we can visit my favorite vender today?"

"No! We'll budget for better potions."

"There is no *we'll* in this, dear brother," I reminded him. "Potions are my responsibility. Not yours, since humans can't even use them."

It wasn't entirely true—some very low-grade potions were safe for human consumption, but they were so low-grade they didn't do much healing and were all but useless. (Humans, apparently, couldn't safely metabolize magic.)

Pat fish mouthed for a moment, and my phone chirped.

"Oh, look! Joy texted us, with the safety emoji!" I held up my phone displaying our sibling safe code—the duck emoji. "Let's go."

I took a step toward Pat's car—ignoring my older brother who was growling under his breath as he resentfully rested an arm on his bloated stomach.

"I never signed up for this kind of disrespect," Pat complained as he ambled over to the driver's side. "To think how cute you were as a kitten."

I looked away for a moment. I swore I could feel a brush of magic, but it hadn't solidified into a specific sensation, so I didn't know what kind of supernatural was causing it.

"You know," Pat started. "I was thinking—"

A noise—a high pitched, throbbing sound I felt in my bones—rumbled down the street. It was loud, but there was something about the noise that felt like it was scratching at the inside of my skull.

I cringed, until the pitch of the sound crawled out of my hearing registry.

Dogs howled and barked, and Pat turned in a circle, his eyes narrowed. "What was that?"

I started to unzip my backpack, preparing to dig out my daggers. "I'm not sure."

The jagged noise of glass breaking filled the air, replacing the ringing left in my ears.

Down the street—in the direction the noise had come from—windows cracked and then shattered, raining glass down on unlucky pedestrians.

None of the windows near us were destroyed—it seemed like we were too far away from the source of the noise.

One block up, someone dropped, falling to their knees as they clutched their ears—I was pretty sure she had to be a werewolf based on her reaction.

What's going on?

Pat put his hands on my shoulders and maneuvered me so I was boxed between him and his car. "You okay?"

I put a hand on his arm, trying to reassure both him and myself. "Yeah. But Pat—I sensed magic before the noise started."

Pat swore. "Stay here. Get in the car, lock it, and then call Joy. Do you understand?" He already had his cellphone out with an outgoing call flashing on its screen.

I yanked his car door open. "Got it. Good luck."

He waved, then took off running down the street. "Hey," he shouted into his cellphone. "We have an incident on main street—it's magic based."

I hit the button on the door to lock the car, then shifted into my cat form so I could crawl into the back seat and peer out the back window.

I don't think this was the tracker's doing. Based on his current patterns, this is too big. He knows just one human will make me stop, so why make such a big fuss that will instantly draw the Curia Cloisters? Unless he's luring Pat away to grab him?

It didn't match his style—he would have found an easier way to grab my brother.

I craned my neck as I peered down the street. The werewolf still hadn't recovered, and based on the number of pedestrians now crouching on the sidewalk, it looked like the shattering glass had caused some injuries, too.

I wonder if any of the elves were caught up in this mess. I remember Noctus or Charon saying some of them worked in Magiford, and I've seen a few downtown over the summer.

I'd been careful to avoid them—which hadn't been hard, I'd only seen them a handful of times.

Now that I was thinking of it, had I ever noticed any elves in Magiford before stumbling on the elven king? Their glamours wouldn't have worked on me, but that didn't mean much since I didn't even know they existed. When I first saw Noctus I thought he was a European fae, and that was when he was cuddling me against his chest.

Peering out of the car's windows, I watched the streets grow crowded with onlookers.

Thankfully, it seemed like the attack hadn't caused a stampede —which was a real possibility as the breakfast crowd and caffeine seekers arrived.

Whoever did this chose the busiest time of the morning to...

The thought died in my brain when I glanced down the sidewalk and spotted two people—both were bleeding and had torn clothes from the glass shower.

They were supernaturals—the tapered ears were a dead giveaway. I probably wouldn't have thought more of it, except one of the elves glanced at Pat's car, and I realized that he had the elven spiral in the pupils of his eyes, and that I knew him.

It was Rodaric. He ran an armory and had made the leather harness I wore under my jacket that kept my daggers and sword in place.

Rodaric wasn't wearing his monocle, but his gray hair and kind smile had marked him out in my memory, so I had no trouble recognizing him. His companion was younger, a female elf with her eyes wide with pain and fear.

Why are they so panicked? Were they hurt badly—wait. I don't feel any magic. Elf, or otherwise. Their glamours aren't working.

The pair crossed the street in front of Pat's car, their fear making their movements quick and jerky. People streamed out of the café Joy, Pat, and I had eaten at, congregating on the sidewalk.

One pedestrian headed toward the chaos while several stayed where they were, talking on the phone. Two, however, were watching the elves with curiosity as the severity of the situation dawned on me.

Their glamours are down. People can see them! If a supernatural notices, they'll know *they're not fae!*

CHAPTER TWELVE

Chloe

I shifted to my human shape and was out of the car before I was registering what I was doing. I looked both ways, but traffic had stopped from the chaos of the attack, so I was free to run after the elves, who were drawing more and more attention.

"Rod—" I bit off his name as I looked around—I didn't want to identify him when his glamour was down and we were on the streets.

Thankfully he looked back at me, his eyebrows moving up when he recognized me. "Chloe!"

"Are you two alright? I have potions." I slung my backpack off my shoulder—I hadn't rezipped it yet in case I needed easy access to my weapons—and dug out my fae potions.

"Our injuries are minor," Rodaric said. "We need to get...get out of the way." He changed what he was going to say and glanced at the humans who were openly pointing to them.

I leaned into the pair as I handed them each a fae potion. "The clocktower?" I whispered.

They nodded.

"But, how? What do we do?" the younger elf asked, her voice wobbling as she popped the cork off her fae potion.

It was a miserable time to admit it, but Pat was right. I apparently shouldn't skimp on my potions, because these weren't going to do much more than take the sting out of their injuries.

I glanced back over my shoulder at the chaotic churn of the crowd that was quickly growing.

Pat is going to be so mad at me for this. I'm taking a chance since we don't know for certain that the tracker isn't tied to this but...

Noctus had sacrificed so much for their people, and this was going to reveal them if they didn't act fast.

I fiddled with my backpack, rezipping it before I slipped it back on.

"Do you think they're fae?" I heard someone behind me ask. "They're so beautiful."

I gulped and thrust my hands out in front of me. "Hold my hands."

Rodaric had uncapped his potion and taken a swig. "What?"

"*Just take my hand!*" I hissed.

Rodaric reached out with his free hand and took mine. His female companion eyed me.

"Do it, Brevlanne," Rodaric hissed.

"She's a shadow," the younger elf protested.

Ahhh, interesting to see not all prejudice is dead.

Rodaric went expressionless, and I could literally see his elfness click into place—replacing his happy charm with something chilling. "*Brevlanne.*"

The elf took my hand with a cringe, but kept her mouth shut.

I took a breath, and looked inward. *Come on magic—I need you to work overtime! Make them as unnoticeable as me!*

I held my breath. The woman pedestrian that had been eyeing Rodaric blinked, then turned to face down the road.

"Someone called 911, right?" she asked.

Another bystander who had been staring at the elves shook his head as if he was trying to clear it. "Yeah. We should probably leave—there are going to be police swarming the area."

One by one the humans turned away.

I let myself exhale, but kept my shoulders bunched up. "Come on. We must get you to the clocktower."

"I don't believe it." Rodaric let me bullishly drag him along. "They're looking away. We're *designed* to pull people in—it's been the biggest fight to just blend."

"Don't think about it," I said. "It could break the effect."

"But magic isn't working right now," Brevlanne frostily said, her disapproval palpable. "There's some kind of block on it."

"As I said, *please* don't think about it!"

"Is your magic shy?" Rodaric asked.

"No, it just does its own thing, and I can't do much more than beg it to work. We're turning." I looked both ways before I hauled the pair along, my thoughts skittering through my brain so fast I could barely register them. "Are you two the only elves in that part of downtown?"

"No, there are at least two others." Rodaric caught up with me, his voice hardening as he set his shoulders, his strides overtaking mine. "Oleander works in a store downtown—"

"A clothing boutique," Brevlanne interrupted as she also started to nearly jog, which meant I had to run. "Lost Garden. She always opens the store."

"She's taller than you," Rodaric began.

"Oh, that is such a surprise," I grumbled under my breath as I struggled to keep up with the elves' long legs.

"Long hair—blond in color," Brevlanne said.

"By long, she means quite long," Rodaric explained. "Past the small of her back—you'll be able to pick her out of the crowd."

I blinked in surprise at the assumption I'd need to find her, and then realized he was right. They couldn't go get this Oleander, or any of the other elves. They needed to get out of the area before any supernaturals saw them.

Hustling like we were, it was a fast trip to the clocktower. We were only two blocks away when I heard the wail of police sirens, and I was willing to bet the Curia Cloisters task force was closer to the accident since Pat had been calling them when he left me.

"You said there were two." I squeezed Rodaric's and Brevlanne's hands when I noticed cars were starting to roll down the street—driving away from the disaster. "Who else is downtown?"

"Jaqleon." Pain flickered across Rodaric's face when he adjusted his arm—one of his injuries most likely. Apparently his half drunk fae potion hadn't done much.

Focus! I can't help with injuries—just the hiding!

"He's as tall and skinny as a bean pole—he comes from a family of summoners, so he's got the tattoos," Rodaric continued.

"Tattoos?" I asked.

"On his arms," Rodaric said.

"Must you tell her *everything*?" Brevlanne hissed.

"Yes," Rodaric said. "She's helping us, and if she can't find Oleander and Jaqleon, there's no telling if they'll get back to the clocktower!"

"They're elves," Brevlanne scoffed. "They don't need the help of a *shadow*."

Normally I would have been way more interested in the conversation. I'd always been a little freaked out by how easily the elves of Calor Villa seemed to accept me. But even the curious part of me couldn't be roused in the middle of an emergency—my survival instinct was way too strong for that.

"Brevlanne," Rodaric growled. "Why do you think she's with us right now? Because *we* need *her* help!"

Brevlanne grimaced—although I think it might have been from the pain.

"She is our king's Ama," Rodaric said.

"Amalourne," I automatically said as I looked up and down the street with practiced paranoia.

Rodaric stopped walking, jolting us to a stop. "What?"

"He calls me Amalourne." I paused, remembering the weird reaction Ker had when Noctus had called me that in front of her. "Though maybe I shouldn't have shared that."

Both Rodaric and Brevlanne were staring at me, unmoving.

Oh boy. Yeah, I shouldn't have said that.

I'd repent of blurting out the nickname later. For now I had bigger problems. "We have to keep moving, please." I tugged the pair forward.

They were silent for several steps.

"His arms," Brevlanne abruptly said, her voice almost sulky.

"I'm sorry...what?" I asked, confused.

"Jaqleon has tattoos on his arms," she said.

Huh. Did my nickname bring about this attitude change, or what?

To my surprise, Brevlanne continued. "He works at, I, I can't remember what it's called." She rapidly blinked, and I could almost see her body start to register the shock from the injury and the situation crawling across her.

"It's a, a computer repair shop. The only one downtown," Rodaric tried to explain, his eyebrows bunching in frustration when the words didn't come easily.

"I know the place," I said. "They do phones and other electronic repairs, too."

We were at the base of the clocktower—we just had to cross the street.

"Will you be okay here?" I asked, peering up at the clock face.

"We'll be fine." Rodaric let me go. He plucked the empty fae potion from Brevlanne's hands. "Thank you, Chloe."

I didn't waste my words as I turned and ran, sprinting back in the direction we'd come from.

Gotta hurry, gotta hurry! I can't let them be seen!

Instead of using the sidewalks, I shifted to a cat and zigzagged my way up an alleyway. There, I found what I was looking for, a fire escape ladder.

I changed into a human to make quick work of it, then cut my way across the roofline of the block before I jumped off and had to shimmy up the next ladder.

It was faster—I could run without worrying about catching anyone's attention or getting run down by a car.

When I was close enough that I could see splashes of blue and red from the police cars over the ledges of the buildings, I hopped down, planning to merge into the chaos.

I jumped down into an alley and popped out on a street, pausing for a moment to get my bearings.

The street was empty, except for a fae walking down the side-walk—away from the accident—on the opposite side of the street.

His hands were tucked into his black jacket, and his stride was casual and even.

He wasn't bothered by what had just happened, even though —if Rodaric was right—he couldn't access magic at the moment.

I studied him, taking in his blond hair and casual fae grace and height.

There's something déjà vu-y about him. Not that I've met him before, but...have I seen him somewhere?

He wasn't a Night Court fae—those guys were way too proud of their Court Alliance, they all wore stars and moons or trash griffin pins somewhere on their clothes whenever they were out and about.

Save it for later.

I attempted to brand a mental image of him, but I could hear cries of people in pain, and raised voices.

I needed to move it.

Sprinting up the street, I slowed down only when my sidewalk merged with main street. The place was a mess.

There were ambulances, police cars—police tape was actively going up—and crowds of injured pedestrians were being shepherded through the now closed street as onlookers stopped to gape and—stupidly—take pictures.

I couldn't tell exactly what had happened, except to say there was shattered glass everywhere, I still couldn't feel magic, and the only supernaturals I saw were three werewolves who were leaning against the ambulances, holding their ears and whimpering.

I think they were among the worst injured—it seemed like everything else was limited to cuts and lacerations from the broken glass.

What was the point of this?

I let the thought fester for a moment before I snuffed it out. It didn't matter now—that was for people like Pat to document and guess. I needed to get Jaqleon and Oleander out.

If I could find them.

Lost Garden is farther up the street. Let's head there first.

I skirted around a police officer who didn't even give me a second glance, and scrambled around one of the parked ambulances.

I didn't see Pat, which was a good thing for me. He was immune to my magic that made me unnoticeable, and if he saw me he would chew me out. But his absence also probably meant he was briefing his task force, so time was of the essence.

When I arrived at the Lost Garden clothing boutique, I sucked in more air than I needed and almost hiccupped.

All the front store windows were blown out. The shattered glass littered the front of the store and was tossed across the wooden floor and the chic rugs that were going to be impossible to clean.

The display mannequins had toppled—probably from the

force of the blast—but the rest of the store's interior was untouched.

Hopefully Oleander wasn't near the front.

I stood in the doorway—which was empty, because the glass door had been blown to smithereens. "Hello, Oleander?"

The shop was silent, but I didn't see any blood anywhere.

Maybe she got out?

The computer repair shop was a little farther up the street—it was nearly out of the blast zone, so Jaqleon was probably fine and just needed help slipping out of the area. Unless maybe he and Oleander had left together?

I skulked away from the boutique store and hurried down the street.

I'll check the computer repair shop first. Then come back—woah.

Across the street, I saw a woman with long blond hair that hung past the waistband of her black slacks. A black beanie was pulled low over her forehead and covered her ears, and she was wearing a giant pair of sunglasses. Ignoring the beanie and sunglasses, she was dressed closer to fae fashion with her knee-high black boots that had metal reinforcing the toe and heel, and the tunic-like cut of her golden shirt with its flowy sleeves, but there was no mistaking that hair.

She was crouched in front of something heaped on the ground next to her, her movements quick and anxious.

I checked both ways before crossing the street. "Oleander?" I called as I reached the sidewalk—I didn't want to startle her.

She swung around, her lips pushed so tightly together they were white, but after a moment she gasped in relief. "*Ama*."

I paused, surprised she recognized me.

She held up her cellphone. "Rodaric called—he said you were coming."

Bless the elves and their adoption of human technology.

"Good. Rodaric mentioned there was someone—"

The heap on the ground groaned.

I joined her as she turned back to it, my eyes tracing over the pile of what looked like rags, until I realized there were legs under the ripped jeans and a face shadowed by a hoodie that glittered with shards of glass.

"Jaqleon?" I asked.

"Yes." Oleander crouched at his side, pushing back the hood just enough to reveal Jaqleon's face. He had some scratches, and his eyes were clenched shut with pain, but he opened them long enough for me to see the glassy look in his spiraled eyes.

"It's Ama," Oleander said.

"Our king's Ama?" Jaqleon asked, his eyes pinched shut once again.

Our king's Ama?

I thought Rodaric's reference was a onetime thing, apparently not. I filed the title away, but I wasn't going to ponder it now. I nervously looked around, watching for Pat—still no sign of him.

"Yes. Chloe Anderson."

Jaqleon nodded, and I saw sweat was dotting his forehead.

"How is he so injured?" I glanced back at the street; no one else looked even half as injured as the elf.

"He was standing inside Lost Garden with me—by the door," Oleander said. "He was flipping the sign for me since I'd forgotten to. When the front window blew out, it ripped him to shreds."

I ran a hand through my hair. "Can he make it to the clocktower?"

"He'll have to," Oleander said.

I exhaled. "Okay. I need to be touching both of you for my magic to work and make us less noticeable. But we'll want to get off main street at the *first* turnoff," I said. "With him injured this badly, my magic probably isn't going to work as well as usual."

"If we both support him with our arms, I'll make sure I'm touching you," Oleander said.

"Got it."

Oleander hefted him to his feet, half lifting him with a fireman's hold before she got him balanced on the sidewalk.

I lifted his right arm and scooted under it, holding him when he teetered. I grabbed the back belt loop of his jeans, but Oleander took the brunt of his weight as he slumped over her shoulders.

We started down the sidewalk, the crunch of glass punctuating each step we took.

Please work, please work, please work.

I had to remind myself to breathe as we hobbled down the sidewalk, heading toward the end of the block.

Both of the elves were so much taller than me that Jaqleon was half crumpled, stretched between us as he was, but Oleander tucked her arm under mine, remaining in contact with me.

In theory, this should work, but I don't know if I need skin-to-skin contact or what.

I stared straight ahead as we limped past an ambulance.

An EMT trotted past, carrying a caddy filled with bandages. She didn't even glance at us.

I peered up at Oleander; her skin was ghost white underneath the flashes of blue and red from the police lights. But we had just one last store to pass before we could take a side street.

"The area is secure, bring the task force in."

Hooo, I know that voice. That is not a voice I want to hear right now!

I tried to simultaneously angle my body and head toward the buildings and crabwalk sideways while looking at the main street out of the corner of my eyes.

Pat stood in the middle of the street, talking on his cellphone.

CHAPTER THIRTEEN

Chloe

I made a noise in the back of my throat, then jolted forward.

Jaqleon groaned, but Oleander matched my pace—she'd been holding back, anyway—and we zipped around the corner, making the turn off to an intersecting street just as Pat turned around.

My heart beat rapidly in my chest, but he didn't call out after me, so he must not have seen me.

"Everything okay?" Oleander asked between clenched teeth.

"I saw my brother," I said.

Oleander paused just long enough to fix her grip on Jaqleon so she held him more securely while we edged past an empty police cruiser that had a tire up on the curb. "Is that dangerous, or...?"

"Seeing him is very dangerous," I said. "Because my magic doesn't affect him. He could have seen me."

"And that would be a bad thing?"

"Yes." I grunted when more of Jaqleon's weight tilted onto me before Oleander cleared the police car. He was a lot heavier than I'd realized, and my already high respect for Oleander jumped.

Cars were parked haphazardly in the middle of the road—stuck by the roadblock—but the sidewalks weren't too full. The few people in the area were also walking away, heading out of the disorder.

"Why?" Oleander asked.

"Sorry, what?"

"Why would it be bad if your brother saw you?" Oleander's brow was furrowed, but with confusion, not effort.

I fixed my hold on Jaqleon's belt loop. "Because I'm helping you two, and my brother doesn't know..." I glanced meaningfully at her ears, covered by her hat.

"Is that why you left?" Oleander asked.

I rapidly blinked. "Is this really the conversation you want to be having now as we're dragging your severely injured friend on a covert route to try to smuggle you two out of the area?"

Oleander ducked her head, and some of her gorgeous blond hair—that was silky smooth with not a strand of frizz, which I would bet was an elf trait—slipped over her shoulder from where Jaqleon's arm had pinned it. "I overstepped my boundaries, I apologize."

"No, don't apologize," I groaned. "It's just...*really*? Now?"

"I am a Mors, and I was an active member of King Noctus's guard," Oleander said apologetically. "Though it's been many years, I am used to active war zones. And Jaqleon is in rough shape, but not critical. He's from the Auron province—not as tough as a regular Mors elf."

"I see," I said, trying not to think about the implications of an ex-guard who now worked for a *clothing* boutique? "We need to turn here," I said. "There are a couple of alleyways we can use—I want to get us off the open streets."

"Understood," Oleander said.

She was silent, and I felt bad for questioning her. It wasn't like she'd really asked that personal a question—I was more shocked that Noctus hadn't given everyone a reason for my sudden exit. Though I suppose he also never explained why he'd suddenly adopted a cat, so maybe his people were used to not getting explanations.

I sighed as we edged down a dank alleyway, the noise from main street fading away. "My family is human. They live like humans," I said. "My brother and sister are involved with supernaturals because of me, but they're *human*. No matter how much I try to protect them, a fae or vampire could charm or daze them with their abilities and anything they knew would be fair game," I said.

"In theory, they could have moved into Calor Villa, but they're *human*." I glanced at Jaqleon—not nearly as convinced of his health as Oleander was. "My parents are traveling around the USA right now, living out their lifelong dream of camping. My brother and sister—as much as they want to be with me—have their own dreams they want to accomplish. They'd move to Calor in a moment if I asked, but they've given up so much for me, I can't ask for them to stay permanently in Calor, and they're too much of a risk to just let them keep living normal lives, knowing about the existence of Noctus and...you all."

We popped out of the alleyway and headed south again. I could see the clocktower getting closer—we were almost there.

"So you fear accidentally revealing...us," Oleander slowly said.

"Yes," I panted.

"I understand." There was something about the tone of her voice, but I couldn't risk looking away from the skyline.

Oleander, apparently, was tracking this complex conversation perfectly while doing most of the work carrying Jaqleon. Meanwhile, I was struggling to keep my brain calm enough to figure out what streets we were following.

"It seems our shortcomings have finally grown consequences," Oleander said.

"What?" I asked.

Jaqleon groaned, and Oleander busied herself with repositioning her comrade.

"We're almost there," I nervously said. "Do you want help carrying him to the gate?"

"Yes, please," Oleander said.

We turned another corner, and I saw the bottom floor of the clocktower. No one was standing outside it, but cars were driving up and down the street, so we had to wait a minute before crossing—I didn't want to risk popping out and testing my magic. Not today!

Once we reached the clocktower, I struggled to hold on to the pair and open the heavy door with one hand, but I did it, and wedged my foot in the doorway before pushing it open with my hip.

Jaqleon's head sagged alarmingly, and he groaned again when we jolted him while scuffling through the doorway.

"I'm sorry, I have one last potion in my backpack. Maybe we should have administered it once we got far enough away." My voice was loud in the near silence of the clocktower—all the businesses in the tower were elf owned, so they must have vacated it based on the dimmed lights.

Oleander shook her head. "Rodaric indicated there would be help waiting once we got through the gate. They'll have elf made potions, which will inherently work better on Jaqleon."

"Okay, I'll trust you on that. Where are we going?"

Oleander nodded to an employees only door that I personally knew had what felt like an endless staircase. "To the basement."

Now that we were in the clocktower, I wasn't so militant on touching them—I was pretty sure no one was going to be lurking around the tower, and if they were my magic wasn't going to do much given the situation.

So I scurried ahead, opening the stairway door, and helping tuck Jaqleon's limbs in when we went through the door.

It was a tricky trek to the basement—I had to pull an ID card from Oleander's pocket and swipe it, and we passed by two magic shields—but it struck me as odd that Oleander was supporting Jaqleon's side.

I wonder why she isn't picking him up like she was planning to when I first found her—holy crap!

When I opened what I hoped was the final door to the basement, I had to pass in front of Oleander, where I saw the streak of crimson red on her shirt that had *not* been there when we first started this moving venture.

"You're injured!" I blurted out.

"Yes," Oleander acknowledged.

"Why didn't you say anything?!"

Oleander smiled, and I noticed she was blinking more. "It's not a bad injury. It's merely growing to be very inconvenient."

She staggered a step, making her and Jaqleon tilt alarmingly. I hurriedly tucked myself under Jaqleon and again grabbed him by the back of his pants, attempting to take as much of his weight as I could.

"You should have said something," I said.

"It wasn't worthy of notation," Oleander said. "It's only because I'm not used to blood loss these days. I'm getting lazy in my old age. Although I imagine being cut off from my magic isn't helping the situation. It's a good experiment, I suppose."

"You're crazy," I muttered as we staggered toward the glowing portal. "All of you elves are crazy."

"Crazy fun!" Oleander declared with a laugh that was all too carefree for my comfort.

I eyed her with concern. *Just how hurt is she?*

I really didn't want to set foot in Calor Villa, but Noctus had returned me to my apartment when I was a cat, so I was pretty sure I could consider this a similar situation. The real risk was that Pat could return to the car at any point and realize I wasn't there. My phone wasn't ringing nonstop, so I was safe for now, but I wasn't sure how far my luck was going to hold out.

More of Jaqleon's weight abruptly shifted onto me when Oleander tripped on her own feet, making up my mind.

"Should I go through the gate with you?" I offered.

Oleander's forehead puckered with worry lines. "Perhaps," she evasively said. "If you don't mind the portal traveling?"

"I'm used to it. Come on. Let's go."

I tried to march faster—we were so close to the gate that the glowing doorway cast a green glow on Oleander's hair.

"I should train more," Oleander said. "I am getting quite soft to be this badly affected. Jaqleon is going to be embarrassed about this after he is treated."

"Less talking, more getting through the gate," I said. "Come on!"

Oleander was letting me take more and more of Jaqleon's weight. I was hoping this wasn't a sign of collapse, but I wouldn't be able to drag one elf through the portal, much less two.

"This is a battle, right?" I asked. "Conquer it! Think of...victorious thoughts."

"I do miss bashing heads," Oleander wistfully said.

I almost lost my grip on Jaqleon at that statement. "Elves really are made differently. Hold on!"

I stepped into the portal, and for a moment the world around me went black and my senses dulled as I was unable to tell up from down.

I barely noticed it, though, I was so determined to hang on to the two injured elves.

The portal spat us out into the weak morning sunlight. I barely had enough time to register the ring of elves around us before Jaqleon's weight crumpled on top of me and the cobblestone ground rushed up to greet me as I staggered.

"No! Nope!" I strained, my arms and legs shaking, but we stayed upright.

Elves wearing armor rushed forward, catching Oleander before she fell and relieving me of Jaqleon's weight.

Other elves—wearing human clothes with their sleeves rolled up—immediately got to work, popping potions out of leather bags and tiny vials off leather belts.

"Jaqleon's shredded," I said to the elves fluttering around me. "And I think Oleander is suffering from blood loss."

"What about you—"

"I'm fine!" I stepped back from the elf who was shaking up a potion as she eyed me. "Just...help them," I lamely said, gulping when I noticed the pallor to Oleander's face as some of the elves helped her sit.

This satisfied them momentarily as they swirled away, crowding around the injured, giving me a moment to finally place myself.

We were in one of the lower levels of the mountain side city that made up Calor Villa. It was one of the levels I hadn't visited before—we were in some kind of square surrounded by tall buildings that were covered in vines and greenery that I was pretty sure I hadn't seen before.

I jumped when someone put a hand on my shoulders, settling only when I realized it was Rodaric.

"—knew we should have left a scout outside the tower. Chloe Anderson, are you all right?" His voice was loud over the shouted orders of the elves wielding the potions.

"I'm fine. I have to go—now—but, will they be okay?" I glanced at Oleander, who shut her eyes as she lay down on the ground.

"They'll be fine," Rodaric assured me. "It's more likely the trauma of being cut off from magic combined with their actual injuries. They'll be given the best care."

"Okay. Do I need to lock any of the clocktower doors or anything?" I asked.

Rodaric shook his head. "The shop employees will be

returning shortly—they're gearing up now with charms and shields."

I absently nodded, until I realized what he was saying. *Holy—they're preparing for another attack!*

My shoulders hunched at the thought, and I assumed that would be the height of my anxiety, until I heard, "*The king!*"

The elves turned as one, facing one side of the square.

A moment later, Noctus appeared—wearing his black clothing, holding a sword that gleamed with magic.

Charon, Aristide, and Ker were behind him.

Ker was in her human form. When she saw me, her eyes lit up, and it was a slug to my gut.

I greatly underestimated how much I'd miss them. But I can't—not yet. I still haven't figured out a way for "us" to work.

"I gotta go," I repeated, pulling free of Rodaric's grasp and staggering toward the gate.

Rodaric let me go, and the shouts were replaced with hissed mutters as the elves organized, electing someone to inform Noctus.

I was almost to the gate—I was so close to it that I could feel the elf magic it radiated dance across my skin—before I remembered the fae.

When I was staying in Calor Villa, Noctus and Charon were keeping tabs on a fae—a male fae. What if...

"Noctus!" I shouted as I swung around, my voice carrying over the crowd.

Noctus flicked his eyes to me, and immediately silence fell over the square.

I gulped, but there was too much at stake to let my awkwardness get the best of me. "There was a fae—a male fae—who left the scene, and was *way* too relaxed considering he had to have been cut off from magic. He was fae tall and lean with their usual graceful way of moving, but the only somewhat distinctive thing about him was his blond hair, sorry."

Noctus nodded. "We'll look into it."

He opened his mouth to say something, but I couldn't stay anymore. My brother was a convenient—and truthfully should have been the *biggest*—concern, but the truth was I didn't think I could stay much longer near Noctus, near Charon, Ker, Aristide, near any of the elves, and not get pulled in.

We still don't have any resolution at this point. My thoughts left me more confused than the abrupt feeling of weightlessness as I stepped into the gate. *But I can't reach out to Noctus—none of the plans I've thought of are all that viable.*

Still...my heart physically hurt when I stepped into the clocktower. Even though the weird feeling that portal travel always smacked me with was gone, I still felt disorientated.

Calor, nestled into the mountains as it was, had been colder despite the morning sun, and the air had a misty scent to it that rolled off the lake.

The clocktower smelled clean, and faintly of flowers from Ker's flower shop, and it was deafeningly quiet compared to the organized bustle the elves made.

I wish there was a way I could tell Noctus and the others that I'm not giving up. But I can't talk to them—or I guess I could if I went back to the cul-de-sac with the Paragon, but I can't say anything in front of him, either. Maybe Charon, Aristide, and Ker will drop by the Book Nookery again?

My steps were quiet and my hackles were raised as I trotted through the abandoned building, making my way to the side doors. I was almost to the door when I realized I could see *my brother* standing outside!

He was planted on the sidewalk with two werewolves—one in their wolf form, one in their human form—and a wizard, all three wearing the task force uniform.

Nope, nope, nope! This is bad! No matter how I exit, they're going to see me.

Normally I would have just skipped out behind Pat's back. But these were task force members. I had a hunch they weren't just standing around out there for funsies. My magic might make me unnoticeable, but if they were intent on questioning people, I doubted it would hold out.

If I could get in my cat form it would be less dangerous, but I can't open the door and then *shift and come out. That would be attention-drawing in a totally different way. But what...wait.*

I was standing in the clocktower. There absolutely was a way out of this in my cat form—jumping from the roof.

I'd practiced falling from it more times than I cared to remember, and I knew the various jumping spots like I knew the toe beans on my paws that people always insisted on pushing.

I'd just aim for an area out of sight, stroll out as a cat, and then I'd be free to sprint back to the car.

I ran to the stairwell and started the climb.

I just hope it wasn't me *Pat followed here. Why else would he be in the area?*

I had a lot of time to worry about this as the climb took forever, but at least I wasn't panting by the time I reached the floor I wanted.

I didn't go all the way to the top, I ducked out at an observation deck that wrapped around the clocktower faces. I had to peer over the side—holding on to the scaffolding with white knuckles—to pinpoint my brother's location—before I chose the area I would leap into.

This is my first jump from this kind of height in months. I can do this.

As I shifted into my cat shape, I was surprised to find that it wasn't anxiety that was making my heartbeat pick up, but excitement.

That is...very unexpected. For me.

I leaped from the railing as a cat, stretching my paws out to help slow down my terminal velocity.

My heart leaped into my throat, but I landed on all four paws with little more than a jolt.

I made it! Okay, I can do this!

My tail erect, I trotted around the corner, joining my brother and his coworkers.

None of them besides the transformed werewolf noticed me, and he just wagged his tail at me before looking back up at Pat who was giving his people instructions.

I ambled across the street and continued up the sidewalk, heading back toward the car.

I was pretty euphoric—I couldn't believe I'd gotten away with it!

The elves were safe, Pat wouldn't know about my little side trip, I'd even managed to tell Noctus about the fae guy.

Thinking of the fae's absolute casualness about the whole situation made my skin crawl—there was definitely something to him.

I should tell Pat, too, in case he is involved with the incident. But how can I tell him? I only saw the fae on that side street, which isn't something I could see from the car.

Some of my good humor wore off at the thought as I dodged around a group of human police officers, who didn't even glance at me.

I couldn't tell Pat I'd just sashayed off into the middle of the crime scene—that wasn't my style, and he'd raised me better than that. I would have happily stayed in the car if I hadn't seen Rodaric—it was better to stay out of the way of the professionals in situations like this.

Whatever I come up with would be a half lie, and I don't like the thought of that either. Especially since there could be repercussions across supernatural society for this.

I was almost to main street by this point, and my elation from my success had almost entirely drained away.

This is why I had to leave when I did. Because the lies, the layers...

I stepped into an alleyway just long enough to swap into my human form. The shift complete, I managed to join a gaggle of humans edging out onto the sidewalk of main street, gossiping and gawking together.

I still haven't given up on finding a way to make this work, but it feels impossible whenever I face a situation like this. I'm not giving up my human family, and Noctus can't risk his people. No matter how much scheming I do, those are constant factors.

I sighed and checked both ways before I crossed the street, approaching Pat's car. I swung my backpack off my back—I had both Pat's and Joy's spare car keys for security purposes, so I just had to dig it out.

I couldn't find them in the inner pocket where I usually kept them. The keys must have fallen into the larger compartment of my backpack—not surprising considering the jostling I'd been through in the last half hour.

I rested my bag on Pat's car and shoved my arm deeper into my backpack, pausing when my fingertips brushed lace before my nails scraped a stony surface.

My collar from Noctus.

I was still carrying it around in my backpack—unwilling to leave it in my studio apartment.

But...what if I put it on?

I pulled the collar out and carefully folded it so it rested on my left palm. The three pomegranate red gemstones that decorated it seemed to glow in the morning light.

Putting the collar on wouldn't restore the bond—that would happen only if Noctus put the collar-necklace back on me. But... wouldn't it send a message just the same?

I'd been prepared to never see Noctus again, but since September began, I'd seen him three times. Yes, I couldn't really move toward him right now. But. If I wore the necklace, wouldn't that be the same as telling him that I was trying?

I impulsively unfolded the collar and tugged it on over my head—the lace stretched like elastic so I could pull it over my ears, though I snapped myself in the nose with the gems in the process.

When I pulled it down my jaw it shrunk, comfortably settling on my throat—though I worked it all the way down to the base of my neck so it looked like part of my shirt.

He might miss it—it's me, after all. Who knows if he'd see it through my magic? But I have to try.

I took a deep breath of air and rested my fingers on the red gems.

"Chloe! There you are!"

I spun around, surprised to see Joy hurrying down the sidewalk, holding an icepack to her head.

"Joy? What happened?" I snatched up my backpack and rushed to intercept her. "How did you get hurt?"

"It's not a big deal," Joy said. "I was near a werewolf when the attack happened. She freaked because of the magic disruption and smacked into me." Joy's tone was sunny, and she swatted at me with her free hand, but I scanned her, taking in every wrinkle and the dirt smears on her clothes.

"Werewolf strength is no joke, whether they mean it or not. How hard did she hit you?" I eyed the icepack.

"She just bumped into me. If I hadn't been wearing heels I wouldn't have fallen over," Joy said. "I smacked my head when I fell—not enough to injure myself, I just have a bump."

I stared at my sister, trying to gauge just how much she was underselling the injury.

Do we need to go to the hospital? The last potion I have isn't human grade, so I can't give it to her...and it probably wouldn't do anything even if it was safe for her.

I wanted to scream. It was so unfair that my human family, with their big hearts and bone-deep bravery, were so *delicate*.

This is just another reminder of why I can't just haul them off to Calor Villa. They're such easy targets, even though Pat and Joy are a million times fiercer than the average human.

"Stop looking so worried." Joy used her older sister/no nonsense tone that she broke out whenever she needed to boss me around. "I'm fine. I promise. The EMTs already cleared me. Didn't you get my text?" Joy asked.

"I changed forms for a bit, that's probably when it came through," I said.

Joy frowned. "Why did you change forms?"

And now I have to figure out what I tell them without feeling like an awful person for lying.

"I thought I saw someone I knew, and I wanted to make sure they were okay." I cringed. "Pat told me to stay with the car, he's going to be furious that I left it."

"It's fine—he's working now. I came back here to find you and take you home. I need to get back to the apartment to change, and maybe take some painkillers."

"I'll drive your car," I volunteered. "You'd need both hands to drive, and it's better if you keep icing that bump."

"I'm only supposed to have it on for ten minutes, then off for ten minutes." Joy beckoned me to follow her as we headed back toward City Hall. "So I'll be done soon. *But* I won't argue with you."

I peered up at my much taller sister, my concern growing. Joy *lived* to argue—it was why she loved her job as much as she did.

She must be hurting more than she's willing to let on.

"What did I tell you earlier—stop looking so worried." Joy elbowed me without looking at me. "I'm not on death's doorstep."

"I know, I know. But are you sure you should go into work?"

"Yes. City Hall is demanding a debriefing from the Curia Cloisters. But I've got a few hours until then, maybe I'll take a shower."

"Just don't take a nap."

"I have a bump on my head, Chloe, not a concussion, you worry wart."

"Sure, just no naps."

CHAPTER FOURTEEN

Noctus

I watched Chloe disappear through the portal gate, fleeing since she had accomplished her goal and dropped off Oleander and Jaqleon.

Rodaric had messaged Charon as soon as the incident had taken place, and we'd mobilized in time to be waiting at the gate when he and Brevlanne stepped through. When he'd said that Chloe had gotten them to the clocktower, and that she'd *gone back* for Oleander and Jaqleon, it took everything I had to stay there in Calor Villa while she risked herself.

I thought that had been bad enough, but this, this was worse.

Do I have to be king? My people don't even like me. Surely they wouldn't care if I abdicated.

"Your orders, Your Majesty?" Charon had his cellphone out, and even as Oleander and Jaqleon received treatment, the others crowded in the square turned to me.

I glanced up at the sky, which glimmered with the pearlescent sheen the spelled barrier made.

No. There's no one else who can maintain the barrier. Furthermore, I am responsible for the plight of the elves. I knew I'd be seeing through the consequences of my actions as long as I lived. I just never thought there'd be a reason I'd want *it any other way.*

"Gather a squad—Charon will lead—and see what footage we can recover from the area," I said, my duties grounding me once again. "Track the incident—I want to know what the radius was of the sound blast and the disconnect from magic," I continued. "If they're different areas, we need to know. Use stealth, but be aware, we must move fast. The Curia Cloisters have likely sent personnel out to the area, and we have visuals of human police. Our window of opportunity will soon close."

"Understood," Charon said. "Will this be our only investigation in the matter?"

"No," I said. "We'll visit again once the area has recovered. I'll lead that trip."

Charon bowed and disappeared into the crowd, tapping the shoulders of those he wanted to join him.

I watched until I was aware of Aristide sidling up next to me. I rolled my shoulders back, mentally bracing for a sarcastic comment about Chloe.

"That was a rather strong response to an issue that technically has nothing to do with the elves," Aristide murmured. "You believe the fae Chloe spotted is indeed the one you and Charon have been tracking—the one you first heard of from the barista at Queen's Court Café?"

"It's a distinct possibility," I said. "Particularly since we have video footage that put him at the scene of the previous artifact explosion."

"It seems like he's stuck on poking the hornet's nest." Ker approached me from the other side, idly twirling the tip of her left braid around a finger. "The Curia Cloisters task force was already quite the power to be reckoned with given how they handled the wizard drama last year. With the addition of Chloe's brother to the force, it's only gotten stronger. That fae is taking a lot of risks with these stunts."

I made a noise in the back of my throat, neither agreeing nor denying.

"I'll bite," Aristide started.

"Not here," Ker said, attempting to lighten the moment.

Aristide ignored her and continued, "You're taking this too seriously for a sudden hobby cultivation in mysteries. What's up?"

I set my jaw and turned away from the crowd, drawing my friends in closer. "You're correct that the fae seems intent on creating a fuss, but for what? There have been injuries, but it hasn't been disastrous. Even with today's incident I expect the greatest outcome will be building expenses from the glass. *Why*? If he is so intent on damage, why not scale it up?"

"Is it possible he's just trying to sow seeds of chaos?" Ker asked. "The artifact ring we broke was small time problems—nothing hugely threatening."

"No, but it rubbed at the relationship between humans and supernaturals," Aristide pointed out. "And it was too carefully set up for it to be entirely accidental. Which proves Noctus's point. If he was the brain behind the artifact ring, he must have a goal in this, too. Is that what you're getting at?"

"Yes," I said. "Which means it is likely each incident is carefully chosen for a specific reason—whether it's for the location or a test run of sorts."

"Test run?" Ker stood straighter in her alarm, all signs of her usual kind demeanor leaving as her wolf eyes hardened. "But we've already covered that he hasn't done anything on a larger scale before."

"That we know of," I said.

Ker tilted her head back and studied me with the intensity of a predator. "So, we really are going to operate under the assumption he's part of that organization the Paragon is after?"

"The organization has already proven to be overly invested in Magiford," Aristide chimed in. "Between all the wizard drama and the attempts on Queen Leila's life. If Chloe's tracker belongs to it —like the Paragon seems to think—they likely have a larger presence here than we assumed."

Ker sighed, which came out as more of a growl. "Every instinct I have says we'd be better off just cutting and running from this place. But that's still not an option, is it?"

"Not just yet," I said. "Though it might be in our future."

"Goodie," Aristide said, his voice sour. "I just love living in indecision. It's my favorite."

His sarcasm broke Ker out of her wolfish intensity. "Indecision? Please, we'd still be living in Calor Villa no matter what city Noctus moved us to. It's his people that must deal with the indecision and if the portal locations were changed."

"I resent that," Aristide said. "You forgot, a good half of the elves in Calor are Mors elves. They roll out of their beds in the morning ready to leave it forever. Minimalists, the bunch of you."

"Calor Villa could never be construed as a work of minimalism," I said.

"Compared to the other elven sanctuaries that used to exist, it's downright dowdy," Aristide stated.

"Ah," Ker said. "Of course, you do keep the past close to your heart, nostalgia—"

"Finish that sentence, I *dare you*," Aristide said.

Ker erupted into a belly laugh, giving Aristide time to sniff.

"Well, now that we've distracted Noctus from his pining, shall we hear what the elves present at the time of the event had to say?" Aristide asked.

I looked back over my shoulder. "Oleander is on her feet, let's start with her."

"You got it." Ker maneuvered herself in front of Aristide so he could take her arm.

"Did you notice, Ker, how Noctus did not negate my accusations of pining?" Aristide said.

"Did you notice, Ker, how last night Aristide went to bed early, near the same time as when the secret history podcast he listens to that he thinks none of us know about drops its new episodes?" I countered.

"You're the worst," Aristide complained.

"Someone's got to keep you company," I said, a slight smile pulling at me despite the situation.

I couldn't stop being king—there was no one else in Calor who could fill the position. It had many inevitable conclusions that I didn't want to face at the moment, but at least I still had Aristide, Ker, and Charon.

And maybe, in a way, I still had Chloe. Because despite the danger the situation presented to her...she'd still come.

CHAPTER FIFTEEN

Chloe

I scuttled out of Book Nookery, bracing myself against the wind as I made my way to Joy's car, where she was waiting for me.

I had to yank hard on the car door to close it against the gusts of wind that made my hair a wild mess and yanked on my coat.

"Wow. October arrives, and autumn is feeling vengeful." I pushed my hair out of my face then buckled myself in. "Any news from Pat?"

Joy had mostly been picking me up for work since Pat had been working crazy hours because of the sonic-boom incident on main street. We hadn't seen much of him in the days since the accident, though he made sure he called us to check in on us.

"No." Joy pinched the bridge of her nose. "I saw he was quoted in an article in the human newspaper today that they're still investigating, and I got a text from him reminding me to pick you up, but that was it."

I studied my gorgeous sister with concern. Although her hair and clothes were flawless, I could see little signs of exhaustion—the way her smile wasn't completely even, the extra perfection of her eye makeup which meant she was wearing concealer to cover her bags, and she was leaving her hair down instead of braiding it or putting it up as she usually liked to do a couple days a week.

"Joy...we have to stop doing this," I said. "You're exhausted, Pat is working a very important case, I can drive myself to and from work."

"The problem has never been if you *could*, it's that crazy psychopath who's stalking you," Joy said.

"I can handle—"

"Before you finish that sentence, remember how your last fight with him went," Joy said, her voice hard.

I snapped my mouth shut, stung at the bitter reminder.

It's even worse than she knows, because I had to be saved by Noctus.

Joy glanced at me, the purplish morning light dimming the glow of her blond hair, before she immediately looked back at the road and turned on her blinker. "You took that harder than I meant for you to."

"It's a valid point," I said around the lump in my throat.

Joy sighed. "Only partially. Look, you don't realize it, but I think you could totally take that creepy stalker."

"Tracker."

"Whatever. Pat thinks you can take him, too."

"Neither of you think that, or you wouldn't be so over the top with the protective measures," I said.

Joy briefly stopped the car at a four way stop sign. "We have the protective measures, and Pat is acting like an ornery mama bear, because you don't think you can take him out."

I hesitated for a moment as I tried to digest what Joy was saying and came up with nothing. "*...what?*"

"You underestimate your capabilities." Joy looked up and down the street before making a turn—we always took crazy routes home to avoid making a routine that the tracker could follow. "You took out two fae monarchs while busting Pat and me out of a kidnapping. You can handle one deranged supernatural, even if he exploits your weakness for bystanders."

I massaged my forehead. "I've been training to make sure he can't attack me."

"Yes, but that's not the same as knowing you could take him out," Joy said. "And when you're not personally convinced, facing him is a dangerous thing to do. I'm not blaming you—you've lived a life in which most of supernatural society was bent on telling you that you were weak, and we, your human family, couldn't say anything about that part of your life since we're just humans."

"You're not *just* humans," I said.

"Oh, we are. Even with everything Pat and I have tried, we're still humans. There's a lot we don't get about you that your boss understands better just because she's a fellow supernatural." Joy turned into a small parking lot. "But that's not the point. What I mean is...we believe in you. But your life isn't something we're willing to play around with, and if you hesitate in your own abilities, facing the tracker is too dangerous. So, I'm taking you to work tonight," Joy concluded before she parked the car in a spot and shut it off.

"Okay," I agreed. "But what are we doing here?" I peered out the window, recognizing the tiny parking lot and the unassuming 'Queen's Court Café' sign posted over the coffee shop.

"I need caffeine." Joy dropped every sparkle she'd had in her voice and face so she resembled a zombie from the movies. "Or I'm going to die. My coworkers told me this was the place to go for supernaturals, apparently. So I thought we should try it! Let's go—woah!" Joy struggled out of the car, working hard to slam the door shut.

I reluctantly got out, and we fought our way across the parking lot.

We'd just made it to the sidewalk outside the storefront when something soft and flabby slammed into the side of my head.

For a moment my heart stopped, until feathers followed by a striped raccoon tail covered my eyes. "French Fry, what are you doing out in this weather?" I struggled with the trash griffin, trying to fold his wings for him so the wind would stop buffeting them around.

French Fry made a cooing noise and tried to crawl onto my shoulder.

Joy darted into Queen's Court Café, and stood by the glass door, keeping an eye on me from the safety of indoors.

She waved to me, a genuine smile back on her face.

I scowled at her, until my attention was stolen by French Fry, who had stuck his butt up into the air in a stupid attempt to balance on me, and then toppled headfirst over my shoulder.

I caught him, but he'd unfolded his wings again in the process, and the wind nearly tore him out of my hands.

"You silly, bird-brained raccoon!" I growled as I helped him refold his wings. "Why would you *possibly*—"

"Is that a trash griffin?"

I looked up, and dropped French Fry on my feet.

Queen Leila—her black hair pulled back in a French braid and her purple-ish-blue eyes wide with surprise—held the door open with one hand. In the other hand she held a pink leash, clipped to the harness of a leopard-sized and shaped feline, except this cat had thick, luxurious fur that was a blinding white, and was dotted with light gray and yellow dapples.

"Uhhh," I said.

"Come inside, the wind is crazy out there." Queen Leila yanked the door open wider.

I scooped French Fry off the pavement. "I can't just leave him out here."

"Bring him in," Queen Leila said.

"But I don't have a leash." I closed my eyes against a particularly powerful gust of wind. "Queen's Court Café requires leashes on all pets."

"Get in," Queen Leila ordered.

I hopped in without hesitation, still clutching French Fry to my chest.

Instantly, I felt warmer.

The dark blue painted walls dusted with flecks of gold and white paint to represent the night sky matched with strings of lights that crisscrossed over the ceiling gave the café a cozy feel that sank into my bones.

The café had updated some of its photographs of Night Queen Leila and her king since the last time I'd come here, but nothing else had changed.

The smell of coffee still permeated the air, softened by the sweeter scent of apples, which Queen's Court kept sacks of by the small drive through window.

Queen Leila's giant cat thing—a gloom, another citizen of the fae queen's Night Realm—sniffed my legs as I stepped deeper into the café.

The gloom, and Queen Leila, were the only customers in the shop—which surprised me as Queen Leila usually traveled with guards.

Maybe there's someone here with her, I absently wondered as I felt the silken sensation of fae magic tickle my elbow. *Because I feel fae magic, but I'm pretty sure it's not coming from her.*

"Hey!" The barista, I recalled his name was Landon, leaned over the counter. "That bird hasn't got a leash." He narrowed his eyes, and his freckles seemed to pop with the scrutiny.

"It's fine, Landon, he's with me," Queen Leila said.

"Doesn't matter if you're the namesake of the café. No leash, no entrance," Landon declared.

Leila rolled her eyes. "Landon..."

"You can't fool me. I know that thing's called a trash griffin! I don't want it pigging the place up, because do you know who will have to clean it up? Me. So take your little garbage pet along, or get a leash."

"Oh, I've got one." Joy flipped open her purse and dug around inside it.

Don't ask, don't ask, don't ask, I internally pleaded as Leila watched Joy extract a purple, cat sized slip leash. *PLEASE, don't ask.*

Queen Leila obviously knew about my abilities, and I wasn't shy about who I was, but. Somehow, I knew that if Joy had to explain how frequently she and Pat had saved me from humane societies that they now kept leashes in their cars/bags to this beautiful fae empress, my dignity was going to die.

I took the leash from my sister, made a loop, and dropped it over French Fry's head.

Instead of settling around his neck, it slid down to his chest, so it looked like a ridiculous necklace.

French Fry preened and cooed up at me as I smoothed his wings for him and restored order to his soft raccoon fur.

"Sorry, he's leashed now." I held French Fry up once I'd gotten him as groomed as he was going to get.

Landon stared at him through still narrowed eyes. "I don't know if we allow birds in here."

"Seriously Landon?" Leila said. "He's leashed, that's your store policy. It says nothing about birds!"

"That would be because we've never had a nut try to *bring* a bird in here—which is saying something since you're a regular customer," Landon said.

"Fine," Leila said. "Then go ask Rhonda about the policy."

"'kay." Landon stood upright, sucked in a breath of air, then yelled. "*Rhonda*!"

"Go *find* her, Landon. No one wants to hear you shouting like that," Leila scolded.

"Geez, okay, okay." Now it was Landon's turn to roll his eyes. "You got super bossy once the fae started calling you an empress, did you know that?" He skulked off before Leila could reply, disappearing into what I assume was a storage room.

Leila shook her head then smiled at me. "Sorry about all of that, Chloe. But, um...do you know that's a trash griffin?"

"Yes." I tried to ignore French Fry, who was staring up at me, bobbing his head from side to side in an attempt to invite me to pet him. "He is...I see him frequently—ouch, French Fry, stop that!"

French Fry, grabbing at my clothes with his beak, hauled himself up the front of my jacket so he could sit on my shoulder. He bit my ear to stabilize himself, then cooed and affectionately rubbed his head against mine.

"Wow." Leila retreated a few steps to pick up a to-go drink—one of two left on a small end table. "Now that is something I've never seen before. He's a pet?"

"More of a friend?" I pushed French Fry's raccoon tail out of my face. "He finds me whenever I walk around Magiford, and he's built a nest outside my apartment window. I call him French Fry. I don't make him do this, or anything. He's just been flying around since I moved here," I nervously explained. "I know he's yours since he belongs to the Night Court."

Leila raised both of her eyebrows as she studied French Fry. "I'd say the trash griffins are my subjects, not my personal pets, though I get what you mean."

The gloom at Leila's side twitched its whiskers before it made this horrible warbling noise that sounded like a goblin getting sat on.

"I'm sorry, where are my manners? This is Muffin." Leila set her drink back down, then crouched down next to the cat, ignored its teeth that were as big as the joints of her fingers, and loosely hugged the creature before scratching under its throat, eliciting a throaty purr from it.

Watching the interaction, I gulped a little. *I am so glad my powers only work on housecats, not all felines.*

Leila smiled at her pet, then peered back up at me. "So... French Fry?"

"It's his favorite food," I said. "He likes to show them off to me a lot."

"That sounds about right," Leila said. "And he just started following you around one day?"

"Yeah. I saw him around a lot and assumed it was a Magiford thing," I said. "We got friendly over the years, and now..." I trailed off so I could catch French Fry when he fell off my shoulder. "I'm sorry," I said.

Leila laughed. "Why apologize?"

"Because he's your, er, subject."

"Yes, and he's free to be friends and find a home wherever he likes." Leila tilted her head as she studied French Fry. "Everyone in my Court treats them like pests, and they can be quite stupid, but I do think they're smarter than we give them credit for."

Considering he was able to find me in Noctus's realm, yes. He's much *smarter than everyone assumes.*

I couldn't say that, though, so I nodded. "Yep!"

I sensed Joy edging toward the front counter, knocking my manners into me. "Oh, Queen Leila, this is my sister Joy," I said.

"Hello, Queen Leila. It's an honor to meet you." Joy smiled before she hissed to me. "I told you this was a good place to see supernaturals!"

"Hello," Leila smiled. "Chloe mentioned you when we discussed her particular background. It's lovely to meet you."

"Why thank you," Joy said.

"Joy works for the human City Hall," I said.

"Ahh, so you also deal with politics," Queen Leila said. "Someone to appreciate my pain."

Joy laughed. "It can be a pain, yes, but I'm grateful for the opportunities and chances my work has provided me."

Leila looked from Joy to me and back. "Yes, I imagine so..."

Everyone was silent for a moment, and I felt the awkwardness start to slip in.

"I'm surprised to see you here, Queen Leila," I said after several moments of silence, struggling for a conversation topic. "Lord Linus stopped by my workplace with a tour bus, he mentioned you'd be leaving soon on another trip to visit the other fae Courts."

"Yeah, it got delayed after the incident downtown." Queen Leila reclaimed her drink and took a big swig of it. "But since we don't seem to have any new leads, I'm leaving tomorrow. Today I'm just tying up a few loose ends, though I'm glad I ran into you, I wanted to make sure Lord Linus and the tours weren't being too pesky."

I absently cuddled French Fry to my chest. "No, not at all. I should be thanking you, since the tours make a visible connection between us."

"Yeah, that was how he tried to win me over to the idea when he first suggested it." Queen Leila threw her now empty drink cup away, but made no motion to finish off the second drink. "Though I won't lie, I was all for it even before then. Anything that gets my Court out of my hair and under someone else's supervision for even an evening is a win. Though I wish Linus didn't know that, as that's how he's made a case for not giving me any kind of cut from all the money he's rolling in."

Leila shook her head at her fae father, most likely unaware that she was displaying some of the same mannerisms as him from the way she shook her head all the way to his same magnetic charisma.

Leila looked around the shop, her eyes lingering on a shadowed area in the back corner before she nodded. "I met with the Paragon briefly," she said, her voice lowered. "He mentioned his *contact* was going to share some resources with you. Did you get them yet?"

"Yes," I nodded. "I got them last week."

"Did you have any problems with the materials?" Queen Leila asked.

"No," I answered her slowly, slightly confused by the question.

"Good!" The fae queen smiled. "The Paragon mentioned he's had...not trouble with him, but that contact has been evasive in his answers before."

"Really?" I asked, faking surprise when I'd witnessed firsthand how much Noctus annoyed the Paragon.

"Yeah." Queen Leila slightly shook her head. "He's been helpful before, giving us insight into magic we'd know nothing about." She fidgeted, moving the second to-go drink around on the table before she itched a spot behind Muffin's ears.

I stayed silent as I waited for her to go on.

"But it's always a reminder...of their capacity," Queen Leila said.

I worked hard to make sure my voice sounded unbothered. "What do you mean?"

"I've encountered *that* type of magic multiple times," Leila said. "It has different forms, but it's always deadly."

I had to bite my tongue to keep from talking.

Deadly, really?

Yes, Noctus had deadly magic—I'd seen him with his heirloom weapons. He could be terrifying.

But the elf portals, barriers, charms, and similar magic I'd seen, all of it had been sharp and strong, certainly, but not *deadly*.

Well...except that outlawed magic those elf teenagers tested out that Noctus nearly smote them for.

The front counter creaked when Joy leaned against it, reminding me that my sister—who didn't know about my visit to Noctus in honor of the Paragon's wishes—was present. I needed to be careful in our conversation.

"Isn't all magic like that?" I asked. "Wizards and their control over elements, werewolves with their insane strength—all magic has the potential to be deadly."

"I don't know. I've seen shadow creatures capable of..." She glanced at Joy and trailed off. Leila tugged on her coat, and I recognized the same, unsettled energy in her that I occasionally saw in upset cats. "The power scale is different," she concluded.

I mashed my lips together as I gazed up at Leila's face.

The Paragon said she's been attacked by elf magic...she's strong, but that doesn't mean it didn't scare her. I get it, I'm terrified of the tracker. But it's not fair. It's elves like the tracker and whoever he's working with that do so much damage, when Noctus works secretly to help Magiford and is treated with suspicion.

This was why Noctus would never risk coming forward.

Because there was no guarantee supernaturals would even give them a chance before they'd judge the elves of Calor Villa.

"Unfortunately," Leila continued in a lowered tone, "it seems like it's also behind many of the troubles in Magiford these days."

I glanced at Joy, who had pulled out her cellphone. "Surely it's not behind *everything*," I said.

Leila looked back to make sure the baristas hadn't surfaced. "I imagine your brother hasn't told you because it hasn't been cleared for public knowledge just yet, but you of all people deserve to know, Chloe. The incident last week? That was elf magic."

By this point I was considering going and finding Landon myself because I wanted this conversation to be *over*—Leila might be thinking Joy wasn't listening, but I knew better, and I didn't want this conversation putting any ideas in her head.

"I thought the elves were gone," Joy said, proving my point.

Leila hesitated, but she must have concluded that Joy would find out from Pat eventually, because she continued, "It seems like some of their magic has survived—which isn't that surprising. Enough time has passed that those who *knew* better than to dabble with danger like that are gone, and our generation is naïve enough to think they can handle it." Leila flashed us a smile. "But, I wouldn't take it to heart, Chloe. You're safe here. I promise."

Joy's shoulders relaxed marginally, and I forced myself to smile, feeling like a horrible traitor.

"Thanks," I lamely said.

French Fry seemed to pick up on my mood, because he suddenly thrust one of his bird feet up, mashing it against my mouth. It took me a moment to realize he was pressing a French fry to my lips.

I cranked my head back to avoid the who-knew-how-old fry. "No thanks, but that's very kind of you...wait." I frowned down at my feathery and furry friend. "Where did you even *get* that? You didn't have any when we got in here!"

French Fry waved his treasure at me some more, still offering it out.

"That's very interesting behavior," Leila said.

"Pardon?" I had to lower French Fry so he was propped against my stomach instead of my chest—he kept swiping his probably germ-infested fry too close to my mouth for comfort.

"I've never seen a trash griffin act so nurturing," Leila said. "He really does care for you."

"I'm sure he cares for you since you're his queen," I said, feeling obligated to attempt to get French Fry in his monarch's good graces, even if French Fry himself was too oblivious to.

Leila laughed. "You don't have to worry about him hurting my feelings. I love my Court animals—all of them—but as I said earlier, they have their own wills. I want them to be happy in their own style, and I couldn't possibly house them all if they all wanted to live with a person, anyway."

"Oh, I wouldn't say he's living with me—"

French Fry took advantage of my open mouth and thrust his stale, cardboard textured French fry in my mouth, earning a yelp from me.

Mindful of Landon's complaining, I rushed to a garbage can and spat the fry out while the very proud trash griffin crawled onto my shoulder and Joy chuckled.

Leila was kind enough to pour me a glass of water from the plastic pitcher and cups the café had set up by their napkins, silverware, and busing station, breaking café rules in the process as she dropped Muffin's leash to juggle everything.

I gulped the cup down, barely registering when French Fry whacked me on the side of the head with his wings.

My bratty sister was too busy wiping tears from her eyes to help. "You should have seen your face," she said. "Your eyes bulged out of your skull, and he just looked so *proud*!"

I eyed my sister. "Next time I visit your apartment, I'm sleeping on all of your pillows in my cat form and will leave my fur everywhere."

"Now, now, it was a touching display." Queen Leila patted my back with her left hand while she refilled my cup of water. "Though you might want to down a fae potion—there's no telling where he was keeping that fry."

Muffin wailed in her goblin-y voice, unnecessarily backing her queen up.

"I'll keep that in mind," I sourly said.

Leila set the pitcher down, then returned to my side, rubbing French Fry on the top of his extra round dome before reclaiming Muffin's leash. "But I think the display proves my point: whatever the reason, French Fry has chosen you. You shouldn't consider him a Night Court creature, but rather yours."

French Fry cooed under the fae queen's gentle touch, but he stayed glued to my jacket.

"Thanks." My voice cracked awkwardly, and I finished off the rest of my water, just to give myself something to do so I didn't have to look at the lovely queen.

I could feel myself rapidly growing awkward the longer the moment lasted, but—*finally*—salvation arrived.

Landon slouched back into the café, a moody frown pulling on his face. "Rhonda says the pest with wings and a tail can stay," he said. "I tried to tell her his existence is breaking health codes, but she cited the precedence of cuteness. I made the argument that he is *not* cute and that her ability to judge cuteness is broken. She informed me that once I have my own café, I can make my own judgment calls." The barista shook his head as he fussed with his apron and took his place behind the counter. "As if I'm crazy enough to ever think of opening a café after working here! Nah-uh! So, what can I get you, owners of the garbage creature?"

"He's a trash griffin, Landon. Don't insult him," Leila called to him before her phone chirped. She glanced down at it and made a face. "I'd love to keep on talking, but I really need to finish a few errands."

"We understand," Joy said in her sunny voice. "We hope your trip to the other Courts goes well."

"Thank you, I appreciate it. Now, if you'll excuse me..." The fae queen smiled one last time, then turned on her heel. "Rigel, are you ready to go?"

The silky sensation of fae magic that tickled at my elbow intensified, and a guy *stepped out* of the shadows in the back corner of the café.

CHAPTER SIXTEEN

Chloe

I nearly turned into a cat—it was only the thought that if I did that French Fry would land on top of me and, with how my day was going, would probably squash me, that kept me from following the instinct.

Tall, with silvery white hair and tawny, copper colored skin, the fae crossed the café and picked up the remaining drink on the coffee table.

"K-king Rigel," I gulped. He was easy to recognize considering we were standing in a shrine to his wife that had his face plastered everywhere.

King Rigel nodded to me and Joy before he sipped his drink.

Queen Leila handed him Muffin's pink leash, and he took it, somehow looking even more deadly with the gloom, despite the bright and happy color of her collar and leash.

"I'll pop outside, hopefully Eclipse will sense that we're ready to go. Goodbye!" Queen Leila waved before she slipped outside, the wind tugging on her ponytail and jacket.

"I'm going to order a drink." Joy headed for the counter, where Landon still suspiciously eyed us. "You want anything, Chloe?"

"Do you have steamers?" I asked.

Landon blinked. "You mean you just want hot, frothed milk laced with a flavor syrup?"

"Yes."

"Weird vibe, but yeah. I can make it. What flavor?"

I shifted French Fry to one arm so I could dig into my coat pocket for my wallet. "Caramel, please."

"I got this one." Joy made a shooing motion before she eyed the chalkboard sign that displayed the café's monthly flavors. "What is the 'Gloom's Glory'?"

"That's a dry cappuccino with a maple flavor shot and a drizzle of raspberry sauce on the foam."

"I'll try that, please."

"Got it, ready for your card when you are..."

My attention waned from my sister and Landon when I realized King Rigel was still in the store with Muffin-the-gloom, and he was studying *me*.

"You should be cautious of the information you received from the Paragon's contact," King Rigel said, his voice a lot smoother than I'd been prepared for. "It's likely to be biased, and unlikely that he shared the greatest of your powers with you."

Thinking of all the training I'd been put through under Noctus's insistence and Charon's watchful eyes, I highly doubted that, but I could see why the Night King would assume that—elves and shadows were supposed to be enemies, after all.

"Thank you for the warning," I said.

Rigel narrowed his eyes. "You're not worried enough about it."

I gaped at him in surprise.

I'm pretty sure this is the first time in my life anyone has indicated I should be more anxious than I already am.

"In fact, you are oddly calm considering you have a half-blood chasing you," Rigel continued.

Shoot—how is he so perceptive? Something must be giving me away, but he can't have a vampire's hearing of my heartbeat, can he?

I backed up a few steps, putting space between us, bouncing French Fry a little so he flapped his wings to explain the retreat. "Um," I said. "I am quite anxious about the tracker, I assure you."

Rigel glanced outside, checking on his wife. "No. You don't get it, elven magic is *deadly*, and while you may be immune to it, everyone around you is not." He nodded in Joy's direction, making my blood turn cold. "They *searched* for ways to subjugate other supernaturals. There has never been another race as power hungry and vile as them, and we will not let their spirit return."

Rigel left, the gloom stalking along at his side, without giving me the chance to respond, though I don't think I could have.

I buried my icy cold hands into French Fry's fluff, unable to banish the cold that had settled in my bones.

I understood why Noctus wanted his people to stay hidden, but I never guessed how much they'd still be hated today. Though it seems like some of the vitriol is because of the organization the Paragon talked about. As a result of using elven magic for evil purposes, they're reminding all Magiford supernaturals why the elves were wiped out.

Even if Noctus wanted to step forward, it would be a PR nightmare with some potentially violent consequences if Rigel's feelings are any indication.

In the past few years, some very beloved, very *powerful* people —like Queen Leila—had been threatened by elven magic. Those who loved those people, were likely to react to the idea of elves like Rigel had.

"I've got your steamer, Chloe." Joy stepped in between me and the door, returning warmth to my heart as she held up my to-go drink. "Do you want to drink it here, or at home?"

I glanced down at French Fry—he'd hunkered down in my arms and appeared to be sleeping, his little paws occasionally twitching. "Here's great. Thanks, Joy."

"Of course, thanks for not minding this pit stop!" Joy set my drink down on an end table before she settled herself on the couch next to it. "Also, we should think about getting French Fry a leg band or something. I'd suggest a collar, but with the amount of puking he does, that's probably not wise."

The icy feeling in my bones warmed under the onslaught of my sister's love. "Why do you think he needs a leg band?" I sat down, splaying the trash griffin out on my lap.

"Because if he starts following you into buildings like this, you're going to need some kind of indicator that shows proof of ownership." Joy winked before she took a sip of her drink. "Gosh, caffeine is better than any fae potion, I'm telling you."

I laughed, mentally tucking away my painful thoughts.

Noctus going public was the longest shot plan I came up with. Realizing it's not viable is okay. There must be a way. I can't give up.

A WEEK PASSED, and as October really settled into Magiford, Pat was still working longer hours.

The first time I finally saw him for more than a few minutes was the first night he'd decided to drive me to work since the attack downtown.

Pat was fiddling with his cellphone, trying to get it to start a music playlist, when I climbed into his car.

"Hey, stranger! How are you?" I kept my voice light and chatty, even though I was studying him with eagle-eyed precision.

He had dark circles under his eyes, but besides a general weariness he didn't seem *too* much the worse for wear. (I was especially encouraged that his clothes seemed clean-ish. Pat was infamous for sacrificing hygiene for work. His namesake of Patience perhaps hadn't been as perfectly in tune as Joy's.)

"Hey, Chloe." He smiled at me and tossed his cellphone into a cupholder, where it bounced off fast food wrappers and used napkins and ricocheted into my lap. "Sorry—I should clean the car out. One of the gophers from the Cloisters could be stowing away in here and I'd never know it."

"Don't worry, you've had bigger concerns. Except for the gophers, that is. The groundskeeper still hasn't caught them?"

"Nope. He tried spraying the lawn with castor oil and they still tore the place up. He's starting to get desperate enough that he asked one of my werewolf coworkers to hunt them down, but none of the shifters want to get near the holes since he threw some mothballs down them and that scent is too strong for their noses to take."

I buckled my seatbelt—Pat wouldn't move until I did—then adjusted the dagger strapped to my side so it didn't dig into my stomach. "If the groundskeeper is asking you guys for help, I take it that means things are finally slowing down?"

"Finally," Pat grunted as he put the car into drive and pulled away from the apartment building. "How's it going with your training?"

"Good." I flipped my satchel open, brandishing the huge three-ring-binder—after testing, I'd discovered neither of my siblings could see its real size, either—that had become my constant companion. "I'm finding there aren't many powers I wasn't already aware of, it's more like I didn't necessarily know the scale."

Pat turned on his blinker, then checked over his shoulder like the perfect driver he was before making the turn. "Like falling from heights?"

"Yes," I slowly answered, again feeling a pang of guilt for not telling my siblings about the hours Noctus and I had spent clock-tower diving.

Thankfully, I'd finally been able to tell them about the ability—Charon had included an incredibly detailed section on the physics behind the ability, complete with drawings of a fuzzy little black cat I was pretty sure Noctus had made based on how big the cat's eyes were and that it appeared to be losing fur while jumping.

"There are opportunities for me to hone some skills." I set the binder in my lap, but refrained from opening it. "As of now, I can just sense magic and supernaturals since most of them ooze some form of it. I should be able to better sense *where* and *who* the sensations are coming from. I also should be able to get my powers to work on others as long as I'm touching them," I said.

My relay race with the elves had proven that I could do it with my ability to escape notice, but what I really wanted was to see if I could get my immunity to magic to spread to others. So far, my practice said no, but I couldn't find anything in Noctus's notes that said I couldn't.

"Any advice for your cat form?" Pat asked.

We were downtown now, so the streetlights lit up his blond hair and washed away the dark circles under his eyes.

"No." My forehead puckered as I tried not to judge my ancestors. "It seems like they didn't value the cat form for much more than sneaking around."

"That's short sighted." Pat flicked on the windshield wipers when a drizzly mist began to fall. "You use that power more than any of your other abilities."

"Yeah," I agreed. "You would have thought they would have at least noted it makes it super easy to smuggle weapons or food or something if you swap between shapes."

"Remember how we used to use you to transport piles of leaves?" Pat laughed as he turned off main street, heading south toward Book Nookery.

"Yes." I laughed at the memory.

Pat and Joy used to rake the leaves onto a tarp, then bundle it up so I could barely hold it off the ground before turning into a cat and one of them carried me to the collection spot farther down our street where I'd turn human and dump the leaves with no effort.

"If a couple of humans and a kid shadow figured out how to exploit your cat form, I imagine your ancestors must have, too. Even if it wasn't recorded." Pat glanced up at the clocktower as we passed by it on our way into the southern neighborhoods.

"Yeah," I agreed. "Though something tells me they probably weren't using their abilities to make yardwork easier."

I felt a prickle of elf magic, followed by an overwhelming sense of fear that rattled my bones.

"Pat! The tracker—"

Before I could finish the warning, something slammed into the front of Pat's car, *crushing* the bumper.

Pat's airbag inflated with a blasting pop that made my ears ring, though I could still hear Pat's mutters.

"Tracker," I repeated as I struggled to unbuckle my seat belt and yank my leather harness and short sword from my backpack.

My danger instincts were lighting up my brain—but it was a little late for that.

"Understood." Pat grabbed his cellphone from me, his thumb almost scraping the call button when elf magic burned in my mind, and seconds later the window of his car door shattered, showering us with glass.

The sensation of fear and darkness was so close, the hair on the back of my neck stood on end. *No, no, no!*

"Drop the cellphone." The tracker stood outside Pat's door, holding a handgun level with Pat's head.

CHAPTER SEVENTEEN

Chloe

All air left my lungs.

"Drop the cellphone and get out of the car," the tracker repeated. "*Now*."

Pat glanced at me, mutiny in his eyes.

"*Don't*," I warned him in a whisper.

The tracker pistol whipped Pat, who grunted as he fell back in his seat.

The tracker pressed his handgun to Pat's temple with one hand and snatched up Pat's phone with the other, flinging it over his shoulder.

"Shadow, get out of the car." The tracker racked his handgun, loading a bullet. "*Now*."

I opened the door and slowly got out, my leather harness only half on and my backpack falling on the pavement. My heart was beating erratically, and already my hands were starting to sweat.

The tracker stayed by Pat's side, his eyes on me as he opened Pat's door. "Out, human," he said.

Pat, his hands raised, eased his way out of the car, uncoiling so he stood next to the half elf.

I watched my brother, trusting him. *He'll make an opening, I just have to take advantage of it.*

"Now," the tracker purred. "Back away—"

Pat struck like a snake, his hands coming up under the tracker's, forcing the gun to point toward the sky.

He tried to knee the tracker in the groin, but the half elf had already leaped backwards, releasing the gun into Pat's hands.

I shrugged on my harness and unsheathed my sword during the struggle, before turning into a cat and darting under the car.

By the time I emerged on the other side, Pat had the gun pointed at the tracker, who seemed remarkably unconcerned with the change of power.

"Drop the gun," the tracker said.

Pat narrowed his eyes and opened his mouth to refuse, and the tracker snapped his fingers.

Elf magic grazed my ribs, and a circle carved into the road lit up, illuminating the five terrified humans sitting in it.

Their hands and feet were zip tied together, and duct tape had been smoothed over their mouths, keeping them silent.

The glowing circle underneath them had to be the source of elf magic. It was an angry red color, made up of interlocking script that I recognized as elvish.

Oh, no. My stomach squeezed into a knot. *He's got us.*

"Drop the gun," the tracker repeated. "Or they'll be destroyed."

A muscle twitched in Pat's jaw, but he flicked the safety of the gun back on, then held one hand up in the air before he bent over, setting the gun down on the ground in front of him.

I flicked my tail, trying to judge if I could scurry back under the car since the tracker seemed most keen on Pat at the moment.

"Stay, shadow." The tracker retrieved his gun and pointed it at Pat.

It still had the safety on, but that would only stop him for a second, and I was not going to play around with my brother's life.

My heart thundered in my chest, and the tracker smiled. "Finally, I have you boxed in. It took long enough to figure out how exactly to pin you—you're so *obnoxiously* unusual. But now that I know the trick, it's simple enough." He kept the gun trained on Pat. "He's your weakness, and those sheep are his weakness. To keep you in line, I just have to threaten a gaggle of humans."

The instinct to run boiled in my gut, rapidly replaced by absolute focus as I stared up at the tracker, who'd just threatened my *brother*.

The tracker flicked the safety off his gun as the magic circle under the humans burned from the angry red to an orange the color of a raging fire. "So, shadow. Answer my questions, or I'll shoot him *and* release the curse on the humans."

I listened, not just to the tracker, but to the sounds of the city, hoping beyond hope that someone would come this way—we were standing in the middle of the street! Just one car, that was all I needed.

I could hear the purr of the car engines, but they were farther away—probably over on main street. Beyond that, nothing except for the occasional explosion of feathers as a city pigeon flew past.

"Shadow, *pay attention*!" the tracker growled. "Turn into your true shape."

I glanced at Pat, but he wouldn't look away—he didn't take his eyes off the tracker.

I tapped the change, and in a moment I was standing next to my brother in my human shape.

"Hands up," the tracker ordered.

I slowly held my hands up, though I didn't trouble myself to keep them away from my body. The second I got the chance, I was grabbing my sword—because I was *going* to get a chance.

There was no way I was letting this creep hurt my brother, or the humans he'd captured.

The question was, could I do it *without* getting myself shot at?

"First question," the tracker said. "Who trained you?"

Something tightened around my heart, squeezing it in my chest. "I wasn't trained by shadows," I slowly said, trying to figure out how to mislead him. I couldn't let him find out about Calor Villa—Noctus had said there was a chance the guy would turn into a full blown zealot if he realized more elves had survived.

I'd go down fighting first.

I licked my lips. "I was self-taught—"

"You use an *elven sword*, shadow," the tracker snarled. "You couldn't be self-taught. You can't even buy an elven forged sword these days!"

Pat finally looked at me, whipping his head so fast in my direction he must have cracked his neck.

Darn it. Even after we get out of this, Pat is going to be all over me.

I'd avoided explaining any details about my sudden sword skills to my siblings, telling them the people I'd stayed with in the spring and early summer had taught me. But while neither of them could have recognized the forge pattern of my sword, Pat knew enough about supernatural society to know that anything elven made would *not* be owned by an unimportant, overlooked supernatural like myself.

"Where did you get the sword, and who taught you to use it?" the tracker continued. "You aren't worthy of wielding it, and yet you *move* so—you don't fight like a shadow, fae, or vampire. Why, *why* do you fight like an elf?"

The tracker swung his gun so it was no longer trained on Pat, but me.

Big mistake.

"I *know* there are more elves," the tracker ranted. "You found them, didn't you? You *killed* them—"

I drew the dagger secured to my shoulder strap, yanked it free of the leather tie that held it in place whenever I needed to be upside down, and threw it at the tracker.

It grazed his free hand—I was more concerned about the spell on the humans than the gun. (I didn't like pain, but I could drink fae potions, so I could rebound faster than Pat or the others.)

The tracker said something in elvish and snapped his fingers, and I noticed the spell circle that had surrounded the humans grew, expanding toward us. Next he swung the gun back to Pat, but I'd reached the tracker by then, pushing his arm down so the gun was pointed at the ground.

Elves are fast, but shadows are faster.

My throat squeezed with anxiety when orange light started to crawl across the paved road, and I realized he'd expanded the circle so *we* now stood in it.

Pat!

I needed to take the tracker out, now. A headbutt would have worked best, but, of course, he was *too tall*! So I ground my heel on his foot.

When he tried to leap backwards and get away—like he had with Pat—I turned into a cat and jumped onto his shoulder, then turned back into a human, landing on top of him.

Unprepared for my sudden weight, the tracker fell.

I landed on my feet, then slammed my left foot down on his right hand—the one that held his gun.

The tracker shouted and reflexively let go of the gun.

I didn't kick it—Pat had raised me better—but I kicked his hand away from the weapon before standing on his wrist again, trusting my brother to secure the handgun.

The tracker pinched the middle finger and thumb of his left hand together.

He's going to snap!

Remembering how he'd made the magic circle appear, I lunged for his left hand and wrenched his fingers apart.

Unfortunately, that put me in a vulnerable position, stretched out across him with my torso and chest unprotected.

The tracker realized this too. He slammed his head into my side—which didn't hurt, but it did make me waver so I was off balance—tipping me just enough so the tracker could yank his limbs free.

I heard Pat move behind us—hopefully he was getting the gun.

I gritted my teeth as the tracker did some tricky self-defense move I didn't know, flinging me to the side so our positions were swapped with me pinned to the ground. Gravel dug into my back, and he held my arms pinned.

"You pestilence," the tracker growled, before he shouted something—presumably in elvish.

I braced myself, but instead of feeling any pain, I heard muffled screaming.

I peeled my head off the ground and saw the humans stuck in the circle were writhing.

There was a clack that sounded like a gun falling, and Pat collapsed to his knees, his jaw clenched and sweat breaking out on his forehead.

The spell was affecting him, too, since it had expanded.

Stop him—I have to stop him!

I turned into a cat, slipping out of the tracker's grasp, but he fell on top of me before I could slide out from underneath him.

"Be still, shadow, or I'll increase their pain," he warned.

I froze.

The tracker smirked as he slowly peeled himself off me, grasping my middle with his hands to keep me secure. "Do you know how little pain it takes to incapacitate a human?" he asked.

I panted, my fear roaring back as I tried to look at Pat, but the tracker blocked my view.

"Just a little tweak," the tracker said in a conversational tone. "Like this." He said something in elvish again, and the bound humans convulsed. Pat screamed, his voice raw with pain.

My instincts yelled at me that I needed to turn human—to do *something* to help Pat and the others.

But if I move, he'll hurt them worse.

The tracker laughed over the moans of pain, and through the confusing haze I felt more elf magic scrape at my ribs—more than I should have sensed since the circle was the only active spell.

Does he have something else up his sleeve? Should I act now because it will only get worse?

Pinned in my feline form, my thoughts were a confused muddle, and still the tracker laughed.

Until a bright magic slammed into his side and sent him hurtling through the air, hitting the asphalt so hard he rolled several times before finally coming to a stop.

I changed into my human form and twisted around, reaching for my sword as I tried to face this possible friend or foe.

Prydwen stood on the sidewalk, his sleeves rolled up to reveal his arm tattoos that glowed yellow like the magic that had smacked into the tracker.

A motion of his fingers, and the bright magic that hovered over the tracker zoomed back to Prydwen, giving me a glimpse of what looked like a bowling ball sized bird that had an enormous head, small beak, and whose very essence seemed to radiate magic.

Prydwen nodded to me, and there was something stony about his expression—maybe it was the way the spirals in his eyes seemed to glitter as he stared down the tracker.

Behind me, the tracker roared.

I pivoted to face him, boosting out of my crouch as I pulled my sword free.

The tracker started to stand, until a spear pinned the back of his jacket to the ground.

Following the path of the spear, I looked to the other side of the street and saw Oleander, pulling another spear out of a book sized portal. I barely recognized her, even though she still had her long, blond hair and was wearing a ruffled skirt and a beige trench coat, her expression was so hard and foreign, like Prydwen's.

It took me a few moments to realize, I was seeing them as *fighters*; this was what they *could* be, not what they chose to be.

"There's a pack of humans two blocks up, coming this way," Oleander called. "We need to finish this fast."

I was already sprinting toward the tracker, my sword drawn.

He'd shrugged out of his coat, and was raising his fingers to snap before Prydwen's shining bird smashed into his hand, stopping the motion.

I was on him before he could do anything more. *I have to disable him—so he can't say anything—or snap!*

I clamped my hand around his mouth and then smashed him on the side of the head with the hilt of my sword. His breath rattled as he fell to his knees.

I ruthlessly kicked him—slamming my heel on the small of his back—and he collapsed to the ground.

I fixed my grip on my sword as I stood over the wheezing tracker.

"I called backup, but we still need to finish this quickly. Aren't you going to kill him?" Oleander asked as she strode across the sidewalk, her heels echoing in the eerie silence of the street.

I licked my lips as I stared down at the tracker.

He'd caused me so much pain—he'd hurt my *family*. My sword felt like it burned my hand, and all my instincts screamed that killing him was the only way.

But...I couldn't.

And not because the Paragon and Queen Leila wanted to question him, but because *I* couldn't.

I'd fight—to the death if my family was threatened. But this was a line I couldn't cross, and I wasn't going to go against everything I was just for him.

I shook my head. "No, I'll call it in to the Curia Cloisters. They're eager to question him."

Oleander snapped off a nod. "Understood. We'll hold him while you make the call?" Holding a new spear, she strode closer, beckoning for Prydwen to join her.

Prydwen's brightly colored bird circled overhead.

I kept my sword at the tracker's throat until Oleander could take my place. Then I jogged over to Pat and crouched at his side.

"Are you okay?" I asked.

Pat waved me off. "Make the call," he grunted.

I retreated to the car, my fingers clumsy with my relief as I unzipped my backpack and grabbed my phone from an inner pocket.

"Y-you're elves," the tracker said as he started to come out of it.

"Don't speak," Oleander ordered in the coldest voice I'd ever heard.

Keeping my sword unsheathed, I unlocked my phone, then headed back to Pat.

"How could you help a *shadow?*" the tracker demanded.

Prydwen held his arm out and his bird landed on it. "He seems unwilling to stop talking. Why don't you muzzle him?" Prydwen idly suggested, his voice lacking emotion and warmth.

"A good idea," Oleander said.

I opened my phone app. *When they get serious, they really go for it.*

I was just about to punch the phone number when the tracker shouted.

Before Oleander could stop him, he yanked some kind of necklace from his neck, breaking the leather cord, and slapped it onto the asphalt.

Onyx colored magic formed under the necklace, then streaked

outwards like a bursting star, shooting branches out at Oleander, Prydwen, Pat, and the humans.

The magic grew out of the ground like tendrils of ivy, and coiled around them. As the tendrils grew around its targets, I saw the magic left scorch marks in Pat's and Oleander's clothing.

It must have been unimaginably painful. Pat's back arched, and Prydwen fell as if he'd been kicked, a keening noise ripping free from his mouth.

The magic tried to ensnare me, attempting to twine around my legs, but the second it touched me, it fizzled and died.

But I wouldn't have minded the pain—the muffled screams of the humans trapped in the circle and Pat's shouts tore my heart open.

"This is forbidden magic," Oleander ground out between clenched teeth. "How does he have it? He can't have this kind of power, not as a half—" She broke off in a choked exhale, too pained to keep talking.

Forbidden? This must be dark magic, then. I need to stop it—now.

I was on the tracker before he could stand, standing over him as I tried to figure out how the spell worked.

The necklace—he used it to start it!

The broken leather cord had a pendant made of a black stone, but it looked weirdly liquid, and it didn't seem to reflect any light.

I aimed my sword at it and thrust down, intending to impale it.

The moment my sword touched the necklace, lights flashed, and the recoil nearly threw me off my feet. The entire sword shook, rattling my hands so hard I couldn't feel my fingers. If it had been anything less than elven made, it probably would have shattered.

The tracker laughed as he picked himself up off the ground, holding the necklace. "It would take a lot more power than *you* can wield, shadow, to destroy an elf made artifact!"

He yanked Oleander's spear from her limp fingers and pointed it at me. "Now, submit—or the pain they're in will only grow, and it will peel away at their bodies, layer by layer."

A sob caught in my throat as the screams grew louder.

I'm not strong enough...I must give in.

"Okay, whatever you want, just stop!" I shouted.

"Not so fast," he said. "First, I want you to suffer—through their pain." The tracker's nose was bleeding—that was probably Oleander's handiwork—and his mussed hair gave him more of a crazy aura than normal, but I trembled as Prydwen's shouts grew in pitch, his voice going hoarse from the pain.

The smell of burnt hair was starting to fill the air—I could only imagine how much pain my brother and the others were in.

"Stop it!" Tears of desperation clogged my throat, and I couldn't arrange my thoughts—did I attack him? But if this necklace was indestructible even if I killed him, would the spell stop?

The sour smell of blood was starting to fill the air, and the screams were growing weaker—they were hurting because of *me*.

"Stop it!" I shouted. "Just stop it! I surrender—just stop!" The last of it came out in a sob as I dropped my sword and held my hands up.

There was a tickle in my elbow that was similar to fae magic, but I was too frantic to trace it.

The tracker swaggered up to me, pulling another handgun from his coat. "I'm going to enjoy this," he informed me when he slid a magazine into the handgun, then racked the slide, loading a bullet.

He aimed at my heart.

I shut my eyes, and I felt a ripple of power followed by a dim roar. Then the tracker screamed.

CHAPTER EIGHTEEN

Noctus

I leaned back in my chair, reviewing an expense report for the clocktower in the quiet of my study. After the artifact incidents I'd decided to risk adding additional protection to the clocktower as it was a possible target considering its size and the sheer number of people who passed through it. But the tower manager had also put in a request for funds to purchase Christmas decorations, and I was struggling to understand how one could spend tens of thousands of dollars on such a thing.

Ker was lounging on the new settee Charon had selected for my office this past summer—we needed it to be the same size as the previous couch for Aristide's sake—eating jerky with a thoughtful expression, the kind that usually meant a Dale Carnegie lecture was incoming.

Aristide set his wine glass filled with blood down on the coffee table with an irritated clack. "*Must* you masticate your food like a dog gnawing on a bone?"

"I am a wolf," Ker said.

"Who chews like a t-rex."

"Hey!"

The argument created just enough noise to cover the never-ending ringing noise of wild magic that still hadn't ceased its pouting, so I ignored it and turned a page in the expense sheet. *Just how many Christmas trees does one building need? And why must they all be themed? Gingerbread, forest animals, Nutcracker, cats—cats? Well...I suppose if they want to put so many trees up, they might as well have different themes.*

Charon threw open the door of my study, his expression unusually tense and grim. He clutched his cellphone with what was nearing too much strength. "Chloe is in trouble."

I stood up before I realized what I was doing. "What?"

Ker had been waving a piece of jerky at Aristide, but at Charon's announcement she rocketed upright. "Where? How?"

"Downtown, by the clocktower," Charon reported. "The tracker has a group of humans he's using as hostages against her and her brother."

Aristide stood from his favorite chair, seemingly fidgeting with his jacket but really checking his daggers. "How did you find out?"

"Oleander called it in," Charon said. "There are humans nearby—if any of them happen on the street the tracker will likely grab them, too, as additional hostages."

Aristide said something in French—a language I'd always been bad at, but I was certain the phrase involved a blight on the tracker's parents for birthing a monster.

"He knows she won't let anyone get hurt," I said.

"Yeah," Ker grimly agreed. "He's got her figuratively pinned."

"Your call, Noctus," Aristide said.

I silently stared at my desk, trying to lock down the roar in my heart that demanded blood. *He's fighting Chloe. Chloe! If he hurts her, I'll rip him from—*

I cut the thought out, grinding my jaw as I tried to balance my emotions. I *couldn't* be impulsive. Acting publicly could reveal my entire realm.

"Noctus?" Ker asked.

"Anonymously call the Curia Cloisters," I said. "Tell them what's going on."

I wanted more than anything to race to Chloe's side, but my entire existence was *for* duty. I couldn't, no matter how badly I personally wanted to.

"That might be problematic," Charon carefully said. "Oleander intended to help her, as did Prydwen. He sent me a text about the issue and had already called his summon. If we notify the Cloisters, Oleander and Prydwen might be seen."

"They're using magic? On the streets of Magiford?" I stared incredulously at Charon. I was a careful ruler, but as I had noted before, I ruled over an anxiety ridden, fearful people who wanted to avoid discovery more than anything else. "Why would they take such a risk?"

"I imagine it's because of *you*," Aristide said. "They know she's important to you."

I shook my head. "I'm little more than the bogey they hide behind to keep the realm running. Why would they risk revealing what they are for me?"

"Because they know why you fought your parents and siblings, dismantling your entire family." This statement, shockingly, came from Charon, his gaze steady and steely as he met my eyes. "Because they know, if you could, you'd risk everything for Chloe. But you feel like you can't as our king, so they will on your behalf."

My fingers itched to reach for the dagger set I had hidden in the top drawer of my desk as I desperately tried to calm the inner turmoil.

Was it really acceptable? Involving myself with Chloe inevitably meant we'd have to come forward, particularly now since supernaturals knew she was a shadow. We'd face hatred for certain. As a king could I really put my people through that, when I was the reason they lived like this?

But Chloe...

"I'll say it again, Noctus," Aristide said. "Your call."

I'd dedicated my life to duty—duty to my lands, duty to magic, and now duty to my people. Could I really allow myself this one thing, even if it changed my life and the lives of my people, forever?

Everyone was silent—even the ever-sulking wild magic held its peace.

I briefly closed my eyes, and I swear I heard Chloe laugh and felt the warmth she brought into my life. In that moment, I made my choice.

"Hoo, I just picked up on an increased heartbeat, we're going!" Aristide crowed.

"We're not just going." I glanced down at the shackles on my wrists and released a bit of my power. The shackles cracked in half, falling onto my paper covered desk with a thump. "We're ending this."

Freed from the constraints on my magic, I extended my hand and reached into my weapon storage portal.

CHAPTER NINETEEN

Chloe

When I opened my eyes, a segment of the top layer of the asphalt had melted and peeled off the road.

The tracker was splayed at the end of the melted patch, his entire body shaking and his clothes smoldering.

The sensation of elven magic was so strong it was hard to breathe, and my heart beat faster in my chest—not with dread, but hope.

Steeling myself, I turned around.

A knight wearing a dark gray tabard that was decorated with embroidery of roaring black lions along the slashed front hem, metal gauntlets, pauldrons, and boots stood there, silent. He held a rapier forged of black metal that had black lions that formed the curved guard and knuckle guard. Three circles formed from glowing black elvish script spun around the pommel of the rapier, the center of the blade, and the point. The script constantly changed and circled the rapier, making me pretty sure it was an elven heirloom weapon.

Noctus.

I knew it was him, even though I couldn't see his face.

He's here. He came! ...and he's using a royal weapon? What is he doing?!

There was no hiding the usage of a weapon like that—there would be way too much magic used. Noctus was practically announcing to all Magiford that he existed!

Questions later, tracker first!

Noctus pointed his head in my direction, and behind him Aristide, Charon, and Ker—in her wolf form—stepped out of the shadows.

"Careful!" I yelled. "There are humans nearby, and he's got a spell—forbidden elf magic!"

The onyx magic was still streaming out from the necklace, crawling over Pat, Oleander, Prydwen, and the humans.

The tracker had dropped the necklace next to me—he must have lost control of his limbs when Noctus hit him with that blast.

I hesitated, caught between running for Pat, trying to stop the necklace, or going after the tracker, but the choice was made for me when Noctus stepped off the curb into the street, heading for the half elf.

I'd better focus on the spell—standing next to Pat isn't going to help him when that pendant is torturing him.

Gingerly, I picked up the necklace. The onyx magic lashed out at me, but, again, it couldn't do anything except drift across my skin. I'd hoped lifting it off the street would stop it, but the magic flowed on, burning everyone within reach.

I twisted around, hoping to ask Charon for a hint, but Charon, Aristide, and Ker drifted off, disappearing into the soupy darkness of the night. It was then that I noticed that the spell hadn't spared Noctus.

The onyx vines of magic crawled up his legs, leaving black marks on his armor, and tendrils of smoke drifted off him where the magic touched his clothes.

Noctus didn't react, but he had to have felt it as he strode across the street, the magic seeping through his armor.

It's affecting Noctus, too? I need to stop it, now! But how?

Noctus picked up the tracker by the collar of his jacket and casually tossed him—as if he were a couch cushion. While the tracker flew through the air, Noctus slashed his rapier, the sword's blade glowing with magic and light.

The black elven script that floated around the weapon lightened to a gray, and a beam of light shot from the blade's point, enveloping the tracker, who screamed.

Still holding the necklace, I scrambled over to Pat—no longer worried about the tracker. I didn't want to touch Pat with the necklace and risk making things worse, so I set it down in the street, then stepped on it. Confident it was secure, I tried to rip the vines of magic off him.

Wherever I touched the magic squashed flat, but it kept on crawling across him, leaving burn marks in its wake. My touch didn't make it disintegrate; it just couldn't touch *me*.

This isn't helping!

Noctus was still whaling on the tracker. The half elf had tried to get up and run, but Noctus got in front of him and kicked his knees out from underneath him before slamming him into the ground with an impact I could hear.

Despite all of that, the spell hadn't stopped.

The necklace must not be keyed into him. To stop the spell, we must destroy it. Noctus could probably pull that off, but he can't right now, so how do I negate it?

An idea glowed in my mind, one that I really didn't like, and had a good chance of not working, but I'd try *anything* at this point.

I impulsively grabbed the necklace and ripped the black pendant off the cord.

The pendant had grit from the street on it, and the flitting thought that I was going to get a disease from this crossed my mind, but the onyx magic still streamed out from it, harming everyone in the area.

I must try.

I took a breath, then popped the pendant in my mouth, snapping my teeth shut so it was completely encased in my mouth.

Abruptly, the magic that had pulsed out of the necklace cut off.

"*What did you do?*" the tracker shouted at me.

Noctus seemingly hadn't knocked him senseless yet. His hair was wild, and blood dribbled from his nose, but his eyes were bulging in shock and maybe five kinds of horror.

He stared at me, until Noctus struck him with the flat of his blade, making him face plant on the ground.

I kept my mouth shut—no way was I opening it and risking the magic getting out.

Please work, please work!

The pendant was smooth like a marble, but it was tinged with the taste of dirt from the street. The sensation of elf magic was so strong it made my ribs throb, but no magic could wriggle past my lips—I'd successfully caged the spell.

As I watched, the onyx tendrils of magic curling around Pat started to shrivel, unable to connect with their power base.

The vine-y spell died on Noctus as well, drying up before disintegrating.

The sense of relief was even stronger than the motor oil taste that was filling my mouth from the street-soiled pendant.

Yes! This is it!

The tracker was still screaming, seemingly unhinged by my actions. "Why would you *do* that? Who even *thinks* like that?" He scraped himself off the road and tried to lunge at me, blind to the danger that was Noctus.

Noctus grabbed him from behind, dragging him backwards and away from me.

I ignored his shouts and concentrated on keeping my mouth shut while I fixed my hold on my sword, my feeling back in my fingers.

Well. Now what?

I couldn't swallow the pendant—it was way too big. But I didn't want to run around with it in my mouth—even now I could feel it fighting to get free. If I didn't keep my teeth clenched shut...

Oleander was able to tear the vine-y spell off her, and after she staggered to her feet—I could see awful burn marks through the new holes in her clothes—she hurried to the humans, grabbing the dying magic and tearing it off them.

Prydwen's bird helped free him, pulling a tendril off his face before he and the creature staggered off to help Oleander and the humans.

Pat, more delicate than the two elves in his human body, groaned. "Chloe?"

I crouched next to him, trying to touch where the magic hadn't burned him.

"What happened?" Pat coughed, his voice hoarse, then looked up, blinking with bloodshot eyes. "Who's the knight?"

I gently patted his shoulder—unable to answer him.

"I'll kill you!" the tracker shouted, his eyes wild as he tried to crawl across the street toward me. "I'll never stop until I've spilled your blood! Leadership said to ignore you, but I knew better!"

"You will stop," Noctus said, his voice so dark and raspy I barely recognized it. "Or you will die." There was something about the roughness of his voice—he sounded less controlled than usual, more on edge.

"No." The tracker ignored Noctus, even though the elf king

placed his foot on the tracker's back and pushed him flat against the ground. "She's a shadow, her blood *must* be spilled, it's my life calling!" The markings on his neck glowed as he—in his apparent insanity—tried to summon magic and pointed his finger at me.

"Then your life is over." Noctus's rapier exploded with light so bright I had to close my watering eyes.

When the light faded, I risked opening an eye.

The tracker was collapsed on the ground, his eyes glossy with the vacant stare of death, his body motionless.

He was dead.

For a moment, my relief was so strong it made me dizzy.

I was safe again. Pat and Joy were safe. My *family* was safe.

It was followed by a swift stab of guilt. I didn't want to be the kind of person who rejoiced over death, and the Curia Cloisters had wanted to question him for his possible connections to that shadowy organization.

But the weight of fear that had dogged my every step for months was gone. It was over!

Noctus nudged the tracker with his boot, flipping him over. With his helm on I couldn't tell what he was thinking, but it seemed like he was following old training as he crouched down next to the tracker—still holding his rapier with his right hand—and searched the body.

I opened my mouth to release the biggest sigh of my life.

A wisp of onyx magic drifted out of my mouth.

Shoot! The spell is still going!

I snapped my teeth shut with enough force that I felt the click inside my skull. *How are we going to destroy this thing? Maybe Noctus can break it with his rapier? I should find my cellphone so I can type out questions and answers since I can't talk.*

I wasn't too bothered by this twist; my trouble was coming to an end, after all. The spell was a problem, but so was the destroyed asphalt, and the captives.

Oleander said there were humans nearby, I can't believe they didn't wander here yet.

I puffed my cheeks as I rolled the pendant around my mouth.

I kept my hand on Pat's back as he recovered and watched Noctus search the tracker, until Aristide reappeared about a block up. I nearly swallowed the pendant and choked when I saw who was with him.

The Paragon, wearing a green cloak and turban, strode at Aristide's side, his hands glowing with magic.

Murphy's law strikes again—the worst-case scenario is here! Not only is he going to see Noctus at full power, he'll see Oleander and Prydwen, too!

Magic swamped my senses as it always did whenever I saw the Paragon, and my powers were all too eager to peel back the magic and show what his glamour hid.

My eyes blurred with tears, and my nose would have probably instantly plugged if I didn't tilt my head back and frantically snort for air.

No! We aren't doing this. I can't open my mouth to breathe!

"The perimeter is secured. Hello, Chloe." The Paragon strutted across the road. "I have a shield up, keeping the noise and mess inside and the general population outside, good riddance. But what is going on here?"

Well, that explains the flicker of fae magic I felt earlier.

Pat was able to stand, his knees shaking, but a stubborn expression settled on his face.

I hovered at his side, wanting to lecture him, but I *couldn't open my mouth!*

Oleander and Prydwen ignored the Paragon—they were too busy cutting the humans free of their zip ties—and now that Aristide had delivered the Paragon he seemingly felt his duties were done, as he slowly made his way up to me.

He tilted his head, likely listening to my heartbeat. "Chloe?"

I reached out to touch him, setting a hand on his arm.

Aristide frowned. "You can't talk?"

"She stuffed a spell in her mouth." Pat's voice was hoarse, and when he coughed, it sounded wet and painful. "I'm pretty sure it's still active, her magic is just holding it back. Who are you?"

Aristide smiled enigmatically. "A family friend."

"I'm her family," Pat said harshly. "*Who are you?*"

"He's trustworthy," the Paragon declared. "What matters is what's going on right now?"

Pat—oblivious to who the Paragon was—put a protective arm in front of me, attempting to make me back up toward his car. "We're not saying anything until backup from the Cloisters arrives," Pat said.

I made an assortment of grunts, which Pat understandably failed to interpret.

The Paragon's frown turned wary as he saw Noctus with the tracker's body. "Wait, someone was killed?"

I wildly nodded as I dodged around Pat's arm.

The Paragon, however, didn't notice me. He was studying Noctus.

"Noctus?" he called.

Noctus turned his head so his helm was pointed in the Paragon's direction.

"It *is* you! You have a lot to answer for!" He strode toward Noctus, and I hurried after him.

"Chloe!" Pat tried to follow me, then groaned—slowed by his injuries.

Sorry, Pat. I'll make sure you get medical attention, but this could be a disaster!

"What is—no—*who* did you kill?!" The Paragon's voice turned angry.

Noctus stood up. "This is the half elf who has been trying to kill Chloe." His voice was still extra deep and growly.

The Paragon didn't seem to notice this. He planted his fists on his hips and puffed his chest up. "And so you *killed* him?"

"As I said, he was trying to kill Chloe."

"He was a lead to the organization—"

"I don't *care* about your personal goals and concerns," Noctus interrupted, his voice even darker than it was before. "He was a threat to Amalourne, he had to be eliminated."

"Amalourne?" the Paragon repeated. "You mean Chloe—wait, *Amalourne*?" The Paragon turned around, this time to face me. "Ama? *You're* Ama? And you pretended not to know each other?"

I saw the stirrings of real anger kindle in the Paragon. Instead of puffing up and getting louder, he seemed to draw in on himself, and his voice got quiet. "What is going on?" he asked. "And why are there other *elves* here?"

This is what I wanted to avoid!

Noctus ignored the Paragon's wrath and stepped around him, drawing closer to me. "You stopped the spell—the one tied to the necklace?"

I nodded.

Noctus slid his gloved hands under my chin and gently tilted my head so I was looking at him again. "It's still going?"

"Mmhmm." I puffed my cheeks and pointed to my mouth. I nervously glanced at the Paragon. He was watching with narrowed eyes, still upset.

Oleander, having finished helping the humans, came trotting up to us, her manner brisk despite her ruffled skirt, heels, and ripped clothes. "Your Majesty, have you any orders?"

Her question made the Paragon's eyes narrow further.

Noctus kept his hand under my chin, but he pivoted slightly so he faced the humans. "The captives?"

"Freed," Oleander said. "And injured. They will require medical attention. I believe Pat Anderson is trying to decide if he should call the Cloisters for medical attention, or come over here to see to his sister."

I had to stand on my tiptoes and peer around Noctus to see my brother. Pat was walking with a limp, and he'd found my cellphone, but he hadn't dialed it yet. His eyes were stuck on me as he tried to make up his mind.

I shook my head at him. *Wait, please.* I motioned to my mouth, and again shook my head. *I need to get Noctus out of here, and we need to get this spell taken care of first!*

"We have to handle the forbidden magic the tracker cast before we can call for backup, or they'll be gravely injured when they arrive," Noctus said, echoing my thoughts. "We'll destroy it now, taking advantage of the barrier the Paragon is maintaining to limit damage. Clear the area—have Prydwen get the humans a block or two up, then find Ker and Charon. They should be patrolling the borders."

Oleander bowed. "Understood, Your Highness." She jogged off, making a pit stop by Pat as she hopefully explained the plan to him before trotting on to Prydwen and the humans.

I was not so accepting of this idea. *Wouldn't it be better to take the necklace to Calor and destroy it there?* I hesitated for a moment, then reached up, placing my hand over the one Noctus held to my cheek.

Noctus looked down at me, still wearing his helm. "You think it would be better to take it to Calor and destroy it there?" he guessed.

How, exactly, can he read me so well? I nodded.

Noctus slid his hand from my cheek, down my neck, so it rested on my shoulder. "No. I won't risk you carrying that vile magic in your *mouth* through a portal."

"She really is Ama, isn't she?" the Paragon asked, his voice flat.

Noctus seemed content to ignore him, but I was all too aware that we'd need the Paragon's help to get through this without Noctus, Oleander, and Prydwen getting discovered, so I nodded.

The furrows in the Paragon's brow were so deep, Aphrodite could have stuck a paw in them. "Given context clues, I imagine there must be a great deal more elves that Noctus *did not* tell me about based on that one's conduct?" He flicked a finger at Oleander, who was leading the humans away.

That I was less inclined to answer. I looked up at Noctus and scooted a step closer to him.

A sigh leaked out of the Paragon, one that deflated him. "Fine," he said, sounding simultaneously young and old. "Fine, fine, fine. We'll handle whatever this wretched spell is, and then I want an explanation. What's the spell?"

"Elf magic," Noctus said, "of the dark variety, tied to a pendant that Chloe is holding in her mouth. It's anchored to the pendant, so we must break it to stop the spell, but fae magic won't work."

"Of course, it won't. I assume it must have some kind of weakness—though if you say the fires of a mountain volcano, be prepared to be tackled."

Noctus raised his rapier. "I can destroy it."

"Of course, you can, Mr. Overpowered," the Paragon groused. "Do you need help?"

"No," Noctus said. "As long as you maintain the barrier. This is going to be...loud."

"It just keeps getting better and better. In that case, I'm moving back." He started to turn away, then paused. "But there *will* be a reckoning for this, Noctus."

Noctus didn't answer him. He faced me, and his hand that rested on my shoulder slipped down my back, settling on my waist. "You'll spit the pendant out, Chloe, and set it on the ground, then get back," he said. "The magic won't harm you, but there will be a collision of power. You're going to feel that, even if you aren't affected."

A collision of power, that sounds fun.

"Chloe?" Pat, still holding my phone, limped closer to us, but hesitated a few steps away.

I pulled away from Noctus so I could approach my brother.

Pat studied me. "There's a lot you haven't been telling us, isn't there? He knows you. *Really* knows you."

I hung my head. *I'm sorry. I didn't know what else to do.*

Pat sighed. "I had a hunch something had happened before Joy and I were kidnapped, but..." He trailed off as he rubbed his face. "We must talk about this, but your knight is right. That spell is awful, and it needs to be destroyed."

I nodded so violently the pendant rattled around in my mouth.

Pat glanced down the street, where Aristide, Oleander, Prydwen, and the humans stood—Charon and Ker still weren't anywhere to be seen. "I'll wait to call—for a few minutes," Pat said. "And then you're telling me *everything.*"

Since I couldn't say anything, I reached up and gingerly hugged him, trying not to touch any of his wounds.

It's going to be okay. I'm not scared, don't worry.

I hoped my feelings got through the hug.

When I pulled back, Pat's face was set as he made the switch from big brother to work mode. He turned on his heel and headed toward the others, digging in his pocket for his wallet and badge. "My name is Pat Anderson, I'm with the task force from the Curia Cloisters..." he called as he walked up to them.

The humans immediately abandoned Oleander and Prydwen to cluster around him.

Excellent, now's the time to destroy the pendant. I did a quick scan of the area, trying to choose a suitable location.

We had to do this fast—the longer we delayed, the greater the chance someone was going to realize there was a giant fae barrier up.

Here. I walked up to the patch of asphalt that Noctus had already destroyed—no sense costing the city extra money for repairs, because if Noctus was afraid I was going to feel this "collision of power", there was no way the road was going to make it out just fine.

I crouched down next to the pavement, then looked up at Noctus, who had followed behind me.

Noctus raised his rapier—still holding it with one hand. The circles of glowing elvish script reappeared around his weapon. "Ready."

I spat the pendant into my palm and set it on the street before it could even flicker with magic, then I turned to a cat—my faster form for short distances—and sprinted off.

Just when I reached the sidewalk, I felt the throb of magic deep in my bones, followed by a horrible roaring noise.

Hurricane level winds ripped at my fur. I had to turn into a human to keep from being blown off my feet. Power rippled through my body, striking my bones and making them vibrate like a tuning fork.

I held my arm up over my eyes as I tried to look back at Noctus, but all I saw was white light. Above all the racket, I heard a click that reverberated through the street itself.

Slowly, the light faded, and silence descended on the street.

The air was thick with magic, which seemed to muffle every noise.

Everyone stared at Noctus, who stood motionless, his rapier thrust into the ground.

Unable to stand it any longer, I spat out the grit the pendant had transferred to my mouth.

This seemed to break the spell as Noctus pulled his rapier out of the ground. "It's destroyed," he announced.

More worried about getting some kind of disease or bacteria from the pendant than I was about social manners, I wiped my tongue off on the sleeve of my jacket as I trotted back to Noctus. "It's dead?"

"Cracked and deactivated." Noctus knelt as I reached him, picking up the cracked pendant that was now in two jagged pieces. "Not as cleanly as I would like, but it will do."

"That took a lot of power to break," I said.

"Destroying any elven artifact requires a great deal of power," Noctus said. "The stronger the artifact, the more power is needed to break it." He handed me the two pieces, dropping them in my palm.

I waited for a moment, tensed, trying to see if I could sense anything from the pendant. When I felt nothing, my shoulders slumped in relief.

It was over.

I exhaled and pocketed the pendant—I'd have to give it to the Cloisters since it was evidence, but I was not going to lose it. Then, my heart painfully full of hope, I threw my arms open wide as I boosted myself onto the tips of my toes.

CHAPTER TWENTY

Chloe

Noctus scooped me up, pinning me against his armored chest with one hand as he swept a gauntlet-clad hand through my hair to cradle the back of my head.

His armor dug into my skin and uncomfortably poked me, but it was the most precious hug I'd ever had.

"Thank you," I whispered. "Thank you for coming." Tears blurred my eyesight as I rested my forehead on his pauldron. It was cold, and the edges cut into my skin, but I didn't care.

"Always," Noctus said.

I started to nod, until his words finally caught up with my brain. "Wait, what?" I picked my head off his shoulder and peered up at him. "But—you can't. Even this—what are we going to do?" I was too afraid to say anything, so I tried to meaningfully glance at Oleander and Prydwen.

I couldn't get a read on Noctus thanks to the helm he still

hadn't taken off, but his hand was gentle as he smoothed my hair. "It's okay, Chloe," he said, his voice mellow and warm.

"No, it's not okay," I hiccupped. "How are you going to cover this up?"

"We won't," Noctus said.

"You won't?" I repeated.

"*We* won't," Noctus corrected.

No, I had to be misunderstanding him. There was no way the elves were coming forward. That would never happen.

"But...?" I started, but couldn't even find the words to say.

Noctus moved the neckline of my sweater, seemingly inspecting me. "Calor Villa will reveal itself."

I was afraid to breathe—anything I did might break the moment, and I'd find out it was all just a dream. "Then...we can...?"

"Yes."

A sob clogged my throat as I threw myself into Noctus's shoulder, holding him tighter.

In one moment, the agony that had endlessly torn at my heart was gone.

Everything wasn't right in the world, but this was what I'd wanted more than anything, and now it had come true.

All this time I spent turning plans over, trying to figure out how we could make this work with the fewest sacrifices possible...and Noctus does this.

A small part of me felt like I was being unbearably greedy and selfish—this was going to change Calor Villa and those living in it forever.

But I'd do everything I could to help them and—probably more helpfully given their positions—if I asked Pat and Joy, they would too.

I wanted to tell Noctus this, but I couldn't find the words. Not that it mattered—Noctus seemed fascinated by something on my neck, he kept rubbing his thumb against my throat.

"Amalourne indeed," the Paragon said, his voice cold enough to make me let go of Noctus and step back. "Well done. The spell is destroyed. How amazing. Now, explain what is going on!" He stalked back over to us, his body stiff. "How many elves are you hiding in that house of yours?"

Noctus adjusted his grip on his rapier. "Don't you want to know what happened here first?"

"No," the Paragon said. "Because right now you're the greater threat. I'm not asking anything the Curia Cloisters won't ask when they arrive."

"I stopped a supernatural who was attacking humans," Noctus said. "That hardly constitutes a threat."

The Paragon curled his bony hands into fists. "Don't try to paint yourself as a hero. You killed the biggest lead I found this year!"

I fidgeted, burning to defend Noctus, but my words were meaningless—I didn't even have the pull in the Cloisters that Pat had! I sneezed—the Paragon's stupid glamour was still affecting me.

"I gave the Cloisters *months* to handle him, and they didn't. If you wanted to question him so badly, you should have helped Chloe sooner," Noctus said, his already steely voice growing darker.

"It was our failing," the Paragon agreed. "We should have reacted faster—if I'd learned sooner what she said she was, I would have. But you—you've been lying this entire time! You're not the last of your kind, and your willingness to wear any kind of shackle on your magic is obviously a farce. You'd best prepare yourself, Noctus, because everything you've been trying to hide is going to come into the light."

Anger flickered in the Paragon's eyes, but Noctus accepted it unflinchingly.

This is just the start, I realized.

Everything I'd seen since returning home had proven to me

why Noctus hadn't wanted to come forward. Queen Leila and King Rigel's suspicions, the assumption that elves were inherently evil—it was going to be horrific.

And yet, he'd done it. For me.

Something wild flickered in me—the same kind of deadly calm that settled on me when the tracker had threatened my siblings, prodding me into stabbing him.

The Paragon and the Cloisters together would try to force Noctus's hand.

And I was going to stop them.

No matter what I do, the elves will have to come forward as part of this—it's unavoidable since the Paragon knows as much as he does. But. I can make sure they do it on their terms, and aren't coerced. And I know just how to do it.

"Do you understand, Noctus?" the Paragon asked. "The time for bargaining is over."

"No," I said.

The Paragon and Noctus turned toward me.

The scowl that had settled on the Paragon's lips tweaked in his confusion. "What?"

I lifted my chin, and whatever it was inside of me that had stirred the embers of strength ignited into a forest fire. "The Curia Cloisters won't be asking anything, because *you're* not going to tell them about this."

The Paragon laughed—his voice a lot younger than his appearance. "You seem to be under a mistaken impression, Chloe. I didn't trust Noctus before, but I thought I knew his situation. Turns out, I was a fool. That makes him dangerous—and you're just as suspicious to me if you really are Ama."

"It doesn't matter how suspicious you think he is." I gripped the belt of my harness with my left hand, using it to put some steel in my spine. "You're not going to say a word about him, Oleander, or Prydwen."

"Oh? Who is going to stop me?" The Paragon leaned in, his voice dark.

I can do this.

I took a deep breath, then answered. "I will."

"Oh?" The Paragon scoffed. "So now you're falling back on your ancestors' ways and are threatening assassination?" He shook his head, his movements a lot faster and more fluid than usual—I was getting to him.

"No. I don't kill," I said. "But I'll finally let my magic take a look at whatever your glamour is hiding, and then I'll tell *everyone*."

The street was silent for several long moments as the Paragon stared at me.

Emotion flicked across his face so quickly, I couldn't even identify the expressions. "You...you know I'm wearing a glamour?" he finally asked.

I unflinchingly met his gaze. "Paragon, I'm a shadow."

The Paragon's face crumpled into something like grief, before he laughed again—this time sounding closer to hysteria. "I forgot—of course, you're immune to magic! You're just so nice and anxious, it never occurred to me! Hah-hah! Such a rookie mistake, and I didn't even think of it!" He was still laughing as he threw his arm over his eyes, smashing his glasses into his face.

Well, I think that worked?

I'd hoped it was a decent threat, but I hadn't expected that kind of reaction. This was kind of extreme. I wanted him to take me seriously, not to have a mental breakdown.

The Paragon was squatting now, still laughing as he rocked forward and backwards.

Too afraid to look away, I cleared my throat. "I think you're misunderstanding what I mean."

The Paragon removed his arm and owlishly peered up at me. "What?"

"I haven't seen what your glamour is hiding," I said. "I've managed to keep my magic from stripping it."

The Paragon stood up, his glasses nearly flying off his nose with his incredulousness. "You haven't looked? Why not?"

I think I'm losing control of this conversation...

I kept my shoulders rolled back. "Just because I haven't looked doesn't mean I won't. If you go after Noctus I will—"

"I get it, I get it," the Paragon said. "Why haven't you looked?"

I hesitated. "Because your secrets should remain yours," I honestly said. "I certainly don't want to be involved in your business."

Because that would be so much more trouble, and I have enough of that already, thank you.

I added as an afterthought, "Also, it's not polite."

"Not polite," the Paragon dumbly repeated. He abruptly broke off in another laugh—this one was flavored more like an amused chuckle, thankfully—and the light entered his eyes again. "Very well, Chloe Anderson. I agree to your terms—not because of your threat, but because of who you are."

"I'm sorry?" I said, confused.

"More than anyone else in our society, you could gather secrets, manipulate, and blackmail," the Paragon said. "However, you obviously don't do such a thing. Because you're too polite, too honorable, and—frankly—too well raised. That *you* want to protect Noctus means something. So, I shall bow to your wishes in this matter, and add my thanks that you have refrained from peeking."

I nodded—it was too dangerous to say thank you to the Paragon as he was a fae, especially since his mood was...off.

"Hold on." Noctus moved in on the Paragon, looming over me. "Let it be known that if you harm Chloe—physically, with your fae tricks, or otherwise—I will *end* you."

The Paragon frowned. "So you really are that close, hm? Then why has Ama been missing from your home for months?"

"That doesn't matter," Noctus said.

"Of course it doesn't," the Paragon grumbled. "But you have nothing to fear, I assure you. Forget you, she's far more terrifying. She drank charmed tea in front of me without batting an eyelash. I don't think my cat would even tell me if she somehow popped into my pocket realm. Menace."

The Paragon gave me the evil eye, but I relaxed.

A sassy Paragon was a good sign. It meant he accepted where we stood, for now.

"I wait in horror to see what the two of you combined do to my mental health," the Paragon griped. "I'm so delicate, perhaps I shan't survive."

"Paragon," I started.

He held a hand up, stopping me. "I jest. However. I want to know the truth about what's going on. Between you two, with your minions, all of it." He rolled his shoulders back as he studied Noctus and me.

"Done," Noctus said.

The Paragon blinked in surprise. "Well, that's unexpected."

Noctus shrugged. "I knew what I was doing tonight, and I refuse to live without Chloe anymore. That means it's not a matter of if we are revealed, but rather how we can do it in a way that gives us the greatest advantage."

My heart warmed, and I felt a blush burn on my cheeks when the Paragon raised both of his eyebrows and looked at me.

"Interesting," the Paragon said. "I never pegged you as a romantic. I'm stopping by your place once this mess is cleaned up —be prepared."

Noctus was silent in his helm.

The Paragon shook his clothes out, then pirouetted so he was pointed up the street. "Okay, let's pack it up!" He clapped his hands as he strode up the street. "Humans! Let it be known that

I'm fae, so if anyone asks, the fae get the credit for this entire rescue operation. Now, who needs tea? That was a rhetorical question because I already know the answer: all of you."

I raised my eyebrows at that nifty bit of wordsmithing—the Paragon couldn't lie, so he'd used implications instead. Pat was the only human who would know better, and he'd go with me on this. For now, anyway, until he made me explain everything.

That's going to be fun...

I frowned as the meaning of the Paragon's words dawned on me. "He's going to use his charmed tea on them, isn't he?"

"Possibly."

Noctus's answer jarred me back to us, and I turned and stared up into his helm—wishing I could see his face or eyes.

There's maybe one regret I have in all of this, and I should tell him now.

"Noctus, thank you—for coming, and for helping. I had the opportunity to end things, I should have just done it, but—"

"Don't apologize for who you are." He took my hand, tugging me a step closer. "Particularly because you shouldn't have to cross that line if you don't want to."

I gulped and nodded.

"That was good thinking, though, with the pendant," he added.

"Thank you," I said. "I was desperate, and so relieved it worked. Though I could really go with some mouthwash right now." I laughed nervously and swung our joint hands—I could practically feel Pat's eyes boring into my back.

Noctus nodded, or at least I think he did. His gestures were always small to begin with, and with the helm obscuring his face I couldn't tell for certain.

We were silent for a few moments.

I nervously fidgeted, before I gave in and spoke. "So...what now?"

"I'll leave with the others. You'll stay to give your statement to the Curia Cloisters, then call your employer to let her know you will not be in tonight," he said.

"Okay." I nodded, trying to act nonchalant even though I wanted to nervously wring my hands. *Is that it? We just part again? Does he feel differently about me now that we've been apart for a couple months? I mean, we never said I love you or anything, but he asked me to be bonded to him. Wouldn't that mean something—*

"And then," Noctus continued, oblivious to my inner panic, "you come home. And you bring your siblings."

"Joy lives in the same building with me," I absently said. "So she doesn't need to be brought anywhere."

"I wasn't talking about your apartment."

I froze as I tried to process what I was hearing. *Not my apartment? What is he talking about—wait...I come home?* "Do you mean—?"

"Our home," Noctus said. "Doubtless the Paragon will spend the night howling on my porch. We may as well make it an event and tell your siblings everything, assuming you want them to know?"

"Yes!" I said. "Absolutely, yes. I'll call Joy. Should we come to your house?"

"Call Charon," Noctus said. "He'll pick you up when you're ready."

"I don't have his phone number anymore," I said.

Noctus frowned. "Yes, you do."

"No." I shook my head. "The number he gave me was disconnected after I left."

"Yes," Noctus said. "For safety purposes. And then he contacted you through Book Nookery. Multiple times."

I started to shake my head again, before it dawned on me. "Wait—is he Mr. Ferryman? The customer who kept purchasing books and never came in to pick them up or answer his voicemail?"

"Yes."

I laughed in sheer relief. "That was him? I never caught on—he even bought a cat book in his last order."

"Chloe," Pat shouted to me before beckoning me over. "You want to come start your statement about all of these...fae?" he asked. "Backup should arrive in five minutes."

He means we have to get our story ready before the Cloisters get here.

"Sounds like we need to get started." I took a step toward my brother, my happiness bubbling inside me like a shaken soda can. "I'll see you at home!"

"Wait."

Noctus caught me by my wrist with his free hand, his grasp gentle so the edges of his metal gauntlets didn't so much as scratch my skin. He hooked his rapier on his belt, then pulled his helm off, tossing it aside.

His hair was tousled, fanning across his forehead, and his hazel eyes were dark in the cover of the night, but I could still see that the spiral pupils were swirling.

He tugged on my wrist, pulling me close.

Gawking at him as I was, I staggered closer, smacking into his chest.

Noctus eased his hand along my jaw, stopping so he cradled the back of my head as he studied me. His gaze flickered down, and I realized the source of his fascination: the collar. Since I'd put it back on, it peeked out of the neckline of my sweaters.

Oh, oh, he knows. He knows I really care about him, and that I—

"I love you, Amalourne." Noctus leaned over and kissed me.

Like, *really* kissed me, his lips on mine, overwhelming all my senses.

For a second, I was stiff like a board.

Is this really okay? Can we really be together?

Noctus tilted my head a little, and I felt the lace of my collar flex with the movement, bolstering me.

There was nothing keeping us apart, not anymore.

I melted into the kiss, my hands gripping the front of

Noctus's tabard to ground myself. Kissing Noctus was like being immersed in elf magic, but the sharpness had softened to a gentle caress.

Wait, he's kissing me...and I just had the equivalent of a gravel pit in my mouth.

I pulled back from Noctus, breaking off our kiss.

"Mouthwash," I blurted out. "I need mouthwash! I haven't rinsed my mouth off since the pendant—"

"I'll risk it." Noctus's voice was still raspy as he recaptured my mouth.

This time I stood on my tiptoes so I could fling my arms around his neck, and let Noctus hold me steady—his arms encircling my back—as I immersed myself in our kiss.

"*Chloe*!" Pat shouted, his voice high-pitched and scandalized, interrupting us.

I reluctantly broke off. My cheeks were no longer just hot with a blush, my entire face was *burning*. I risked sneaking a peek up at Noctus. The spirals of his eyes were swirling, and although he raised an eyebrow in irritation, his smile was so warm I could bask in it.

We edged closer together again, drawn like magnets.

"Chloe!" Pat yelled again.

"Coming," I laughed as I backed away from Noctus.

"Don't *laugh*," Pat yelled. "That makes it worse!"

"I'll see you at home," I said to the elf king.

"Home," he agreed.

"*Chloe*!" Pat hollered. "I'm not equipped to handle this. *Stop* flirting!"

I couldn't stop laughing as I hurried down the street, feeling better than I had in months.

The tracker had been eliminated, my family was safe, and Noctus had come for me.

The only thing that dimmed my joy was the nagging reminder that the elves had essentially promised to come forward into a society that still hated and resented them...and that the tracker had mentioned leadership.

Just how big was this organization...and how great a threat was it, not only to supernaturals and humans in general, but to the tenuous relationship between us?

CHAPTER TWENTY-ONE

Chloe

It took some time to corroborate my statement with Pat's, tell the Curia Cloisters what had happened—painting Noctus and the others as good-citizen-fae-nobles who stepped in when they heard the screams—and call Ms. Booker. By the time I'd gone back to my apartment to gather the essentials—including my sister—and finally waited for Pat, we didn't get to the Cape Cod house until after midnight.

I stepped through the portal gate fitted into the front door, my muscles still twinging a bit from the fight—I only drank a lower tier fae potion since I hadn't been seriously injured in the scuffle.

I had just enough time to look back to make sure Pat and Joy had made it through the gate—both looking a little green-faced from the experience—when I was scooped off my feet, dropping the backpack I was holding in the process.

"Chloe!" Ker's voice was loud and joyous as she hugged me so tight I'd probably need a chiropractic adjustment. "You're back, I'm so glad you're back!"

"Ker!" I hugged her back, enjoying the heat she radiated like a furnace.

"Oh, of course. All your greetings go to the *wolf*. I see who the favorite is."

I laughed when Ker finally released me, then staggered over to Aristide, who stood with his back to a hallway wall, resting his hands on his white cane.

"Hi, Aristide. I'm so happy to see you." I set my hands on top of Aristide's—I wasn't going to hug him without an invitation since the vampire was far less touchy-feely than Ker.

To my surprise, he slipped his hands out from underneath mine, rested his cane against his side, then took my hands in his so he could squeeze them. "Welcome home, Ama," he said.

While Aristide still held my hands, Charon picked up my backpack and started down the hallway. "I believe His Majesty wishes to meet in the library. I shall gather refreshments, and see to it that rooms are prepared for the Andersons."

"Thanks, Charon," I called after him.

Charon stopped his progress long enough to turn around and bow to me. "Welcome home, Chloe," he said, echoing Aristide's greeting.

Tears blurred my vision as Ker laughed and threw an arm over my shoulders.

I'm back, I really am back. I thought I'd never set foot in this house again, but I'm back!

Pat coughed, jolting me back to the present.

"Oh, I'm sorry. Aristide, Ker, this is Joy and Pat—my older sister and brother." I pulled my hands from Aristide's so I could shuffle out of the way.

"It's a pleasure," Aristide said, his voice surprisingly empty of sarcasm for the moment. "Chloe has spoken much of you both."

"Welcome to Calor Villa!" Two steps and Ker was at my

siblings' side. "You have no idea how excited we are to have you here—it's like we already know you!"

Ker gave first Joy then Pat an enthusiastic hug.

Pat's eyes bugged with the experience, but Joy hugged Ker right back with obvious delight.

"Perhaps we should continue the introductions in the library? If we engage in any more mushiness, I believe I will expire," Aristide announced.

"Yeah, we shouldn't get too into it without Noctus," Ker agreed. "He'll be upset he missed greeting you as it is. Come on—this way."

Joy sped up so she could walk with Ker, her voice pleasant and casual as she started pumping the werewolf for information. "So how long have you known Noctus?"

"For quite a while—Aristide has been around much longer, naturally."

"Have you been with him for years?"

"Closer to centuries."

The pair happily gossiped while Pat and I settled into the middle of our little caravan, and Aristide took up the rear.

I glanced at my older brother, trying to gauge his reaction.

I hadn't had time to explain to my siblings my relationship with Noctus and the others—plus I'd wanted to wait for backup. Pat and Joy could be merciless, and I selfishly didn't want to face them alone.

But now, as I studied Pat's carefully blank face, I wondered if maybe that was a mistake.

"I'm sorry," I blurted out.

Pat glanced at me. "For what?"

"That I didn't tell you and Joy about any of this. But there are a lot of secrets, and a lot of them weren't mine to reveal..."

Pat simply nodded.

Yep, he's upset. Maybe not mad, but he's not happy about any of this.

Cowed, I was quiet until we reached the library, where Ker opened the double doors and ushered us in.

The library was just as awe inspiring as the first time I'd seen it—any book lover would have been awed no matter how many times they saw it considering it was two stories and the room itself was larger than some houses.

The glass ceiling showed off the dark sky outside the villa. The mountain the villa was built against pierced so high into the sky, it felt like the ceiling nearly scraped the dark clouds that covered the night sky, and the gentle tap of falling rain pitter pattered on the spelled ceiling.

Bookshelves were arranged throughout the room in an orderly layout and lined the walls of the second floor.

There were more lanterns than I remembered—some of them were made of brightly colored paper and glowed like they contained flickering candles, while others were made of stone and were set in solid, guiding pathways.

The tree at the far end of the library was no longer flowering. Instead, its leaves were a mix of searing scarlets and bright yellows. A few fell off a branch and fluttered down, landing in the moat of water that surrounded the tree.

The giant glass globe—as big as I was tall—that was positioned in the center of the room still spun, though today it glowed like it was lit within by clusters of fireflies.

"Woah." Joy stared up at the moving platforms that glided over our heads, following a pattern that led them to connect to the various staircases that led to the second floor. "Chloe, did you date this Noctus guy just for his library? Because if not, you should."

"*Joy*!" I squeaked.

"I'm just sayin'," Joy said.

"Don't worry, Chloe," Aristide said. "I'll be sure to pass this wisdom on to Noctus."

"Don't, please," I warned him. "We're not—I don't—"

"Chloe," Aristide said. "I may be blind, but that doesn't mean I'm deaf. Even *I* heard of your illicit street kiss."

"Aristide!" I groaned.

"I thought it was cute," Ker said. "Just like a movie. But while I'm certain Noctus would be very willing to give you a library—eventually, that is—the next step in your courtship should be him giving you flowers."

"You're just saying that because your flower shop is the only one in downtown Magiford," Aristide said.

Ker winked at me. "I'll order something special for you—and all of my flowers are sourced from elven arborists, so you know they're high quality!"

"Elven arborists?" Joy asked with interest.

Desperate to change the topic, I charged deeper into the library. "Why don't we sit down?"

"Over here," Ker called. "There's a nice fire this way."

Ker marched past the spinning globe and turned into the maze of books.

She led us to a back corner, where a fire pit already lit with blue and white flames and filled with glass stones was positioned in the center of a circle, surrounded by plush cushions made of satin and silk with silver tassels and embroidery lining the edges.

Ker plopped down on a tufted cushion, then gestured to the other cushions. "Make yourselves comfortable!"

Aristide shuffled purposefully around the circle, using his cane like a measuring stick to find a mound of embroidered pillows that, when he settled down on them, propped him up and supplied a semblance of back support.

Joy chose a cushion that was as large as our parents' dining table from our childhood home. I thought maybe she just wanted to sprawl out, but she grabbed me by the hand, tugging me onto the cushion as she sat down. "This is fun," she said. "But doesn't the fire need ventilation?"

"The flames are magic," Ker explained. "Noctus's magic, to be precise. So it doesn't burn the way regular fires do."

"Does it not need energy to burn?" Pat asked. He'd put a polite expression on as he sat down next to me, sitting so close his leg scraped mine and I was essentially pinned between my siblings.

"It does, but Noctus's magic serves as the energy source," Ker said. "That means it's technically a limited resource, but Noctus is strong enough to heat the mansion this way."

"Enough polite prattle," Aristide interrupted. "I'm sure there's got to be some questions you're dying to ask. What do you want to hear? The foundation of our friendship, or tales of our sordid past? I'm afraid it will be rather disappointing: Noctus's greatest concern in the past decade has been trash collection and disposal within the city."

"City?" Joy echoed.

"Village." Noctus emerged from the bookshelves, his hair damp and his charcoal gray suit dotted with what I was assuming was—based on the ceiling—rain.

My entire body tensed—I didn't know if I should get up and... what? Hug him? That kiss meant something, and I knew we were something, but I didn't know what that something was.

In the end, it didn't matter—Pat and Joy had me wedged so tightly between the two of them I couldn't get up, and neither of them seemed inclined to move.

The air was tense, until the Paragon bustled out from behind Noctus—his robes similarly rain spattered, except for the baby sling that covered his front. "Village? You call that a *village*? You need a refresher in English vocabulary terms."

Judging by their appearance, I was pretty sure Noctus had just given the Paragon a tour of the city.

The Paragon used a swatch of his long hair to wipe off the sling, and—as expected—a pink head and triangle ears popped out of it. Aphrodite tilted her head so far back she was looking at us upside-down, and chirped at us.

"*Mmert*!"

Noctus ignored the Paragon and walked past our little circle, and instead drew back a thick curtain from a window.

The wall we were next to was technically an interior wall, but thanks to the wonders of elven portal magic, the window showed a view of Calor Villa, the white, cake-like tiers of the city going all the way down to the base of the mountain.

Rain puddled in the streets, but despite the murky night sky, the city was bright from lamps that burned with white and blue flames, reflecting off the white stone that made up the city walls and some of the buildings.

Even at this late hour a few elves were out and about. I saw two squads of what I was guessing were guards based on their dark clothing, and a few civilians huddled under brightly colored umbrellas.

"This is Calor Villa," Noctus said. "Located within the fae realm, and connected to the human world with portals."

"A hidden elf city," Joy breathed. "But...how?"

I took a deep breath to fortify myself, then started what was going to be a difficult conversation. "First, I need to introduce you. Joy, Pat, the guy with the baby sling is the Paragon, the top fae representative in the USA. And that's his cat, Aphrodite."

"Very pleased to make your acquaintance." The Paragon bowed to my siblings, then started patting Aphrodite's rump.

"And this," my voice cracked with anxiety, "is Noctus—the Mors elf king, and ruler over all the elves who live here—the last remnants of the elves. Noctus, Charon, Ker, and Aristide were the friends I stayed with when the tracker first found me."

"How? And why?" Pat asked. "Did you know him before?"

I glanced up at Noctus, wondering if he wanted to step in. But the elf king tucked his hands into the pockets of his slacks, his shoulders squared and his thoughtful attention on us.

I guess I get to run this storytime.

"No," I said, working to keep my voice even. "I met him in my cat form when I let a bunch of Seelie fae take me in order to escape the tracker. He rescued me...and then adopted me as his pet."

"He *what?*"

TWO HOURS PASSED before Pat and Joy were satisfied with my story and felt they'd gotten enough information about Noctus and the others.

They'd asked questions about everything from how I'd managed to fool everyone into thinking I was a cat, to clarification questions about the bonding magic Noctus had originally cast on me, to asking how the elves managed to live within human society without other supernaturals realizing they existed.

The Paragon was shockingly silent through most of the talk—he'd only complained when he let Aphrodite out of her sling and she chose to leave him to sit on my lap. Even now he was lying belly down on a pile of cushions, frowning at a row of books organized on a bookshelf that was nearly within arm's reach as he listened.

"—been able to avoid detection from supernatural society as supernaturals haven't historically been keen on sharing spaces with humans," Aristide explained. "And besides shadows, no human or supernatural can see through an elf glamour. Realistically, it's the invention of the cellphone and the age of information that has proven to be the largest threat to elven secrecy, but elves from Calor Villa have been able to use the cover story of fae nobles. Magiford has been a bigger challenge, mostly because supernaturals here are starting to adopt human technology."

"You mean with the power of human technology and the new spirit of mingling that's taking over Magiford, supernaturals are much more likely to notice the patterns of your people, and they'd know enough to question your people if they tried to use the excuse of fae nobles as their front." The Paragon's eyes nearly disappeared under the shelf his furrowed eyebrows made. "Which is why your people are in such a precarious situation. You could probably hide here in Magiford for another five, maybe ten years, but if things follow the current trajectory, it's inevitable that you'll be discovered."

"Precisely," Noctus said. "Although that doesn't pertain to this conversation. We're here to satisfy Pat and Joy, not discuss the future of the elves."

Silence enveloped the library.

I looked back and forth between my siblings, trying to read their polite expressions.

"Do you have any more questions?" I petted Aphrodite, my fingers gliding over her wrinkled body as I tried to push down my building anxiety.

During the talk, I sensed a change from my siblings.

Joy had become quieter instead of chatty and inviting—signaling she was thinking.

Pat had thawed to Noctus and the others, but sitting next to me like he was, I could still feel the tenseness that radiated off him.

They were upset, but I had the nagging feeling that the target of their anger had switched from Noctus, to *me*.

They're not happy I hid all of this from them.

"I think that's all of the important things." Joy leaned forward to set her empty china teacup on the stone edge of the firepit. "Or at the very least, that's all I'm going to understand tonight."

"It's a lot to take in," Ker said, her voice soothing. "I'm sure it's a surprise to learn that elves still exist, much less our part in Chloe's fight against the tracker."

"It certainly makes me feel better about the weeks we didn't know about him," Joy said.

"Yeah." Pat had been reaching for a piece of jerky—Charon had brought *a lot* of snacks—but he abruptly dropped his hand into his lap. "We owe you our thanks for keeping her safe."

"It was my honor," Noctus said.

"So, why don't we wrap things up here for tonight?" Ker sprang to her feet. "Everyone must be tired—and you're spending the night, of course."

Pat inhaled deeply, drawing his shoulders up. "Just for the night," he agreed. He stood up, gathering his teacup of decaf coffee and empty plate—ignoring Charon hovering over us.

"I believe I shall also take my leave—for now," the Paragon said.

"If you show up on my porch within the next week, I'll call the police and tell them you're an escapee from a residential home," Noctus said, his voice devoid of feeling.

The Paragon scowled. "I have my answers, so I'm satisfied —*for now*. And I'm all too aware of Chloe's personal warning to try to poke my nose in this beehive. But you'll need my help, mark my words, when you decide to reveal yourself to supernaturals."

"Certainly a person with your power would be advantageous to have on hand when King Noctus and the elves do come forward," Joy said, instantly switching into her work mode as she smiled sunnily and her voice became bright. "However, since you and Pat magnanimously allowed them to use a cover story for tonight's event, they have the luxury of choosing *when* to come forward, which, naturally, I assume they'll do when they have a story they can use to their advantage to make the maximum positive impact. Am I correct, Your Majesty?"

Both Joy and the Paragon swiveled so they faced Noctus.

Noctus—who had remained standing for the entire talk—didn't even bat an eye. "Naturally," he said.

The Paragon grunted. "Who needs a story—you just need to make a social media campaign and you'll win the humans' love and affection immediately with your looks and wealth. Why do you have all the luck? It's unfair." The Paragon groaned as he stood up, his knees cracking. "Come, Aphrodite. I've had my fill of elves for the day. We're going."

Aphrodite, cradled in my pretzel crossed legs, lifted her head up, twitched her tail, then flipped to her other side so she was looking at my stomach.

"*Aphrodite*!" the Paragon said, his voice shrill. "Are you ignoring me?"

"*Mmert*," Aphrodite said.

The Paragon staggered a few steps backwards, as if he'd been hit. "So this is how deep your affection for me goes—when you are faced with a shadow you abandon me?"

"Don't take it personally." Pat stood up, finally freeing me from the jam between my siblings. "All cats love Chloe—unreasonably so. We went to New York City for a family vacation when she was seven, and she was nearly carried off by a feral cat colony."

"I'd believe it," Ker said with great seriousness. "It's an unexpected superpower—as is her cat form. Cuteness is a power you must be careful with."

"Why do you say that as if it's something *you're* burdened with?" Aristide asked. "I remember what your wolf form looks like. It's terrifying. It matches your name."

"I could have gotten cuter since you were cursed," Ker said.

"Impossible," Aristide said. "You make me brush your teeth in your wolf form nearly every day. I know how big your canines are."

I leaned Aphrodite against my shoulder and supported her with one hand as I stood up. I took a moment to shake my legs out—that pins and needles feeling had numbed my calves—then staggered over to the Paragon, who was still clinging to a bookcase.

"Here, Paragon. Do you want me to hold Aphrodite while you

get the baby sling ready, or are you just going to carry her?" I asked.

"Ahh yes, my duplicitous cat and her new object of admiration. Hello." The Paragon weakly sighed, as if he had lost the will to live, then winked at me and straightened up. "I'll use the sling—it's always better to have one's hands free and available for anything. If you wouldn't mind holding her for just an additional moment?" The Paragon reclaimed his sling—which he'd abandoned by the pile of pillows he'd sat on—and started shrugging his way into it.

"Sure." I moved so I supported Aphrodite with both hands—she was pretty hefty to hold. "I'm glad you were here to hear the explanation."

"Of course." The Paragon's glasses nearly slid off his nose as he secured the sling. "It let me judge what kind of a threat Noctus and his elves are."

I paused, Aphrodite's considerable bulk pulling on my arms as I tried to figure out the most diplomatic way to phrase my question. "Paragon? Please don't take this the wrong way, but...why are you so accepting of all of this?"

After his attitude when he'd first found us, I'd assumed he'd be demanding that Noctus put the shackles back on, or accept some kind of limitation on his power or observation spell cast on the city so he could keep an eye on them.

Instead, the Paragon was practically his jolly self, and didn't seem bothered at all by Calor Villa, when just hours ago he'd been ready to blackmail Noctus.

"You mean why am I no longer ready to throw hands with Noctus?" the Paragon blithely asked.

"Well...yes," I said.

"It is partially because my greatest concerns are no longer valid. That stalker of yours croaking is not the massive loss I thought it was because of what I learned tonight," the Paragon said. "I now know it was Noctus who took out that artifact ring—

which, it's always good to know who is active in your backyard, but also works as a testament that he is willing to help supernaturals. Given what was said about the fae who might be behind the current artifact trouble, I suspect the fae's days of freedom are also numbered, and he will be another connection to the organization that I can question once Noctus catches him."

"Oh." I blinked, surprised.

Not that the argument was so valid, but because the Paragon had seen this and made the pivot in mere hours.

I always knew he could be dangerous, I guess I just didn't know on how many levels. And suddenly I'm really glad it never occurred to him I could see through his glamour...

"But the biggest reason I am no longer uneasy," the Paragon grunted as he tied a knot, "is because of you."

I blinked rapidly. "*Me?*"

"Yes. When I first saw Noctus, I assumed he'd somehow put you under his power as well, and that he was the driving force behind all of this."

"He is," I said. "He's the Mors king."

"Ah, you missed the distinction," the Paragon said. "Yes, he is the most powerful force involved in this delightful circle of trust we just experienced, but he is not the drive behind the entire situation. You are." Finished with his preparations, the Paragon peered at me.

"Me?" I asked.

"Yes," the Paragon said. "Noctus might have initially started things by choosing to adopt you without knowing what you were, but the truth is his decision to come forward, your relationship, and the elves revealing themselves are all because of you. You are not under his power; rather, he is under yours. I had some concerns he was trying to claim you in an effort to control the last known shadow, but it is abundantly clear to me that instead, it is you who chose him. All that tips the scales to keep Noctus from being all powerful and untouchable, which means he's a great deal safer to cooperate with than I initially estimated. Savvy?"

I stared at the Paragon, trying to digest everything he'd just told me. "I guess?"

I'm pretty sure he didn't share this out of the kindness of his heart... which means this is a political move. One I don't think I get.

It was just as well I'd come clean to Pat and Joy. Joy would understand the political undertones of this, but I'd wait to ask her for advice on a less traumatic day.

The Paragon crouched so his eyes were level with Aphrodite's. "If you'll excuse me, milady, might I remove you from your new favorite? It is high time we head home." He gently lifted the sphinx cat from my hold, tucking her into the sling with practiced movements.

"I appreciate what you've done tonight," I said.

The Paragon glanced at me. "I could say the same thing."

"But I didn't do anything tonight."

"You have, but that's not what I was referring to." The Paragon tilted his head, and for a moment his eyes had that simultaneously young and old look to them again. "Not every supernatural would have refrained from peeling back my glamour. Most, in fact, would have done exactly that."

"I already told you, it's not my business," I said.

"And you only mind your business?"

"I try to," I said. "Staying in my league is a practice that has considerably lengthened my life."

"You will likely have to question that if you continue your relationship with Noctus."

"Because the elves are going to reveal themselves?"

"No." The Paragon patted Aphrodite's back as he gave me a pitying look. "Because you'd be a *queen*."

I was going to argue, until I realized what he meant, and my voice died in my throat.

The Paragon raised his eyebrows. "What's wrong—cat got

your tongue?" He laughed at his own joke, then paused. "I never understood that human saying. Do you know what it means?"

"Charon." Noctus's deep voice came from directly behind me, inciting a jump from me. "Please see the Paragon out."

The Paragon smoothed his mustache. "Oh, I see how it is. I'm being pushed out, am I?"

"Yes," Noctus said.

"Of course, Your Majesty." Charon bowed to Noctus, then adjusted his customary hood before ushering the Paragon away.

"Very well, I suppose it is well past my bedtime. Good night, everyone. I look forward to a working relationship with you all in the future." The Paragon benevolently waved, until he and Charon disappeared into the maze of bookshelves.

We were quiet around the fire pit, exchanging awkward smiles. I was deeply aware of Noctus's gaze on me, but for some stupid reason, I couldn't muster the courage to look at him. Nobody said anything, until I heard the groan of the wooden doors, signaling the Paragon and Charon had left the room.

"That went better than I expected." Aristide peeled himself off his cushion and reached for his cane before standing.

"With the Paragon?" I asked.

"Indeed," Aristide said. "He was quite angry out on the street. I thought for certain he'd complain more about the death of the tracker."

Noctus shrugged. "After hearing how much he harmed Chloe, he's likely thinking Magiford is lucky I chose to only mete out justice on the tracker, and not the Curia Cloisters for failing to be any kind of help."

"They helped," I said. "They would have helped more; it just took them forever to confirm that I really was a shadow."

"Ahh yes, more of their stupidity. Politically speaking, as soon as they realized there was a possibility you were a shadow, they never should have left you alone," Noctus said.

"Yes," I said, finally able to look up into his hazel eyes.

"Except I wasn't the most encouraging since I was trying to avoid their attention for *your* sake, too."

"Is that why you were putting off meeting with the Paragon and Queen Leila for so long?" Joy asked.

Pat frowned. "You were that worried, and you still didn't tell us?"

Feeling like a deer blinded by a car's headlights, I froze. "Um..."

There was that feeling of disappointment—tinged with anger—again.

I guess we still need to talk more.

Ker—envoy of charisma and kindness that she was—rolled to her feet. "How about I show you Andersons to your rooms?"

Joy smiled as she gracefully stood, standing just as tall as the werewolf. "Thank you, Ker."

Pat held up his cellphone. "I need to make a few calls with my unit first. Could someone show me to the lawn?"

"You can make calls from within the mansion," Noctus said. "We have perfect cell reception and town-wide wi-fi."

Pat whistled. "Impressive, how'd you manage that?"

"Magic," Noctus said. "And a lot of money."

"With a dash of bribery and more than a few memory charms," Aristide added.

"Mmm," Pat said. "In that case, then, I'd appreciate a guide to our rooms."

"Great!" Ker smiled, then pushed her braids behind her shoulders. "Let's get going."

I smiled at my siblings, then turned to Noctus with a nervous smile. "So..." I trailed off and nervously rubbed my palms together. "I guess we should talk—"

"Nah-uh." Pat snagged me by my wrist and pulled me along. "Not tonight."

"Pat, no. I need to talk to him." I planted my feet and leaned back, resisting.

Pat stopped. "I'm not stupid," he said. "You told us about your bond, so now I finally know what that necklace you're wearing is. You need to talk alright, but it's *not* going to be tonight."

I stiffened. "That's not a choice you get to make for me."

Ker, standing in front of us, shifted her gaze back and forth and looked nervous. "Maybe we should give the siblings a few minutes?"

"No, everyone's just tired." Joy smiled. "We just need to get some sleep. Thank you for showing us where to go. Come on, Chloe."

I stared at my siblings for a moment. "I'll talk to you tomorrow, Noctus."

"I look forward to it," Noctus said.

Ker nodded. "Okay, then. Let's—"

"It's fine, Ker," I interrupted her. "I'll show my siblings where our rooms are. Same hallway?"

Ker, feeling the tension, fidgeted. "Yes."

"Their rooms are the two rooms next to yours," Noctus said.

"Got it. Thanks!" I flashed them a smile, then strode through the library as fast as my much-shorter legs would carry me. "Goodnight, everyone!"

I didn't wait for a response, and Joy and Pat caught up with me before I even had time to duck around the first shelf.

I was quiet up until we left the library and closed the door behind us—I was certain neither Ker, Aristide, nor Noctus could hear us this far away with a wall between us.

"Look," I began as I led the way down the hallway. "I know you're disappointed with me, but I'm not going to apologize for this."

"None of it was your fault," Joy said.

"Except for choosing to leave us in the dark," Pat said.

I sucked in a deep breath. "Yeah, I'm not sorry about that."

Pat tucked his hands in the pockets of his coat. "Oh?"

"No. You're my family. I was protecting you." We popped out

of the maze of hallways, ending up by the immense staircase that led up to the second floor where the luxurious bedrooms were.

"We don't want you to sacrifice yourself for our sake, Chloe," Joy said, her voice softer and kind.

The gentle tone of her voice nearly undid me—I was aware it was a little silly that I was starting to get upset when I was the one who'd lied to them...until I remembered they'd done the same thing.

"You mean like you and Pat have?" I asked as I started up the stairs.

"What are you talking about?" Pat asked.

"The way you two chose careers and planned to move here without telling me," I said.

"We wanted to help you," Pat said.

"Yeah, and I wanted to protect you!" I climbed an extra stair to give myself a height advantage, then turned around to face them. "The Paragon's reaction to the elves is *mild*. Supernaturals hate them. Associating with them is a major risk, and you both already were kidnapped because of me. I wasn't going to tell you because I had to choose between Noctus and everyone, and keeping my family safe. I chose you!"

Pat and Joy exchanged glances.

"It's not that we don't understand where you're coming from," Pat said. "It's just...you're our little sister. We want to protect you."

I briefly pressed my hands to my eyes. *They don't get it. They're just on autopilot, trying to take care of me like they have since I was little.*

I couldn't blame them. I was an anxious existence. I'd never been bold, or the type to stand up for myself.

And in their defense, I'd let Pat make all the decisions about how to handle the tracker, passing off what should have been my responsibility.

But I'd always been willing to sacrifice for my family.

While I knew I was still weak in comparison to the new

leagues I'd been thrown into—with the likes of Noctus and the Paragon—I was already starting to see the way my abilities could be advantageous, like helping the elves when they were cut off from their magic while downtown.

Yes, I needed to keep on leveling up my skills so I could protect my family from any threat, but I already had the potential to protect them. (Even the tracker knew that—it was why he was so upset whenever he fought me.)

It is my fault that I've been so passive in all of this, but I guess it's time that Pat and Joy stop seeing me as the cute kitten from our childhood. They don't have to understand how hard I intend to train so I can protect them, but I'm not going to put up with them trying to pry me apart from Noctus. I just got him back.

CHAPTER TWENTY-TWO

Chloe

I dropped my hands to my side and frowned at my siblings, trying to figure out how to tell them all of this. "Have the two of you ever stopped to think about what I can really do?"

"What do you mean?" Joy warily asked.

"I beat up not one, but *two* fae monarchs, after breaking into a compound full of fae without getting caught," I said.

"Unseelie and Seelie monarchs are the least powerful of the fae rulers," Pat started. "Even we know that—"

"How many supernaturals on your task force could have done what I did?" I asked. "On their own, without help?"

Pat looked at his feet. After several long, uncomfortable moments, he sucked in a deep breath. "Not many."

"The tracker had to take hostages—*multiple* hostages—in order to pin me down. He had to cheat because he knew he couldn't face me head on," I reminded them. "In the supernatural world, the elves were the bogeyman to everyone, and I, as a shadow, am the bogeyman to the elves. Only I could be even scarier than my ancestors, because I'm elf-trained."

Joy's eyes were crinkled at the corners—not with joy, but pain. "Chloe...I'm sorry if you thought we don't think you're competent. It's not that. It's just..."

"We're humans," Pat said. "Even though we've tried our best to learn everything we can, we're not supernaturals."

"Yes," Joy agreed. "And since we can't ever fully understand what you go through...all we can do is try to help you. Although maybe, in our own fears, we've been a little suffocating."

I softened my stance, the stiffness leaving my shoulders. "You're not ignorant. Being a supernatural isn't like an exclusive club or anything, it's just..." I started plodding up the rest of the stairs, trying to buy myself time to think. "It's just that you two make decisions and you don't ask me. I didn't know how you'd react to Noctus, and even if we ignore the danger factor and that it was partially his decision to make, or that in telling you I would have been dooming you both to a life in an elf city—"

"There are worse fates than that," Joy muttered behind me as we reached the top of the stairs.

I wanted to grin, but I made myself push forward—this was important. "Recently, whenever I talk to you about any trouble I encounter, you two create an action plan that you think is best without even consulting me, and expect me to roll with it."

We reached the top step, Pat and Joy both wearing thoughtful expressions.

"Normally I don't mind following your leads, but I should get to have a vote, too," I said.

"We should have told you what we were planning with our careers," Pat abruptly said.

Joy had been playing with one of her silver bracelets, but with Pat's declaration, she grimaced. "We didn't want to make you feel like you owed us," she said. "But I guess we should have talked to you about it."

"I'm so happy you guys moved here." I stopped outside the door to my bedroom. "I love living near each other again. But…I need to be able to make my own decisions, and I need to be able to talk to both of you and know you'll listen and not try to make the decision for me."

They nodded, and the last bit of tension between us evaporated.

"Our little sister is all grown up." Joy reached out and pulled me into a hug. "It's simultaneously so amazing, but weirdly emotional."

I hugged Joy back, laughing when Pat ruffled my hair.

"You're a good kid, you do great for yourself," he gruffly said.

"Just remember that, because I'm including romantic decisions in this discussion," I warned him.

Pat made a face. "Let's talk about something else, please."

I scrunched my nose at him. "You're the one who keeps interrupting me whenever I try to talk to Noctus."

"Hey, I was there downtown. You were not *talking* with him," Pat said. "Joy, back me up here."

"Oh, after I met him, you were never in any danger of getting interference from me," Joy assured me.

Pat scowled. "What are you talking about?"

"He's out of this world gorgeous, unbelievably wealthy, an *elf*, and a king?" Joy ticked off her fingers as she recited the list. "Little brother, let me tell you, it doesn't get any better than that."

Pat uncomfortably scratched the back of his neck. "Yeah, but isn't he going to complicate her life?"

"He's an *elf*," Joy said with reverence. "She gets to date a real-life Legolas, except he's even cooler! It's a blessed romance."

Pat made a strangled noise. "At times like this, I can't believe we're related."

Joy cackled as I tapped the wooden door to my bedroom.

"This is my room," I said before going down the line. "And then these two rooms will be yours. Look inside and take your pick."

"What do you mean take your pick?" Pat opened the door to the first room and kept his eyes on me as he stepped inside. "A room is a room, isn't it—holy luxury! Are those *silk* sheets?"

"Noctus—through the work of Charon—is a very welcoming host," I said.

"See?" Joy called in after Pat. "What did I say? A blessed romance!"

She waited a few moments then turned to me and spoke in a lowered tone. "I know we just promised to stay out of your love life, but if you decide you don't want what the bond means—what a relationship with a *king* means—just say the word, and we'll get you out."

I blinked as I tried to process what she'd said. "Pardon?"

"I get good vibes from that elf king of yours," she said. "He's not a nice guy—he's way too deadly for that—but I'm not against you being with a dude who could eviscerate any psychos who try to stalk you in the future because you're the last known shadow or something. *However*. Just because Noctus is a fairytale come to life, doesn't mean his story is the one you want. So, don't be afraid to say something to us."

I laughed, but Joy's bluntness cut to the truth.

There was nothing keeping Noctus and me apart now. But our relationship didn't exactly have a solid foundation. We were going to have to talk and figure out boundaries—and where we stood—before I got too caught up in everything.

I guess it's just as well I'm not trying to hash things out with him right now. Noctus is charismatic enough to get me to let him press my toe beans when I was a cat. I need to be in my right mind when I face him.

"Thanks, Joy," I said.

Joy winked at me. "Anytime, little sis." She reeled me in for another hug.

"Joy!" Pat shouted from deep within the room. "You have to see this! There's a fireplace in the bathroom!"

I WAS HALF ASLEEP when I heard the door snick open.

Who? What?

I didn't know what time it was—it took a lot of work to peel my eyes open and see the slit of sunlight visible between the heavy drapes.

But I was aware enough to brace myself when I heard feet trot across the carpets.

"Chloe!" Ker flung herself onto my bed, landing half on top of me and bouncing hard.

I tried to speak, but only grunts escaped my mouth.

"Good morning!" Ker sat up, her feet hanging over the side of my bed. "Charon sent me to tell you 'home means training'."

"What?" I pushed my sleep-snarled hair out of my face as I sat up. "What time is it?"

"Seven in the morning, Miss Merry Sunshine," Aristide said.

I groggily peered across my bedroom and spied him leaning against my door frame. "Is Charon mad at me?"

"No." Aristide languidly twirled his white cane. "Rather, I believe he has barely been able to contain himself in his joy that you're back."

"Ah." I rubbed my eyes, then reluctantly pushed back the thick duvet spread across my enormous bed. "Okay."

"Didn't you get enough sleep?" Ker asked. "I mean, I know it was a late night..."

I staggered over to one of the giant windows and flicked a shade back, filling the room with bright sunlight and instantly blinding myself. "We were up until after two in the morning," I said. "Plus, I didn't go to bed immediately after we finished. I called my parents—we'd told them about the tracker, but Mom wanted the details and said I had to call, no matter the hour, once I got a chance."

I stumbled through my luxuriously furnished room, and fumbled my way into my closet—which I'd noticed the night before was still stuffed with the clothes Charon had bought for me.

"Never cross a mother," Ker wisely said, following me into my closet. "Do you want us to tell Charon you need to reschedule?"

"Nah, I'll be fine." I grabbed the first exercise/training clothes I could find, then tottered toward the bathroom. "I wasn't really sleeping anyway. Just dozing."

"Same here!" Ker reported. "It's so exciting—things are coming together!"

"Yes," I said.

"You better gird your loins," Aristide said. "Ker is not the only enthusiastic one. Noctus was up the entire night, so Charon was as well—likely plotting your training demise."

"Goodie," I said.

Ker patted my shoulders, then pushed me deeper into my bathroom. "Don't you worry a bit. Charon is quite proud of how you've handled the tracker. Now you get changed, and Aristide and I will escort you down to the training area!" She stepped out, closing the door behind her, sealing my fate.

Sooner than I thought possible, I stood in the villa's stadium-sized training facility, and pondered the possibility that my end might not be from Charon's training, but from the exhaustion likely to occur when I had to climb up the seemingly endless stairs to get out of this pit and back up into the villa.

"I can't believe he's not here." Ker jumped off a large rock formation—one of several sprinkled around the stadium. "He was very emphatic that you needed to be down here post-haste."

The fake sun—which must have been the work of magic since we were deep in the mountain—shone above us, hanging in the ceiling that was bright blue like the sky.

A breeze—which shouldn't have been possible since I didn't see any ventilation shafts anywhere in the room—ruffled my hair, which I'd pulled back into a ponytail, and the green grass that covered half of the arena.

"It's Charon," Aristide said. "Noctus might have sneezed and distracted him with the need to contact all elven apothecaries in the city."

"Hmm." Ker frowned thoughtfully at the door, until she brightened, standing straight. "I'm sure he'll be here shortly," she said with a sudden confusing conviction. "Come on, Aristide. Let's go."

"Why?" Aristide said. "Hearing Charon lovingly minister to Chloe with merciless training is going to be our best source of entertainment all day."

"We need to be up top," Ker said.

"No, we don't."

"Yes, we do," Ker said. "What if Chloe's siblings wake up? We need to be prepared to greet them as hosts."

"This is just because you want to influence them or win them or whatever your Dale Carnegie fellow says, isn't it?" Aristide asked.

"It's a part of it, yes," Ker acknowledged. "We need to make a good impression on them. Now, come on."

Aristide didn't look convinced, but he let Ker nudge him along, guiding him out of the stadium. "Fine, but only because then Noctus will owe us," he said.

"There's an idea." Ker yanked the door open for Aristide. "Have fun, Chloe!"

"Thanks," I weakly said.

Aristide shouted back to me, "If you die, we'll be sure to tell your family!" The door closed behind him, muffling the sound of his laughter.

I shook my head, then shuffled my feet on the barren turf for a moment.

Well, I suppose I should start stretching.

I checked my harness, sword, and daggers, then started warming up.

I was stretching my arms out behind my back—an excellent stretch for my arms and shoulders—when the door creaked open again.

"Good morning, Charon," I called as I released the stretch. "I wanted to thank you for the translations and the binder. I learned a lot from..." All thoughts in my brain died when I turned around and saw not Charon, but Noctus standing in the doorway.

CHAPTER TWENTY-THREE

Chloe

He was wearing his black, utility clothing, and although I didn't see any weapons on him, he was probably carrying several. His blond hair was damp—he must have just showered—and his hand was still set on the half open door.

We stared at each other for a moment, but it felt like a day.

"Good morning," Noctus finally said.

"Hey," I said. "Hi. I mean, good morning."

I gulped, then took a step toward him—which must have been what Noctus was waiting for.

He was across the arena in the blink of an eye, his arms closing around me.

I had just enough time to grin up at him like an idiot before he leaned over, pressing a searing kiss against my lips.

Given that I wasn't worried about the diseases I would share from effectively licking the pavement, like I had been for our first kiss, I relaxed into this one faster, linking my hands behind his neck and resting my arms on his shoulders for extra stability as I was starting to feel lightheaded in my giddiness.

The kiss was consuming, killing every thought in my overactive brain and making my toes curl in my boots.

Even though our bond hadn't been renewed, I swear I heard wild magic humming, and deep inside of me, something finally relaxed.

I was with Noctus. Finally.

In all my planning and hope, there had always been a part of me that was terrified that this day would never come. But we were here, together, and the sense of loss I'd been nursing all summer long was gone...because of what I had deemed the "impossible-never-going-to-happen plan" of the elves going public.

I felt such a hurricane of emotions—absolute, perfect delight, sheer relief, and a morose sense of thankfulness for what the elves of Calor Villa were going to give up to make this happen.

To my embarrassment, tears started dripping from my eyes, burning a searing trail down my cheeks.

Noctus pulled back long enough to fix his arms around me. "Amalourne, what's wrong?"

"Nothing," I said—crying harder. "I'm just so happy! My family is safe. And I get to be with you when I didn't know if that would ever happen, but what about everyone in Calor Villa? I just—" I couldn't speak anymore I was crying too hard.

Noctus picked me up—literally sweeping me off my feet—then sat down where we stood on the grassy field, tipping me against his chest before settling me in place on his legs.

I was still crying after all of that, but at least I wasn't sobbing and snotting all over his shirt as I rested my cheek on his chest. "Why am I crying?" I asked, bewildered.

"Relief, likely," Noctus said. "You also probably haven't had a chance to process everything that happened last night."

I shut my eyes—which were starting to feel swollen. "That sounds right," I agreed. I hesitated, then made myself ask the question that I wasn't sure I wanted to hear the answer to. "Noctus...are you sure about this?"

"About us?" Noctus asked.

"No—well, yes, in a way—but I meant are you sure about revealing yourself to supernaturals? About all the elves revealing themselves?" I scrubbed at my face, trying to wipe the tears which I could feel were turning my face red and splotchy.

"Ah." Noctus bent one of his legs, angling it so it supported my back. "Then please allow me to assure you it was not a decision made under duress. It wasn't even fully my decision. My people made it clear they felt we could—and should—reveal ourselves. They will not resent you for this, and you can still walk away if you want."

That took the sniffles right out of me. "Why would I walk away?"

"Because very few people in supernatural society are likely to welcome us given our history," Noctus plainly said.

"The transition might be messy, and I think initially it could get ugly. But eventually I think it'll even out." I tried to discreetly rub my nose as I considered the problem. "Supernaturals are obsessed with power. They'll respect you because of what you can do, or they'll realize—like the Paragon—that there's a lot more to be gained by being on friendly terms," I concluded.

"We can hope," Noctus said in a voice that meant he didn't share my optimism. "But it likely won't improve for years, and I don't want to drag you down with us." He hesitated, and while I was still leaned against him, close to him, I felt a distance open up between us. "Additionally, as part of going forward there are sure to be things about me revealed to the public that you might not...appreciate."

He's bracing himself for rejection, I realized when his arm slid off my back.

"I assume you're talking about killing your family?" I asked.

Noctus didn't respond.

I peeled myself off his chest so I could look him in the eyes, then took his right hand, squeezing it so he would look at me. "I know you call yourself the kingslayer," I said. "And I know the death of your family is the reason why supernaturals won the war."

"Yes, I slaughtered them," Noctus said. "But that is not the full sordid tale, and you deserve to know it all before making any kind of commitment."

I studied Noctus, taking in the tiny movements he made: the hardening of his jaw and the resignation in his hazel eyes.

This is going to be hard for him. And something tells me that maybe it's not the right move for right now.

We were finally together after months apart, and Noctus was making a huge sacrifice as part of our relationship. Was it emotionally healthy to hash this out *right now*?

I know roughly what happened, and from my weeks spent as Ama I'm aware Noctus works as if it's his reason for living—not because he likes it, but because it's his atonement.

Now—knowing Noctus, even knowing the elves of Calor Villa—I already knew there was nothing Noctus could tell me about the issue that would make me feel differently about him. And between the death of the tracker and the need to make plans for the elves, there was already a lot going on.

I wanted us to be supportive, not to feel like there were certain hoops we had to jump through in order for us to be "solid". I'd experienced enough of that from the Curia Cloisters.

Besides, there are things I need to tell him—like the fact that Ms. Booker knows about him. It doesn't matter so much now that the elves are going forward, but I should still tell him. But I refuse to use now—the first moments we're finally alone together—like we're representatives meeting to strike a bargain.

"I do want to hear about it," I said, slowly, trying to follow my gut instinct. "But...I think that's something that can wait."

Noctus didn't even hesitate. "It might make you think differently of me."

"Except it won't." I relaxed, already feeling more confident with my decision.

"It's what Aristide has informed me is called a giant red flag."

I pulled on his hand to get his attention and make sure he was looking me in the eye. "Noctus, I might not know your centuries-ago past, but I know who you are right now. That's who I want my relationship to be with. We *finally* are together again. For right now, that's more than enough."

Noctus's eyes didn't narrow per se, but the intensity in them kicked up a notch. "Are you certain?"

"Yes," I said.

"Truly?"

"I want you to tell me when the time is right," I said. "And I know that time is not right now. Besides. There's some stuff I need to tell you, too."

"Understood."

Sitting as close to him as I was, I felt Noctus's entire body relax.

"You really are my Amalourne," he said, his voice a velvety caress.

I was going to finally ask what Amalourne meant—everyone who knew elvish always reacted weirdly whenever Noctus said my nickname—but I didn't even get a chance to open my mouth before I was dumbstruck by my own shyness.

Noctus's hand grazed my side as he wrapped an arm around me again. "So, you say it is not the time to air dirty laundry—a thought I am both thankful for and grieved by."

"Grieved?" I managed to ask.

"Yes. Because if I told you about my role as kingslayer, I was hoping that would give me the right to ask, given you are wearing the collar I gave you, does that mean what I think it does?"

All thoughts of my nickname died as I puffed up, turning red with embarrassment, while leaning into him once again. "Um."

Noctus laughed—making a pleasant rumble I felt since I was tipped against his chest. "You'd better speak your mind, Amalourne. What does it mean?" He pressed his head close to mine, his breath fanning across my ear and neck. "Unless this is something else you'd rather wait to discuss."

"No, we don't have to wait," I gulped.

"Oh? Then what does it signify?"

"It means yes," I blurted out. "Yes, I want the bond. Yes, I want to be with you."

"As my queen?" Noctus asked as he shifted, somehow drawing me closer.

I babbled—literally: I couldn't summon the brain cells to say actual words.

"Because you would be queen—a very different sort from what perhaps I initially imagined since Calor Villa will be revealing itself," Noctus continued. "But being bonded to me would make it unavoidable."

"Queen seems like an awfully important role to give someone who couldn't even get a job at the Curia Cloisters," I said.

"Is that a no?"

"No, it's an 'I'm questioning the wisdom of this,' but if that's the only way we can be together..." I trailed off.

"Then you wish to renew the bond?" Noctus asked.

I nodded.

Noctus said nothing, waiting in silence.

Ah, he needs to hear it.

I shifted so I could peer up at Noctus, unflinchingly meeting his hazel eyes. "Yes, Noctus. I want to renew the bond. I love you, and I'll do whatever is necessary as part of loving you. Even if that means being a queen."

A small part of me wanted to hyperventilate at the idea, but what I'd said was true.

I'd been prepared to give up so much more to be with Noctus. Granted, being queen means I'll be submerged in the politics I've spent years avoiding, but if that's what I must do in order to have both my family and Noctus, I'll do it. I am definitely unprepared for it, but I'll have Noctus, Charon, Ker, and Aristide to help me and make sure I don't fumble things too badly. Besides...being queen might put me in a position to make their transition to going public easier since I'm a shadow, but that might be an overestimation of my personal power.

Noctus paused. "Are you sure you don't want to wait to hear more of my past?"

"Like I said earlier, it's not necessary. I know who you are, Noctus. That's all I need."

Noctus brushed his fingers against the base of my throat. "Then...may I?"

I sucked in a deep breath, then exhaled. "Yes. Please renew our bond."

Noctus gently pulled the collar-necklace up my neck, the pads of his fingers scraping my skin. He pulled it over my head, then studied it for a moment before threading it through his fingers and stretching it wide again.

When he reached to slip it back over my head, I leaned away from him. "Don't you have to reactivate it?"

"Yes, by putting it on you myself," Noctus said.

"You don't need to say anything?"

Noctus blinked. "No."

"You don't have to give it a spark of magic or anything?"

Noctus looked down at the collar then up at me. "It's always had my magic."

"*...what?*"

"I told you when I explained the bond, this has a piece of me in it."

"Yes," I said.

"It never stopped having a piece of me in it. While the bond can technically be revoked, the magic is permanent."

I stared at him, a feeling of incredulity replacing my giddy anxiousness. "Do you mean to say that you stuffed that necklace —which was effectively a part of you—in my backpack, *and let me wander around Magiford at will*?!"

"It wasn't that dangerous," Noctus said. "Although a part of me is in the necklace, the bond would only reactivate if I put it on you."

"What would have happened if the tracker had noticed it and tried destroying it?" I asked.

"He would have died," Noctus said.

"So it has some protections on it?"

"No," Noctus said. "But I would have felt it since I'm connected to the collar, and realized you were in danger."

I mashed my fingertips into my temple. "You are unbelievable."

"Thank you."

"I just can't even process this insane behavior."

"Aristide will be glad to hear that. He feels like he doesn't have any backup when it comes to questioning my decisions."

"*Noctus*!"

A smile tugged at Noctus's lips as he held his hands—and the collar—up. "Ready?"

I exhaled deeply, then nodded. "Ready."

Noctus lowered the stretched fabric over my head, smoothing it back on my neck.

Even though I'd been wearing it seconds ago, it felt warmer, and prickled with elf magic. Something clicked into place, and then a familiar warmth flooded me, grounding me to Noctus's presence.

I exhaled, relaxing into the magic as it seeped into my bones. "This connection stuff is amazing," I said. "I know there's a necessary trust factor, but it feels incredible. I'm sorry it's just so one-sided."

"It is possible we might be able to figure out a way for you to return the bond," Noctus said.

I perked up in his arms, shaking myself free of the drowsy stupor the warm embrace of his magic threatened to lull me into. "Really? Even though it's an elf thing?"

"The process requires elven magic, but since I'm an elf, in theory, you should be able to tap into my magic to cement your own magic to me," Noctus said.

"And how would I do that?" I asked.

Noctus glanced at the sunny ceiling. "I suppose the same way I did it. I summoned a portion of my magic, used it to trace it back to my very essence, and then used my magic to transfer that essence into the necklace."

I rubbed my thumb over the three jewels affixed to my collar. "That'll be a problem. I don't actively use my magic, except when I make the swap between my forms."

"Interesting," Noctus said.

I narrowed my eyes as I tried to hold on to Noctus's magic. "Let me just try something quick."

I tapped my shape-swapping powers before Noctus could say anything, briefly feeling my magic as I shifted into my cat shape. Unfortunately, the sensation was over faster than a single beat of my heart. It was so fast, I didn't even have a chance to really grab my magic, much less hold it.

Well. That could be a problem.

I meowed as a cat, then swapped back to my human shape.

Again, I didn't have a chance to do anything with my magic, because the moment was still fleeting. (For that matter, I wasn't sure I was even using Noctus's magic correctly. I felt the warmth of it, and was hoping that was enough.)

I switched back and forth several times—nearly smashing my head on Noctus's jaw on more than one occasion—before I was forced to take inventory of the situation while balancing on Noctus's leg in my cat shape.

I can feel Noctus's magic, but my magic is so intangible. I just can't get a grip on it.

I flicked my tail back and forth, thinking hard.

"Amalourne, relax," Noctus said. "I just got you back. I don't care if it takes us a decade to figure out how to get your half of the bond cemented, you're with me. That's all I truly care about."

I drooped, my little cat ears flattening in my disappointment. *I suppose he's right. It's not like we have to rush this.*

I jumped off his leg, then tapped my magic, turning human. "Sorry," I said. "I was just hoping it would be an easy fix."

Noctus slipped an arm around my back, scooping me closer to him. "There is nothing to apologize for," he said. "I'm delighted you want to prioritize returning the bond."

I curiously peered up at him. "I said I was in love with you, of course I'd want to prioritize it."

Noctus smiled enigmatically. "Shall we go?"

"Go where?" I asked.

He squeezed me close in a brief hug before letting me go. "To the kitchens for breakfast, or maybe my study. There's not really any point in sitting around here when we could be somewhere more comfortable—and more ready for when your siblings rise."

I scrambled to my feet. "Good point. Sure."

I brushed my legs and rear off so I didn't shed grass inside the immaculate mansion, and watched as Noctus stood with a lot more grace than I had.

On an impulse, I stood on my tiptoes so I could again throw my arms around his neck and hug him as tightly as I possibly could. "We're together again, Noctus," I said. "This next part…it might not be fun, but it's because we're not going to do this by halves."

"You're right." Noctus scooped me up again, holding me propped up against his chest so he could look directly into my eyes. "And you deserve to know—everything."

"As do you," I stubbornly said—I was *not* going to forget to tell him about Ms. Booker!

Maybe I should just get it over with.

I glanced up at Noctus, wondering.

He smiled at me, dazzling me so badly I just sat there like an idiot while he leaned closer, his lips brushing mine.

"Hold up," I said, even though I leaned closer to him. "Charon should be here any moment, and I'm pretty sure I'd die if he saw us kiss."

"He's not coming," Noctus said. "He sent Ker and Aristide to wake you up because he knew I wouldn't."

I pressed my forehead against his neck. "Are you *certain*?"

"He's been very invested in returning you to Calor Villa since the night you left." Noctus settled for kissing my earlobe since I was trying to hide my face.

"Yes, but he's a very diligent teacher." He was winning me over, so I leaned back—practically an invitation, or as close to one as I'd get.

Noctus's chuckle was deep and throaty, and he kissed his way from my cheek toward my mouth. "Maybe, but I'm his king." His lips brushed mine, and the doors slammed open.

CHAPTER TWENTY-FOUR

Chloe

I yelped and teleported a good ten feet away from Noctus, who looked unimpressed as Charon strode into the arena in a grand entrance.

"At least it's not a ridiculous *clock* this time," Noctus grumbled. "Charon, what are you doing?"

"Your Majesty, I would have thought it was obvious, I'm here to train Chloe," Charon said. "It's been months since she's had a session, she needs a refresher. Also, I wish to see what she learned from the materials you sent her."

"And you couldn't wait a few minutes more?" Noctus asked.

"I gave you twenty minutes, Your Majesty," Charon said. "Given that you spent half of the night pondering what you'd say to her, I assumed that would be plenty of time."

"You failed to add in extra minutes for all the things I want to communicate that don't involve speaking," Noctus said.

"Do that on your own time, Your Majesty," Charon said. "Chloe, defend yourself!"

I turned into a cat and ran, my tail aloft and my fur puffed up.

Charon unsheathed a sword, until Noctus stepped in front of him.

"I'll fight her—you observe, *teacher*, so you can tell her what needs work," Noctus said.

Charon tilted his head. "That's not as much fun."

"Yeah, well you ruined all of the fun I had planned, so it's a fair turn." Noctus shoved his hand into the small, glowing portal that appeared in front of him.

He pulled out a sword—its blade was made of glass while its hilt appeared to be made from a single, shining gemstone.

Ooh, I recognize that one.

It was the first heirloom weapon I'd ever seen him use.

As it had the first time, a curl of smoke formed around the sword, and then engulfed Noctus, hardening into armor: a helm that covered his skull and eyes and cut off at the bridge of his nose, a chest plate, chainmail, boots, and gauntlets, all dark and all ornamented with a feather-like design.

The armor was stunningly beautiful and deadly, and with his eyes hidden, Noctus's smile seemed almost feral.

"Here, kitty, kitty," he said.

I was so outraged by this turn of events that I switched to my human shape so I could shout—from the relative safety of one of the rock formations placed strategically throughout the arena. "He's fighting with a royal weapon? That's not even giving me a sporting chance!"

"It will be a valuable experience for you," Charon said. "So you can see an heirloom in action, and know how to fight on the chance that one responds to you after you renew the bond."

I shuffled around to the opposite end of my pile of boulders. "We already renewed the bond—and I've tried pulling royal weapons in the past without luck!"

"Well, then, this will encourage you to try harder the next time you attempt it," Charon said.

I would have yelled some more, but Noctus had found me, so I turned back into a cat and ran around the rocks. Once out of sight I turned into a human and jumped, scrambling on top of the lowest boulder in the formation, before turning into a cat and climbing higher.

Tucked deep into a crevasse, I waited until Noctus passed below me before turning human and springing on him from above.

I was trying to land on his head, but Noctus heard me and pivoted, angling his body so I landed on his shoulder.

He was able to roll with my momentum—a move that would have flung me off. Except I turned into a cat and dug my claws into his chainmail, so I flopped, but stayed in place.

When he moved to slam his back into the rock formation, I released my claws and changed into a human, dropping behind him, then changed back into a cat to run between his legs, before changing to a human again so I rammed into him with the unforgiving force of my magic.

This proved to be a slight miscalculation—I hit my head on his armored thigh in the process and barely managed to unsheathe my sword—so I turned back into a cat and staggered away as Noctus backed off, trying to put space between us and regain his sense of balance.

Changing back and forth so quickly was a testament to the growing hardiness of my stomach—I'd been working on the rapid switches for weeks, and the hardest part about it was the frantic changes that came with my viewpoint from shooting up and down instantaneously.

"You've improved your abilities," Noctus said.

Suspicious—in my experience Noctus and Charon were both honorable, but unbelievably conniving—I made a run for the rock formation again.

"But still inclined to run rather than fight, I see," Charon said.

I backed into a small space that was just big enough for me to change in, swapped into my human form, then crouched, waiting for a chance.

Noctus drew even with my hole, and I lashed out, stabbing my sword through the greaves of his metal boots.

"Maybe not so inclined," Noctus said. He stabbed his sword straight into the rock formation. I heard a click, and then a blast went off.

I curled into a ball and covered my head as rocks and pebbles pelted my body.

When everything had settled—except for the cloud of dust—Charon called out to me. "Do you know what you did wrong there?"

I uncurled, then staggered out of the cloud of dust. "I didn't follow up my attack, so Noctus had plenty of time to counter?"

"Indeed," Charon said. "It was a good initial attack, you just need to be fiercer."

I made a noise in the back of my throat. "Fierce. Right. That's me, the fierce housecat."

"You were fierce when you took down Harel and Darina," Charon said. "I saw the footage."

"You can be very fierce." Noctus rested the point of his sword on the ground. "The problem is you constantly underestimate your skills in comparison to your enemy's, and you only truly go for it if you feel backed into a corner—something that happens to you with shocking frequency."

"I imagine it would be easier to be fierce if you could wield a royal heirloom," Charon said with too much complacency for it to be an offhanded remark.

"He has a point," Noctus said. "Since we renewed the bond, you could try reaching for a royal weapon again."

"Oh, because I haven't already failed enough today?" I asked.

"It seems you must learn the lesson that a poor attitude begets poor results," Charon said.

"Fine. Fine. How do I do it again?" I asked.

"Follow the sensation of my magic through the collar, back to me," Noctus said. "Through me, you should be able to access the gate to my weapons—it'll feel different from my magic because the weapons have powers of their own."

"Okay." I squeezed my eyes shut, and followed his magic.

It was easier, this time, to trace his magic through the collar back to him and find the gate to his weapons. I don't know if it was experience, or just because I knew him even better now.

My shadow instincts started rolling around in my gut, but I ignored it as I reached—both physically and mentally—for the gate.

I felt magic engulf my hand—a prickly sort of magic that was even sharper than the general sensation of elf magic.

I pried an eye open and saw my right hand was thrust into a tiny portal that glowed white. My hand had that weird topsy-turvy sensation portals always produced, but when I opened both of my eyes and crouched like some kind of swamp creature I could look inside, where I caught sight of shadowy shapes that I recognized as Noctus's various weapons.

"I know you have hundreds of them, so statistically there should be one that likes me, but I think they can tell I'm a shadow," I said. "They don't seem very keen to approach me. None of them are even getting close this time."

"Can you hear anything different?" Noctus asked. "Not in an auditory sense, but rather something you feel?"

I tilted my head sideways as I struggled with the concept of hearing without my ears. "No. Nothing."

"Perhaps with time they will grow more accustomed to you," Charon suggested.

I shook my head as I pulled my hand from the small portal.

Just before I pulled my fingertips free, I heard it.

Truck.

The word unfurled from my heart, in a voice that I didn't recognize, and was strangely hard to pin down and describe. It was low pitched, I think, but it was almost more like I felt the word than I heard it.

"I take it back, I'm hearing 'Truck' again," I said.

Charon narrowed his eyes. "Truck?"

"Yeah, I know," I agreed with his unspoken judgment. "I heard it the first time Noctus had me try this, too. He told me then there wasn't a weapon with that name—which makes sense since motor vehicles weren't invented until after the elven war. I'm probably mishearing it. Maybe they're cursing at me in elvish and I just can't hear it well enough?" I tried wriggling my fingers, but I didn't feel anything solidify within my grasp.

Hello? I tried to think it with all my mind, but I wasn't entirely sure how heirlooms chose to communicate with their chosen wielders. *Are you there?*

Nothing.

I didn't even hear the name again.

"The heirlooms are not cursing at you," Noctus said. "That's not how their limited sentience works."

"Well, whatever weapon it is, it isn't coming closer. It's probably a hallucination," I said as I finally pulled my hand free.

"You are too sane to hallucinate," Noctus said.

Charon neither agreed nor disagreed with him. "Since it seems using an heirloom is not possible at this stage, we shall continue with a review of your strategy in the fight against Noctus." He turned a page in his journal, reviewing some of his previous notes. "Let us begin with your attempt to jump on top of Noctus from the rocks. A smart move to use the terrain to your advantage, but it would have worked better if you had thrown a distraction and *then* jumped. Let's practice. Use the rock formation over there..."

SINCE PAT and Joy had both taken the day off after the fight with the tracker, when dinner was held in the early evening (early, because I had a shift at Book Nookery I needed to get to) they both were still hanging out at the mansion.

I didn't know if it was because Noctus was trying to put his best foot forward, or Charon was chuffed to finally have guests, but we ate in a room I had never seen before.

A cross between a dining room and a conservatory, the ceiling and one wall were glass held in place by metal welded to look like vines, while the solid wall was covered by darkly paneled wood and torches that flickered with Noctus's white and blue flames.

The windows showed a view of the mountains, city, and lake—all cast in orange and pink from the setting sun—and were lined by greenery: wild roses, hydrangeas, and bushes I didn't recognize with delicate pink, white, and purple buds.

"Thank you for inviting us to dinner, Noctus." Joy selected another piece of fresh focaccia bread and added it to her plate—patterned light blue and gray with golden fleurs. "The food is phenomenal."

"Yeah," Pat agreed. "Everything is amazing. But I still want to know, Chloe, are you moving back here?"

"Yes," I said without thinking as I selected a Romanian cabbage roll. (The mysterious chefs I never saw but seemed omnipresent had thoughtfully labeled everything.)

"If either of you, Joy and Pat, should wish to move into the mansion as well, we have plenty of room," Noctus said. "Regardless, we will keep your rooms open for you in case of any visit."

"Huh," Pat said. "Interesting. Ker, could you pass the baked salmon?"

Charon, who had been talked into sitting by Joy and was seemingly shell shocked she'd accomplished it—I couldn't remember if I'd ever seen Charon *sit* before—bolted to his feet. "I can fetch them—"

"Sit down, Charon, I've got it." Ker handed the plate off to Pat before Charon could move.

"That is a very kind offer, Noctus, but I believe we need to talk with Chloe before taking you up on it," Joy said.

I peered at my sister—who I sat next to—in surprise and with some suspicion. "Why?"

Joy leaned in and whispered. "I don't want to make you feel pressured, or like you think we don't trust you."

Oh...she's giving me the space to be...like I asked them to.

They were trying—it had only been a day, and they were already trying.

I really do have the best family.

I cleared my throat. "The villa is gorgeous, there's an entire city outside the window, the food is the best I've ever had, and it's free. I'd think you moved because you'd be crazy not to. But I appreciate what you're trying to do."

"In that case..." Joy straightened up and smiled at Noctus. "Perhaps in a month or two, I will make the move. I'll have to decide if I want to break the lease or find a subleaser."

"That won't be a problem," Noctus said. "I own the building. I'll let you out of the lease."

I choked on my cabbage roll. "*What?*"

Noctus tapped a finger on the stem of his crystal wine glass. "Didn't I tell you? I bought it when you were staying here."

"*Why* would you do that?!"

"Because it badly needed a security upgrade since the tracker was on your tail, and I knew the original owner wouldn't be open to the suggestion," Noctus said. "It's just as well. When we go public, my people won't be forced to live in Calor anymore, but I'd need to offer an equally safe and secure alternative."

I almost stood up in my shock. "Wait, you own it! That's how you got in when you brought me home from the pet shelter!"

"Indeed," Noctus said.

"What did I tell you, Pat? A rich Legolas," Joy muttered.

Pat didn't acknowledge Joy's observation, but he did look at Noctus. "Unlike my sisters, I'll have to stay where I'm at." He awkwardly stared at the butter—which had been sculpted into a flower shape and drizzled with honey. "As much as I complained when I first moved, having an apartment close to work has been a huge advantage. But, thank you for the offer."

"Of course," Noctus said.

"You'll just have to visit lots," Ker said from farther down the table. "The elves have all kinds of fun festivals you don't want to miss!"

The scent of the rose bush behind me tickled my nose as I took a thick slice of what I recognized from my previous stay as elven sweet bread.

"Chloe, don't you want any chicken kabobs?" Joy asked. "They're amazing, and I don't think you've tried them."

"Sure, I'll take a skewer, thanks." I took the plate she passed and added a marinated chicken kabob to my plate.

"Finally got over your avoidance, hmm?" Aristide lifted his wine cup of blood and smiled enigmatically.

"Her what?" Pat asked blankly.

"I suppose she hasn't had time to tell you." Aristide's chuckle worried me. "When Noctus first adopted her and didn't know she wasn't a cat, for *weeks* all we fed her was roasted chicken."

"Is that why you refused to eat chicken for several weeks after we first moved here, Chloe?" Joy asked.

"Yes," I slowly said, half unwilling because I knew my siblings were going to rib me about this for weeks.

"It took us some time to realize she had a wider palate than we gave her credit for, considering she would not eat the cat food or raw meat the internet told us to offer," Noctus said. "She nearly fell out of my arms in her exuberance when an elf child offered her a strawberry."

Pat found this so funny, he made a honking noise.

I scowled at him. "It wasn't funny. I didn't even get any milk because they knew cats are lactose intolerant. I'm still bearing a grudge over that, *Aristide*!"

"I'd apologize, but if you had gotten sick, Noctus would have turned the entire villa upside down trying to cure you," Aristide said. "And that sounds messy."

Pat nodded in approval. "Diligent pet ownership is important."

Desperate to change the flow of the conversation, I cleared my throat. "Hey, Pat, were you able to close the case on the tracker in a way that the Curia Cloisters accepted?" I asked.

"The guy is dead," Pat said. "There's not much they can do."

Aristide snorted into his wine glass of blood at the observation.

"It's good timing, actually," Pat said. "The Regional Committee of Magic isn't happy about all the artifact incidents, so we've been wanting to put more resources on the issue. This will free some up."

"It'll free *you* up," Joy corrected.

"I had guys looking for the tracker," Pat defended himself. "And I hate to break it to you, sis, but I work with folks who are more than capable of pulverizing me." He paused, then added, "Though I am the only human, so they were stoked that I'll be primarily working on this case now." He fussed with his cloth napkin—like I said, they were going all out—then glanced at Noctus. "If you find anything, I'd appreciate it."

Noctus nodded. "Then I should let you know that—thanks to Chloe's visual of him—we were able to confirm that the fae we believe was responsible for the first artifact attack, and was involved with organizing the illegal manufacturing ring we broke at the end of spring, was present downtown the day of the most recent attack."

Pat sat up straighter in his chair. "Do you have any pictures of him? Anything I can share with my guys?"

"Yes," Noctus said. "We'll see to it that—"

Charon immediately stood. "I could fetch them now."

"Sit down, Charon," Ker said.

A muscle in Charon's jaw twitched, but he sat down and reluctantly picked up the cup of tea he'd poured himself.

"Do you know where he was downtown?" Pat asked. "Because we were able to trace the epicenter of the explosion on the sidewalk. If we can pin him to that area, we'd have a case."

"What stores is the spot near?" Ker asked.

"Just outside a pet grooming salon," Pat said. "Paw & Order."

"I'd have to see a map, but I don't know that we had any footage from that particular area," Noctus said.

Charon shook his head. "None of our people work in a grooming salon."

"That's a shame," I said. "With the elves' natural aptitude with animals, I bet they'd be fantastic at it."

"All elves don't have animal magnetism," Charon said. "It's a skill that varies."

"Oh," I said. "Is that why Noctus made such a big deal about it, because it's rare?"

Aristide laughed as he leaned back in his chair. "He made a big deal about it because Noctus is one of the most intense pet parents walking this world. Something I had no inkling of until you came into our lives, so we have much to thank you for, Chloe."

Pat awkwardly cleared his throat. "Yeah, Chloe is great. But thank you for sharing information...Noctus and Charon."

Charon just nodded, but Noctus flashed a polite smile at my brother. "Of course. Is there anything else we should know?"

Pat frowned as he thought. "We recovered the artifact used to make the noise, too: a green gem—that apparently couldn't handle the spell because it was cracked pretty badly."

"Do you know what kind of gem it is?" Charon asked. "Perhaps the cut, or size?"

"I happened to see it, and it was smaller than a ping-pong ball, but I don't know enough about rocks to make any kind of guess whether it was an actual jewel or just a crystal, sorry," Pat said.

"Don't be," Noctus said. "Crystals can hold spells as well as jewels, so the type doesn't necessarily matter, it just makes it easier to track."

Pat nodded, but he'd dug into his dinner, so he couldn't reply.

The rest of the table was silent, except for the rattles of our plates and the crystalline noises our cups made.

I was digging into my food—Charon had worked me *hard*—but I did finally notice when Joy wiped her mouth for the third time in a row as she eyed our hosts.

"I hope I'm not overstepping any boundaries," she cautiously started, "so please excuse my boldness, but it occurred to me that if the elves go public, it might be ideal for them to use a situation like this fae setting off artifacts to their advantage."

Pat—his mouth once again full of food—eyed our sister.

I—on a similar wavelength—asked in his place. "What do you mean, they could use it to their advantage?"

"If the elves helped the Curia Cloisters capture this fae guy and went public at the same time, you'd be able to assure humans of your good intentions. It'd be an excellent PR opportunity," Joy said. "And with the supernaturals set against you, you'll want to focus, first, on appealing to humans before then attempting to restore your reputation with supernaturals."

"And you have an idea for that, too?" I guessed.

"Yes," Joy said. "But not one I'm willing to share just yet." She glanced at Noctus and Charon, then uneasily shifted in her chair.

"It's a worthy suggestion," Noctus said. "Though it's to be hoped that the artifacts case is closed well before the elves need to come forward."

"What kind of a timeline are you thinking?" I asked.

Noctus frowned. "I'm not fully certain, yet. We just had time to inform the city leaders of all that happened last night, and I'll have to include the Paragon in some of the conversations—unfortunately. I'm hoping we'll be able to wait until next year—to give the elves who work in Magiford time to prepare. But I'm aware time is not necessarily on our side."

"In that case, I apologize for bringing up such a grim topic," Joy said.

"No apologies are necessary," Ker assured her with a grin. "This is something that needs to be talked about. And I'll fess up that we researched you and Pat when you moved back to Magiford, so we know you're speaking from a point of knowledge. By the way, I find your work with supernaturals so fascinating and encouraging!"

"Oh, thank you." Joy smiled as she dipped her focaccia bread in olive oil that was seasoned with fresh herbs. "I'm happy I can help them. American systems—particularly the red tape that goes into owning a small business—can be confusing for humans, it's no wonder there aren't a lot of businesses that are supernatural owned."

"Yes!" Ker nodded vigorously as she cut into her baked salmon. "I own several businesses myself, and it took me decades to learn how to correctly and legally integrate them into human society. I'm so excited that more supernaturals are starting to follow suit. Has anyone from Magiford approached you for help yet?"

Oh. I ate my elven sweet bread. *I'm pretty sure I know where this is going.* Grinning, I peered down the table to find Noctus watching me.

Slowly, he smiled back, his humor making the spirals in his eyes swirl.

"Yes, actually," Joy said. "There is a brownie bakery—I mean a bakery run by fae brownies, not the dessert—that's opening in a new apartment building soon. They had a fae lawyer who helped them, and I believe the fae Night Queen had some of her people help them, too, but they wanted to know the particulars about advertising, and they had a few questions about obtaining a liquor license."

"That's marvelous!" Ker said. "And exactly the kind of thing I love hearing. Let me ask you, have you heard of Dale Carnegie?"

Yep. She went there.

Aristide groaned and picked his cloth napkin off his lap so he could dramatically toss it at the table. "Ker, must you discuss *that man* at the dinner table?"

My cellphone alarm went off, so I took a sip of water from a crystal chalice—elves, man—then hurriedly stood up. "I hate to eat and run, but I've got to head out for my shift." I pulled my phone from my pocket and flicked the alarm off as I hip-bumped my chair back into place, then grabbed my jacket, which I'd thrown over the back of it.

"Bye, sis." Pat didn't even look up from his plate of Brazilian BBQ and grilled pineapple.

Joy leaned back in her seat so she could look up at me. "Have a good shift, Chloe!" This was accompanied by a little handwave before she turned back to Ker.

Charon's gaze narrowed on me—a practical excuse to stand and stop picking at his food—and he leaped to his feet.

Before he could say anything, Noctus spoke. "I'll drive you, Chloe."

Aristide had been lounging in his chair, taking delicate sips from his goblet, but at this proclamation he snorted, spattering blood around his cup. "Do you even have an up-to-date driver's license?"

Noctus rolled his eyes as he strolled across the garden room, joining me by the door. "Yes. I just never drive *you*, because you endlessly complain I take corners too fast."

"Because you do," Aristide said. "Make certain you buckle up, Chloe."

"Thanks, Aristide. Goodbye, everyone!" I stepped through the door Noctus held open for me, and waited for him to close it. "That was fun."

"Yes," Noctus said, leading the way down the long corridor. "It was interesting to see you have your own variation of teasing from your siblings that I experience from Ker and Aristide."

"Interesting?" I asked. "How?"

Noctus shrugged. "I'm not very familiar with healthy family relationships, so I didn't know how they would act with you. I will confess, it makes me glad. I don't think Aristide will ever pick on you the way he does on me—he's too grateful for your existence. It warms my heart to know there is someone in your life capable of similarly embarrassing you."

"Noctus!" I said, caught halfway between laughter and surprise. "The scandal of it!"

The smile Noctus gave me was softer and relaxed the tense air around him more than any of the polite smiles he'd bestowed upon my siblings. He held his hand out, palm facing me.

For a moment, I didn't know what he wanted—we'd been apart for months—until my muscle memory kicked in, and I tapped my palm to his.

Noctus entwined his fingers with mine, holding my hand so I couldn't let go, and swung it with a relaxed air.

It's because he's happy, I realized. *He also didn't think we'd ever work, but because of his people, we are.*

I mean, I was pretty happy, too. I obviously had missed Noctus a lot, but I hadn't realized how much I missed our bond.

Even now, my collar—or necklace as I was describing it to my siblings—was a warm reassurance.

Noctus might think his past is a red flag, but we got through me pretending to be a cat and him making me his well-fed prisoner. We're going to be fine.

It occurred to me that it was perhaps a tad hypocritical to be assuming that, when I hadn't told him about Ms. Booker.

But the status of our relationship—and my trust in Noctus—

weren't really my biggest worries. Trying to figure out how to return the bond was.

Still...it's not like I'm looking forward to this.

"Hey, Noctus? I need to tell you something." My voice wobbled as we walked down the hallway, Noctus moving more slowly to set a pace that was comfortable for me.

"Yes?" Noctus asked when I didn't immediately continue.

"I told someone about you—I never mentioned Calor Villa or even Charon. I just told them I was living as your pet, and that you were from the Mors royal family."

CHAPTER TWENTY-FIVE

Chloe

Noctus thought for a moment. "Your employer?"

My eyes grew wide. "Yeah. How'd you know?"

"I didn't. It was the most logical guess," Noctus said. "You hadn't told your siblings or family—you wouldn't want to put them in danger—but you have the sense to know your cat act was potentially dangerous and seek help. Book Nookery has an odd sort of power to it, and I knew the Curia Cloisters actively stonewalled you, so Ms. Booker is a reasonable supernatural you would look to for advice." His face had lost the relaxed expression, but he didn't seem angry.

"She hasn't told anyone," I quickly said, though I was pretty sure that based on the way Noctus hadn't let go of my hand, he wasn't upset. That thought cheered me on as we started down a spiral staircase. "But she did help me research the collar once I realized you were able to track me, and she knows about the bond."

Noctus slowly nodded. "When did she learn of it?"

"The bond? Well, she didn't know the details and precise type of bond—I never did tell her, since I left shortly after you explained it to me, and she very kindly never asked."

Most likely because I acted like a nutcase with a broken heart when I got back to work, but Noctus doesn't need to know that.

I convulsively tightened my loose grip on Noctus's hand, but was too embarrassed to look at him as I stared straight ahead while we cleared the last stair. "But Ms. Booker realized it was an elven bond pretty shortly before I revealed myself to you."

"I see," Noctus said.

Silence stretched between us as we turned up a hallway, still heading for the front door.

"I'm...I'm sorry, but also not sorry I didn't tell you when I was still living here in the villa," I continued. "For so long, I didn't know what was going on, and I needed someone in my corner, or—"

"Chloe." Noctus stopped and turned to me. He tugged me closer with his grip on my hand, then slid his free hand under my chin, tilting it up so I'd look at him. "You did what was right for you. I was keeping you captive in Calor Villa. You would have been an idiot to let yourself be so entirely isolated when you had no reason to believe I'd protect you."

I took a breath, then nodded. "Thank you for understanding."

"It was a smart—and reasonable—thing to do," Noctus said. "It was a way of protecting yourself—something I would rather you be proactive in."

He smiled finally, and there was almost a sly quality to the twitch of his lips. "Besides, I'm proud that you were able to carry the entire thing out right under my nose. Charon will be furious he didn't catch on."

I shyly smiled back, relieved I'd finally told him.

Noctus brushed the gems on my necklace with his thumb before he reluctantly started off for the front door once again.

"And while I'm grateful you told me for the sake of our relationship, the fact is it doesn't particularly matter that you told your employer since she refrained from attempting to blackmail us, and we will be going public shortly, so there isn't a chance to use this information to her advantage."

"Well. I was going to ask if I could tell her about everything that happened," I said. We were almost to the front door by this point—I could see the giant golden gate we'd have to pass through to get out to the Cape Cod's front lawn. "Including Calor Villa."

Noctus slightly narrowed his eyes. "And you believe she will use *that* information to her advantage?"

"Sort of?" I said. "I'm pretty sure she'd start ordering more elf books—both fiction and nonfiction—in advance to prepare for what's going to be a book-boom. So she'd economically use it to her advantage?"

Noctus laughed. He laughed so hard we stopped all forward progress.

"Chloe," he said, swinging our joint hands when he finally recovered. "That isn't the type of advantage I was referring to."

"Yeah, I guessed that," I said. "But I wanted to be forthright."

Noctus pulled the golden gate, which opened without so much as a creak. "Then thank you for your forthrightness."

We stepped through the portal, and I was able to keep a semblance of balance this time as we passed through the dizzying swirl and stepped onto the cement porch of the Cape Cod house.

The chill of October nipped at me through my jacket. "Oh," I said, thinking of my workplace. "Charon and the others probably told you, but Lord Linus—father of Queen Leila of the Night Court—has bus tours that stop by Book Nookery to see me since I'm the last shadow. Once we go public, there's a good chance he'll also advertise the fact that I'm your girlfriend to try to get even more gawkers."

Noctus dug a garage door opener out of his pocket and clicked it, so the garage door slowly rattled into motion, winding back to reveal the black SUV in the garage. "Then he'd be better off advertising our bond—that's more impressive than a paltry title like girlfriend," Noctus said.

"You can give him that business advice." I tugged my jacket closer with my free hand as we approached the garage. "I'm just telling you, so you can decide if you want to produce Mors Elves merchandise or something."

"Ahh, yes. Ker has already been badgering me to begin merchandising efforts. And she keeps leaving copies of *How to Win Friends and Influence People* in my bedroom. As if she didn't make Aristide, Charon, and me read it every decade."

"Chloe?" Shiloh stood across the street, squinting in the evening light as she rested a hand on her mailbox. She stared at us for a moment, then brightened—her entire face lighting up. "You two made up?"

"Um," I said.

"Yes," Noctus said. "I finally groveled, and Chloe has graciously accepted me again."

"That's not *at all* what happened," I said, and was ignored.

"Way to go, Mr. Shade!" Shiloh winked and gave him thumbs up. "I'm so happy for you—the whole neighborhood is happy for you, aren't we, uncles?" Shiloh turned on her heel and expectantly peered at the house next to hers.

A light abruptly turned on over her neighbors' porch, lighting up where the neighborhood "uncles" typically hung out.

Three shapes were planted there, and it took me a second to realize it was the uncles. They were wearing dresses, bundled in shawls, and had surprisingly well styled wigs perched on their heads. All three of them had balls of yarn in their laps, and appeared to be wielding large knitting needles.

"Boo!" cackled the uncle with a mustache. "What do you think of our Halloween costumes? Scary, eh?"

"Forget that." The second uncle poked him with one of his needles. "Look, the sonny finally got his girl back!"

"Bravo!" the third uncle shouted. "We never thought we'd see it!"

"That's hardly supportive," the mustache uncle said.

"Oh, right," the third uncle said. "Let me clarify: it's not that we thought it wouldn't ever happen, we just thought we'd die first!"

Shiloh shook her head as she traipsed across the street, joining us on the driveway. "Don't listen to them," she said. "We were all pulling for you. And welcome back, Chloe!"

My cheeks heated with a blush. "Thanks," I said. "How are you doing, Shiloh?"

"Couldn't be better!" Shiloh grinned. "My classes are going swimmingly—thanks for helping me with that book."

"Of course," I said. "I'm glad we had it in stock. Are you deep into midterms now?"

"Yes, but most of my classes just have papers this semester." Shiloh glanced back at her house, a brief frown flickering across her face before she smiled at me. "Hey, I wanted to ask how you like the renovations at your apartment complex, and about apartment life in general."

"Oh." I blinked, trying to remember exactly what we'd said to Shiloh when Noctus and I had first used the excuse of apartment renovations to explain my sudden neighbor appearance. "Um..."

"The security system finally got a well needed update, so the place is quite safe," Noctus said.

"Yeah it did," I muttered under my breath.

"That's great since safety matters," Shiloh said. "How expensive is apartment living—if you don't mind me asking?"

"It varies a lot depending on the type of apartment," I said. "My studio is pretty cheap, but my sister, Joy, has a two bedroom in the same place with a walkout patio, and it's way more expensive, but reasonable considering the size. The closer to downtown you go the more expensive it will get, though."

Shiloh nodded slowly, her expression still less than her usually bright and bubbly self.

She's alone—both of her parents died. I assumed her dad must have left her more than the house, but maybe the finances are becoming a strain?

I offered her the most reassuring smile I had in my arsenal. "Magiford has shockingly affordable rent. If you want to try an apartment, this is the city to do it in."

"It's the supernaturals," Noctus said. "Although they make up a large portion of the city's population, very few of them would be willing to live in an apartment, so there's not much of a demand."

"Really?" Shiloh asked.

Noctus nodded. "Werewolves would feel too cramped, and vampires are too snobby. Wizards would, but by nature they live in Houses, so that leaves fae. The big fae Courts all live on their sovereign's land, so they wouldn't be competing for housing either."

"Mmm, but what about that supernatural apartment complex that's newly opened?" I asked.

"That's different. Those apartments are designed with supernaturals in mind, and it's specifically for the outcasts of society." Noctus's expression wasn't *watchful* exactly as he studied Shiloh, but he was definitely catching on to whatever I was feeling, too. "Is everything all right, Shiloh?"

"Oh, yeah." Shiloh laughed. "Everything is as sharp as sharp cheddar! I'm just curious."

"You know you can ask me for help," Noctus said. "*Any* kind of help, yes?"

"Yep." Shiloh grinned as she started to back toward the sidewalk. "I know, Mr. Shade. Dad told me you were one of the good ones."

"I've told you before to call me Noctus," Noctus called after her.

Shiloh laughed. "Not gonna happen, Mr. Shade. I'm hedging my bets that Chloe doesn't have any young relatives, so I'll get to be the flower girl at your wedding if I act young enough!"

"The *what?*" Noctus said, his forehead wrinkling with confusion.

"Ask Chloe about it," Shiloh advised as she crossed the street.

"Please don't," I said.

"Then ask Charon," Shiloh yelled back to us.

"Definitely not that, either!" I yelped.

Shiloh laughed. "Have a great night, you two!" She grabbed the mail from her mailbox before heading inside.

Noctus and I waved to the uncles before heading into the garage.

I waited until we got into the car and I was buckled in before asking. "Do you think Shiloh is doing okay?"

"No." Noctus braced his arm on my seat so he could look through the back window as he backed the vehicle up. "And it frustrates me that she won't tell me why."

I tapped my feet on the rubber car mat—it seemed Charon had switched the mats out in preparation for the incoming winter weather—puzzling it over.

While Noctus has been concerned for humans in the past, it's more in a detached sort of way as it usually comes from his concern for his people living amongst the humans. He's protective of his entire neighborhood, but he seems to treat Shiloh with the same care he treats one of his people...

"So," Noctus prompted me. "What is a flower girl?"

I slumped in my seat in defeat. "Oh boy."

BECAUSE OF SOME scheduling for one of the afternoon workers, my shift at Book Nookery started later than usual, so I didn't finish until about six thirty in the morning, which was when Ms. Booker came mincing down the stairs to relieve me.

"Good morning, Chloe, dear," Ms. Booker said.

"Good morning, Ms. Booker." I put the last book away that I was restocking, then collapsed the now empty box I'd been carrying it in. "Thank you so much for giving me off my previous shift. I'm sorry about the last-minute change."

Ms. Booker smiled and adjusted her pearl necklace—this time matched by a pearl bracelet. As usual she was nothing less than genteel and tidy with her black skirt and orange sweater—which was about as close as Ms. Booker got to embracing the seasonal changes.

"It was no trouble, dear," she said. "The other clerks have already informed me you took on two extra shifts they needed covered as thanks. You are quite conscientious about such things. I am glad for you that you are back with your elf."

"Yeah, I mean yes." I awkwardly folded the collapsed box in half, then opened the closet where we stored recyclables and tossed it in. "He's coming to pick me up this morning, so I was hoping you'd be interested in meeting him."

Ms. Booker raised her penciled-in eyebrows. "You told him I know about him?"

"Yes." I darted back behind the desk so I could sign out of my checkout ID in the system. "I told him yesterday when he dropped me off, but my shift was so late that you'd already retired for the evening."

"The wise are early to rise," Ms. Booker said. "But yes, I'd be delighted to meet your beau."

"Um," I said.

A hint of a wicked smile tugged at Ms. Booker's lips—colored with perfectly applied red lipstick that had a hue of orange in it to match her sweater. "There is no need to be shy, Chloe, dear."

"It's not that, I just wanted to tell you..." I took a deep breath in, then let it out. "There are more elves alive than just him," I said. "Some work for him, others he's protecting. There's a whole city, actually, that lives in a corner of the fae realm he's carved out with barriers. I've known for a while, but I didn't tell you because I didn't want to endanger you."

Ms. Booker set a hand on the desk. "I see," she said. "Then I assume you must believe it's safe to tell me now?"

"Because they're going to go public within the next year," I admitted. "I wanted to tell you now, though, since I know you won't share the information."

Ms. Booker nodded thoughtfully. "You are correct. But I will be forthright and say I won't share the information, only because these elves are all attached to your King of the Mors."

I blinked. "You trust my judgment of him?"

"Partially, yes," Ms. Booker said. "It is more that I trust his judgment of character for choosing *you.* But also because as a scholar of history, I am fairly certain we have that king of yours to thank for the supernaturals winning the war against the elves."

I mashed my lips together—I'd gotten hints that Noctus was indirectly responsible for the win before, because he'd wiped his family out, and they'd been the elves' strongest fighting force with their death magic.

But I haven't talked to Noctus about it yet, and that's something I want to hear from him.

Ms. Booker glanced at the clock. "Your beau I assume won't arrive for another minute or two. Why don't we retreat to the kitchen? A revelation such as this warrants a cup of tea, and we will hear the bell if anyone enters. Then you can tell me more of what has happened."

"Okay."

I followed Ms. Booker into the back and filled her in on the Calor Villa, the clocktower, and the elves' presence in Magiford.

It took less time to explain things to her than it had to Pat or Joy, because Ms. Booker had already been aware of Noctus and had a much better reference of elves in general as a wizard with a penchant for history and books.

"I appreciate your candor," Ms. Booker said when I finished.

"I shall not abuse your trust—although you are right, I will do my best to order elf books in preparation. Mr. Gleevers will be thrilled," she dryly predicted.

"Yes, it's a shame there aren't many books about elves in existence," I said.

"Nonfiction books? Oh, yes. But there are a shocking number of fiction fantasy romance books that feature elves," Ms. Booker said. "Those will be the best sellers. We'll have to plan for a special display once the announcement is made."

My mouth dropped open at the thought of my elegant employer making a display of fantasy romance books—Ms. Booker had always favored nonfiction over fiction, so it was already a bit of a shock that she knew about the elf romances—so even though I heard the bell attached to the front door, I could only stare at her.

Ms. Booker, having finished her cup of tea and begun bustling around the kitchen, peered through the doorway. "Oh," she said. "Judging by his stature and appearance, I would say this is your beau, Chloe, dear?"

I bolted from my chair and zipped in front of Ms. Booker—a protective measure drilled into me thanks to Pat—and relaxed when I recognized Noctus.

He smiled when he saw me. "Chloe," he said. "Charon and the others are waiting in the car. Shall we leave?"

Others? Aren't we just going home? Or were Aristide and Ker that desperate to get out for the day?

Despite being a vampire, Aristide was shockingly prone to being awake and active in the mornings. I suspected it was because he was just that old and powerful based on all the jokes Ker and Noctus made.

Ms. Booker ignored my surprise and took advantage of the situation.

"Just a moment, sir." She scooted around me and marched toward Noctus. "I request a chance to meet you."

"Of course," Noctus said, standing still as Ms. Booker appraised him. He was wearing a suit today—his typical clothing whenever we ventured into Magiford, unless it was for training—and his golden hair was slicked back with more of a businessman look to it than its usual artfully tousled state.

He took off his aviator sunglasses, and he must have dropped the glamour that hid his ears—longer and more tapered than the average fae's—since Ms. Booker startled.

"I am Noctus Mors," Noctus said. "Last of my line, King of the Mors, Bearer of Destruction, and ruler of Calor Villa."

Ms. Booker dipped in a perfect curtsey. "Mildred Booker," she said. "Owner and proprietor of Book Nookery."

I was average height, and I looked short in comparison to Noctus, but Ms. Booker was petite, so standing in front of Noctus, she looked *tiny*.

"Ms. Booker." Noctus slightly inclined his head. "I have heard much about you and your store. It's an honor."

"Thank you. I have heard some varied reviews of your conduct," Ms. Booker frankly said. "But it seems that you have finally settled things."

"We're attempting to settle them." I grabbed my backpack and jacket from the cupboard I used to stow my stuff, then shuffled into the lobby. "There have been a few hiccups."

Noctus held his hand out to me. I took it, and *tried* to hear the choir of magic I knew Noctus heard, but even with my collar activated I still couldn't hear it.

"I see," Ms. Booker said. "You aspire to have a full bond together, then?"

I almost dropped my backpack, and the only noise that could make it out of my suddenly collapsed lungs was a pained wheeze.

"Yes," Noctus said—not at all embarrassed. "The irregularities of Chloe's relationship with magic mean the common way of bonding isn't possible, but we'll figure out a way to overcome it."

"You think it's truly possible for her to bond with you?" Ms. Booker asked.

"Given magic's favoritism toward shadows, I could not imagine it wouldn't allow it," Noctus said. "It's too advantageous for her—something I hope to capitalize on."

I hemmed and hawed some more, but the corners of Ms. Booker's lips turned up—which meant she didn't just like him, she approved of him. (Ms. Booker was not a woman who was fast to smile.)

A car horn honked outside, followed by silence, then three additional short blasts.

Noctus looked back at the front door. "We'd better get going. It seems they're getting restless."

"Indeed. It was good to meet you, Your Majesty," Ms. Booker said.

"It was my honor, Ms. Booker." Noctus tugged me out of the bookstore, and when I popped out into the dreary morning light—the sun hadn't risen yet, and the sky was cloudy, so everything was a gloomy gray color—I saw the familiar black SUV...rocking wildly on its wheels.

I clutched my backpack to my chest. "Woah."

"Ker is excited to be going into Magiford in her human form," Noctus said. "Charon isn't one for appreciating exuberance."

The windows were tinted, so we couldn't see what was going on inside, but I wasn't too surprised when Noctus opened the side door, revealing Aristide cackling as he poked his cane up by Charon, smashing it on the steering wheel.

Ker had her hands flush against the ceiling and was bouncing up and down in the car, while Charon pulled a handgun from a shoulder holster hidden in the folds of his cloak-like shirt.

"Stop disturbing the peace, or I'll shoot you," Charon told the vampire.

"You'd hurt *me*?" Aristide asked, planting a hand on his chest in horror.

"You'd survive," Charon grimly said.

"You sound disappointed about that," Aristide said.

"I might be," Charon said. "Good morning, sir. I'd get out to open the door for you and Chloe, but Aristide's cane is blocking my way."

"It's fine, Charon. Chloe, do you want to ride up front with me as a cat?" Noctus asked.

"No way, sit in the back!" Ker scooted into the tiny middle spot on the bench seat, smashing Aristide into the side of the car in the process. She smiled welcomingly and patted her vacated seat. "Then we can all *talk*!"

I grinned as I hopped in next to her, buckling myself into my seat before Noctus closed my door for me, then opened the front passenger door.

"I feel like this would be the perfect opportunity to make a joke about wolves loving car rides, but I will refrain," Aristide said.

"Good." Noctus slid into the passenger seat and closed the door with a thump. "Because otherwise you'd find a nostalgia vamp joke in the sponsored-by section of your favorite crime podcast."

"You wouldn't purchase a sponsorship just for a joke," Aristide scoffed. "That would take too much of your precious time away from ruling."

"You're right," Noctus said. "I wouldn't, but Charon would."

Ker belly laughed as Charon turned the car on and pulled onto the street.

"Where are we going?" I asked.

"Why do you assume we aren't going straight home?" Aristide asked.

"That seems like a pretty unexciting thing for you and Ker to tag along for," I said.

Aristide made a noise in the back of his throat. "A valid point."

"We're going to stop at the animal grooming salon your

brother mentioned—Paw & Order. They open at seven," Noctus said. "Since we're more familiar with the fae we believe is behind this, we might pick up something the Curia Cloisters missed."

"The Cloisters didn't even know to look for him in the first place," Ker pointed out, swaying into me as Charon executed a right turn.

"We'll also be going in with a cover story," Noctus said. "Provided, Chloe, you are willing to play a role in it."

"Sure," I agreed, then paused when I realized we were going to a pet grooming salon, and Ker wasn't in her wolf form. "Do you mean—?"

Aristide's grin was positively gleeful. "Oh yes. We do."

CHAPTER TWENTY-SIX

Chloe

"Welcome to Paw & Order! Who do you have a grooming session scheduled with?" A friendly looking human guy with a bright smile, a bushy beard, and a bright red shirt that read "Proud Paw Dad" greeted us when Noctus walked through the door.

The place smelled like wet dog and pet shampoo, but it was cute with the walls lined with framed photographs of cats and dogs in their before and after shots, posed so they looked like mugshots.

I clung to Noctus's fancy suit, my claws threaded through his button up shirt as I held on in my familiar cat hug stance, with Noctus's left arm supporting my rear.

I had to be leaving holes in his expensive suit, but I was too anxious to care. I wasn't sold on the idea that this plan was actually going to work.

"Good morning," Noctus greeted the man. "I don't have an

appointment. Ama doesn't need to be groomed today, rather, I wanted to see if you'll suit her needs."

"Oh, in that case, welcome!" The man leaned against the half wall that divided the small lobby from the grooming area behind him.

There were five tables, and although they'd only opened a few minutes ago, two of them were already occupied, one by a Scottish terrier, and another by a smiling mix who was wagging his tail so hard he whacked a brush out of his groomer's hand.

An empty doorframe let me peer back at the washing area—which was filled with stainless steel washing stalls and a full shower for large dogs. A sheet of opaque plastic hung from the side of the doorframe. The door most likely had been glass and was destroyed from that terrible noise spell.

The front door and nearly all the windows that showed a view of main street were whole, but they'd already been replaced if the picture window that was stapled with the same plastic sheeting as the door was any indicator.

At least I don't see any cats. That'll make this easier.

"My name is James. I work reception and help with the baths when the groomers need an extra hand," front desk guy said. Confusion briefly flickered across his face when he saw Charon, Aristide, and Ker slip inside, joining Noctus in the tiny lobby.

Noctus glanced back at them, unconcerned. "These are my friends, who are very concerned about Ama's grooming experiences, and wished to be here to inspect the place."

Yeah, they would be why I'm not sure this is going to work.

Charon—for once sans his ever-present cloak-like shirt and instead wearing a button up shirt, slacks, and a suitcoat that was the same watery gray color as his cloak-like shirt—bowed slightly to James.

Ker, standing so Aristide could hold the back of her right arm, waved to James with her free arm. "Yes!" she said. "Ama is such a sweet creature. I need to see for myself that she'll be comfortable. Isn't that right, Aristide?"

"No," Aristide said. "I'm here because I need to find a new place to take my seeing eye dog for her grooming sessions," he announced, going entirely off script.

"You do care deeply for your seeing-eye dog," Ker said. "One might say she's your closest friend."

"Goodness, *no*," Aristide shuddered. "She's a hellion—much like the famed Kerberos who guarded the gates of Hades. But she is a large dog and has an unfortunate tendency to collect mud on her underbelly."

"She does not," Ker said.

"She does too," Aristide stubbornly said.

"How would you know?" Ker challenged. "You can't see it!"

"Smell, my friend. It's all in the nose," Aristide said.

And this just raises more concerns. I knew only Noctus and I should have come in here.

I had suggested the plan, and was shouted down by Ker, Aristide, and Charon with such vigor I was certain Noctus must have suggested that plan before picking me up.

James—apparently recognizing what level of pet parents stood before him—just smiled and nodded. "Bellies on large dogs do commonly collect debris, particularly if your dog has long fur. If you have any questions, I'd be happy to answer them!"

Charon whipped out his tiny notebook and pen. "Firstly, you take cat clients, yes?"

"Absolutely!" James nodded. "Cats—particularly elderly cats and long-haired cats—cannot always groom themselves well enough, so we maintain grooming services to help such clients."

Charon wrote in his notebook and asked, without looking up, "How do you keep the cat comfortable during the process?"

"Depending on your cat's comfort, we will either bathe them in a basin or let them stand in a wash stall. Additionally, we use tools like the Happy Hoody to quiet the noise of the dryers, and will use positive reinforcement with owner-approved treats," James said.

Charon, perfectly playing his part, looked up so he could eye James from head to toe. "How can we trust she will like you and the groomers?"

"As I mentioned, whenever possible we use positive reinforcement," James said. "But you are correct, there is a certain chemistry that is needed for the cat to trust us so we can work on her. If you want to set her on the partition, we can see how comfortable she is?"

I unhooked my claws so Noctus could slide me off his chest. He set me down on top of the wide partition, rubbing under my chin.

Okay, it's showtime.

I needed to engage James enough that he felt he was accomplishing something so Noctus could then casually ask him questions about the attack.

"Hello, Ama." James smiled at me. "If you don't mind, I'll fetch a treat—"

No, no, no. Stay here!

I purred as I ambled up to him, sniffing the hand he had resting on the partition, before rubbing my face on his fingers.

"Wow, you're such a friendly girl—and so beautiful, too!" James gently petted me, a smile blooming underneath his massive beard.

I sat down, tucking my tail around my paws, then rubbed my head on his arm.

"She is remarkably friendly. You've done a wonderful job socializing her." James turned his smile onto Noctus, who was staring at me.

"Yes," Noctus said. "Some might say I did too good a job."

If I had been anything less than serious—and I was always serious when pretending to be a housecat—I would have flattened my ears at him. *What, did you want me to hiss and bat at him with my claws? He'd boot us out of here before we could ask anything!*

I got my revenge—with Aristide's help.

Aristide whacked Noctus in the back with his cane. "Oh, did I just hit you, old friend? So sorry!" he said, his voice syrupy with zero regrets.

Charon—reliable, wonderful Charon—turned on his heel to gaze at the front of the store. "I see you're doing some remodeling." Using his pen, he pointed to the picture window—the only one that still needed replacing. "Will that affect your grooming schedule, or are you open during the remodeling?"

James ignored the little drama playing out in front of him—he was focused on petting me—but Charon's observations roused his professionalism. "Yes, we're getting that and the door replaced—our contractor is just waiting for the last of the windows to come in. But they'll be installed after grooming hours, so it won't affect our clients or our store hours."

Ker made a noise of sympathy. "Is this from that magic explosion that happened downtown recently?"

James still petted me, but it seemed to be more automatic than his actual focus.

Good. Keep on petting me, I'll lower your blood pressure and *make you more relaxed and likely to answer!*

"Yeah," he said. "Since everyone needs new windows, it's making a bit of a local shortage. Thank goodness the weather isn't too cold yet!"

I thought I heard a meow, so I suspiciously peered over the partition, looking into the grooming area, but it was still just the two happy dogs. *Hmm...*

"It's unfortunate that it so adversely affected so many small businesses," Noctus said.

"At least no one died in the accident," Ker said.

"Maybe," Noctus said. "But they haven't found the perpetrator."

I heard the meow again, and this time, a round, plump face popped up over the edge of the desk pushed against the half wall, no doubt called out by my magic that attracted cats to me.

Oh, darn it. They have a shop cat. This could complicate things.

The cat—a dusty gray color—jumped onto the desk. His tail was missing, and his face had a distinct "mix" look to it, so I was betting he was a rescue.

"Perhaps the spell was set up by someone who owned a window business," Aristide suggested.

James watched me as the store cat hopped on top of the wall, making its way toward me. "It wasn't as bad as it could have been. As you said, I'm just glad no one was killed. Is Ama friendly with other cats?"

"She is," Noctus confirmed.

"Great, then if you don't mind I'll let Wallace greet her. He's harmless, he's just very shy, and it's unusual for him to greet our feline clients."

Ahah you don't know how unusual this is about to get, I thought as the store cat sat down, mirroring me, then kept scooting closer and closer.

He so deeply invaded my space I had to lean back so we weren't knocking heads. *Yes. Hello.*

A hint of a smile hovered on Noctus's lips, giving away his amusement at my predicament. "Yes, it's good for Ama to greet other felines, too. Speaking of the attack, it seemed like an odd bit of magic to use—a loud noise to break glass? What is the point? It caused mayhem for the day, but after the injuries were seen to, the biggest problem is all the property damage."

James thoughtfully petted Wallace as the cat mashed his head into my chest. "Yeah, I was working that day. It was odd—we didn't actually hear much of the boom in here."

Wait, what? How? Pat said the epicenter was just outside! I kept staring ahead and purring as Wallace started licking my ear.

"What do you mean?" Charon asked as he turned to a new page in his notebook.

"The noise started a few seconds before the glass broke," James said. "And it made all the dogs we were grooming at the time absolutely lose it. They went crazy barking. We were afraid the noise might have damaged their ears, but every last one of them got checked by the vet two streets down, and he said their ears looked fine—well, except Holy Terrier. He had an ear infection, but his groomer noticed that when she bathed him and was already going to tell his owners."

Ker shifted from foot to foot, her eyebrows furrowing. "When they barked, was it from fear, or something else?"

"It didn't seem like fear," James said. "We had two extremely shy clients that day. They would have bolted if they were scared. But they barked like the others."

Something flickered across Ker's face.

She's got something, I realized, turning away from Wallace since his sandpapery tongue was starting to scrape at my ear. *All the barking...is she thinking about werewolves?*

James frowned. "I really just hope all our clients are fine, and they weren't in pain despite what the vet said."

"When they do catch the perpetrator, I'll be glad to see him pay for his crimes," Aristide said.

"Yes," Noctus said. "I heard they even have a few suspects."

"Really?" James brightened again. "The Curia Cloisters is so tightlipped about this, I haven't heard anything about that!"

Aristide tapped his cane on the floor. "As a vampire, I've heard a few whispers. Nothing official, mind you. Apparently, they're looking for a tall, blond man. He's a supernatural, but they believe he initially posed as a human."

Noctus adjusted his aviator sunglasses and scoffed. "As if that kind of description narrows it down. You said you were here, James. I imagine you saw a number of blond men walk past."

"Yes," James agreed. "But there was one outside just when the dogs started barking. I noticed since I looked to see if there was something that set them off."

"Really? What did he look like?" Ker asked, sounding harmlessly curious.

"Tall," James said. "Taller than me. He was wearing what I'd call casually expensive clothes. I didn't see his face—his back was to me by then, but I remember wondering what his hurry was because he was walking ultra-fast, and I thought he might have done whatever set the dogs off."

Hm. Yeah, I think we can assume that fae is responsible for all of this.

"I see," Charon said. "Perhaps he was fleeing the scene of the crime?"

"Seems likely," Aristide said.

James shrugged as I backed into him in my effort to escape Wallace's tender ministrations.

"Mind your manners, Wallace," James told the shop cat, who meowed pitifully before rubbing his head on my chest.

Good to know my magic is working just fine.

James petted me for a moment. "You know, I'm noticing her fur is a little thin. We sell powder supplements you could sprinkle over her food to help her skin and coat."

Aristide broke off into a suspicious cough, and even Ker was struggling not to snort.

I narrowed my eyes at them. *Go ahead, laugh. You all are at least partially responsible for the stress that makes me lose my fur!*

"That won't be necessary. Her hair is thin because she's been stressed," Noctus said. "But I figured out the source of her stress and eradicated it."

Wallace, in his almost violent eagerness to snuggle, nearly knocked me off the wall, so James had to scramble to support me. *Too strong words, Noctus, too strong! But you're not wrong.*

"Eradicated?" James repeated.

Noctus's smile was as sharp as one of his many weapons. "Precisely."

"Crazy pet parent," Aristide accidentally-on-purpose loudly muttered.

Realizing Wallace wasn't going to back off, James picked him up, so he didn't notice when Ker nonchalantly tipped her head toward the door, signaling we could leave.

Yep, she figured something out.

"Thank you for your time," Noctus said. "I am delighted that Ama seems calm in this establishment."

"Of course." James, still holding Wallace, watched as I walked down the half-wall, heading for Noctus. "Give us a call when you're ready to schedule her."

Noctus scooped me up, placing me in my usual cat hug position. "Thank you," he repeated as he headed for the door, which Charon held open in anticipation.

"I like this place," Aristide announced as Ker also guided him toward the door. "You can be sure I'll make an appointment for my guide dog."

"I look forward to meeting her!" James smiled, before the door swung shut behind us, and our little band of merry supernaturals stood on the sidewalk of the still-quiet street.

Ker looked up and down the street—besides Paw & Order, the only places open on main street were Dream Bean and a few eating places, none of which were on the same block. "I do *not* get mud on my belly," she announced.

"No, but you kick up lots of grit and sediment when it's wet outside, and it sticks to your sides," Aristide said.

"That's hardly my fault!" Ker said.

"No," Aristide agreed. "But you make me brush your teeth *and* your coat. Why not get a professional grooming?"

"Grooming is a Pack bonding thing," Ker said.

"I drink your furry-tasting blood. Isn't that bonding enough?"

"No," Ker said plainly.

"Then what about everyone else?"

Ker stopped next to the SUV and waited for Charon to unlock

it. "Noctus plays fetch with me, and Charon rubs my paw pads with balms when they get rough."

"What about Chloe?" Aristide asked. "She's Pack now, isn't she?"

"Yes," Ker said. "And I'm hoping she'll take naps with me in our alternate forms. I miss having naps with other furry packmates."

"Ah." To Aristide's credit, Ker's wistful observation immediately shut him up.

I waited until everyone had piled into the car before I climbed off Noctus's lap and made my way to my open seat, where I changed into my human form.

"What did you get from that visit, Ker?" I asked.

"Wow." Ker shook her head as she studied me from head to toe. "I just can't get over how convenient your changing powers are."

"They are." I hurried to buckle myself in as Charon turned on the car and pulled out onto the street. "But you figured something out—I saw it in your eyes when James was talking about the dogs going nuts."

"I might have," Ker said. "But it's a bit of a long shot."

"What is it?" Noctus asked.

"Well, we already knew the few werewolves who were downtown at the time were adversely affected by the noise, right?" Ker asked.

Noctus removed his aviator sunglasses. "Yes. They reported ringing ears and hearing loss. Though there may be more to it than I recall. Charon?"

"Those symptoms were all temporary." Charon checked his mirrors before turning off main street. "They were given clean bills of health within the hour, and it was ruled as being a side effect of the noise used to take the windows out."

"What if the sound's purpose wasn't to break windows, but to test how well the noise disabled werewolves?" Ker asked.

"That's a chilling thought," Aristide said.

"But not out of the question," Noctus said. "One could conclude the first artifact was similarly built for vampires." Although I couldn't see Noctus's face since he sat in front of me, I could feel his frown forming. "Chloe, you were downtown during the attack. How adversely did the werewolves react at the time of the event?"

I stared up at the ceiling of the car as I tried to recall that frantic day. "They were on their knees," I said. "They weren't attacking anyone, that's for sure."

"Did they make any noise, like James said the dogs did?" Charon asked.

I furrowed my eyebrows as I struggled to remember. "I don't think so, but I also don't know that I would have heard it since there were so few of them. It was mass chaos down there. Pat would know, though."

"So we have two artifacts, one of which mostly did property damage while the other seemed to be intimidation and terror purposes, but both of which also have small side effects that seem aimed at two different kinds of supernaturals," Aristide concluded. "That...that's not good."

"If our observations are correct, it means we can assume there will be similar incidents focused on wizards and fae," Charon said.

"Before what?" I asked. "Why would they do this?"

"If the Paragon is correct about the organization he's trying to stop, it is possible they have an end goal in mind. Most likely something that would turn humans against us," Noctus said.

The car was filled with a suffocating, grim silence.

I hope we're wrong, I thought. *I hope we're overly reading into things. Please.*

SINCE THE CHAT with James made it obvious that whatever the aim of the artifacts, downtown was going to continue to be targeted, Noctus ordered a review of the security measures of Calor Villa at large, and all the properties he owned—including the clocktower.

That was how, three nights later, I stood on the observation deck of the clocktower, watching the glittering street and sign lights give a muted glow to the gray, low hanging clouds that filled the sky.

The wind was icy, making my nose and cheeks red. It was a lot colder than it had been when Noctus and I had gone tower-hopping back when he was first teaching me how my powers worked. The wind ripped at my warm jacket and gloves—all new, compliments of Charon.

But despite the cold, I watched the glittering lights with relief.

The tracker is gone. Pat and Joy are safe.

Life had been so crazy since that night, besides my cry fest with Noctus I hadn't really processed it. But the tracker was *dead.*

I hadn't wanted him dead, but I wasn't sad he'd been permanently dealt with.

My siblings were safe. We didn't have to have all the drills, all the codes anymore. I could walk around without worrying about my safety—or theirs.

I rubbed my cold nose, noting that the prickle in my ribs that warned me of elf magic grew stronger. I'd been feeling it all night while Noctus adjusted the barriers, but based on the growing concentration, Noctus was probably coming up to see me.

Everything is perfect. The elves are going public, my siblings know about Calor Villa, I won't ever get chased by Seelie or Unseelie fae again… it's all so much more than I ever dared to hope for.

I set my hands on the low wall, peering over the side so I could watch the streets below. Even through my gloves I could feel the icy cold of the stone, and the sensation of elf magic drew even closer.

Well, I guess everything isn't perfect. There's the fae on the loose using elven artifacts, obviously, and I still have to find a way to return my bond with Noctus. I just don't know how to hold on to my magic long enough to share it. Maybe I can ask Ms. Booker before my next shift. Noctus will have to check the books in his library since I can't read elvish...though maybe I should start to learn it?

"You seem deep in thought."

I smiled at Noctus, unsurprised by his presence as he joined me on the walkway beneath the clock face. "Yeah, it's been so crazy the last few days, I don't think it's even sunk in that the tracker is gone, and I'm safe after he's been dogging me for so long."

Noctus nodded, the wind playing with his dark gold hair. "You're right. But you ought to know, there may be more zealots like him."

I winced. "Yeah. If more elves survived the war and are a part of that organization the Paragon is hunting, I imagine there must be some who share the tracker's sentiments."

Noctus moved closer, tucking an arm around my waist, instantly warming me. "But you'll have our help—mine, Charon's, Ker's, and Aristide's." Noctus looked out over the city. "And although I don't look forward to revealing Calor Villa's existence, knowing you are important to the elves of Calor Villa will also further assure your safety."

Thinking of Brevlanne, I rested my head against his shoulder. "Yes, but not all of your people like or trust me."

"No," Noctus agreed. "But those individuals most likely don't like me either. If they respect us and follow the laws, that's good enough for me."

"Why wouldn't they like you?" I asked. "When everyone else in Calor Villa hero-worships you?"

"They don't hero-worship me," Noctus dryly said. "They're merely too scared to do anything but fall in line."

Thinking of Oleander and the other elves I met, I shook my head. "That's not what I've seen."

"That's because you don't know any better," Noctus said. "I'm a—"

"Kingslayer?" I guessed.

"Yes."

"Because you killed your family?"

"... Yes."

CHAPTER TWENTY-SEVEN

Chloe

I looked up at Noctus, taking in the way the lights cast a muted glow on his face that seemed to soften its usual sharp angles.

The elves of Calor Villa aren't the ones who hold that against him, Noctus is.

"Noctus, why did you kill your family?" I asked.

Noctus raised an eyebrow at me. "This is the time and place you want to get into this?"

"Yes," I said. "Because it bothers you more than I realized."

"Very well." Noctus slid his arm off my back and took two steps away from me, putting some distance between us. "What do you know about it?"

I kept my expression bland, but it bothered me that he'd backed away. "Not much. Aristide and Ker said it wasn't their story to tell, and every record I found of it just said the Mors royal family was wiped out in one incident—which I assume was your doing."

Noctus glanced up at the sky. "It was. I acted on an evening when I knew my family was going to be together—my parents, brothers, and my few remaining cousins and aunts and uncles. It was a feast. I destroyed them." His voice was detached, as though he was talking about someone else, but I saw the spiral—the pupils of his eyes—swirl. He had feelings about the situation, even if he didn't display them. "I used Destruction—the Mors' ultimate weapon, which had chosen me to wield it shortly after I reached adulthood. Nothing can stop Destruction, so it was child's play. They were gone within minutes."

I linked my hands behind my back as I listened, watching for any flicker of emotion on Noctus's face, but his expression was icy.

"My father lasted the longest," Noctus continued. "Since he was the king at the time, he had some magical resources I did not. But he still couldn't last against Destruction. I thought for sure he'd use his last breaths to warn our allies. To warn *any* elven family what I'd done. But no, even in his last moments he was selfish and bent on revenge. He cursed Destruction—a blood curse of suffering and torment, but never any death. He was trying to put it on me, but Destruction absorbed the curse, and I separated my magic from it before it spread to me."

"I saw the painting of you with Destruction," I said. "Ker mentioned it was cursed."

Noctus turned so he looked out over the city, which took him yet another step away from me. "Precisely," he said. "I'll never be able to use it again. No one will."

He keeps getting further and further away. Is he really dreading my reaction that much?

"So that's how you did it." I pulled the zipper of my jacket up just a little higher so my collar fitted snugly under my chin. "But *why* did you do it?"

Noctus stared out at Magiford and said nothing.

"I know there's more to it—everyone I've talked to has said

you did it for a reason, but no one will tell me exactly what it was."

Noctus didn't even stir.

He's locking up. I'd better make a move, or he's going to convince himself I'll leave him over this.

"Noctus, I *know* you." I crossed the distance between us, and grabbed his arm so he wouldn't back away again. "You're just and responsible. You didn't do it out of a thirst for power because you don't like being king. And the elves had been winning the war. Without your family to act as the deadliest army in existence, they lost. You were the crown prince, you knew they'd lose without the Mors," I confidently said.

Noctus had been raised in death and war. There was no way he didn't know that in eradicating his family, he would make it possible for supernaturals to win.

Wait...is that why?

"Is that why you did it?" I asked as I struggled to verbalize my thoughts. "You destroyed your family because of the war?"

Noctus was quiet for a moment. "Magic made its choice. It loved—loves, still—humans above everyone else. Attempting to subjugate magical humans—wizards and oracles—and regular humans alike was folly. Despite our many talents, eventually magic would abandon us elves because of that folly. I saw the signs after the mass extinction of the shadows."

"What do you mean?" I asked. "The elves were at the peak of their power then."

"Yes," Noctus said. "And we were slowly losing our ability to interact with wild magic."

"Like what's happening now?" I asked. "Everyone is freaking out because wild magic is dying out."

"Not the same, but similar, yes," Noctus said. "Power struggles bring death, which inevitably brings the loss of magic." He laughed—a broken sound. "You'd think someone would have come up with a different plan by now, but no. Brokenness begets brokenness, I suppose."

"Your family wouldn't have listened if you'd talked to them about it," I said. "Ker and Aristide made it clear, they only cared about power and blood."

"Maybe," Noctus said. "Or maybe it's because supernaturals still don't value humans, and magic will abandon them for it."

That doesn't make sense, though, because as it's dying off, it's leaving humans, too. I wasn't going to argue this point, this wasn't about the state of supernaturals, but Noctus and a burden that had plagued him for years.

"I've wondered if there was another way I could have taken. Something else I could have done to turn elves off their single-minded quest to dominate humans," Noctus said. "That night... wild magic *sang* to me. It wanted me to do something. So I did what I knew: bloodshed."

I started to shake my head, but Noctus interrupted me. "No, it really was all that I knew at the time, Chloe. If you listen to Aristide and Kerberos, they'll paint me as a tragic hero, but there was nothing noble about the slaughter I created that night. It was necessary to stop the plans of all the royal elven families, and I don't regret it, but so many innocents were killed in the massacre that followed as supernaturals won the war. There were elves who wanted nothing to do with the subjugation of humans. They just wanted to live peacefully. Yet, they were forced to pay for the greed of those who ruled over them."

"And that's why you're obsessed with being the most dutiful, perfect king," I said. "Because you feel like you owe it to the elves of Calor Villa."

Noctus finally looked at me. "Yes."

"Even though, if your predictions were right, what you did was the only way to save them?"

"Yes." Noctus raised his hand—as if he meant to touch me—then abruptly dropped it again. "I've wondered in the centuries that followed, was it really the only way? It seemed to be at the time."

"Noctus, you can't spend your life torturing yourself because you aren't perfect," I said. "You acted—to save them, to save magic. No, it wasn't a moment that should be reveled in—there's never any glory in bloodshed. But you *protected.* Prydwen's daughter who offered me the strawberry when I was Ama? She exists because of you. *I* probably exist because of you—if the elves had won I doubt even the best shadows would have been able to stay hidden."

I dropped his arm and linked my hands around his neck, desperately trying to ground him. "What is it that makes you so cynical about that?"

Noctus wrapped his arms tightly around me, as if he thought I was going to run. "Because I killed my family. And I never heard wild magic address me again after that night."

That's what this is about. He thinks because wild magic didn't speak to him, he did wrong. Even though he knows there weren't any *good options at the time.*

"I should correct myself. I never heard wild magic again," Noctus continued, "until the day I picked you up, a beleaguered cat taken hostage by local fae."

I blinked in surprise. "Really?"

"Yes," Noctus said. "It smugly sang the entire time you were under my roof. And then it wailed like a banshee after you left, day in, day out." Noctus squeezed me, before relaxing his hold on me. "I tried to save you from me, you know."

"What are you talking about?"

"Wild magic encouraged my plan to bond you to me. Even after I realized you were a shadow, it sang in your presence and pushed me to you. There's no way being with me could be any kind of advantage for you, which is why I tried to give you up, but it seems my nearly endless strength runs out when it comes to you."

"No advantage?" I laughed. "Noctus, you're filthy rich, you're a *king*, and no one could protect me better. You have every advantage anyone could ever offer, believe me."

"Except I am the king of the race that decided to kill shadows, and from the very family line that was sent to exterminate your race," Noctus pointed out.

At this point, I would have happily strangled wild magic—if it was physically possible. How *dare* it guilt Noctus like this? In fact, I was sorry I'd ever thought that hearing it was pretty!

"Noctus, that was hundreds of years ago. You might be an immortal, but most of the world is not. Dragging that kind of burden, harboring rage over it for so many years, won't be any good for anyone. You just forget that because Ker, the only mortal you've known for all these years, is being kept alive by you and Aristide!"

Noctus tilted his head.

"And did it ever occur to you that perhaps wild magic wasn't so excited to see me because I am a shadow, as much as it was excited that *you* were choosing to adopt a pet because you wanted one? You were actively seeking out a tiny creature for the sole reason of wanting to be loved—and don't lie to me, because I heard nearly every time you complained that I wasn't warming up fast enough because you had high expectations of your annoying animal magnetism powers!"

Noctus probably wanted to say something by this point, but I was really on a roll. "Maybe it was never about me, about what I was. Maybe it was all about what wild magic wanted for you. If I was magic's favorite as you like to say, then why would it be on board with you bonding to me if it was so angry with you?"

I strained, standing on my tiptoes so I was just a little bit taller as I peered up at him. "Maybe wild magic loves you more—and don't you dare say you're unlovable because I, Noctus Mors, happen to be unbelievably in love with you!"

Noctus raised an eyebrow. "Even after everything I've told you?"

If I were in my cat form, my hair would have puffed up. "Of course!" I said. "I said I'm *in love* with you! I renewed our bond, and I'm actively trying to figure out how I can return it!"

Noctus relaxed, his shoulders losing their tenseness and his hazel eyes finally softening. "You really are my Amalourne."

There's my nickname again, but let's put a pin in it for a minute. I have to make sure we have closure on this issue, or it's going to fester in him.

"So you get it, then?" I asked. "You accept that I'm not going to judge you about your family and I'm thankful you made that kind of sacrifice?"

Noctus paused, tilting his head. "I can see what you're saying, and I'm gratified you can view it that way. And..."

"And?" I prodded when he trailed off.

"And perhaps you are partially right about wild magic," Noctus said.

"That it loves you more than you think?" I asked.

"Yes." A slight smile tugged at Noctus's lips as he leaned over so he could rest his forehead against mine. "Because ever since you've returned, it's been singing in joy, just like my own magic."

I started to laugh, until Noctus's lips brushed mine.

"Woah. Hi." I gulped.

"Did you have any more questions?" Noctus asked, his lips brushing my cheek when he spoke.

"Just one." I could feel my thoughts melting like butter, but I had to stay focused! This was something I needed to know! "What does Amalourne mean?"

Noctus abruptly straightened, surprise flickering across his face. "You don't have any more questions about what happened with my family?"

I reviewed our conversation, then squinted up at him. "No?"

"That's really all you wanted to know?"

"No, I also want to know what Amalourne means," I said.

"But nothing more about my family?"

"No."

Noctus stared at me, furrowing his eyebrows so much a line on the bridge of his nose appeared.

"So." I let go of his neck and rested my hands on his shoulders for my own comfort. "What does it mean?"

Noctus settled his hands on my waist, and while he smiled there was something about his expression. He wasn't pulling back, but he also wasn't turning on the charm. "Ama—as I assume you heard from your time as my pet—is the elvish word for sweet. It references sweet as in sugary things and baked goods. It is a mildly affectionate term."

Something seemed to ignite in Noctus's eyes as he watched me, taking in every move I made. "Amalourne is different as it's not a term of endearment, but rather a statement about living. The direct translation is 'the sweetness of life,' although its meaning is slightly more complicated. It's used to refer to things like the laughter of a child, the bloom of a flower, the first snowfall of winter, the smile of a loved one—all the small things of beauty that make life worth living."

I was quiet as the significance of the name sank in.

"Amalourne isn't used to label one specific thing," Noctus continued. "My friendships with Charon, Ker, and Aristide—though I will deny it if you ever tell him—are also Amalourne. But elves privately treasure such things, and we don't publicly label it because they can be so fleeting, and it gives others power in knowing what's important to us."

That's why everyone was so shocked whenever Noctus called me Amalourne in front of others. Because in naming me Amalourne, he had openly been deeming his pet cat as a great joy in life.

"No wonder you were bitter when you realized I was a shadow," I said. "I thought you'd be angry, but you seemed...*disappointed.* I get it now. The cat you'd decided to let past your defenses wasn't what you thought."

"No," Noctus agreed. "But you became my Amalourne in a different way. I felt peaceful and warm while holding you when I believed you were my pet. But each time you reach for me, every shy smile you give me, every time you blush, is so much better and richer." His voice wasn't teasing—he was being genuine.

"So." Noctus let go of me and picked up my right hand, which he bowed over—like a knight swearing his allegiance. "Will you continue to be my Amalourne, Chloe Anderson?"

I was so overwhelmed by emotion that, for a heartbeat, my answer was clogged in my throat. "Yes. Of course."

When Noctus straightened up I pulled my hand free and hugged him, my heart singing. "Thank you for explaining it to me," I said.

"Naturally," Noctus said. "When you think of it, it was quite hilarious: I would call you Amalourne in front of others who understood the implication, but you—the object of my adoration—were clueless."

"It's not funny, it's romantic," I said. "Let me have this moment."

"So you favor romantic things? That's useful to know," Noctus said.

I lost some of the reverence for the moment as I suspiciously peered up at him. "Why would that normally sound like a sweet observation from most people, but closer to a declaration of war from you?"

"Perhaps because most people wouldn't know how to use such a fact to the greatest advantage, whereas I will make full use of it for the sake of your happiness," Noctus suggested.

"Yeah, no, it's because you *will* use it to your advantage when you want something," I grumbled. "I can see it now."

"That's just your paranoid shadow instincts," Noctus said. "I don't want much. Just you, and maybe some additional training sessions."

A noise of aggravation escaped me as we officially left the

romance behind—run over and dead. I pointed myself in the direction of the elevators and broke out of Noctus's grasp with the plan of rejoining civilization. "Why would you want me to get more of those?"

Noctus took my hand in his and followed me as I marched toward the elevators. "Because once we find a royal weapon or heirloom of mine that you can use, we can have personal matches."

"Does it have to be personal? Why not impersonal?"

"It would be fun."

"It would be terrifying," I countered.

"It would improve our relationship!"

I stopped to look up at him. "You're not going to let this go, are you?"

"I haven't met another elf capable of wielding an heirloom in centuries. Forgive me for my excitement."

I heaved a sigh, and my shoulders drooped as I gave up. "Fine. I can try sticking my hand in the pocket realm again, but I don't think any of your weapons intend to."

"If they don't, then that will merely be a good excuse for us to *look* for one that will," Noctus said. "There are still a few elven strongholds that are hidden—abandoned and teeming with trap spells and the like. But surely we could plunder something from one of them that would be interested in a shadow."

"They'd have to like you, too," I reminded him as I started for the elevators again. "Because I can only wield weapons using your magic."

"True," Noctus said. "In that case maybe time would be better spent appealing to the weapons I already have."

"Get Charon to make them a PowerPoint presentation," I suggested.

"You think they'd listen?"

"I don't think anyone would dare not listen to Charon, including nearly sentient weapons," I said.

Noctus didn't laugh like I assumed he would, instead he stopped—our linked hands pulling me to a halt, too.

"Is something wrong?" I asked.

"No," Noctus said. "But there is one more thing I should tell you—something important."

I gulped. "Oh?"

"I know where the elf princess—the one the Paragon seeks—lives," Noctus said.

I was going to give him a simple okay—that fact wasn't too surprising given how stubborn the Paragon had been in approaching him—when the thought struck me.

It's Noctus. There's no way he'd just keep tabs on someone he believes needs protection, which means she must be nearby, and there's one person who fits that description. "Is she...Shiloh?"

"Yes," Noctus said.

That would be why Noctus thought they might leave Magiford in the future—Shiloh was considering leaving.

"Wait." I frowned. "Isn't she human?"

"Half," Noctus said. "Her father was human. He never told her the truth."

"Why not?"

"Because he knew his daughter. She'd feel honor-bound to find her mother's family, even though her elven grandmother is just as shrewish and hateful as my own mother was. In their pride, arrogance, and greed, Shiloh's maternal family would consume her."

"And if the Paragon finds out, you think he'll just sacrifice her in a different way," I guessed.

"Yes."

I mulled over that for a moment, before I asked, "Similar to how—in a way—you were sacrificed to end the war?"

Noctus looked away, but I saw a muscle in his jaw twitch. "The Paragon would use Shiloh to try to rebuild wild magic—which would be a temporary fix, if it even worked at all. No matter how righteous his intentions are, I won't let him bleed her in such a way."

"And you're telling me this because protecting her is important to you, so it needs to be important to me, too," I said.

"The time I can protect her is coming to an end," Noctus said.

"Yeah," I agreed. "And eventually you'll need to tell her what she is—it's not fair to Shiloh to keep her in the dark." I narrowed my eyes as I thought of the sunny student, who had already experienced so much pain. "But I'll help you to protect her. I know what it's like to be vulnerable. I wouldn't want that for Shiloh, either."

Noctus watched me for a moment, studying me with a scrutiny that almost made me feel shy. "How did you learn to be so compassionate, despite being so thoroughly abused by other supernaturals?"

I smiled. "It comes with the territory of being raised by humans."

"Not all humans are compassionate," Noctus said. "In fact, I would argue that the majority of them are not."

"There are bad humans—just like there are bad supernaturals," I agreed as we started strolling toward the elevators again—we were just a few steps away from them. "But they can be kind and loyal in a way most supernaturals wouldn't understand," I said.

"If you say so."

I glanced up at Noctus, trying to gauge his reaction. "Now that we're on the topic of humans," I began. "There's just one last thing I'd like to ask you about."

Noctus's open skepticism morphed to something warm as he studied me. "I believe I told you before: ask me for anything, and it will be yours."

"Well." I cleared my throat as my cheeks burned in a blush. "I still really don't think humans are magic's favorites," I said. "I know we've talked about this before, but I don't get why you're so stuck on the idea of magic playing favorites."

"I've told you why I know it has favoritism—in the way it grants humans the ability to use magic."

"That's really vague and not really an answer," I said.

"Very well, then I'll explain in a more concrete way. Vampires have a few powers, but they cannot wield magic. Shifters have abilities, but all of those are innate and come with being a shifter, they can't command magic. Fae and elves can both use magic, but fae need something to wield it—an artifact of some sort. Elves can also use artifacts—or weapons—but we can also use things like cast spells, runes, tattoos, et cetera. However, our emotions impact and can entirely cut us off from magic which we still require tools to reach. Wizards—and all their subclasses—can innately use magic without any need for interference of any kind, and without any kind of failsafe. They can just reach for it."

"Okay." We slowed to a stop in front of the elevators, and Noctus pressed the button to summon the elevator while I considered his argument. "I can see what you mean. It's not about strength of supernaturals, it's about the ability to access magic without needing any kind of go-between."

"Precisely."

"But why do you say that humans are magic's favorite, not just wizards?" I asked. "Humans technically get the worst deal out of everyone because fae, vampires, wizards, shifters—all supernatural powers and abilities work on them, and they can't even really use potions and glamours for themselves."

"Because," Noctus said, "wild magic is the most potent and the most present among *humans* than anywhere else in the world."

"What?"

"Yes. You'll find more wild magic around humans than you could find in the most pristine, untouched land, or even in what used to be the fae realm," Noctus said.

The elevator dinged, and the doors opened.

I stepped in, Noctus right behind me. “That seems kind of backwards.”

“Indeed,” Noctus said as the door closed. “I suspect it’s also why my kinsmen wanted so badly to enslave humans.”

I played with the zipper of my jacket as I considered everything he’d just told me. “Are you saying you think it wasn’t just greed for power, it was jealousy?”

“Exactly.”

CHAPTER TWENTY-EIGHT

Chloe

Days passed, making it a full week since the dinner my siblings had at Calor Villa. While Pat wasn't able to find the fae guy—or even secure any additional information about him using Cloisters resources, since apparently he wasn't registered in the Midwest—the Cloisters had their people on the watch for him.

But while we might not have gotten any farther on the case, my life had suddenly become an intricate balancing act between shifts at Book Nookery, my siblings, and life at Calor Villa.

None of that was bad—I was happier than I'd ever been. But it meant I didn't have much time for thinking, and I hadn't been able to find any resources that would help me figure out how to cement my half of the bond to Noctus.

That was really starting to bother me.

"Hey, Ker?" I fidgeted as I stood next to her. I was supposed to be watching Noctus and Aristide—Aristide had decided since

Pat gave me a foundation with handguns, it was time for me to adopt them into my fighting style.

I was not so sure, particularly as I watched Aristide shoot at Noctus—who was wielding an heirloom weapon for the occasion.

"What's up?" Ker asked.

I glanced at Aristide—he was cocking his head, listening to Noctus's heartbeat no doubt, as he adjusted where he pointed his handgun. "I was wondering," I slowly began. "Wolves don't have magic, right?"

"Correct," Ker said. "Well, I guess Alphas have maybe a form of it, but it's been debated whether alpha powers are magic or something else entirely."

"Except you can shift," I said. "Isn't that magic?"

Ker paused, then turned toward me. "Are you thinking about how to return the bond with Noctus?"

"Yes," I said. "Since transforming back and forth between human and cat is the only active magic I have, I've been trying to forge the connection during that moment, but it's so fast I don't have a chance to grab my magic, much less do anything with it."

Ker tucked both of her braids over her shoulder and pursed her lips as she thought. "I guess it would make the most sense to think you have to use your transformation magic. But is that really your only active magic?"

"Yes," I said. "All of my other abilities run on autopilot. I can't control them."

"But you can feel when they kick in?" Ker asked. "Because for wolves, all our abilities just are. All the time. There is no ebb or flow because they aren't magic based, it's sheer physical ability."

"I guess that's a good point." I frowned as I thought. "My powers will turn off and on to a certain extent, though a few of them are always going—like magic not working on me."

"Do you think that's maybe the problem, that you need to lower your guard against magic so you can return the bond?"

I shook my head. "I don't have to do that to make things like fae health potions work, and Noctus had no problem forming the bond with me when he thought I was just a cat." I fidgeted, watching Noctus run serpentines as he avoided more of Aristide's gunfire. "I'm not at all blocked from Noctus, either. I just can't scoop up my own magic to direct at him."

"Good point." Ker went back to watching Noctus and Aristide as Aristide switched out his magazines—instead of letting it fall out like I'd seen in the movies, Aristide was careful to take his empty magazines and put them in the back pockets of his pants.

Probably so he doesn't trip on them while moving around, I idly noted.

"Using your transformation magic is worth a shot—haha, a shot," Ker chuckled to herself before her expression turned serious. "But don't let yourself be consumed with it, Chloe. Noctus wanted to bond with you because he's a tad obsessive and overly protective, and being able to track your location suits him. He won't be upset if you can't return it."

"I know," I said. "And that makes me feel *worse.*"

Ker threw an arm over my shoulders, squeezing me in a warm side hug that seemed unique to her and raised my spirits even though I hadn't figured anything out. "Hey, if all else fails, you *are* magic's favorite. Just ask magic!"

"How?" I asked. "I only ever heard magic when Noctus used his magic to heal me."

"What about when you try to use one of his heirlooms?" Ker asked.

I paused. "I don't think so, but I haven't tried to listen—I was too focused on attempting to draw a weapon."

"Then give it a shot," Ker coached, her eyes on Aristide and Noctus even though she still had her arm on my shoulders.

"Okay," I agreed.

"There you go." Ker patted me on the back, then cupped her hands around her mouth so she could shout. "Better watch yourself, Noctus! He nearly got you, and you need to be looking cool for your future queen, or she'll be disappointed!"

I didn't see Noctus's reaction. I shut my eyes—focusing on the warm sensation that oozed from my collar.

Using the collar as a starting point, I traced Noctus's powers back to him, engulfing myself in the inferno of magic that was his being.

Since I'd done this a few times now, I was faster at finding the pins-and-needles sensation that marked out the gateway to Noctus's arsenal, and when I opened my eyes again, the portal of hazy white magic had opened around my right hand.

As usual, I could see a little around my wrist—just enough to catch a glimpse of a few of the shadowy shapes of Noctus's many, *many* magical weapons and heirlooms.

Okay, so I'm tapping Noctus's powers...can I hear magic?

I stared at my feet as I tried to mentally shut out the sounds of Aristide's cackles, Noctus's low voice as he responded to whatever potshot the vampire had said, and the occasional thunderous noise of a gunshot that echoed in the enclosed training grounds.

There was no choir, no song played by the wild magic. I couldn't hear magic at all.

Well, that's disappointing.

I did, however, feel the attention of Noctus's many heirloom weapons. Their scrutiny seemed to hit me in the chest.

"Hello," I said out loud, having concluded thinking a greeting to "Truck" in my earlier rendezvous didn't seem to work at all. "I apologize for interrupting...whatever you are doing. It's just me again. Chloe Anderson," I said, speaking to them as I would Ms. Booker—pandering, maybe, but I wasn't about to upset Noctus's magical weapons.

Ker was watching me with raised eyebrows, but I didn't care.

Truck.

Once again, I felt the low-pitched word bloom inside my chest.

"Ah, yes. Greetings, Truck," I said.

Whatever weapon was saying "Truck", it didn't bother to follow up with anything helpful or useful.

In fact, just as they had every time I'd tried this, I could see the shadowy forms of weapons whisk past my fingertips. Noctus had said that meant they were judging me, but I knew it for what it was: whatever test they were using I was failing because none of them stopped or attempted to forge a connection with me.

Concentrate. This isn't about judgmental weapons, but the bond!

Since I couldn't hear magic, I couldn't really ask magic for help, but the weapons did represent a different part of Noctus's abilities. Maybe I could get my magic to react to it?

I stood still as the weapons kept on judging me, and I tried to sense if any of my magic was stirring.

Come on, I helpfully thought. *Go to Noctus! Follow the connection!* I could feel Noctus's magic through my collar, and I thought of routing my powers through it.

I waited, holding my breath.

Nothing happened.

I tried two more times, but I still couldn't feel any tangible sensation of my magic moving.

Disappointed, I started to withdraw my hand from Noctus's pocket realm, freezing when the ten-thousand-needles sensation that brushed my senses intensified.

Oops. Better explain myself to the weapons.

"I was attempting something involving Noctus's and my magic, but it's not working. I'll just go now. Thank you. Sorry. Excuse me."

Truck.

"Yes, goodbye, Truck," I hastily said—just in case.

I yanked my hand out of the portal, relaxing once the gate faded.

"I'm impressed," Ker said. "That's the first time I've seen Dale Carnegie's teachings applied to an elven weapon."

"I want to stay in their good graces," I said. "Especially since some of them might hate shadows, being made by elves and everything."

"Wise, but I wasn't criticizing you," Ker said. "I am genuinely impressed with your unique approach. You know, once elves go public, we could teach a Dale Carnegie class at the Cloisters! His wisdom should be shared with the supernatural community. They need it."

Before I could say anything more, the doors to the training stadium clicked open. Charon stepped inside, back to wearing his hood, though this one appeared to be a new model because it was less of a watery gray and closer to a cream color.

When Charon saw me he nodded his head. "Chloe," he said. "Kerberos."

"Hey, Charon!" Ker waved. "Is something wrong?"

"I was going to inquire with Chloe to gauge her interest in a tour of Calor—specifically the levels of the town she has not seen," Charon said.

I blinked in surprise, trying to adjust Charon's behavior to my mental schematics.

Charon always did whatever Noctus wished—like training me, which I knew he enjoyed in a twisted kind of way given how he delighted in making me take stairs—and things that would benefit Noctus's kingship.

Noctus must have come up with the plan. But it would be a good idea. I refuse to think about what would happen if I became que—no, I won't even think the word. However, no matter what the future holds, it would be smart to be familiar with the whole city.

"That's very thoughtful, Charon. Thank you." I smiled, hoping to show him I was willing. "I'd be delighted to see the rest of the city."

"That's an excellent idea, Charon," Noctus called, surprising me.

Not because he and Aristide weren't fighting—I hadn't heard

a gunshot since I tried talking to Noctus's weapons—but because Noctus's statement implied the tour was Charon's idea.

"But the timing is off," Noctus continued. "Give us twenty minutes. Aristide and I need to clean up and reset the hall."

"Forgive me, Your Majesty, but the invitation was for Chloe. Not you." Charon bowed to Noctus. "Your presence is unnecessary."

Noctus paused mid-step, staring at Charon as if he'd suddenly grown another head.

I gaped at Charon, and even Ker seemed shocked.

Aristide, however, cackled. "That was beautiful. Well done, Charon! The first time you ever refused His Greatness over here, and you just *handed* it to him!"

Noctus blinked. "What." He didn't sound angry, but genuinely bewildered.

Aristide caught up with Noctus—who still hadn't moved—and bumped his shoulder. "I'll tell you what: your place as Charon's favorite golden child, with whom the sun rises and sets, is not just in jeopardy, it is weeks away from ending."

Noctus let Aristide manhandle him, his eyebrows sliding up with the vampire's colorful description.

Aristide, however, was just getting started. "You are the King of the Mors Elves, the ruler of Calor Villa. But Chloe is very likely to become your consort—the *Queen* of the Mors Elves. No longer will you have sole custody of Charon's affection. Nay, you shall be forced to share it! It's possible that she may even eclipse you—she's a lot nicer and less sarcastic than you!"

"She wins friends and influences people," Ker said.

"I'm only sarcastic and mean to you, Aristide," Noctus said. "Because you have the personality of a lemon that has been pickled in a vat of vinegar."

"See! That's what I'm talking about," Aristide said. "But that's fine! I'll just wait. Your comeuppance is on the horizon!"

"It is not," Noctus said. "Because you cannot possibly be right. Charon?"

"Of course not, Your Majesty." Charon bowed deeply to Noctus, and then in the same breath pivoted to face me. "Shall we leave for the tour now, Chloe?"

"Oh, we can wait for Noctus," I said.

"If you wish," Charon said. "I will wait for you at the main entrance to the town."

"Thanks, Charon," I said.

"Of course. Excuse me." Charon bowed at large to the group, then slipped out of the doors, leaving a stunned audience behind him.

"Oh, this is positively delightful!" Aristide laughed. "Life is going to be so much more interesting from now on!" He slapped Noctus across the shoulders, then continued on his way toward us, still snickering as he tapped his cane on the smooth ground.

"I don't think—Aristide's obviously wrong," I said as Noctus approached me.

Noctus chuckled, his expression bemused. "No, I've seen the signs for a while that Charon was starting to take an interest in you—your wardrobe marked the beginning. And Aristide is correct. Perhaps I have grown too comfortable in my assurance of my position. If I had asked my people earlier about coming forward, I could have saved us both a considerable amount of misery."

I glanced at the door Charon had shut behind himself. "I'm pretty sure he's also playing it up—for the fun of it."

"He does have a very twisted sense of humor," Noctus said. "But he also doesn't look well at tardiness, so I'd better get cleaned up, or he'll come to whisk you off without me out of spite."

White magic formed around Noctus's hand as he returned the saber he'd been using to his heirloom arsenal. His armor faded, leaving him the black boots, pants, and shirt he usually wore for training.

He kissed my temple, then headed for the door, which Aristide was already prying open.

Ker, instead of following them, closed in on me, sweeping me up in a tight bear hug that made my bones creak. "I'm so glad we met you, Chloe."

"Thank you?" I said, my lungs starting to burn from the compression. "I'm just very thankful that you all have welcomed me."

"Of course," Ker said. "You're important to Noctus. We'd love you no matter what, for his sake, and with your powers you perfectly round us out as a group. But it's more than Noctus and your abilities." She finally released me, stepping back so she could look down into my eyes.

"You value us. You listen to us. And you don't see us as a threat—you don't see our *friendship* as a threat. Instead, you work to understand it."

"Well...my closest friend in Magiford is a trash griffin," I said. "But I have Pat and Joy. So I understand both loneliness, and the kind of love that's so special it's like magic."

Ker's smile shrunk from her big, wide grin, to something smaller but truer. "Yes," she said. "It's *just* like magic."

"I'M TEXTING you an interactive map of the next city level," Charon announced as we turned off from the huge white staircase that started at the top of the city, at Noctus's villa, and marched down the entire mountainside.

I swiped my phone screen open just as my phone chirped. "Got it," I said. "...why are the aqueducts marked as usable paths?"

"Because the Mors elves are a paranoid bunch who like to have contingency plans for all possible pathways and places of combat," Aristide said.

"At least once a year he makes us practice fighting while standing in them," Ker said. "It is not as fun as you would assume it is, and then we have to clean the aqueducts to keep the water purified."

"The first structure on the left is the overhang for food carts," Charon continued, ignoring the dubious background to his rules. "Food carts are allowed to begin service at dawn and must close by the midnight hour. The apartment over the structure belongs to Maven and Cedaric, the representatives of this tier. They have two children and four grandchildren. Maven is an embroiderer, while Cedaric serves in the guards and was once a member of the Mors army."

I looked up from the map displayed on my phone. "Charon, I'm sorry but I'm never going to remember everyone's names."

"I will create flashcards for you, to aid you in your memorization of the city representatives," Charon thoughtfully said.

"Is there going to be a quiz on this?" I joked.

Charon took just a touch too long to look at me. "Of course not," he said with absolute insincerity.

There's absolutely going to be a quiz on this.

"So you really think I'm going to be queen?" I asked.

Charon stared at me as if I were an idiot.

"I mean, the elves of Calor Villa will *want* me to be queen?" I clarified.

"Of course," Charon said.

"You don't get just how happy everyone is that there's someone in this world who can actually tame Noctus," Aristide said. "We all had written him off as a bachelor forever. I thought his adopting Ama would mark the beginning of his 'crazy cat guy' years, eh, Noctus?"

"It only occurred to me to adopt a cat because I was becoming concerned you were in your dotage, and I needed something to cheer me from that depressing thought," Noctus said.

"Lies," Aristide declared.

"Oh really?" Noctus said. "Then why did you suddenly start complaining that your blood drinks tasted off and begin acting paranoid?"

"Because the blood drinks *were* off! Ker kept spiking them—she added her own fur once! That's beyond petty, that's just mean."

"You told me my blood tasted furry," Ker said. "I thought you should taste what real furry blood was like."

"I had to hack up a hairball after drinking that concoction of yours."

"Yes, well, I didn't know your digestive system was so delicate or I wouldn't have tried it. And I did apologize."

I watched the chaotic exchange of friendship for a moment longer, then turned back to Charon. "I don't suppose there's a chance I could just be a symbolic monarch, and not actually get involved in the political side of things?"

Charon frowned at me. "Do you not care about the elves and our fate?"

"I do, I just don't know that I should be making decisions with Noctus for them," I said. "It feels...wrong."

"Don't worry," Ker assured me. "The elves will benefit from you as their queen—you'll do more for PR than Noctus's pretty face ever could since you're a shadow living among elves."

"I object to that," Aristide said.

"On what basis?" Ker asked.

"That Noctus has a pretty face. My memory tells me he's striking, perhaps a bit terrifying, but not pretty."

Ker bowed her head. "You are correct. I will amend my language in the future."

"Both of you are idiots," Noctus said.

I smiled at the trio—not because of the content of the stories, but the way they were telling them.

Noctus, Aristide, and Ker were acting extra chaotic, and it was because they were relaxed and happy, and were reveling in teasing each other.

I might not be looking forward to becoming a queen, but it means a lot to know they're all for it.

Charon led me further down the street. "If you look closely, you'll notice this section of the town uses different architecture and building materials compared to the rest of Calor Villa. That is because this part of the town was renovated about a hundred years ago after a landslide flattened several buildings."

Noctus strolled along behind us, Ker and Aristide trailing in his wake.

"Is the reconstruction important?" I asked. "Are other levels jealous?"

"No, rather, it is notable because Maven and Cedaric are paranoid about further rockslides, and request that defensive spells be strengthened by His Majesty on an annual basis," Charon said.

I nodded at the sound logic. "That makes sense. Do landslides happen a lot?"

"Your Majesty?"

Our group turned as one, looking back at the white stairs we'd left.

Oleander—her long hair swaying in the chilly breeze—jumped down the last step while Prydwen more carefully trotted behind her.

The pair bowed to Noctus, Oleander holding the pommel of her sword to keep it from slapping the side of her leg.

"I beg your pardon for the intrusion, Your Majesty," Oleander said to the ground. "But Prydwen and I just received messages from the Curia Cloisters that they have officially closed the case of the tracker."

"Good. Well done, both of you. Thank you for your help that

evening—it was appreciated and will be remembered," Noctus said.

I thought Oleander with her chill personality would smile or something, but she just stood up straight, her expression serious. "It was my honor."

"Mine as well," Prydwen added, nerves making his voice thick until he cleared his throat. "I'm glad we were present at the time." He slightly nodded to me, his facial muscles relaxing just enough that it seemed like he was thinking about smiling, until he straightened up again and stared at Noctus's chin.

Charon considered the pair. "Did Pat Anderson tell you the case was closed?"

Prydwen shook his head. "It was an automated text message. Although, I also got an email about it."

Now everyone pivoted to stare at me.

"Pat is probably avoiding calling attention to them by not personally reaching out," I offered.

"An intelligent move." Charon made a note in his notebook that, knowing him, was most likely a foundation for a plan he would hatch that involved using both of my siblings for the sake of Calor Villa.

Ah, well. Pat and Joy can handle themselves, even against the likes of Charon. They were probably the only duo I knew of that could take him.

"How are the new patrols at the clocktower going, Oleander?" Noctus asked.

"Good," Oleander said. "The guards have settled into the location, and we've drilled them on what areas are safe to use magic in and what places are public. There has been no sign of the fae near the premises at this time."

"That makes sense," Aristide said. "The fae likely doesn't know what the clocktower hides. He's too preoccupied with his fun and games in the rest of downtown."

"Yeah, but he may attack it just because it's a recognizable symbol of downtown," Ker said.

"That's true," Aristide said. "But it seems like the types of spells he uses are the focus more than the location. Though maybe not, it's possible he placed the most recent spell where he did because he wanted to see the dogs' reaction in the grooming salon and scale it for werewolves."

"Possibly," Noctus said. "Regardless, we can safely assume next he'll be targeting either wizards or fae."

"Would he really target wizards?" I asked. "Or would he write them off as not being worth the attention?"

"A thoughtful argument," Charon said. "However, there's already proof that the organization he works for has harassed wizards in the past."

"If that's true, maybe he already has a spell in mind to affect wizards," Noctus said.

"That's an unsettling thought," Aristide said. "Though very possible. Let's just hope he doesn't have a particular target in mind."

"The Curia Cloisters is the one place that has all of those races present," Ker said. "Though with all the defenses on that building, he'd be insane to even try targeting it."

"Pat said they're raising defenses just in case," I said. "But I think he's half concerned they might be targeting the Regional Committee of Magic."

"That would be even more insane," Noctus said. "All the committee members are the magical equivalent of monsters. They would end him without blinking an eye."

Aristide snorted. "That's pretty rich coming from you."

Ker laughed, her rich voice echoing over the bustle of the city.

I smiled too, but there was something about the conversation that bothered me.

Not anything anyone said, rather...it was like we were missing something.

The first attack could have been written off as an attempt to scare humans, but it had a twist that was solidly aimed at vampires. The most recent attack was probably aimed at werewolves and shifters based on the noise...but if his aim is to do a larger attack, wouldn't it be better for him to launch it sooner instead of keep experimenting? He'd have a higher chance of having an element of surprise if he did it now instead of continuing with his experiments.

Unless this is all maybe an intimidation tactic and he intends to drag it out and turn the public against supernaturals—that seemed to be the goal of the artifact ring. Except that was undeniably run by stooges, not leaders like the fae probably is.

And if that was the goal, why did they make the second attack markedly bigger than the first? It affected the whole street, which was entirely unnecessary as there weren't many shifters downtown. It affected more fae—and elves—with the spell that cut off magic—wait...

"What if the second attack was aimed at the werewolves *and* the fae?" I asked, interrupting the friendly banter.

Noctus's shoulders straightened as he considered my suggestion. "Did the fae suffer any kind of adverse reaction? I didn't hear of any of them being harmed outside of collateral damage from the broken glass and chaos."

"The no-magic zone," I said. "The elves got caught in it, and we assumed it was done so supernaturals wouldn't be able to heal as quickly as normal. But what if it was to cancel fae glamours and magic, and test how they responded?"

"Oh." Aristide grimaced. "I do *not* like that idea. There's a good chance you're right. But I do not like it."

Noctus and Charon exchanged looks. "If there was a test for the fae threaded in that attack, what are the chances there was something in the first incident that targeted wizards?" Charon asked.

"The shadow creatures," Noctus said. The certainty in his voice sounded grim. "Vampires and shifters could use raw strength to destroy them, while fae are typically trained in some form or fashion of weapons and could defeat them with their training if they were cut off from their powers. Wizards, however, are generally only ever trained in the use of magic."

"That means the fae has tested attacks that would affect each of the four magic supernatural races," I said. "Unless we're wrong and this really is just about small incidents."

"The Paragon might have a better idea given that on the whole, he's more familiar with how this group operates, but I suspect we're correct," Noctus said.

"Great, so they really are planning something on a large scale," Aristide said.

"Could be targeting the entire city?" Oleander asked.

Noctus shook his head. "Even with elf magic at their disposal, it's too big a target."

"Then it must be the Curia Cloisters," Ker said.

"We need to go back to my study." Noctus turned away from the city, herding us back in the direction of the stairs. "Chloe, would you call Pat?"

"Sure," I said. "What are you going to do?"

"Contact the Paragon," Noctus said. "He's got a direct line with the Regional Committee of Magic. I need to move in and offer my help so he doesn't panic and reveal Calor Villa in the process."

A WEEK PASSED, and thankfully—blessedly—nothing happened.

I went to the Book Nookery as usual, Pat still spent too many hours on duty, and Charon continued with my training.

The only change was that Noctus now always had a squadron of elves on standby at the Cloisters with the Paragon's help—he insisted they were an elite fae guard unit and thankfully no one had asked him why he hadn't summoned them before now given all the past incidents in the Curia Cloisters. (Of course, knowing the Paragon, it was unlikely anyone wanted to risk asking him and then be forced to sit through whatever long-winded, chaotic tale he spun to suit the fae inability to lie. The Paragon, I was starting to suspect, used his eccentricities as a different kind of glamour.)

"If you'd like to get out here, Chloe, I'll go park the car," Charon offered. "I texted His Majesty before we left, so he'll be expecting you. Aristide and Ker should be waiting."

I snapped out of my reverie. "Okay. Oh, and thanks, Charon, for picking me up from work."

"Of course." Charon shifted the car into park after rolling to a stop outside the main doors of the Curia Cloisters. "The chance to escape the Paragon's presence was most appreciated."

I grinned at him as I unbuckled my seatbelt and then tossed my backpack onto the bench seat of the SUV.

While I was working the night away at Book Nookery, Noctus, Ker, Aristide, and Charon had spent the night meeting with the Paragon for a discussion about the elves' future.

"See you inside," I said as I slipped out of the car.

"Of course," Charon nodded to me as I slammed the car door shut.

I gave him one last wave, then headed for the front doors. Since it was barely six thirty in the morning, the sky was still a dark blue, but any sign of the stars had faded, and the horizon line was rimmed with an anemic pale yellow, promising the sun would soon start to rise.

Thankfully there was no wind, and even though I could see the silvery puffs my breath made in the cold air, the chill pleasantly hung in the air instead of burrowing into my bones like it did when there was a strong wind.

I guess it's encouraging that the Paragon wanted to discuss the elves. He must feel like the Curia Cloisters is secure enough if he wanted to talk about something besides the artifact-spell issues.

Personally, knowing that at any second the blond haired fae could spring his trap was rubbing my nerves raw. But that was probably due to the power difference between the likes of me and the supernaturals with power, like the Paragon.

Walking through the front doors of the Cloisters was like getting slammed by a wall of magic—there were so many spells I couldn't even tell all the types at work.

Maybe I'm just paranoid, I wondered. *Maybe the Paragon isn't worried because there's just no way anyone is stupid enough to target the Curia Cloisters when it has* this much magic *on it. It would be a suicide mission.*

My eyes abruptly watered, and my nose filled, something that happened only when I encountered the Paragon's ridiculously strong glamour. But if the Paragon was near, that meant so were Noctus and the others, so I blinked through the tears, looking for my friends.

"Chloe!" Ker waved with her left arm, careful not to jostle her whole body as Aristide held the back of her right arm. Behind her walked Noctus and the Paragon, with a group I recognized as elves thanks to my magic-canceling abilities.

That must be the squad on Curia Cloisters duty right now, I realized when I saw Oleander in the ranks.

I scuffed my shoes on the rubber mats arranged just in front of the doors. "Hey, Ker, Aristide. Are you all finished?"

"We are," Aristide confirmed. "Did Charon already drive off?"

"Yeah." I peered through the glass door, but the SUV was gone. "He was going to find a parking spot. Want me to call him?"

"Sure," Ker said.

"Yes!" Aristide said with a great deal more enthusiasm. "If I have to listen to one more question from that conniving old fae, I'm going to bite someone."

I paused in the process of patting down my pockets in search of my cellphone and looked from Aristide to Ker, hoping for an explanation.

"The Paragon had a few questions about why I'm still alive," Ker said. "He was curious about the process."

"He wasn't curious, he was nosey," Aristide groused. "And he refuses to take no for an answer. It's high time that someone teaches him that just because he's the Paragon does not mean we have to answer all his questions," Aristide said. "Ker, why didn't you try to convert him to the ways of Dale Carnegie? If anyone needs to learn how to win friends, it is that odious fae."

"I considered it," Ker said. "But I concluded it would be dangerous for the world if the Paragon was armed with that kind of life-changing knowledge."

"I get the feeling he probably wouldn't care about learning how to better appeal to people, because he doesn't care what others think of him." I leaned against the door, holding it open for Aristide and Ker to pass through. "But, I have some bad news. I apparently left my cellphone in my backpack, which is in the car with Charon."

"Of course you did. This is not our night," Aristide announced.

Ker peered up at the sky as we walked out from underneath the overhang that stretched over the entrance. "The sun is starting to rise, so it's morning now," she said. "Not night."

"Thank you, Channel Four Wolf News, for that ever-so-important update," Aristide said. "Why don't you dig out your phone?"

"Why don't you get out yours?"

Aristide tugged on Ker's arm and then tapped his cane on the ground. "With what hand?!"

"Good point," Ker said. "Okay, I'll call him. But you need a drink. You're stressed out."

"Do *not* talk about my beverages in front of the Paragon," Aristide complained. "He'll be inspired to ask more questions."

I laughed as I looked back at Noctus, the Paragon, and the guards.

Noctus left the Paragon—who was still talking—in his dust, increasing his pace so he could catch up with Ker, Aristide, and me.

He smiled at me, stepping into my space—though he gave me plenty of time to retreat—before wrapping his arms around me and scooping me against his chest. "Good morning, Chloe."

"H-hi." My cheeks burned as I met Noctus's gaze. Recognizing what the light in his eyes meant, I pressed my face into his shoulder when he lowered his head toward mine.

He laughed and made do with kissing the top of my ear—eliciting a squeak from me and a gagging noise from Aristide.

Judging by the rumbling in his chest, I was safe to show my face again, so I peered up at him. "Was the night productive?"

"Marginally," Noctus said. "I'd like permission to call your sister to ask for her help—it seems the Paragon's ideas are unrealistic at best."

"I beg your pardon?" The Paragon—in the process of fluffing up his mustache—scowled at Noctus's back.

"Has anyone called Charon?" Noctus asked.

"I'm working on that." Ker winked as she got her phone out of her pocket.

I leaned into Noctus's hug, threading my arms around his waist. My senses were still smarting from the ocean of spells that oozed around the Curia Cloisters, but I was able to anchor myself on Noctus, relaxing slightly. (It helped that leaning into him made the warm feeling produced by my collar blossom so it covered my entire body.)

"So, did you decide on anything?" I asked.

Noctus shook his head. "Actually—"

Magic shimmered in the air, followed by a sonic boom—exactly like the one downtown but *louder* and seeming to be coming from every direction.

CHAPTER TWENTY-NINE

Chloe

I cupped my hands over my ears, but the noise only lasted for a few long moments, just as it had downtown.

The Cloisters are under attack!

Anxiety nearly closed my throat as the noise rattled the entire building—I swear I felt the sidewalk buckle beneath our feet. Then, the Cloisters' defensive spells kicked in—they were so strong they made my teeth ache. The barriers enforced the building's walls and many windows, holding it together.

I clung to Noctus as I looked back at the front door, afraid to see what would happen. The glass doors shook, but the spells held. The doors didn't even crack.

Ker, however, collapsed to her knees, her hands slapped to her ears and her entire face twisted with excruciating pain.

No—the building might be okay, but the werewolves aren't!

"Ker!" I shouted, but she didn't seem to hear me.

Her ears must be hurting.

I pulled away from Noctus, intending to crouch at Ker's side, until Aristide slammed his cane into the ground and gritted his teeth, seemingly resisting something.

What—oh, no.

The smell of blood filled the air.

I turned in a horrified circle, spotting blood spatters that dotted the edge of the Cloisters' property line like a red fence. It looked like the spatters encircled the entire building, and they were neatly arranged with maybe twenty to thirty feet between each patch of blood.

I thought I saw the sparkle of a green gem in the pool of blood closest to us. It was half shoved into the ground, but it looked like when the sound spell went off, the power of the noise blew the grass turf off it.

How could so many artifacts be buried without anyone noticing? Wait—the holes, from the supposed gophers the Cloisters kept fighting! But that started weeks ago. Just how long has this attack been planned?

Despite his clenched teeth, Aristide didn't seem too affected by the spell. He backed up, positioning himself so he stood back to back with the squadron of elf guards.

But not everyone had his strength. I saw another vampire—a young woman—rush out of the Curia Cloisters, her eyes bright red and lips peeled back, revealing her pronounced fang teeth, as she wildly looked around for the source of the blood.

Noctus pointed to the hungry vampire. "Contain her!"

Oleander was on her in an instant, delivering a kick to her knee that made her fall to the ground, and then planting a foot on her back to keep her pinned against the cement sidewalk.

"The blood spell and noise spell were used," I said. "But I can still sense magic, and there aren't any shadow monsters—"

Faint screams echoed across the parking lot, coming from the backside of the Cloisters.

"Apparently they are in a different part of the building," Aristide grimly said. "Am I incorrect, Noctus?"

"No." Noctus raised his head and appeared to listen—maybe to wild magic, or perhaps to his own powers. "Shadow magic was definitely just dropped on the premises."

"From the uncovered artifacts?" the Paragon asked.

"Possibly," Noctus said. "I can't isolate its location. It's possible they spawned inside the building. Can you smell anything, Aristide?"

Aristide twitched his nose. "Nope, there's too much blood nearby to smell anything from any kind of distance, and I can't hear a ruddy thing over all these bells and sirens."

The Paragon reached into his pocket, likely reaching for an artifact. "If we could only be that lucky—"

I stiffened as nearly all the different sensations of magic that rubbed in my senses evaporated. "Magic is down!" I shouted over the Paragon. "A bunch of spells just cut off."

"Holy Neapolitan," the Paragon hissed—apparently he cursed by ice cream flavors. "I can't access my magic. Noctus, can you?"

Noctus flexed his hands, and I felt it through the collar when he accessed his magic. "Yes. Can you sense any spells at all, Chloe?"

"A few. There are some deep, heavy spells that are still operational inside the Cloisters." I stared at the sidewalk as I tried to pin down the sensations in my body—they were so rough in their power it was difficult to tell them apart. "I feel dragon shifter magic, so I'm guessing some dragon seals are still up, and I just felt some pretty intense fae magic."

"The inner barriers likely just went up," the Paragon said. His glamour was still up and operational, which made me wonder just what kind of magic went into his look. "There will be no way to get into the inner sanctum with those activated."

Sirens started going off—loud, tolling sounds that rang like bells in a tower.

Noctus muttered in elvish as he turned to the Paragon. "What should we do?"

The Paragon already had his cellphone out and was dialing a number. "I'm telling the Regional Committee. Hello—Killian!" He turned his back to us and held his hand over his ear as he tried to hear his phone call over the noise.

Noctus turned to his squad.

Oleander had trussed the hungry vampire up, and the squad had captured three more hungry vampires, but they turned as one unit when they felt Noctus's attention.

"Illona, Silient. See if the task force office is within the boundaries of the inner shields, and try to notify Pat Anderson of what's happening out here," Noctus ordered.

"Your Majesty!" Two guards saluted him, then broke ranks and charged back into the Curia Cloisters.

"Oleander, call Charon," Noctus ordered as he started to bump me away from the Curia Cloisters.

"Did the noise spell damage the Cloisters?" Aristide shouted over the ringing bells, his jaw still gritted.

I hurried to his side since Ker was still kneeling on the ground, whimpering. "No—all the glass held. It looks like we were right and the noise spell was meant for werewolves."

I mentally kicked myself—I still carried fae healing potions in my backpack, which would help Ker right now, except they were in the car!

When this is over, I'm going to buy myself a belt so I can have healing potions strapped to myself at all times!

"We need to move," Noctus said. "We can't see any attacks coming as long as we stand this close to the building."

"I'll help Aristide," I said.

Aristide reached out, and I maneuvered myself so he could hold the back of my right arm, like I'd seen him do with Ker.

"We're going to step off the curb, Aristide," I said. "I'm sorry, I don't know where the ramp is."

"It's fine." Aristide hit his cane on the edge of the curb, then stepped down off the sidewalk and into the parking lot. "We'll manage."

"I've got Ker." Noctus picked the werewolf up in a fireman's hold, balancing her on his shoulder.

The Paragon hung up his call, then growled a long list of ice cream flavors. For a moment his glamour grew smeary. "Killian and Hazel are in Drake Hall," he said. "They'll get here as fast as they can, but Drake Hall is well outside Magiford city limits."

"Queen Leila?" Noctus asked.

"Out on a Court tour," the Paragon said.

"Try her dad, Lord Linus," I called. "He's in charge while she's gone. Do you have his number?"

The Paragon opened his contacts and thumbed a number, then held his phone up to his ear.

We were halfway across the parking lot by this point, with Noctus leading us and the squad of elf guards guarding the rear—their weapons drawn and gleaming with magic.

"Noctus, put me down," Ker gruffly said, her voice tightening with pain.

"Can you even hear right now?" Noctus asked.

Ker, blithely proving his point, wriggled in his grasp. "I'm not some drooly puppy that needs to be minded, I can take this kind of pain."

Noctus bent over, and Ker landed on her feet, tottering a step as she winced—her ears had to be ringing. "Aristide, keep track of her," Noctus said.

"Got it." Aristide let go of me and reached out, snagging Ker's arm.

Ker startled, then relaxed when she realized it was Aristide. She took his hand off her arm and instead clasped it, threading their fingers together. The contact seemed to soothe her as she gave in to the werewolf instinct for contact and crowded close to the vampire.

I backed up to give the pair some room and glanced up at the Cloisters.

Now that we weren't underneath the front overhang, or directly next to the Cloisters, I could see the entirety of the building.

The Curia Cloisters was fairly sprawling, several stories tall, and constructed of very solid materials—brick and stone. The highest point of the building was the domed ceiling that covered the largest assembly hall.

At the apex of the dome was a flickering bubble of magic, colored deep red, but translucent enough to show someone was inside of it, standing next to a glowing smudge.

"There!" I pointed to the roof, then belatedly remembered Aristide. "Someone is on the roof—hiding in a defensive barrier."

"That sounds ominous," Aristide grumbled. He bumped Ker, who saw my pointed finger and followed it up to the roof.

The sight made her growl in her throat. "What do you want to bet that's the fae we've been tracking hiding in there?" Her voice was a little louder than necessary, but she tilted her head back—scenting the air.

The elven guards exchanged rapid fire barks in elvish, and the Paragon yanked his glasses off so he could squint up at the roof. "Is that...?"

"Yes, he's got an elven heirloom," Noctus said.

"You can see it?" the Paragon asked.

"No," Noctus said. "But the wild magic in the area is reacting to it."

"But he's a fae! I thought elven weapons couldn't be wielded by anyone but their owner?" I desperately asked.

"Wielded, yes," Noctus said. "But some royal weapons can be hijacked, so to speak. Use the right magic and techniques and you can harness it for a spell—though it takes forever to power up and as a result isn't very worthwhile."

"It seems not everyone agrees with your estimation," the

Paragon grimly said. "Where are the Cloisters Guards, and why aren't the remaining defensive spells activating?"

"Because shadow creatures are spawning at the back of the building," Charon grimly said.

He stepped out of the shadow of a truck, his hood off, sporting a cut on his cheek that bled a little and made his barely existent frown extra grim. His linen shirt was singed in places, and he held both of his handguns—barrels pointed to the ground.

"I knew the bloodshed would be impossible for Aristide to smell with the blood spell in the air, but I thought Ker would have heard..." Charon trailed off when he glanced at Ker, who glanced from him to the roof with worry but no recognition of his words. "The noise spell?"

"The noise spell," Aristide confirmed.

Charon pressed his lips together, then rolled his shoulders back. "The wizards are struggling to contain the shadow creatures, but I expect the monsters will soon make it up here. I suspect they were supposed to swarm the building based on their attack pattern, but a group of House Medeis wizards were loitering around in the back parking lot and apparently not only carry handguns but are crack shots."

"That would be the Drake influence, thank goodness," the Paragon said. "Any idea what we can expect from the charging weapon?"

Noctus shielded his eyes from the dawn of morning as he stared up at the weapon. "No. I'll have to get closer."

Noctus activated his magic and reached into his pocket realm, pulling out two small swords—at least, small for him. Both were the size of the short sword I used.

The swords activated, the blades igniting with blue and white flames that erupted to swallow Noctus's entire body before the flames formed armor.

The twin blades' armor set appeared to be made of leather—a leather chest plate that covered his upper chest, armguards, and leather boots, with black clothes underneath that were embroidered with blue and white flames. The flames also formed a cloak with a weighted hood and a mask that covered most of his face.

By the time Noctus was ready for battle, the shadow creatures had made it around the corner of the Cloisters.

Humanoid, but with impossibly broad shoulders, clawed hands, and dragon-paw-like feet, the monsters were horrifying to look at. Shadows writhed in the skull where facial features should have been, and there was an oily flatness to them that felt so wrong it made me shiver.

These are the same creatures those teenage elves made in Calor with forbidden magic.

The sensation of elf magic stabbed at my ribs, and I watched with horror as the monsters loped up to the front doors and tried to break in.

"Charon, stay with Chloe—get as far away as possible." Noctus barked a few elvish words at the guards, who rearranged themselves in a new formation. Half of them stalked toward the Cloisters, aiming for the shadow monsters, and the other half fanned out around us.

Noctus stepped away from our group, heading back to the building.

Charon, meanwhile, nudged me ahead. "This way, Chloe."

I looked back, watching Noctus scale a brick wall. The Paragon—still on his cellphone—had followed him and stopped at the sidewalk.

"I should have worn my harness," I said miserably.

"You were going into the Cloisters," Charon said. "Where there is a strict no weapons code because of the threat. Your conduct made sense."

The elven guards reached the group of five monsters attempting to break in the front doors. One guard speared a creature through the heart, another shot one with a crossbow, their movements efficient and coordinated as they pinned the monsters against the wall.

The endlessly ringing bells and scream of the sirens abruptly cut off.

Hopefully that's a good thing, but I doubt it.

"Come on, Chloe," Aristide called as he—using his cane—tapped his way across the parking lot, toting Ker along.

"You're coming with us?" I asked, hurrying to catch up with him as Charon prowled along at my side.

"In a fight of this scale against enemies that don't have heartbeats?" Aristide shook his head. "It's too hard to track, unless they start splitting off and following us. Hopefully they don't have the numbers to do that."

"I'm afraid they do," Charon said. "Do you hear that?"

Ker followed along behind us, but had her nose raised as she tried to use it in lieu of her ears. "Guys," she called. "There's something going on inside the Cloisters!"

"What?" Aristide asked. When she didn't answer, he pitched his voice louder. "WHAT?"

"Because I smell more of the shadow creatures...and fresh blood," Ker said.

The front doors slammed open, and a young woman with black hair staggered out, carrying an oversized metal stapler. She used the stapler to bludgeon a hungry vampire who grabbed at her arm, then ducked out of the doorway to avoid a shadow creature that streaked out through the open doors.

Charon said a word I recognized as an elvish swear word since Oleander had said it multiple times at the first sign of the fight. "This is a larger scale than anticipated."

"Yes," the Paragon said, making me jump. I hadn't realized he'd rejoined us. "It seems the organization had a great deal more firepower than I estimated. And now we're going to pay for it."

More monsters appeared—a few coming from the back of the

Cloisters, but most of them emerging from inside, chasing those who escaped through the Cloisters doors.

Charon, standing on the edge of our group, raised his guns and shot, picking his targets with precision so they only took one bullet to destroy.

The monsters gurgled, clawing at their chests as they fell before their shadowy bodies evaporated. "At least they aren't overly difficult to exterminate," Charon said.

"Maybe so, but with these kinds of numbers, does it matter?" The Paragon pulled what I recognized as a blue slip leash that had the name "Aphrodite" bedazzled on the hand strap, then stalked toward an incoming monster.

I watched with morbid fascination as he wrapped Aphrodite's leash around the shadow creature's neck, and effectively garroted it. The monster didn't die—as a shadow creature I don't know that it was capable of suffocating. But the Paragon used the leash as leverage to drag it to the ground where he savagely kicked at its chest, until its shape collapsed and the monster evaporated.

I burned to do something—*anything* to help. But I didn't have any of my weapons, and unlike the Paragon I didn't carry any spare leashes in my pockets. To make it even worse, my instincts were burning in my gut, urging me to turn into a cat and to run from the danger that was swarming the area.

When we reached the far side of the parking lot, Ker picked up a decorative pumpkin arranged in one of the parking lot flower beds and javelin tossed it at a shadow monster that was stalking a human Cloisters employee running toward us.

Behind us, the elven guard had made a stand, and were slicing through any of the monsters that got close.

Some of the supernaturals running around were fighting back. A wizard had started her car and ran over three monsters that two shifters herded in front of her.

It looked like most of the shifters hadn't recovered their hearing quite yet, but they were on their feet and fighting.

Unfortunately, about three fourths of the vampires who emerged from the Cloisters were too affected by the scent of blood in the air—some of them were even attacking other supernaturals.

"Charon," Aristide said over the gurgles of the shadow monsters and the roars of the fighting supernaturals. "Phone."

Charon shot another shadow creature. "I'm busy."

"No, your phone is vibrating—I can hear it in your pocket," Aristide said.

Charon exhaled deeply, but flicked the safety on the handgun in his left hand, stuffed it in his shoulder holster, then yanked his cellphone free. "Your Majesty," he said as a greeting. He paused, then glanced at me. "Very well." He removed the phone from his ear, pressed a button to turn the phone onto speaker mode, then held it out to me.

I gingerly took it. "Noctus?"

"*Chloe, you have to run*," Noctus said. "*The weapon is a Mors family heirloom, a spear called Pestilence. It's loaded with an explosive spell strong enough to collapse the Cloisters, threaded with a secondary spell that is its specialty: a death magic that will kill anything within its cloud zone. It's going to kill all supernaturals within a several mile radius*."

The Paragon popped up at my side, the wrinkles in his forehead turning trench deep. "Can't you stop it?"

I searched the roofline of the Cloisters and found Noctus, standing on a higher section of the roof. He was facing the red barrier, which glowed from within, lit by the ominous yellow light the spear was starting to shed.

Below Noctus, the stone gargoyles—more of the Cloisters' defensive magic—had woken from their slumber despite the daylight and were attacking the shadow creatures that were now swarming the building.

"*No*," Noctus said. "*I can't get to it. It's got a double barrier protection—a dragon seal followed by a defensive shield we elves commonly used to enhance our fortifications. The fortification spell can be dismantled, but it takes hours, if not days. We have less than five minutes.*"

"Five minutes?" Aristide asked. "That's not enough time to evacuate the Cloisters. Could we open a gate?"

"Not with the magic dampener," the Paragon grimly said. "My pocket realm won't even open."

"*No one in this area is surviving,*" Noctus said, his voice flat and emotionless. "*Not even me. The spell is tied to the weapon's core, and it's a death weapon. Chloe's the only one who has a chance because the death spell most likely won't kill her. But she needs to clear the blast zone to stand a chance.*"

"Couldn't I get through the barrier and get the spear out to you?" I asked.

Noctus was silent for a beat. I could see him up on the roof when he twisted, stabbing a shadow creature through the chest. "*Not a chance. The weapon will kill you on contact—regardless of your abilities.*"

"Maybe, maybe there's something I could carry in," I said, desperate. "Can you make an explosive spell that I could put inside the barrier?"

"*No,*" Noctus said. "*The only thing capable of actually destroying an heirloom is another heirloom.*"

It's like the tracker's pendant, I realized. *Too much magic went into the creation of it for a simple spell to destroy it.*

"*I heard back from the scouts,*" Noctus continued. "*Pat is out on a call inside Magiford. He should be safe.*" He had to know I was starting to mentally shut down, but he mercilessly continued. "*You need to go, Chloe. You can survive this.*"

I thought the Paragon would interrupt, but he merely closed his eyes, and his shoulders sagged before he shuffled off, pulling out his cellphone and making another call.

The Paragon knows...Noctus is right.

"No." I shook my head, fighting the sudden deluge of tears that burned at my eyes. "No, there has to be a way."

"*We're not giving up*," Noctus said. "*I'll keep fighting until the end. But you don't have to. Please, Chloe*."

I shook my head, my breath coming in a choked sob.

Looking up at him, I saw him briefly turn in our direction. "*You are my Amalourne. I can face this, knowing you survive. Run. Promise me*."

Ker, despite her inability to hear, must have picked up on what was going on, because she slung an arm across my shoulders and tilted her head against mine. "Go, Chloe. Please. For all of us." She smiled at me, her brown eyes shiny. "We knew we'd go down like this someday."

"We've been prepared for it since the day the war ended," Aristide added, unflappable with his wry grin.

Charon studied me, and for a moment I saw a raw vulnerability in his eyes. "Calor Villa..."

"I'll help them," I said.

"Thank you." Charon infused the words with so much feeling, I started crying in earnest. Gently, he put his hands on my shoulders and turned me toward the edge of the Cloisters' property. He then pulled a hidden dagger from the top of his boot and handed it to me. "Here, take this for protection, and go."

"But your cellphone," I said.

Charon shook his head. "I won't be needing it. You can keep talking to His Majesty for a little longer."

Until it's over.

I wanted to break down into great sobbing tears, but I'd fall apart later. I wasn't going to do anything to drag my friends—the first group of supernaturals who had ever accepted me—into a miserable memory.

I scrambled over the hedge, then looked back at them.

Ker waved, then turned to Aristide as Charon drew closer to the pair.

"*Chloe?*" Noctus asked.

"I'm here!" I carefully pointed my dagger away from my face

and wiped my eyes on the sleeve of my sweater, then started running.

"I love you. Thank you for all the ways you changed my life, and thank you for surviving."

I almost stopped running—it felt like my heart was physically shattering. *I can't do this.*

"Chloe?"

I forced myself to keep running. "I love you, Noctus. More than anything. I'm so glad we met."

Something crackled on the phone line. "*I have to go*," Noctus said. "*But don't stop running. Survive, Chloe. You'll become the most stunning shadow the world has ever seen. I love you.*"

CHAPTER THIRTY

Chloe

A click severed the call, leaving me alone as I kept jogging, struggling to breathe through my brokenness.

I'm running. Always running and leaving others in danger. My head pounded with each step I took. *It's so unfair. If only I was more capable! I'm so useless!*

The truth was, even if I had my harness and weapons, I wasn't that special. I could fight, but while I could have taken out shadow creatures, that was it.

I hadn't even been able to stop the tracker—Noctus had.

I was powerless.

Charon said I underestimate my powers, but he was wrong. So wrong.

It felt like betrayal. Noctus, Charon, and the others had always treated my abilities with respect, but in the end I couldn't even protect them.

What's even so great about shadows? Our ability to assassinate others? I can't even protect what's important to me! I'm so scared, my friends are about to die, and I can't do a thing! What right do I have to even think *I could be Noctus's queen?*

Something small hit the side of my head, making me scream in surprise.

It took me a second to recognize a charred, stale French fry had bounced off my head, and fallen on the ground. "French Fry?" I gulped, wildly searching for him.

The trash griffin collided with my head.

I caught him before he fell to the ground. "No, no, no. If Noctus is right, you'll die, too. French Fry, you need to get out of here! Fly—fly far!"

French Fry affectionately nibbled my finger, then launched himself from my arms.

He nearly fell to the ground before his wings caught enough momentum and he soared over me, heading for the Curia Cloisters.

"*French Fry*!" I screamed, my voice raw.

I was going to lose my friends, and Noctus—who I was in *love* with. I couldn't lose French Fry, too. But I was powerless to stop him.

I'm always powerless, and always running. Why am I always running?

I knew the answer in my bones: because I was afraid.

I'd spent my life being afraid. And while this past year I'd been frightened into fighting back, it was still my gut instinct, my shadow-genetics, to *run*.

I was a coward.

I'd trained, learned to jump off buildings, taken on two fae monarchs, and I was still a coward. I'd pompously said I could be Noctus's queen, when the reality was I didn't deserve the title.

I was going to be afraid for the rest of my life.

But couldn't I be brave...despite my fear?

I stopped in the middle of the sidewalk, the thought echoing in my mind.

Just because I'm afraid doesn't mean I have to act on that fear. Just because I'm afraid, doesn't mean I have to run.

I looked back over my shoulder.

My fears and instincts are trying to keep me safe, but I can listen to them and choose to fight anyway, even if it means I might get hurt. Always running away—being the only one to survive—would wreck me so much more.

But could I help, when I couldn't even really wield magic?

I had the flickering, pins-and-needles-sensation of the gate to Noctus's royal weapons.

I can help. I just have to be bolder than I've ever been in my entire life.

I turned back the way I came, my movements so rapid I nearly tripped on my own feet.

My heart twisted with fear, and I knew every step I took went against what my friends had asked of me.

But I was going to try to destroy that weapon. I wasn't going to stand by anymore.

French Fry cooed encouragement as he circled overhead, keeping up with my sprint.

We reached the shrubbery that marked the edge of the Curia Cloisters a lot faster than it had taken me to flee.

The area was crowded with supernaturals, fighting off the shadow monsters despite lacking any kind of magic power.

A vampire in a suit who was able to resist the call of the blood gave me a curious look as she punched her fist through a creature's chest.

"Here! Use this!" I tossed Charon's dagger to her—I had a bigger weapon I needed to get.

I jumped the shrubbery, searching for Noctus, Charon, Ker, Aristide, or even the Paragon. I didn't see them anywhere.

My heart pounded, and my brain was so scared I just heard panicked screaming inside my skull. I ignored it and threw myself at Noctus's magic, accessing the portal to his weapons and shoving my hand in.

"Truck!" I screamed, my voice shrill as I ran across the parking lot, zigzagging to avoid shadow creatures. "I need you to choose me! I'm not getting out of this otherwise—*Noctus* won't get out of this!"

My loud screams got me a lot of attention from some deeply confused supernaturals—including a handsome, brunette fae who had to be a Court monarch based on the soldiers who flanked him, but I ignored them as I reached the base of the Cloisters.

I felt something play at my fingertips, but nothing solidified in my hand.

I growled, but turned into a cat so I could claw my way up the Cloisters' wall, using tiny grips from the bricks and the gutters to make it to the top of the overhang.

Standing there, I swapped back to my human form, and again summoned the portal. "I need your help, Truck! I can hear you, so that means you're considering me, right? Please, let me draw you out!"

"Chloe?" Noctus shouted. He was making a stand on a higher section of the roof, with Aristide, Charon, and Ker. I didn't see Oleander and the elven guards anywhere—Noctus had probably sent them inside.

"Chloe, what are you *doing* here?" Noctus yelled despite the shadows swarming him. He stabbed one shadow and beheaded another in one smooth movement, but three of the monsters crowded closer, replacing the fallen creatures.

"Chloe!" Ker screamed, her voice panicked. "Get out of here!" She stood back to back with Aristide, facing off with the shadow creatures that clustered around them.

I ignored both Noctus and Ker as I strained my ears and listened for Noctus's heirloom weapons.

I couldn't hear anything over the frantic beat of my heart and the shouts and crunching noises from the desperate fight that surrounded me.

"Truck!" I screamed like a lunatic. "I'm not asking! You talked to me, so this was your choice, partner! *Come here or I swear I will crawl in through the portal and pull you out myself!*"

I felt something harden, solidifying in the palm of my hand. I closed my fingers around it, barely registering the cylindrical shape, and yanked the weapon out before it had a chance to second guess its decision.

The portal widened, opening as I drew the pole weapon out—it was so long I had to physically back away until the top of it finally exited the pocket realm, revealing an enormous scythe blade. Taller than me, decorated with rubies that sparkled in the rising sun, the scythe's blade had what looked like flecks of dry blood on its curved blade. Despite the scythe itself being *massive*, the weapon was light, and I could bear its weight in one hand—though I had to hold it with both for balance purposes.

Truck.

"Nice to meet you. Work, please, now. We're on a deadline, I promise we'll have proper introductions later!" I said, my words fast and almost hysterical as I glanced up at the ominously glowing heirloom.

This close, I could see the light that drifted up from the spearhead that was stabbed into the Cloisters' roof. I could also make out the blond haired fae standing in the barrier with the weapon.

Fear threatened to choke me, but I took a deep breath and tapped the base of the scythe on the ground. "Let's go, Truck!"

Black fog drifted off the weapon and wrapped around me, forming into plate armor that was veined with glowing red magic. A long cloak—black exterior with a blood red interior—that was undoubtedly going to choke me and get tangled on things dropped from my back, stretching so long that it dragged on the ground behind me.

A helm formed around my head—black and slashed through with enough red magic that I was starting to feel like some kind of dark lord. It left from my nose down completely uncovered and had two holes I was supposed to look out of, but instead blocked my vision.

Whatever. I'm not going to complain about usability features now. We've got to go!

"Chloe—NO!" Noctus's voice was torn with anguish. "That's Destruction! It's cursed!"

I broke out in a cold sweat, but Noctus's warning came too late.

Magic that was a deep, rust color—like dried blood—dripped off the scythe's blade, forming a pool around my feet before climbing up my new armor.

"*Death!*" I heard a voice yell. I knew the shout wasn't in English, but I felt the translation wrap around me like a python. "*For my body you have carved up, with the power contained within it, I curse the sweat of your brow and the veins of your body with death!*"

It was the curse Noctus's father, the King of the Mors, had tried to put on him. And now, it had caught me.

I stepped out of the puddle and tried to shake it off, but the magic stuck like oil, glossing over everything as it defied gravity and climbed my body.

"*Your life will leak from your bones as your very breath burns your lungs.*"

"No." I felt my stomach acid scald my throat as a sour taste infected my mouth.

The red magic twirled around me, tightening like a noose.

"*You are nothing but dust, and now your body shall return to it as you drown in screams of pain and crack your teeth from gnashing them.*"

The red magic boiled—a heat I felt through the plate armor.

"No," I repeated, louder. "Magic doesn't work on me." My voice wavered, but my determination to survive this made me lift my head.

"*Who are you to believe you are stronger than the power in the blood of King Tanus, Monarch of the Mors, the Bloodletter, Scourge of Death, General of the Undin Army—*"

For a moment, my fear spiked.

I wasn't anyone. I was just a clerk at a bookstore, with a trash griffin for a friend. I wasn't powerful, and I didn't even have wieldable magic.

My heart thudded in my chest.

But I love Noctus. And I love Ker, Aristide, and Charon. And I'd do anything to save them—including defying an elven curse.

"I said *no*!" I shouted over the rambling magic. "You can't stop me with a curse—you can't stop me with any magic. I'm an Anderson, raised by humans, trained by elves. I'm a *shadow*!"

Something deep in my heart buckled, and for a moment I felt it: the magic that swam in my soul.

It roared with the power of a hundred tigers, and a golden light erupted at my feet, bursting into teeth-like fangs that reached above my head. My magic snapped up around me like the jaws of a beast engulfing its prey.

The curse shrieked, and I felt it claw at me, but my magic was merciless, shredding it, consuming it until not even a drop remained.

Something in Truck—the scythe—shifted. It didn't change, but my armor did.

Most of the plates melted away, solidifying into a few pieces that covered up key areas, but no longer restricted my movement. The chest piece remained—though it grew less bulky—but the pauldrons disappeared, and the armguards shrank so they only covered my forearms, the top of my hands, and my knuckles. The armor on my legs faded entirely, and the metal covered shoes were replaced with low cut leather boots with whisper-quiet soles. Best yet, the armor went from a tar black color to something softer that was closer to the black fur of my cat form, and the red magic that veined the armor changed to a golden color that matched my cat eyes.

Even the helm changed, the eye holes widening to accommodate my sight.

The tripping-hazard cloak disappeared, but something fluttered at my waist instead. I nearly laughed when I realized it was a ribbon threaded through my belt: gold, with tiny black cats on it.

"That's settled. You ready, Truck?" I shifted my gaze to the red barrier, which was starting to pulse.

As I scrambled across the rooftop, my borrowed scythe made a low noise—an eerie mash of a groan and a moan.

Welp. Ker did say the heirlooms communicated with their wielders.

I jumped from the overhang to the actual roof of the Curia Cloisters—which was a bit higher. I almost didn't make it as balancing Truck during the leap threw me off.

I squinted up at the barrier—which was at least two stories higher than the roofline I was standing on now. "We've got a problem. You're light, but bulky to carry. I don't suppose you'd mind if I just tossed you up there?"

Truck made the moaning noise again, sounding like a ghost in a human horror film.

"I'm going to interpret that as an affirmative. Here we go—we're aiming for the barrier!"

CHAPTER THIRTY-ONE

Noctus

Charon made a sharp inhalation of air.

For a moment I thought one of the shadow creatures had stabbed him, but I followed his gaze just in time to see Chloe *throw* Destruction—the most bloodthirsty weapon I'd ever handled. It scissored across the rooftop and struck a wall that supported an upper level of the Cloisters.

Chloe pumped her fist at Destruction—as if it was a coworker she was encouraging—before she zipped across the roof after it.

"Did she seriously just *throw* Destruction?" Ker asked. "Or was my sight also affected by the spell?"

"She threw it," I confirmed—shouting so she could hear me.

"What did you tell her about heirlooms?" Aristide asked.

"Not enough, apparently," I said.

"I told her it was a partnership," Ker said. "Maybe that gave her the wrong idea."

"I can't believe her luck—or lack of it. Of all the weapons she could pull, she gets Destruction." Aristide casually leaned backwards, narrowly avoiding a swipe one of the shadow creatures made for him. He then rebalanced and lunged forward, stabbing the monster through with his daggers, making it evaporate and disappear.

Isolated on the roof as we were—where there were no civilians or other fighters—Aristide could fight with less worry, and despite the creatures' lack of a heartbeat their gurgles and snarls were more than enough noise for the deadly vampire to track.

It had taken a few hits before Aristide had figured out exactly how low to stab from their crunching maws, but now he was more effective than Charon, who'd run out of bullets and was down to a single dagger.

"I've got to go after her." I raised my twin swords, then lunged forward, stabbing a shadow creature in the chest. I yanked my swords free before it could begin to fade and dodged a second creature, ducking under its arm. Using the easier maneuverability of my shorter blades, I stabbed them up into the monster, instantly ending it. "She's going after the spear."

Ker grabbed a shadow creature by the wrist, threw it over her shoulder, then stomped through its chest. "She could save us all."

"And die in the process," I said. "Destruction can destroy anything, but that close, with the initial blast contained by the barriers? That much raw power will burn her alive. Besides, I might be able to draw the fae out."

"And do what?" Aristide snorted. "He's obviously prepared to die with the rest of us."

"He's got an escape route, or he wouldn't keep hiding behind the barrier whenever I get close." I glanced up at Chloe—she was climbing onto the next level of the Cloisters, using Destruction as a handhold.

Fear—an emotion I hadn't felt in *centuries*—uncurled in my gut. Chloe—my Amalourne—was in so much danger, I was nearly out of my mind.

Aristide tilted his head, listening carefully before he lunged forward, stabbing a shadow creature in the gut. He listened to the rattling hiss that escaped its face, then stabbed it again, this time landing a hit in its chest. "A fair argument."

"We'll cover you." Charon—using one of his emptied handguns—pistol-whipped a shadow creature in the face, then shoved his bare hand through its chest cavity. "Go with blessings, Your Majesty."

I ducked out of the perimeter we'd established and raced across the roof after Chloe, but while the monsters seemed to ignore her—the bonus of being a shadow even if she was decked out in elven armor and holding the strongest weapon I owned—they were drawn to me.

With my twin swords, it was easy to carve a whirlwind path through them—stabbing ahead of me while simultaneously swiping behind me. But it was so *slow*.

Meanwhile, Chloe had cleared another section of the roof and had—insanely—thrown Destruction again.

I must reach her. Now!

CHAPTER THIRTY-TWO

Chloe

I stood at the base of the dome and stared up at the flickering barrier.

Despite everything—the armor, that my magic literally ate a curse, all the training I'd been through—my knees were still shaking.

I can feel the power pulsing from the spear, even with barriers screening it. This is...a lot. I'm scared.

I fixed my grasp on Destruction.

But I'm going to fight anyway.

"The barrier, Truck." I raised the weapon high over my head, and it made its spooky agreeing noise.

I nodded, leaned back, then threw forward with my entire body.

Truck helped somehow. I couldn't throw a football as far as the deadly scythe had traveled since I'd started the climbing process, but somehow the weapon traveled farther and farther each time.

Either Truck itself, or the curved blade cutting through the air made a low wailing noise. It hit the barrier with a tremendous crunch, the point of the scythe digging into the pulsing magic.

I sprinted after Truck, relying on my shadow-given grace and experience to keep me safe as I scrambled up the sloped roof.

I was halfway up the dome before the fae—the tall, blond guy I'd seen in Magiford—momentarily lowered the barriers so he could step out of them.

He carried a polearm that was topped with an ax-like head for smashing and a spike for thrusting.

And now he's standing between me and Truck.

"You're not an elf," the fae called to me as I changed my path so I started to sidle around—maybe I could circle around to the back of the barrier?

He followed me, keeping pace.

"You need to stop this," I said.

"*Why* would I do that?" the fae drawled. "I'm going to win. The Curia Cloisters will be dealt a blow they'll never recover from, Magiford will collapse as the supernatural capital of the USA, and as luck would have it, I'll even take down that pesky Paragon." He thrust his polearm at me.

I turned into a cat—taking me far out of reach of his strike—then sprinted up to him, turning human.

I rammed my shoulder into his gut.

He tried to elbow me on the back, but my chest piece encased my entire torso, so I didn't feel anything besides a vibration.

I turned back into a cat, and avoided his kick by pressing myself against his other leg.

He twirled his polearm and swung the ax down at me.

I tried to slip past him to step through the barrier, but he stomped on my tail, making pain radiate up my back.

I turned human, and tried to dodge, but the fae abruptly stopped his attack and was suddenly…not there.

I turned cat again—giving myself more maneuverability—and scurried closer to the barrier before I dared to look back.

Noctus—one sword stabbed into the stone dome, the other resting loosely in his left hand—held the fae's neck in his right hand.

The fae had dropped his weapon and was scrabbling at Noctus's hand, the tips of his toes barely grazing the rooftop.

I relaxed for a moment, until the feeling of Noctus's power hit me.

I'd been practicing with him, so I was used to the inferno that was his power. But this…this was different. I could feel his seething anger, and the magic in his swords glowed brighter.

This is like the time the Unseelie tried to grab me, when he still thought I was just a cat.

He'd nearly blown up the neighborhood with his rage. I'd had to turn human to reveal myself to get him to stop.

I swapped to my human form. "Noctus!" I shouted.

Noctus didn't even acknowledge me as the fae started to turn purple from the lack of air, and the sheer amount of magic in the air made my skin prickle.

I skidded down the curved surface of the dome and nearly smacked into him. "Noctus—I'm fine! Snap out of it!"

He ignored me, his burning rage fastened on the fae. I couldn't even see his eyes since they were shadowed by his hood and mask.

I glanced back at the spear, my heart pounding in my throat as I tried to weigh out how much time I had left with how badly Noctus was going to blow.

"Noctus, stop it! You've got to vent your feelings, but not like this!" I tried to hug him, but it was like hugging stone.

My breathing came faster, and I was close to a panic, until

something feathered and furry smashed into the side of Noctus's head, plastering against his face.

My jaw dropped. "*French Fry*?!"

The trash griffin peeled himself off Noctus's face, cooing at him before whacking the elf king in the face with his striped raccoon tail.

The stretched, tense feeling in the air evaporated, and Noctus's jaw softened. He dropped the fae, who collapsed in a heap.

French Fry bit a part of Noctus's mask, then launched himself at the fae, grabbing fistfuls of the comatose fae's blond hair with his front bird feet and savagely ripping them from his skull.

Looks like they have this handled.

I scrambled back up the dome.

"No, Chloe, wait!" Noctus chased after me. "It's too dangerous!"

When I felt him lunge for me I turned into a cat, avoiding him. When I reached Truck I jumped, landing on its long pole. *Pretty sure I'm going to have to be touching it to drag it through the barrier.*

Noctus had nearly caught up with me, so I leaped at the barrier, turning human mid jump. I reached back behind me and grabbed Truck's pole, yanking it free from the barrier and pulling it through the barrier after me.

We passed through without a ripple, and I landed in a crouch, tensed and waiting for any traps the fae might have planted.

"Chloe—if you try to destroy it, you'll die!" Noctus shouted. He tried to stab the barrier with the sword he still held, but the barrier flared, and the blade ricocheted off the surface.

"You always told me I was more powerful than I believed," I said. "Aren't I magic's favorite?"

"Yes, but you have limits!" Noctus's voice was twisted with anguish. "No matter if you're immune to magic, the raw power that's released when a weapon is destroyed is dangerous beyond measure. It could strip you to the bone."

I gulped as I stared at the spear. This close to it, I could see the glowing spiral inscribed into the pole's shaft was glowing runes, and they had turned nearly white.

It's going to go any second.

"Maybe you're right," I said. "But while I don't have it in me to kill, I also won't walk away when I might be able to stop this. You must trust me, Noctus."

Noctus stood unmoving on the other side of the barrier, his image warped by the way the spells rippled.

"Take the fae into custody, grab French Fry, and get everyone off the roof," I said. "Please. You trained me for this."

Noctus twitched his sword in a gesture of frustration. "Promise me that you'll come back."

The spear made a high-pitched whining noise, and I felt the air change. "I promise."

"You're my sweetness of life, Amalourne, and my queen."

"And you're my king, and my strength. Go!"

I blinked, and Noctus was gone, sheathing his twin swords in scabbards that hung at his sides before picking up the fae and flinging him over his shoulder like a giant box of books. He snatched French Fry out of the air and cradled him in his arms like a baby, and that was all I had time to see before I turned to the spear—which was almost entirely white now.

"We've got this, don't we—Truck?"

The weapon howled an affirmative as I stalked toward the spear.

"Then let's destroy some magic."

I tapped the pole of the scythe in what I hoped was a friendly manner, then swung it.

The jewels on the scythe flashed, and when the curved blade collided with the glowing spear, the area inside the barrier exploded with magic.

The shockwave blew me off my feet. I hit the ground like a rag doll, bruising my body. The only reason I wasn't tossed head over heels was that I clung to Truck—even though I was face down and it felt like my arms were getting pulled out of their sockets.

Raw power dug through my skin, burrowing straight to my bones as the air turned beastly hot.

The pressure built, and the top of the barrier exploded—the elven shield evaporated while the dragon seal shattered—shooting the excess power straight up into the morning sky.

The elven spell was gone, but the sides of the dragon seal held for a few seconds longer, and the overwhelming scent of sulfur layered the air so thickly I gagged.

My hands started to slide down Truck's pole. I scrabbled for a hold, trying to catch my gloves on the jewels embedded in the weapon, but my fingers were too sweaty to keep my grip.

Terrified, I turned into a cat and dug my claws in, hugging the weapon with my entire body.

The rest of the dragon seal gave, creating a vacuum until the pressure equalized, and the sheer strength of the wind created in the clash of magic nearly stripped me off Truck and plastered my whiskers to my face.

I swapped back to my human form and managed to brace myself with my knees.

The heat of the air made me feel like my lungs were baking with each breath I took, and my magical senses were so overwhelmed it was hard to see straight.

It was still too bright to look at Truck and the charged weapon—but I could feel the resistance of the spear. Truck hadn't sliced through it. It was still active.

The rooftop was starting to buckle underneath me—I could feel the shift in my balance.

If we don't wipe the spear out soon, it's going to kill everyone, and turn the Cloisters into rubble.

"Come on, Truck!" I screamed. "This is what you're supposed to destroy! You're not a blood weapon, you're a protector! Isn't that why you chose me, a shadow who doesn't use her powers like she's supposed to?"

I was crying. My arms numb from the pain of struggling to hold on against the power that tried to push me back.

Truck.

The thought echoed in my brain, and I knew what I had to do.

Ker had said heirlooms were partnerships. I couldn't just jab Truck at the spear, I needed to help.

Bracing myself against Truck, I pulled myself to my feet.

When I tried to reach out—intending to grab the spear—moving was like swimming in molasses. The air was thick and resistant.

When my fingers grazed the spear, the flood of magic hit me like a lightning bolt.

I could only see white, and every nerve in my body felt like it was on fire.

"Better together, right, Truck?" I shouted, but I couldn't even hear my own voice over the roaring blast of the magical battle.

I grimly planted a foot on the shaft of the spear, straining to push against it, then pulled Truck back and redirected it so it would smash into the actual spearhead.

Using both arms, I swung.

The blast of ensuing magic consumed the world.

CHAPTER THIRTY-THREE

Noctus

"What happened? *What happened?*" Aristide shouted, his hands on Ker's shoulders as he shook her. "I can't hear her heartbeat—did she make it?"

"I-I can't tell." Ker held a hand up, trying to see through the brilliant magic that still blanketed the section of roof we'd last seen Chloe on. "It's too bright."

"Noctus." Aristide zeroed in on me. "She's wearing the collar, right? Can you feel her through the bond?"

I mentally reached out and tried to ping the spell, but the sheer amount of magic in the air made it impossible to hear anything.

Impatience, fear, and rage simultaneously slammed into me, but I let them ride through me instead of partaking—noticing them but not giving them control.

Whenever I even thought of letting a sliver of my rage in, Chloe's precious trash griffin—which had claimed a spot on my shoulder—stuck its round head inside my hood and pecked at my ear.

I gritted my teeth as I dragged the blond fae after me while I backed up, trying to get a better view of the roof. We'd retreated to the ground level, but I was seconds away from running back to Chloe.

I couldn't see her, much less hear her—wild magic was alternately keening high and howling, and the persistent humming noise that Destruction always made was present.

If Destruction is still out and active, isn't that an encouragement?

"There!" Charon pointed to the roof.

Chloe was upright. Her shoulders were hunched in a way I didn't like. She seemed to be in pain, and she was tipsy, but she was standing, her armor still in place, her hands gripping Destruction as she stood in a burnt circle—that part of the roof was undoubtedly going to collapse if it didn't get some magical support soon.

The claws that dug into my heart eased, and I felt like I could finally breathe.

"There what?" Aristide asked. "*There what?*"

Ker exhaled a deep whoosh of relief. "She's standing on the roof. With Destruction. She made it!" She laughed as she hugged Aristide, her laugh fading into a dry sob of relief as she pushed her face into the vampire's shoulder.

Aristide—relaxed now that he knew what was going on—slung his arms around Ker. "Of course she made it. Our little shadow is as resourceful and brave as they come."

"Your Majesty." Charon plucked at the unconscious fae—I had not been the kindest in my handling as we disembarked from the roof. It was possible he'd hit his head on several beams and gutters on the way down. An accident, of course.

"I will handle this fiend," Charon said. "Perhaps you should see to—"

I tapped Charon on the shoulder in thanks before I left, running before the rest of his offer was out of his mouth.

The trash griffin—French Fry—jumped off my shoulders, taking to the sky so he could flap ahead of me.

I scaled the side of the building, watching for any damage the shockwave of magic might have caused.

The Cloisters were holding together admirably well—it seemed the Paragon was right to be proud of its defense spells.

But my heart sputtered in my chest when I heard the groan of faltering building materials. "Chloe!"

CHAPTER THIRTY-FOUR

Chloe

For a moment I thought I had died.

I only saw white, and there was a persistent ringing in my ears. That didn't really sound like what I would picture Heaven was like, but I'd also never been skilled at music, so maybe my ears were out of tune.

It was only when I realized how much it hurt to breathe that I figured I was probably still alive.

I planted the butt of Truck's pole on the ground, then leaned against him for stability as I waited for my eyesight to return.

"Way to go, Truck," I croaked. My mouth felt numb—blistered by the heat.

The white started to clear from my vision around the same time Truck's moans pierced the ringing noise in my ears.

The spear was in pieces at my feet—just a bunch of unrecognizable coals and a lump of metal.

Spurred on by my usual brand of paranoia, I ignored the pain and the swimming sensation of my head and slammed my heel down on the coals.

They exploded into embers under my boot, cooling into black ash that the wind blew away.

It worked. It actually worked.

I leaned my head against the scythe's giant blade. Its metal was a cool sensation on my head, chasing away some of the pain. "Everyone lived. We did it." I coughed then folded over from the pain a single cough created.

The roof under my feet creaked, and I felt it buckle through the soles of my boots.

Oh, it's about to cave in.

The roof cracked, and for a moment I thought I was going to fall through the hole.

But my gut instincts—still alive and well—roared to life. I threw myself to the side, rolling down the dome, and nearly impaling myself on Truck in the process. (Charon had taught me a lot of weapons. Scythes were not one of them.)

I was half concerned I was going to roll down the entire roof, but I smashed into something hard that stopped me.

There was the guttural heave as the dome roof collapsed—or at least the portion I'd been standing on.

When I finally recovered, I realized I was plastered against Noctus's chest, who was holding me very carefully so he didn't brush Truck.

"Thank you. I'm pretty sure I was going to swan dive headfirst if you hadn't stopped me." I strained my arm trying to hold Truck away from Noctus, but then let myself face plant into his chest. "You already know Truck."

"Destruction, yes," Noctus said.

Truck uttered a new "woo-woo" noise that still had that spooky many-voice quality to it—most likely his way of saying hello. I'd be grateful to have Noctus act as my interpreter until I got to know the weapon better.

"...what was that?" Noctus said.

"Truck talking?" I said, confused by his confusion.

"Weapons don't talk," Noctus said.

"Ker said they did." I peeled myself off Noctus long enough to look up at his face, then to look at Truck. "She said they can communicate with their wielder."

Truck made a happier sounding "woo-woo" noise that inspired a whole new furrow of wrinkles on Noctus's brow.

"Not like this," Noctus said. "It's usually an inner kind of understanding."

"Oh." I stared at Truck. I swear the jewels on the scythe were sparkling more than they should have in the morning light. "Maybe he's having to adapt, because I'm a shadow so I don't have all the elf qualities he's used to?"

Noctus was quiet for several long moments. "Sure," he finally said. "That must be it."

"You don't sound convinced."

"Frankly, I'm not going to question anything about you and the Mors' family heirloom. You survived what you shouldn't have. If Destruction wants to call itself Truck and start talking, I'm certainly not going to deny it anything," Noctus said.

I laughed, then coughed, and finished with a cringe. "Oh. That hurts. I'd love to just sit here in your arms, but I need a fae potion. Pretty sure I burned my lungs."

"Will it hurt you if I carry you?" Noctus asked.

"Nope. I'd appreciate it, in fact. I think my legs are about to give out—oop, yep."

As if on cue, my legs started to fold underneath me, and Truck fell from my hand.

Noctus caught me, so I was free to watch in comfort and surprise as Truck glowed, then disappeared. My armor faded away, too, leaving me in the clothes I'd worn to my Book Nookery shift.

"He's fine," Noctus said. "He just went back to storage. You're too weak to keep him out."

"Oh, good," I said. "Though I didn't say goodbye to him."

"That's important to you?"

"Shouldn't it be? It seems like a good policy to be polite to heirlooms," I said.

Noctus carried me princess style, picking a path across the Cloisters' roof. "I suppose it's not an unwise sentiment."

I smiled—the moment was too perfect. I couldn't let it slip away.

"I think," I started. "What you mean to say is—"

"Don't say it," Noctus said.

I ignored him. "Being polite is—"

"Not you, too."

"A good way to win friends and influence people," I said.

Ker's hearing must have made a comeback because I heard her "HAH!" echo across the rooftop, even though she was standing in the parking lot with the others.

I laughed, then coughed and slumped against Noctus. "For real, though, I need a potion."

"Nonsense," Noctus said. "Just relax."

I was considering turning into a cat to see if it would maybe hurt less, when I felt my collar start to warm on my throat, and the three red jewels started to glow. The warmth grew, covering my entire body, and soothing the pain away.

He's healing me, I realized, when I heard the happy giggle of wild magic—which was soft, melodic, and had the same multi-toned facet to it that a singing choir did.

"Thank you, Noctus."

"For healing you?"

"Yes," I said. "You're not my Amalourne."

"Ouch," Noctus observed.

"You didn't let me finish," I said, aware I needed to get my words out fast—the healing magic made me feel bubbly and a tad tipsy. I was going to start acting silly soon. "You're not my Amalourne, you're something even more rare and necessary for me. You're my bravery, the steel in my spine, my reason to pick up a weapon that scares the tar out of me and fight anyway. You're my trust, and my safety. Is there an elvish word for that?"

Noctus kissed the top of my head. "Not directly. The closest is perhaps Nutis—the blade that protects."

"Yep, that's perfect." I sagged in his arms. "You're my Nutis. Woah!"

French Fry fell out of the sky like a furry boulder, splatting against my stomach.

He cooed at me and walked his way up my chest so he could snuggle in against my neck.

"Hi, French Fry. Yes, you did a magnificent job," I said as the trash griffin flicked me in the face with his striped raccoon tail.

Noctus's chuckle was low and velvety—and the only warning I had before he jumped over the side of the building.

Charon, Aristide, and Ker were waiting. When Noctus straightened up out of the jump they clustered around us.

Ker pulled me straight out of Noctus's arms so she could hug me, flattening French Fry between us. When she finished, French Fry slid to the ground with a plop and immediately began pecking at the ground.

I tickled him under his wing, but stood up straight when Aristide approached me next.

"You are an idiot," Aristide said before he slid his arm across my back in a gentle side hug. "Don't ever scare us like that again."

I smiled as I leaned into the rare hug. "Thanks for caring, Aristide. How'd I do, Charon?"

The enigmatic elf just stared at me, his expression flat, but I wasn't fooled.

"Am I worthy of being Noctus's consort now?" I teased.

A smile so small that it could barely be measured settled on Charon's lips. "No," he said. "You're worthy of being Your Majesty."

Whether from the healing, or the rare show of emotion, my eyes teared up. "Thank you." I lurched forward and hugged Charon. He stood for the sign of affection, even going so far as to pat my back.

I let him go with a laugh, which turned into a scream when the double doors beneath the Curia Cloisters' front overhang were thrown off their hinges.

The Paragon marched through the door, Oleander and the elves moving with him.

"Noctus!" The Paragon beamed. "You saved us—the building is cleared, too, so I believe the shadow creatures have been taken care of." His smile abruptly died. "But you have to get out of here—now!"

Ker adjusted her stance so her feet were spread wider apart. "Why?"

Seconds later, Curia Cloisters employees and forces streamed out behind the Paragon, zeroing in on Noctus.

"Don't move!" shouted a wizard, who was armed with a sword—magic hadn't returned to the area, so thankfully no one was wielding magic. "Put your hands up—do not reach for any weapon!"

"Wait, wait!" I struggled to slip past Charon and Aristide, who had stepped in front of me. "It's okay—we got the fae who did this!" I pointed to the blond fae—who was unconscious and looked way more bruised than when I'd last seen him.

"Ma'am, there are *elves* on the premises," the task force member said. "Step out of the way!"

No. My lungs twisted in my chest as I realized that with magic being cut off, so were the elves' ability to make glamours. *This can't be happening. We just saved everyone, but they're not going to see it like that.*

"Oh, *stop it*," the Paragon shouted. "Adept Hazel Medeis and the vampire Eminence Killian Drake are on their way over—they'll handle things."

None of the task force members took their eyes off Noctus, or the elf guards.

"With all due respect, sir, you have no authority in the Midwest Curia Cloisters," the wizard said.

The Paragon grimly set his shoulders. "Don't be an idiot, wizard. You saw the elf squad destroy the shadow creatures the same as I did. They *saved* us!"

"We have no proof that they didn't do this, either," the wizard said.

"Of course, you do!" My shoulders puffed up with the very real terror that was starting to set in. "We got the guy who did it! Question him!"

"We will," the wizard said. "In the meantime, we'll be taking all elves into custody!"

No, no, no. I whipped around to look up at Noctus. With his gear on, his expression was unreadable, but I could tell by the set of his mouth that he was resigned to the situation.

This isn't fair—they revealed themselves to save everyone. How did this happen?!

I thought my ears were ringing in my terror, but it wasn't until I saw the flashing blue and red lights that I realized it was police sirens.

CHAPTER THIRTY-FIVE

Chloe

Magiford police cars turned into the Cloisters' drive, tires screeching as they stopped.

Pat popped out of the first car, holding his cellphone up.

"Juggernaut, stand down!" Pat shouted.

"But sir—"

"Don't you 'but sir' me! They just saved the Cloisters—or did you miss everything that just happened?" Pat stalked across the parking lot, and with every step he took tension left me, my friends, and the Curia Cloisters' force. "And that's my little sister you're holding a sword at—which, don't kid yourself, she could use it better than you can!"

Pat reached our spot on the sidewalk and paused long enough to clasp me on the shoulder. "All good?"

"All good," I echoed. "Except that guy—please take him into custody. There's no one officially watching him. He could technically get away if he woke up." I again pointed to the unconscious and very bruised fae.

Pat squinted as the sun finally topped the tree line, shedding light on the Cloisters. "Yeah, I don't think that'll be a problem, but you're not wrong. *Juggernaut*! Take the fae into custody—cuff 'em, too. We don't want him using magic once...whatever it is you all need comes back online."

He jogged over to the fae, beckoning for a few other task force members to join him.

Meanwhile, Joy kicked open the door of a second police cruiser, brandishing a briefcase. She shielded her eyes with her hand as she peered across the parking lot, visibly relaxing when she saw me. She waved, then turned to an unmarked car that pulled up and rolled its window down. "It's fine," she called to the car. "They'll have to give a report to City Hall about this anyway, you may as well take notes. Get out here."

Two humans piled out of the car, and it took me a moment to realize that—between their cellphones that they were using like recorders and the large camera one of them toted—they were human reporters.

If they're reporters, that means Joy is essentially forcing supernaturals to tell humans about elves, too. That's way safer for Calor Villa—if the Curia Cloisters thought they could cover their existence up, they might be tempted to do some nasty things.

The last bit of adrenaline that was making me feel prickly left, and I let my shoulders sag with my relief.

I love my family. So much.

Noctus—now that he no longer had a sword pointed at him—stepped closer to me. "So it seems our timeline of revealing ourselves to the public has just drastically been moved up."

I slid my hand into his, threading our fingers together. "It's okay," I said. "We've got Pat and Joy. This might not be the PR campaign we were hoping for, but they'll help us make the best of it."

"No kidding. I have a feeling the two of you are going to turn out as right as rain." The Paragon shuffled up to us, eyeing first Pat and then Joy with alarm. "And we think humans aren't to be feared. Pah! They're terrifying! How did your sister even *know* any reporters?"

"She works for City Hall," I said. "So she interacts with the local reporters a lot."

"We are lucky both of your siblings arrived when they did," Noctus said. "Charon called Pat, but we intended for him to find you fleeing the area." He glanced down at me. "He doesn't seem surprised to see you here."

Warmth bubbled in my chest. "Pat said he and Joy would trust my choices. I guess they meant it."

"Regardless, I'm glad they came," the Paragon said. "Once I realized we were going to live through this debacle, I knew things were going to be dicey for you elves. I'm sorry about the lack of preparation, but it'll all turn out."

"Yes," Noctus agreed.

"Oh, and if you were wondering, we've got video footage of everything. The Cloisters boosted their security measures after all the fun and games of last year, including putting cameras everywhere." The Paragon gestured to the tree line, probably pointing to some of the hidden cameras. "You'll be credited for what you did, and if I have anything to say about it, we'll send some clips to the human news channels."

"That is very kind of you, Paragon," I said, choosing my words carefully so I didn't thank him.

The Paragon grunted. "Well, you two are alright. And you did end up getting me the lead I wanted, so I might as well throw my weight around a bit to help you. But mark my words, don't let Empress Leila figure out how loaded you are, Noctus. She'll make a case to add elves onto the Regional Committee of Magic and bring you in under the Cloisters umbrella just so she can get the region to tap your funds."

"That wouldn't be the worst thing for your public image," Joy said, stepping into the conversation with a smile. "Hello, Paragon, Noctus. Chloe!"

I let go of Noctus's hand so I could step into Joy's hug.

"I was so scared when Pat told me—I'm glad you're okay." She squeezed me tight, then stepped back, scrutinizing me from my head to my feet. Once assured I was fine, she smiled. "And I'm so proud of you! Once we're through this you'll have to tell me the whole story: I just know you pulled a weapon and saved everyone."

"How'd you hear about it?" I asked.

"Pat texted me updates. One of his people here in the Cloisters was keeping him apprised of what was happening." Joy said.

"Mm, what did I say? Terrifying," the Paragon said. "Now, if you'll excuse me. I have a fae to question. And wake up, it would seem." He swept off, heading inside. He had to duck around a few staff members who were emerging with buckets of water and scrub brushes—since no one besides Noctus and myself could access their magic, it seemed they were going to get scrubbing at the blood the old fashioned way.

"Okay." Joy clapped her hands together. "You haven't officially hired me on, but I took the opportunity to reach out to some human reporters to make sure this gets covered the way we want it to. It will take them about ten or fifteen minutes to do some interviews and figure out what happened here, so we have that long to craft a statement about elves and how they saved Magiford."

"Chloe actually saved Magiford," Noctus said.

"Yes, I am aware of that, and I'm counting on that—we're going to use the angle that you two are bonded to solidly attach her to the idea of elves," Joy said. "Any objections?"

Noctus and I shook our heads.

"Do you really think this will work?" I asked Joy.

"Pretty sure," Joy said. "I would have preferred more time, but the two of you did save the day, and I'd already thought up a few things to say in case something like this happened."

"I appreciate your help," Noctus said. "Despite the possible tenseness in the situation."

Joy swatted her hand at him. "Don't worry—we're eventually going to be family. Oh, and I've still got one trick up my sleeve to help your image. One that will knock the socks off any smear campaign supernaturals could ever come up with—speaking of which, might I add, the bonus to all of this being so sudden is that they also won't have any time to come up with any negative press about you."

I frowned as I puzzled through her explanation. "There's really a story that would go over even better than a rescue-save-the-day story?"

"Oh yeah." Joy smirked. "Humans like a good rescue story, but this? They'll go crazy for it."

Puzzled—because I had no idea what she could possibly be thinking—I glanced up at Noctus—who appeared equally confused.

"What's the idea?" he asked.

"Two words," Joy said. "Royal wedding!"

EPILOGUE- CHLOE

Chloe

Our wedding was held in January—which was a lot sooner than I thought we'd be able to pull off, but apparently when Joy is given a nearly unlimited budget and an entire city of elves willing to help her, she can do miracles.

The day of the ceremony I was sick with anxiety. Yes, I was thrilled that I was about to marry the love of my life, but my life was about to forever change in a huge way. There was no way I—ever anxious cat that I am—was going to experience that without some mild hyperventilating.

I was still questioning my sanity when my wedding actually started.

We were holding it outdoors, on the very edge of a terrace in the top level of Calor Villa. The terrace overlooked the lake and would make Noctus and me visible to the residents of Calor, who crowded the streets far below so they could watch their king marry.

(In reality, I was pretty sure Joy had chosen the spot because of the excellent framing opportunity. She could get Noctus, me, the lake, *and* the crowded streets in one shot. Our wedding was being livestreamed on the internet thanks to Calor's impossibly perfect wifi, but there was also a slew of human TV reporters—some of them were even international and had translators present.)

I was brought to the terrace in a sleigh, pulled by eight white reindeer as snow fell from the sky, making everything quiet while covering the ground in a sparkling dusting.

Ker, Aristide, Charon, Joy, and Pat were waiting for me—all of them wearing polished armor and chainmail and armed with swords—except for Charon and Pat who had both opted for handguns.

Their appearance followed the elven tradition of a blood-shield—something Noctus and I had opted for instead of a traditional wedding party. Blood-shields were essentially our closest friends who would be willing to shed blood to protect us in an attack during the wedding. (Noctus told me it was from an ancient custom when elves commonly tried to attack one another during wedding ceremonies, so you wanted only your closest allies with you to limit the chance of a betrayal.)

"You okay, Chloe?" Pat asked as he helped me disembark from the sleigh.

"I think so." I grabbed fistfuls of my dress—an elven made, white gown that had long, off the shoulder sleeves and a full skirt that was covered in gorgeous white netting embroidered with flourishes and a few hidden cats—until I realized I was going to crush it in my fists and wrinkle it, so I made myself let it go. "I'm just nervous."

"It is a most joyous day," Charon acknowledged.

Joy circled around behind me to fuss with the train of my gown. "Ignore the reporters and the cameras. Today is all about you and Noctus, and you look gorgeous."

Ker pressed her forehead against mine in a brief sign of werewolf affection. "Like a true queen."

Aristide offered me his arm—he'd been chosen to walk with me—while the others settled into place around us so I was surrounded on all sides by our friends in a bubble of reassurance. "Don't sweat it, Ama," he told me, smiling impishly. "Just look at your bond partner, and all your anxiety will melt away."

He probably meant it as a joke, but I looked across the terrace, hoping for a moment of reassurance.

Noctus stood at the edge of the terrace—dressed in a black chest plate and gauntlets, with a jet-black crown settled on his head and his elven splendor on full display.

Even from this distance, I could tell the spiral pupils of his eyes were swirling, and when our eyes met his gaze heated. He slightly tilted his head back, wordlessly beckoning me toward him.

Instantly my shoulders settled, and I was able to push my anxiety to the back of my mind.

It's okay. I have Noctus. I don't need to worry.

Shiloh, standing just a few feet in front of the blood-shield formation, looked back at me with a teasing smile. "Are you ready, Your Majesty?"

My answer was softer and more solid than it would have been before I saw Noctus. "Ready."

Shiloh winked at me, then started down the walkway that would lead me to Noctus. Armed with a basket full of charmed pink, purple, and red petals, her wish to be the flower girl had come true...though it seemed like my explanation of the role had fallen short and the elves had taken the title literally as wherever she dropped a petal, a flower sprouted up through the snow and bloomed, filling the air with a light, sweet smell.

Aristide patted my hand before the blood-shield—moving as one unit—started to follow behind Shiloh.

A small crowd stood between Noctus and me. Of course, my parents—beaming and teary eyed—were at the front, as was Ms. Booker and a bunch of my Book Nookery coworkers, and the neighborhood uncles. I even spotted French Fry, flapping over the terrace like the loon he was.

A good half of the crowd was made up of the Midwest Regional Committee of Magic and their entourages, as well as the Paragon—who had brought Aphrodite with my blessing.

I was vaguely aware of the music—a bunch of stringed instruments and a small choir—though I couldn't have told you what the music sounded like; I was too busy smiling at Noctus.

Noctus stepped out of his spot and came to claim me before we reached the very front. Together we walked the last few steps, coming to stand beneath a wisteria tree that was blooming despite it being the middle of winter.

"Finally." Noctus squeezed my hand, then raised it so he could kiss it—his lips brushing my fingers as he watched me with a gaze that was heated with love. "Finally, you will stand with me—as my wife and queen."

"I just hope I can be worthy of the title." I smiled up at him, keeping my voice quiet—this exchange was between the two of us, not meant for our guests.

"You aren't having second thoughts about us?" Noctus cast a meaningful glance at the reporters and many cameras.

"Never," I firmly said. "I might get indigestion thinking of politics, but I will never regret choosing you, Noctus."

"Good." Noctus stood straighter, satisfaction lining his voice. "And I will never let you go, Amalourne."

We took our positions, facing each other. I paused long enough to peer over the low, knee-high railing to wave to the elves who crowded the streets of Calor Villa, then turned my attention to the ceremony.

The sun was setting over the lake, casting the terrace in a

golden light, but despite the night air sweeping in and the snow, it was still a comfortable temperature thanks to the many braziers that crackled with white and blue flames.

By the time we went through the biggest Mors traditions and a few human traditions, the sun had disappeared, leaving the sky a velvety tapestry of starlight with swirls of teal, aqua, and purple as the elven version of the northern lights swirled over our heads.

"As shadow and elf have become one in bond and marriage, King Noctus—ruler of the Mors and Calor Villa—you may crown your queen," the officiant said—we were again following the elven tradition of crowning me queen within our wedding ceremony.

My heart in my throat, I nervously smiled at Noctus as Charon appeared at his elbow, carrying my crown—which I hadn't been allowed to see before—on a pillow.

Noctus removed the crown and held it up—for our guests, the elves, and the cameras to see.

"The crown, forged for Queen Chloe. It will serve as a reminder to all how she is treasured and beloved by our people, whom she will rule over with a kindness and compassion that we have never been gifted with before. May her reign be long."

Noctus then turned to me, holding the crown out for inspection.

"It's gorgeous," I breathed, staring at the priceless tiara.

The crown was made of gold, forged to resemble branches and vines. The leaves on the vines and branches were made of white diamonds. One diamond hung low off the crown, so it would be visible on the top of my forehead while the rest of the crown would rest on my hair, but there was also one large jewel nestled at the apex of the crown. It glowed first blue and then white—much like the flames of Noctus's magic.

Noctus's smile turned just a little roguish. "It has perhaps a few finishing touches the public won't notice." He brushed the hanging gem with his thumb.

I laughed when I realized the jewel was a cluster, fashioned to resemble a cat pawprint.

Noctus gently nestled the crown on my head. It weighed a lot less than I assumed it would be considering it signified a major shift in my life.

With the tiara secured, Noctus took my hands and said in a raised voice, "I call you, Chloe, my queen, and my heart. My power is yours, as is my kingdom and my life."

Then, he kissed me—a scorching kiss that took my breath away and made me lightheaded with happiness. I leaned into the kiss, breaking away only once trumpets blasted from the villa.

"Long live Her Majesty, ruler of the Mors, Queen Chloe!" Charon said in a voice that pierced the silence of the snowy terrace and city.

"*Long live Queen Chloe*!" the elves thundered in the city below.

Our guests stood up and clapped, while our blood-shield unsheathed their weapons to salute us.

French Fry—sitting proudly in the wisteria tree with the handful of cats my presence had summoned—cooed and dropped bits of a shredded fast food paper bag.

I smiled as I waved first to our guests, then turned to address the elves in the city.

Now, time for my royal vows.

"I thank you—elves of Calor Villa—for placing your trust in me," I shouted once the cheers subsided. "I vow, as queen, to protect you with my every breath, to be worthy of the power and faith you have entrusted in me, and to stand between you and your enemies—not just as queen, but as a shadow and wielder of Destruction!"

I extended my hand and barely had to think of Noctus's magic before the white magic encircled my wrist and Truck solidified in my hand—since I'd first managed to call him out, he'd become overly eager in answering any summons.

Smoke surrounded me, replacing my wedding gown with Destruction's dark armor, run through with veins of gold magic.

At my side, Noctus pulled a weapon of his own—his crystal sword—also taking on magic armor.

Standing together, the two of us hummed with a magic power I could feel in my bones.

"Ready to end it?" I whispered to Noctus.

"At your leisure," Noctus said.

I raised Destruction over my head, smiling when I saw the rivets in my gauntlets—the weapon, in its own statement of delight, had made every rivet in my armor into a tiny stamped pawprint design.

As if sensing my attention, Destruction's jewels glittered, and it cooed its now familiar and happy "woo-woo" noise at me.

I affectionately patted the pole of the weapon, then turned my attention to the elves below.

"May the glory of Calor grow," I shouted. "May the kindness of the elves be known throughout the world!"

I swung Destruction down. The scythe exploded with magic, sending a ripple of power slicing through the sky, cutting a path across the top of the city like a falling star.

Noctus raised his sword, but instead of loosing an attack of his own as we had planned, he spoke.

"Let it be known," he began, "that in crowning Queen Chloe, we, the elves of Calor Villa, are accepting her as our own, which means we accept her family—human and shadow alike."

What? This wasn't part of the ceremony?

Slightly confused, I lowered Destruction, leaning the scythe's curved blade against my shoulder before I patted it like I would comfort a small child.

Noctus continued, "The gates of Calor Villa will be open to any shadow who seeks refuge. Your enemies shall be our enemies, and we will protect you with every drop of blood in our veins, with all the ferocity of our kind."

Out in the streets, the elves *roared.*

Not the cheers of approval they'd made when Noctus and I had kissed, but something far fiercer and much closer to a war cry.

Noctus turned so he looked directly at the cameras, and I finally realized why he'd been so insistent along with Joy that we livestream our wedding—because he was issuing a challenge to the world. *Stop hunting the shadows, or else.*

"If ever a shadow has need of protection, come to Magiford, find Calor," Noctus said. "We will protect you, and wipe out *any* who would seek to harm you."

The air was filled with a metallic chorus, and it took me a moment to realize that the elves—every last one of them—were unsheathing weapons, holding them aloft so they stabbed the sky.

"*Calor*!" they yelled, their promise bouncing off the mountain and echoing over the city with a strength that felt like it imprinted the entire valley.

My throat ached, and I nearly cried.

In less than a year, I'd gone from being an outcast—a supernatural so low that I had to hide from others or I'd risk getting roughed up with no one to help me—to being part of a people who accepted me, who rejoiced in the oddities of my magic.

I've been dreading becoming queen, but I should have been looking forward to it. They accept me. I'm not alone anymore.

The air felt full with magic, and in that moment I heard the song of wild magic—a quiet hum of pleasure arced through my heart.

Noctus finally stabbed his crystal sword into the sky—releasing a slash of power, and changing the future of Calor forever.

Yes, this was a celebration of myself and Noctus, but it was also a mark of change.

The elves, who had once hunted the shadows to near extinction, were offering themselves as the shield and swords—the protectors—of the people they used to fear.

And as Noctus grabbed my free hand and together we raised our intertwined hands into the sky, it finally dawned on me.

I think...I might know how to return the bond with Noctus.

EPILOGUE- NOCTUS

Noctus

According to the Mors tradition, royal weddings were supposed to be followed with days of feasting and celebration, with no work being done by the public or the newlywed couple.

Life, it seemed, would not allow us that relaxation, so the day after our wedding found Chloe and me standing at the barrier halfway up a mountain, tracking the five mantasps that had been ramming into the perfectly sound barrier, terrifying my citizens enough to make them disturb us to request their extermination.

I don't just hate mantasps, I despise them. I unsheathed a sword and stared at the hazy wall that protected my realm. *No, I completely and utterly loathe and abhor them.*

The shadowy figures of the mantasps moved on the other side of the barrier, and my eyebrow twitched in my irritation.

Now that I'm free from the Paragon's shackle, perhaps I should spend a week in the wasteland outside the barrier, tracking all the mantasps I can find and forever curbing their population. They must be unusually prolific given how often they enjoy banging into my barriers, even though it's to no avail as they are too weak to get through.

"Are you sure about this?" Chloe—holding Destruction and already wearing her weapon-granted armor—fidgeted at my side. "I've heard a lot about the fae realm being infested with a toxic miasma. Just because I'm immune to negative magic doesn't mean that will equate to being immune to all that ooze."

"If you aren't, Destruction will offer some basic protection," I said. "And your immunity to magic still means you'll be able to move through the barrier at will. If you start to feel *any* pain, simply cross back into our realm, and Charon will administer a potion to you."

I motioned back to where Aristide, Ker, and Charon were waiting for us with two all-terrain vehicles we'd ridden in to get up the mountain.

Aristide, apparently, was choosing to keep the wedding celebrations rolling even if the newly wedded couple was not. He was sipping at some kind of blood drink that had a paper umbrella in it, lounging in one of the vehicles.

Ker lounged with him, eating a piece of our wedding cake that she'd brought along in a Tupperware container. She offered a gob of frosting to Chloe's trash griffin, who had taken up residence on Ker's boot.

Charon, at least, had the decency to be standing at attention, watching us.

"If you're sure, we can at least give it a shot," Chloe said. "Isn't that right, Truck?"

Destruction—a weapon that had once struck fear in the heart of the strongest monarchs, who had been beheld in terror and spoken of like a curse—made a low, moaning-groan noise, and its jewels practically shone when Chloe used the ribbon tied around her waist to buff out a fingerprint on its pole.

I watched the interaction with a removed sense of disbelief

and pride. *I mean, I find her absolutely charming and lovable, so I suppose it's not so out of the realm of possibilities that she would similarly tame the elves' most dangerous weapon.*

"I'll head in first," I said. "Step through when you're ready." I squeezed her hand, then stepped through the barrier.

The wall—made of my magic—hummed, strong and solid. The vibrations of the magic made bones buzz, but it didn't feel unpleasant until I stepped into the unprotected portion of the fae realm.

Past my barrier, everything was dead. The ground was a burnt black—there was no plant life or regular animal life that could survive the all-consuming miasma, which sucked the magic out of the living. Only monsters like the mantasp could live in it.

The air was acidic and sour, and as soon as I breathed it in a barely noticeable pain bloomed in my lungs from the poisonous fumes.

My sudden presence startled the mantasps, who retreated a few steps, clicking their giant mandibles in anger.

The monsters were an unsettling mixture of wasp and praying mantis. Standing upright on their back legs, mantasps were roughly the size of an average human. They were covered in a grayish brown exoskeleton, and each possessed a stinger the size of a small dagger that stuck out of their bloated abdomens. Their favorite method of killing was to grab their prey with the four limbs they didn't walk on and hold them—since each leg was tipped with scythe-like claws—before finishing them off with their stinger.

I watched the mantasps as I absently adjusted the black, collar-like leather necklace Chloe had given me the night before as a wedding gift. It fit comfortably around my neck, snapping shut magnetically, but I was most—and probably stupidly—pleased because it somewhat resembled the bond collar she wore, making us match.

"Okay, partner," Chloe blithely said, her voice slightly warped as it floated through the barrier. "Let's take out some mantasps."

She stepped through the barrier, pausing—her muscles tensed as she adjusted to the wasteland.

I smiled—temporarily distracted by my smugness that she was so easily able to pass through my barriers. She was truly the only one who could go anywhere she wanted with me.

"Are you okay?" I studied her, looking for any sign that she was in pain. While I couldn't see her eyes—the bridge of her nose up was covered by her helm—I could read her every movement.

"No...I think I'm fine?" She stood up straight, then sneezed. "I can tell there's no magic here." She paused for another sneeze. "And I can feel the miasma searching for magic." Another sneeze. "But it can't seem to dig into me. Although." Yet another sneeze. "It smells weird out here."

Two of the mantasps were apparently less intimidated by Chloe than they were by me, and they started scuttling in our direction.

"Ahh, yes. That would be the poison in the air," I said. "Are your lungs hurting?" It was what I was most concerned about for her. I had so much magic, it would heal me faster than the miasma could harm me. Chloe—while tougher than a regular human—didn't have such healing powers.

Chloe hunched her shoulders. "Maybe a little? My nose hurts more than my lungs."

"I see. I'll use our bond to encourage healing when we're finished. Are you comfortable taking on the mantasps by yourself?" I asked.

"Maybe," Chloe said. "Let me see how Destruction and I can handle one of them first."

"Woo-woo," said Destruction, most disturbingly.

Chloe didn't share my estimation of the weapon voicing its opinion. Not knowing any better, she merely nodded as if it had offered sage wisdom instead of being a weapon that was *making verbal noises*.

"Here we go!" Chloe singled out a mantasp that stood away from the pack, raised Destruction, then used the scythe to slice through the air.

The blade glowed golden before exploding with power, sending a burst toward the mantasp. The blast incinerated it, leaving not even a husk of the creature's exoskeleton behind.

The two mantasps that had been skittering toward us made a very abrupt U-turn and ran in the other direction.

The two that had hung back burst off in opposite directions, fleeing their certain death, angrily clicking their jaws as they went.

If I were as cat inclined as Chloe, I'd be purring where I stood. I had a life partner who was as capable as myself—something I didn't know even existed.

Ker, Aristide, and Charon were my closest friends, yes. But over the centuries, I'd become tired of standing alone. Tired of the curse of endless power and duties that came with it.

And now, I have my Amalourne.

Chloe watched the mantasps run and sneezed. "Yeah, I think Truck and I can handle these guys."

"Have fun." I smiled at her.

She grinned, then trotted after the monsters—Destruction making weird gurgling noises as it tried to chatter at her.

I waited with my sword unsheathed while she easily finished off the second and third mantasps. She was starting to chase the fourth mantasp around when I felt a presence behind me, on the other side of the barrier.

I stepped back through, nearly ramming into Ker—who had apparently wandered closer with Aristide to get a better look.

"Sounds like she's doing well," Aristide said. He was looking at the sky—most likely tracking the heartbeat of Chloe's trash griffin since it was flapping around up there.

"Indeed," I said. "She's ripping through them with ease—with some help from Destruction."

As if the weapon could hear us, it made its unsettling "woo-woo," noise that was audible through the barrier.

Charon, gripping a pen, his tiny notebook, and looking quite pained—pained for him, anyway—peered from the shadowy shapes we could see through the barrier to me. "Do you intend to ever tell her that weapons aren't supposed to really *act* like partners and that they shouldn't make any kind of noise?"

A bright light flashed on the other side of the barrier as Chloe killed the fourth mantasp.

"No," I said.

Aristide rattled the ice of his nearly empty drink. "And are you ever going to explain to her how elves used the weapons with reverence and handled them with care?"

Chloe chucked Destruction, which scissored across the barren land and hit the last remaining mantasp in the abdomen with enough force that it sent it sprawling and cut through its carapace.

I tugged at my new black necklace. "No."

"*Way to go, Truck*!" Chloe called, her voice warping from the barrier, as she trotted toward the pinned monster.

Ker slightly hunched her shoulders—if she'd been in her wolf form she'd be whining with pinned ears. "Are you sure you shouldn't say anything? I mean, I told her a slightly optimistic version of heirloom weapons because I didn't want her to fear your power. But I didn't know...this would happen."

Destruction made happy gurgling noises as Chloe pulled it free, then finished off the last mantasp with another burst of raw power.

"I'm never going to say anything," I concluded. "Not because I don't want to disappoint Chloe, but because I have never seen Destruction so happy. And if she *stops* treating it in this way, I'm afraid it may choose to...express its anger. At us."

"Oh." Aristide almost dropped his drink. "Yeah. That might be an accurate worry. Unless, do you have any wisdom to share with the classroom, Charon?"

Charon delicately turned to a new page in his notebook. "In all of my searching, I have never found any record of Destruction doing such...*things* before, and it is undeniably pleased with Chloe as its new wielder."

"In Truck's defense," Ker said, already starting to fall into Chloe's habit of calling the most dangerous weapon in elfdom after a human made vehicle, "he hasn't been used in centuries—not since Noctus fought his family. He was probably getting lonely, especially since he's used to being the weapon of choice for the Mors family. Maybe he's just excited that he's getting used again?"

"*Thanks for your help, Truck,*" Chloe said, her voice growing louder as she approached the barrier. "*I appreciate it.*"

"*Woo-woo,*" groaned the ancient, deadly heirloom.

"Yeah," Aristide said. "Excited."

Chloe popped through the barrier with a sneeze, followed up by a cough that rattled her lungs. "The mantasps are all gone—I used one of the new methods you taught me, Charon."

"Well done, Your Majesty." Charon—with the growing ease of experience—caught the trash griffin before it could smack into Chloe, holding the creature like a baby.

"Thanks—hello, French Fry." Chloe tickled the trash griffin's belly, then coughed again.

"The poisonous air affects you more than I thought." I frowned as I reached out, pressing my fingers to Chloe's neck to feel for her pulse. "It seems it will be worth improving my ability to use healing magic on you for future fights."

"Can you really use it on me in battle?" Chloe rested the butt of Destruction's pole on the ground, breaking millennium old practices that used to be observed for the weapon. "It makes me kind of loopy. I don't think that would be very helpful when I need to be careful."

"We'll experiment," I assured her.

Destruction groaned, and Ker shivered in response.

"Well then." Aristide saluted in my general direction with his ice filled cup. "The monsters are defeated, and the barrier is safe, shall we get the blissful couple back to the celebration?"

"Sounds good to me." Ker took Aristide's cup so he could focus on his cane. "I could go for another piece of cake or five. Charon, you driving?"

"Always," Charon firmly said. He walked quickly so he was the first to get back to the all-terrain vehicle he'd driven up the mountain, still carrying the trash griffin—who cooed at us from over his shoulder.

I watched for a moment, before turning to my new bride. "Before we head out, might I use my healing magic on you?" I held out my hand to Chloe—needing the contact to heal her.

Chloe set her hand on mine. "Yes, thank you."

I tapped my powers, getting them to kickstart before I used the collar to push a pulse of my magic into her, concentrating on her lungs.

Chloe fidgeted, waggling Destruction. "Hey, Noctus?"

"Yes?" I'd been staring at her chest—making sure my magic got to her lungs—but at the sound of her voice, I looked at her face.

Chloe chewed her bottom lip. "Could I try something, quick? With magic?"

"Of course," I said. "You need not ask, Amalourne."

She stood a little taller. "Okay, thanks." She held Destruction away from me—even if Chloe could use it with abandon, it was still cursed—then stretched up so she was standing on the tips of her toes. She tugged her hand from mine just long enough to throw it around my neck.

I bent forward to make it easier on her and rested my hands

on her hips, closing my eyes and enjoying the peace and warmth she radiated to me through the collar.

I felt her fingers caress the back of my neck, and something *changed.*

The sensation of the collar on my neck didn't change, and I still observed the world in the same manner. Chloe's closeness produced the warmth in my chest that it always did...but it seemed to be *more*.

I could still feel the inferno of my magic, but there was something else there now. Something soft, that twined around me like a cat.

"It worked!" Chloe said.

I blinked as I felt the soft, feline-esque magic pulse, and I realized it was Chloe's powers. "What?"

"I returned the bond!" Chloe said. "I can feel it now. I made a direct line to you, tied to *your* collar. It worked!"

For a moment, I held her closer—shocked at her success. "How?"

Chloe squeezed me tight, then released me so she could back up and beam up at me. "Two ways. Firstly, Truck. Because Truck is cursed, more of my shadow magic is active whenever I use him, so I can see it for more than a heartbeat and reach for it. Secondly, wild magic gave me the hint. I kept trying to reverse engineer what you'd done for me, but I hear wild magic whenever your magic is active in me. It made me suspect that mingling our magic was what I should be shooting for."

I rolled my shoulders back as I tried to track how things felt different. "It makes sense you would have to use a different method, given that you aren't an elf."

Chloe exhaled, her smile relaxed. "I'm just so glad it finally worked! Thanks, by the way, Truck. I'll see you next time?"

Destruction made the alarming "woo-woo" noise, before it started glowing, then disappeared—returning to storage, taking

Chloe's armor with it so she was once again dressed in the practice clothes we'd donned for the journey.

With her face visible once more, I could read the shy joy in Chloe's eyes as she grinned up at me. "Can you feel anything?"

"Yes. Your magic is very different from my own, I can easily isolate it." I paused when I again felt her soft magic twine around me. Carefully—I was half afraid it would shy away from me—I mentally reached for it.

Through the collar, I could feel the link to Chloe—which was just as beautiful and warm as she was. Rather than flee, Chloe's magic flooded me, rumbling in a purr.

After a moment it disappeared, but not without an affectionate rub.

No wonder she's had trouble making the bond—her magic is surprisingly responsive, but fast.

"Any day, you two," Aristide shouted to us from the all-terrain vehicles. "Take your time. It's not like we're missing out on the party of the century or something."

Chloe laughed, and the pleasant noise made the wild magic around us twitter and sing. "We're coming." She grinned at me before walking toward the all-terrain vehicles.

As I watched her approach my friends, a peace I hadn't experienced—maybe ever before—making me relax.

Charon bowed to her as she got closer. "Your Majesty."

"Are you really going to keep calling me that, Charon?" Chloe asked.

"You are the queen of Calor Villa—my queen, the life partner of my king," Charon said.

"What he's saying is, 'yes'," Ker interpreted.

"Believe me, we're all thrilled," Aristide said. "We've known for centuries Noctus needed something—we just didn't know it was a pint-sized shadow."

I raised my eyebrows at the declaration, but said nothing—he wasn't wrong, after all.

"I'm not that small," Chloe said. "You are just all really tall."

I prowled after Chloe. "Don't worry, you are the perfect size to make you an armful," I said before I swept her up.

Chloe squawked as she wriggled in my arms. "Noctus, put me down!"

Laying a slow kiss on her neck, I considered her demand. "No, I don't think I will."

Chloe alternately stammered and gulped, then abruptly turned into her cat form.

Unfortunately for her, I could start to feel it when she tapped her transformation magic thanks to our complete bond, so it was an easy thing to adjust my hold and tuck her even closer to my chest in her fuzzy and undeniably cute cat form.

This made her hair puff up, and she turned back into her human form. "Noctus!" she said, scandalized.

"Look at it this way, Chloe," Ker called to her with a cackle. "You'll never have to sleep in the sink again!"

THE END

For free short stories and more information about the Gate of Myth and Power Series, visit kmshea.com!

If you enjoyed Gate of Myth and Power, please check out Hazel's story in the Hall of Blood and Mercy series. Book one: Magic Forged

OTHER SERIES BY K. M. SHEA

The Snow Queen

Timeless Fairy Tales

The Fairy Tale Enchantress

The Elves of Lessa

Hall of Blood and Mercy

Court of Midnight and Deception

Pack of Dawn and Destiny

Gate of Myth and Power

King Arthur and Her Knights

Robyn Hood

The Magical Beings' Rehabilitation Center

Second Age of Retha: Written under pen name A. M. Sohma

ADDITIONAL NOVELS

Life Reader

Princess Ahira

A Goose Girl

ABOUT THE AUTHOR

K. M. Shea is a fantasy-romance author who never quite grew out of adventure books or fairy tales, and still searches closets in hopes of stumbling into Narnia. She is addicted to sweet romances, witty characters, and happy endings. She also writes LitRPG and GameLit under the pen name, A. M. Sohma.

Hang out with the K. M. Shea Community at...
kmshea.com

Printed in Great Britain
by Amazon

38967029R00235